"FAMILY VALUES"

Reading, throwing a ball, riding a bike . . . these are the things most parents look forward to teaching their children. But in some families what the parents teach their children is murder. There are fathers, mothers, children, grandchildren—entire families linked by bad blood and driven to slaughter innocent people. They shoot, stab, strangle, or beat their victims to death—and do it as a family!

FAMILIES WHO KILL tells the bizarre true stories of America's first families of murder. From Ma Barker and her bloodthirsty sons, to the Gallegos, who abducted young girls as "sex slaves" and murdered them when their lust was slaked, to the Benders of Kansas, whose sexy daughter was the bait to lure men in for her father and brother to rob and kill, these are shocking tales of perverted families who violate every taboo.

FAMILIES WHO KILL

FAMILIES WHO KILL

BERNIE WARD

PINNACLE BOOKS
WINDSOR PUBLISHING CORP.

PINNACLE BOOKS are published by

Windsor Publishing Corp.
475 Park Avenue South
New York, NY 10016

First Printing: August, 1993

Printed in the United States of America

ACKNOWLEDGMENTS

Irene Clark, Judy Dickerson, Joe Fanculli, Bruce Ferg, Susan K. Forbes, Stan Gilliam, Kevin Higgins, Dan Hunt, Sgt. Rick Knight, Jessie Lickteig, Det. Jerry McMenemy, Mike Miller, Robert N. Miller, Bruce Mowday, Sgt. Al Padilla, Denise Pangborn, Bernard F. Pasqualini, Sheriff Frank Reyes, Lt. John Thayer, Orville Trainer, Richard Wagner, Det. Charlie Zagorski.

INTRODUCTION

Families who kill. . . . These are our worst nightmares.

American history is drenched in the blood of countless murders committed by lone assassins, serial killers, or mass murderers, both male or female. They kill for passion or profit. They murder to feed monstrous sexual drives or merely for the thrill of the kill.

The dead are friends, neighbors, loved ones or total strangers, victims of a random and capricious fate who find themselves in the wrong place at the wrong time.

But rarely do entire households—fathers and sons, mothers and daughters, husbands and wives, brothers and sisters—engage in the business of murder as a routine family affair.

Families Who Kill tells the bloody stories of those rare exceptions.

These are not the extended, ethnic "families" of the Mafia, nor the cult, quasi-families made infamous by Charles Manson and his grotesque clan.

These are blood kin who kill others, not each other. Some of these families might, on the surface, pass for any typical American brood—except that each is the spawn of bad seeds—an Ozzie and Harriet nightmare on Elm Street.

Incredibly, these ten bloodthirsty families accounted for about one hundred killings, counting conservatively. Their victims were shot, stabbed, and strangled. Many were sexually tortured before their lives were brutally snuffed out.

The Benders of Kansas is the prototype American family killers. Pa and Ma Bender, a dull-witted son, and daughter Kate, the buxom star of the deadly dynasty, suddenly appeared on the Kansas frontier in the 1870s to seek their fortune.

A dozen or more travelers who visited the Benders' Inn had their heads bashed in by the Bender men while distracted by the sexy Kate. Shallow graves in the Bender orchard eventually gave up their ghastly secrets, but by then the murderous family had vanished into the myths of the Old West.

In the Chicago of the Roaring Twenties, Al Capone made the headlines, but it was the Terrible Genna brothers who made the streets run red with blood.

The Gennas slaughtered scores of competitors and innocent bystanders, although the venomous family has been largely overlooked by history in the glare of publicity generated by Capone. But at the height of their power, even "Scarface" feared the Terrible Gennas who smeared their bullets with garlic to induce, they believed, a ghastly death from gangrene if the victims weren't killed outright in the barrage of gunfire.

Arizona Donnie Clark Barker was never arrested for a crime in her entire life. But before she was cut down in a blazing, forty-five-minute gun battle with vengeful FBI agents, "Ma" Barker had spawned an outlaw gang of murderers, kidnappers, and bank robbers who terrorized the Midwest. Their name became synonymous with the gangster-ridden Thirties.

The McCrary-Taylor clan, a loathsome family of Texas nomads, wandered around the country robbing, raping, and murdering with a shockingly nonchalant cold-bloodedness. They favored young women working alone in donut shops and roadside cafes. Incredibly, the women of the clan calmly watched the violent sexual assaults and then sorted through the victims' belongings for items they could use.

The Lewingdon brothers, Gary and Thaddeus, casually launched a year-long reign of terror and murder in Central Ohio that was dubbed "The .22-Caliber Murders." In a series of apparently random robberies and murders, the brothers butchered ten people—each victim shot multiple times with .22-caliber handguns. Their motive: Something to do on weekends.

In 1978, the three sons of convicted murderer Gary Tison busted their old man and another serial killer out of the Arizona State Prison, touching off the wildest manhunt in the history of the Southwest.

But it was the maniacal murders they committed on the run that forever marked Gary Tison and his sons as among America's most merciless and nightmarish family killers. They slaughtered a family of four (including a two-year-old whose head was blown off by a sawed-off shotgun) who stopped to help the escapees when their car broke down in the desert. Later, they kidnapped and murdered a young honeymooning couple. One Tison boy died in a shoot-out with cops at a roadblock. Gary Tison, the leader of the violent clan, fled on foot and died of thirst in the desert.

Gerald and Charlene Gallego wallowed in a mind-numbing orgy of sadistic death that may be unequaled in the annals of American murders. The

Gallegos are the only known husband-and-wife serial killers. The couple is responsible for ten barbaric murders in California and Nevada. Both of them spent long hours raping and sexually torturing their victims before killing them.

The Johnston family, headed by brothers Bruce, Sr., David, and Norman systematically looted the rural countryside of Southern Pennsylvania and Northern Maryland for more than a decade. Threatened with exposure and blinded by greed, the Johnstons murdered several members of the gang—including the fifteen-year-old girlfriend of Bruce Johnston, Jr., who was also shot to pieces in a bloody ambush but lived.

In *Mass Murder: America's Growing Menace,* authors James Allen Fox and Jack Levin said the Johnston clan was sending a message when they went out to kill: "No matter what, you don't rat and especially not on the family . . . the Johnston killings were truly a collective effort . . . the norm of family loyalty had been severely violated. Death was the rightful punishment."

The same could be said of the Lundgrens—patriarch Jeffrey, wife, Alice, and son, Damon, and all the followers the bearded, wild-eyed Lundgren duped into joining his religious cult.

On one bloody, horror-filled night of April 1989, the Lundgren cult sacrificed five of its own in a grotesque blood atonement ceremony. Cult members Dennis and Cheryl Avery and their three children, Trina, fifteen, Rebecca, thirteen, and Karen, seven, were ritually slain—one by one—and their bodies tossed in a common grave.

Joseph Kallinger, the psychotic Philadelphia cobbler, formed a rape and murder team with his teenage son, Michael, that preyed on housewives in the

Northeast. As a tune-up, they practiced killing another Kallinger son, thirteen-year-old Joseph, Jr., then kidnapped, mutilated, and murdered a ten-year-old child because Kallinger wanted to see what it would be like to cut off someone's penis.

Some of the bloodthirsty monsters depicted in *Families Who Kill* are long dead themselves. But many are still alive, doing time in prison or waiting their turn on Death Row. Others have served their sentences or soon will be set free to kill again. A few simply vanished, leaving in their wake a trail of gore and a lasting mystery.

Ten horror stories. All terrible; all terribly true.

ONE
THE BLOODY BENDERS

Dr. William York was missing.

The fact that the doctor was a popular and prominent figure with social and political connections reaching all the way to Washington was enough cause for alarm. But good doctors were few and far between on the Kansas frontier, so when one of the best simply vanished off the face of the prairie in the spring of 1873, the folks in the southeastern corner of the state felt the loss deeply. Scores of farmers and towns people joined the doctor's brother, Civil War hero Colonel A.M. York, and went looking for him.

The search party located Doctor York—but not in the condition they'd hoped to find him. Rather than alive and well, the good doctor's remains were rotting in a hole in the ground, planted in a garden out back of a crude hostel on the Osage Mission trail known as the Bender Tavern. The Tavern was of a type commonly found on the frontier, family-owned enterprises where travelers could stop for a night's sleep, a meal, and a few supplies before proceeding on their way.

This particular family consisted of John Bender

(some accounts give his name as William) and his wife, known only as Ma Bender since neither contemporaries nor historians ever learned her Christian name; son John, who may actually have been the son of Mrs. Bender from a previous marriage to someone named Gebardt or Gebhardt; and daughter Kate, the notorious leader of one of the most monstrous families in the history of American crime.

The Bender family, it turned out, had concocted a fiendish method of murder that was simple and direct. Doctor York was only one among many who tumbled into their hellhole. A traveler who stopped the night, or was lured to the Tavern by the deadly charms of the voluptuous Kate, was invited to sit for his last supper at the Benders' table with his back to a canvas partition that divided the Tavern. With the guest's attention on food and drink, or distracted by Kate's amply exposed bosom and the tempting promise it held for later in the evening, the Bender men crept up behind the curtain and shattered the visitor's head with a mighty blow from a sledgehammer. Sometimes the Bender men struck a double blow guaranteed to kill instantly, with one swinging the sledge, the other a heavy blacksmith's hammer.

Usually, the victim's throat was also slashed. Then a trapdoor was thrown back and the body dumped into a large pit that had been dug beneath the Tavern's floor. Later, the Benders picked over the dead man's belongings, and, under cover of darkness, dragged the remains outdoors and buried them in shallow graves. To further conceal their bloodthirsty business, the Benders kept the graveyard freshly plowed so passersby wouldn't notice the freshly turned earth.

The searchers who went looking for Dr. York stumbled over this unholy cemetery and thus unearthed a ghastly tale that remains shrouded in mystery more than a century later. Surrounding Dr. York's burial site, they found more hastily dug graves, about a dozen in all, including one that held the bodies of a man identified as George Loucher (or Longchos) and his eighteen-month-old daughter.

As with the other male victims, the back of Loucher's skull had been smashed in and his throat cut. But the body of the toddler bore no marks other than a silk scarf knotted around her neck. The child may have died from strangulation, but searchers who uncovered her body doubted it. Instead, it appeared that the tiny girl had been thrown in the grave, her father's bloody body tossed in on top of her . . . and then she was buried alive.

As days passed, additional graves were discovered on other parts of the Bender property. Most of the remains uncovered were of men, but one grave held the body of a young woman who appeared to have been in her twenties when she fell into the Benders' evil clutches. She was never identified.

And yet another makeshift grave yielded a horror beyond belief—the body of what appeared to be an eight-year-old girl; so advanced was the decomposition that even the sex was difficult to determine. But the torture inflicted on the child before she died was beastly clear to the men who dug her up. She had been tortured so violently that her bones had been yanked from their sockets and the body sexually mutilated. A reporter on the scene for the *Springfield (Missouri) Times* informed his shocked readers that: "One of the corpses was so horribly mutilated as to make the sex even a matter of doubt. The little girl was probably eight years of age, and had long sunny hair, and some traces of beauty on a face not yet entirely disfigured by decay. One arm was broken. The breastbone had been driven in. The right knee had been wrenched from its socket and the leg doubled up under the body."

This revolting slaughter of children, as much as anything, inflamed the Kansas border towns with a raging howl for vengeance against the demonic Benders.

As searchers continued their ghoulish chore, some twenty bodies in all were unearthed in the area around the Benders' loathsome slaughterhouse. However, as time cooled passions, Kansas authorities admitted that the Benders may not have been responsible for all those deaths. On the other hand, no one knew for certain one way or the other.

The instant the first spadeful of dirt was turned in the macabre graveyard, the story of the Benders entered the mythology of the American West: a gruesomely true and bizarre tale of mind-boggling butchery; black magic spells; weird tales of grotesque, nude romps through midnight graveyards; sex orgies; spiritualism; and cold-blooded extermination that made the Benders of Kansas this nation's original family of murderers.

Upon the grisly discoveries near the Bender Tavern, newspapers from hundreds of miles away rushed reporters to the Kansas border to file eyewitness accounts as the graves were opened. The *Springfield Times,* for example, warned its spellbound readers that:

"What follows in its facts may read like the recital of some horrible dream, wherein nightmare mirrors upon the distempered brain a countless number of monstrous and unnatural things, yet what is set down in the narrative is as true as the sun . . .

"In an hour all the town was at the scene of the discovery . . . but the horrible work was not yet completed. The iron rod was again put in until six more graves were discovered. . . . The scene was horrible beyond description.

"The search went on unabated. . . . A fascination impossible to define held the spectators to the spot . . . the crowd increased instead of diminished . . . the whole country is aroused. Couriers and telegrams have been sent in every direction with the descriptions of the Benders. . . ."

A *Kansas City Times* correspondent breathlessly reported that "The scene at the graves surpasses anything in horror that could be possibly imagined. . . . Nothing like this sickening series of crimes has ever been recorded in the whole history of the country. People for hundreds of miles are flocking to Cherryvale and enormous rewards are to be offered for the arrest of the murderers."

But for all the intense press coverage and public clamor, the main questions raised by the discovery of the heinous crimes remained unanswered: Exactly who were these Benders, these grisly butchers from hell who appeared out of nowhere and then vanished into thin air? Incredibly, for all the unspeakable atrocities they inflicted on a score or more of innocent wayfarers, very little is known about this criminal family. It seems that once their gruesome business of wholesale murder was discovered, the Benders simply closed the door on their house of gore and rode off.

What is known is that the Benders appeared in Labette County, Kansas, in the fall of 1870. No one ever knew where they came from exactly, although later wild, bizarre rumors abounded that the family sprang from devil-worshiping covens who practiced black magic witchcraft among the Pennsylvania Dutch.

The only real clue to their background was the Dutch or German language they spoke. Kate spoke English fluently with only a light German accent. Brother John's English was much more broken and guttural. Pa Bender spoke only German and Ma Bender spoke not at all, at least to outsiders.

Descriptions of the Benders were drawn after they disappeared and therefore vary widely. However, a poster in which the governor of Kansas offered a $2,000 reward (a vast sum in those days) for the return of the family was circulated only days after the Benders' butchery was revealed. It described the family members as:

"John Bender, about sixty years of age, five feet eight or nine inches in height. German speaks but little English, dark complexion, no whiskers, and sparely built.

"Mrs. Bender, about fifty years of age, rather heavyset, blue eyes, brown hair. German speaks broken English.

"John Bender, Jr., alias John Gebardt, five feet eight or nine inches in height, slightly built, gray eyes with brownish tint, brown hair, light moustache, no whiskers, about twenty-seven years of age, speaks English with German accent.

"Kate Bender, about twenty-four years of age, dark hair and eyes, good-looking, well formed, rather bold in appearance, fluent talker, speaks good English with very little German accent."

The fact that a wanted poster went so far as to describe Kate Bender as "good-looking, well formed, rather bold in appearance, fluent talker," indicates the enormous impact her charms made on the mostly male settlers in that pioneer society.

* * *

One account of the Benders, described Kate as ". . . the inspiration of the crimes—the tireless one, the leader of the rest—the killer. She was about five feet five or six, and weighed around one hundred and twenty-five pounds. She held herself proudly erect, head high, deep hazel eyes, wide and very bright. Her lips were red, very red, and pouting. It was a mouth to disturb the dreams of young men who saw her.

"Her hair was a crowning glory. It was a deep auburn, coppery in the shadows, flashing gold, glinting in the sunlight, a sleek silken crest. The men of her time called her mighty good-looking. A man of today would unhesitatingly pronounce her beautiful. She talked freely, laughed a great deal, and moved very quickly. She was vivacious and courted the attention of those she met.

"Kate was an alien in the midst of the slow-moving, silent German family, in fact she was so different that she must have seemed like a changeling child. Probably a throwback in the family. . . ."

On the other hand, no one had anything good to say about the rest of the family of killers.

Despite the specific description contained in the wanted poster, Pa Bender has evolved through time into a huge, powerful, Neanderthalish brute, more gorilla-like than manlike. He was once described as having ". . . the frame of a giant—broad shouldered and large boned. He had a heavy jaw, high cheekbones, a low forehead. His eyes were black and piercing, set deeply under huge bushy brows."

Ma Bender was characterized as ". . . heavyset, with a sickening, white, unhealthy fat—stooped—stolid demeanor. She had dark, heavy-lidded eyes, and her black hair was streaked with white. Her expression was so sullen and savage that it repelled even her nearest neighbors, so she was regarded with much disfavor long before any suspicion became attached to the Benders."

The younger man was a carbon copy of Pa Bender—surly, ill-tempered, and, although not big physically, was known to possess the strength of an ox that raged out of control when he was provoked. John, Jr., had a troubling habit of staring through people and ending his conversations with a demented, high-pitched giggle that, according to one Bender visitor who lived to tell about it, ". . . had the fierce malice of a hyena."

In the aftermath of the Bender atrocities, rumors about the secret life of the killers engulfed the Kansas prairie settlements like wildfire. John, Jr., and Kate were really lovers, not siblings, claimed one. An even darker tale had it that the two were, in fact, brother and sister but living in an incestuous relationship while they plotted their murderous schemes.

On one point the various descriptions of the Benders do agree: Except for Kate, the family was a collection of surly, mean-spirited, suspicious louts for whom murder came as easily as slaughtering a pig.

The Tavern was built just off the heavily traveled road linking the major trading centers of Fort Scott, the Osage Indian Mission, and Independence, Kansas, or about seven miles northeast of present day Cherryvale. The cottonwood-lined Drum Creek ran nearby with a grove of apple, peach, and plum trees planted between the cabin and the creek.

Stretching beyond Independence was the vast and lawless Indian Territory and, beyond that, Texas. Thus, the trail attracted not only Kansas settlers, but the hoards of immigrant fortune seekers pushing westward and casting envious eyes on the wide open spaces of Texas and what was to become Oklahoma.

The robbery-bent Benders undoubtedly were attracted to the site since it lay along the route cattle buyers often followed on their way to Texas to buy longhorn beef—buyers who were known to carry large sums of money with them.

The Bender Tavern was positioned ideally to exploit that flow of traffic. As taverns go, it wasn't much, although it was typical of the overnight way stations of the era. But unlike others of its kind, the Bender place was built with murder in mind. The inn's single room was divided in half; a large piece of wagon canvas stretched between the walls.

The front section hosted travelers who were seated at a large, rough-hewn table and were served the meals prepared by Mrs. Bender and Kate. A counter along one wall held a small stock of supplies which travelers could buy: tinned goods, tobacco, crackers, powder, and shot. Neighbors in the area also came to rely on the Benders' inventory rather than making the long drive into town.

The Benders obviously selected their victims with care. Usually men traveling alone, strangers who appeared prosperous enough to be worth killing.

Once marked for murder, the visitor was invited to sit at the table to be served, his back flush against the canvas wall. Behind him, in the dark, Pa and son John Bender waited silently until the unwary guest leaned back against the curtain, his head plainly outlined through the cloth, making an easy target for the Bender men to aim their powerful hammer blows.

Afterwards, they dragged the dead or stunned victim beneath the canvas and stripped him of his clothing and valuables.

* * *

Beneath the back room, the Benders had dug their death pit and concealed it with a trapdoor held in place by leather hinges. The excavation, some six or seven feet in diameter and about the same depth, was lined with stones. Even though the victim died instantly from the blows, the Benders still made sure of their work by slitting the throat and tossing the body into the pit so the blood wouldn't stain the cabin floor.

The pit served a dual purpose: Victims who were not killed outright were left in the hole to bleed to death. Secondly, it served as a holding pen until the bodies could be carried outside and buried at night or when no passersby were in sight.

One lurid historical account of the Benders described the pit as ". . . the highlight, the most important thing in this house of horrors, for it was into this ghastly hole the Benders threw the bodies of their victims until they could safely be disposed of. The pit was stained and discolored with the blood of many foully murdered men . . .

"Still limp and warm, the bloodstained body was dragged to the trapdoor of the pit, and the poor, mutilated thing that had so lately been a living, breathing man was pushed or kicked into a pit by the fiendish group. Then the trap swung shut. The body lay, huddled, grotesque and silent on the stones, while Kate perhaps hurried smilingly to greet a friend, neighbor, or customer.

"Then later that night, with the dull glow of their windows the only gleam of light in the great darkness of the lonely prairies, the robbery would take place when the body, now stiff, cold and blood-clotted, was lifted from the pit and carried through the night to be dumped into a shallow, hurriedly dug grave."

* * *

Apparently, murder was part of the Benders' stock in trade from the time they first opened for business. No one knows who the first victim was (or how many in all), but it may be that the Benders switched to burying their evidence in the backyard when abandoned corpses began turning up around Cherryvale and causing too much commotion.

In the winter of 1872 the first body was found in Big Hill Creek, about four miles from the Bender Tavern. The corpse was never identified, but the cause of death was obvious: skull crushed/throat cut. Crimes of violence were still all too common on the frontier, so the victim was quickly buried in an anonymous grave and forgotten.

A month later, another body surfaced in the Verdigris River not far from Cherryvale. This time there was more concern since the body was identified as a local man who had been reported missing recently. An inquest was conducted, and a town meeting held to discuss the murder, but no further action was taken.

Certainly, no one suspected at the time that the Benders might be connected to the brutal slayings. By now, the family was fairly well-known, although widely regarded as "peculiar." The men were surly and unfriendly. The old woman never spoke to anyone and those neighbors who did come in contact with her left feeling as if they'd just been exposed to something malevolent and unnatural. "Her expression was so sullen and savage that it repelled even her unimaginative neighbors, and so she was regarded with much disfavor long before any suspicion became attached to the Benders," said one account.

Despite the unsettling effect Ma Bender had on outsiders, she became known, throughout the sparsely settled communities, as possessing magical powers to heal the sick. At times, neighbors sent for Ma Bender to visit their sickbeds and work her spells or deliver her potions. On those occasions, Kate went along to translate, help with the spell craft . . . and collect the fees.

Kate, unlike the other members of the family, began attending church and social functions where she proved to be a captivating dancer, and, so went the rumors, an aggressive and insatiable sex partner.

About this time, Kate Bender also blossomed into a local, if somewhat bizarre, celebrity as a faith healer, medium, and psychic capable of some astonishing feats. She began lecturing and holding seances and became so popular she took her act on the road, appearing in small theaters and saloons around Parsons, Labette, Oswego, and Chetopa. The charade not only separated the gullible from their hard-earned dollars, but also was highly effective in luring more potential flies into the Benders' hideous spiderweb. Several came seeking Kate's soothsaying powers; many more were enticed by the scent of her steamy sexuality.

Kate had handbills printed and distributed throughout southeastern Kansas, parts of Missouri, and even down into the Indian Nations. The notices proclaimed:

"Prof. Miss KATIE BENDER

"Can heal all sorts of Diseases; can cure Blindness, Fits, Deafness and all such Diseases, also Deaf and Dumbness.

"Residence fourteen miles East of Independence, on the road from Independence to Osage Mission, one and one-half miles South East of Morehead Station.

"KATIE BENDER June 18, 1872."

There were those who were convinced Kate really did possess supernatural powers. Hindsight may have overrated her, but, according to local legends, Kate not only cured diseases, but also located lost articles and people, practiced astrology and numerology, read palms, told fortunes by means of sticks-and-buttons, cast spells, and sold infallible luck charms and love potions.

Wary neighbors whispered that the Benders had no milk cows, but always had plenty of milk, butter, and homemade cheese. One man claimed to have the answer. Passing by the Tavern one night, the man said he peeked through a crack in the window and saw the Bender women squeezing milk from rags hanging on a string! A farmer living ten miles away insisted that his cows were being milked at night by invisible hands, an obvious case of witchcraft that surely must have originated with the strange Bender family.

Another fantastic story circulated that Kate Bender was a shape changer who often assumed the guise of a cat when she crept through the night to visit the home of a male friend. There, she changed back into Kate. After an all-night sexual romp, she became a cat again and returned home with no one the wiser.

After the murders were discovered, even more sinister tales about the Benders circulated. One, widely accepted as gospel at the time, claimed that the family had been driven out of a German settlement in Pennsylvania by neighbors who believed the Bender women were practicing witches.

According to this fanciful yarn, Kate and Ma Bender visited graveyards at midnight on the full moon, stripped naked, and, in a strange German dialect, cursed the Christian God and swore fealty to the devil.

Once the vows were taken, the women then submitted their bodies to the "Dark Stranger," some ominous figure who conducted the ceremonies. After the group sex, all three chanted obscene phrases and unspeakable oaths that bound them to the Demon for all eternity in exchange for their supernatural powers.

The story, of course, was complete fabrication, but that didn't stop scores of superstitious Kansas homesteaders from soliciting Kate's mysterious powers to make crops grow or swearing by her mystical third eye that foretold the future and found lost objects.

The wife of one farmer claimed she was alone at her home when two valuable rings vanished. The woman rode many miles to the Bender Tavern, paid her $5 consultation fee (a huge amount in those days and one that few farmers could afford), and watched Kate fall into a trance. In the trance state, Kate told the woman the rings were in the wooden gutter attached to the roof of the house.

The woman, skeptical and ashamed of herself for throwing away so much money, returned home. But on the off chance that Kate really did possess the second sight, the woman climbed a ladder to search the drain. Sure enough, one of the missing rings glittered in the sunlight. The second was found in the bottom of the rain barrel where it had been washed during a recent storm.

This story of the recovered rings, true or not, carried great impact and was one of the many such stories that established Kate Bender as a powerful sorceress; stories that Kate undoubtedly set in motion herself to drum up business. If so, her primitive public relations campaign clicked. Word of her occult powers spread, and a stream of customers soon was knocking on the Bender door, eager to hand over their hard-earned $5 for a dose of Kate's pseudo psychics.

With Kate's reputation, deserved or not, as finder of lost items and strayed or stolen livestock, the next logical step was to ask her about missing relatives and vanished friends. An unusually high number of people for this sparsely settled part of the country had dropped out of sight about the same time Kate began offering her occult services, a coincidence that went unnoticed at the time.

The fact that so many relatives of the missing persons came to consult with Kate is a sure sign that no one suspected the Bender family of any wrongdoing. In these consultations, Kate "saw" that the missing men were alive and well, but off on an adventure in the hazardous Indian Territory, or had left on their own for parts unknown, somewhere far enough away that the likelihood of them ever returning was slight.

It was a masterful scam: First rob and murder the travelers. Next, con relatives who came searching for loved ones out of a few more dollars by conjuring up visions of the missing men in distant lands when, in reality, they lay in shallow graves only a few yards from where Kate Bender sat consoling the grieving relatives.

At any rate, the wild stories of witchcraft, spells, second sight, and nude midnight romps in cemeteries helped make the Benders and their Tavern sources of intense curiosity and speculation (but not suspicion) long before the real horrors were revealed.

Since the dead don't talk, most of what happened when potential victims dropped in on the Benders was pieced together later from tales told by survivors who, for one reason or another, had escaped their clutches.

One of those was John Wetzell, a local Independence businessman, who went to see Kate hoping she could cure a nagging backache. At least, that's what Wetzell later claimed, but since a friend named Gordon accompanied him, it's more than likely that the pair was more interested in Kate's physical wares than her miracle cures.

At the Tavern, Kate greeted the men warmly and invited the men in for a good home cooked meal before she performed her magic. Plates were set at a table with the only chairs available placed with their backs against the canvas partition so closely that both men noticed their heads touched the canvas when they sat down.

While Kate chatted gaily with the visitors, she and her silent, scowling mother prepared the meal. About that time, both Bender men entered the cabin, stared intently at Wetzell and Gordon for a moment, and then ducked behind the curtain without speaking.

Uncomfortable with the scuffling, clanking sounds behind them, Wetzell and Gordon stood up and moved to a small counter that held the supplies the Benders peddled.

Incredibly, Kate, who moments before had been a charming and witty enchantress, suddenly changed into a snarling she-devil, cursing the men and their rude manners.

"Sit down!" she screeched. "Only animals eat standing up."

Startled and frightened by the astonishing transformation, the two grabbed up their belongings and fled to their waiting horse and buggy. As Gordon whipped the horse away from the Tavern, Wetzell, pistol at his side for protection, turned and saw the Bender men run from the inn. In the dim light cast by the glowing oil lamps, it appeared they carried weapons of some kind and, in the fading shadows, Kate stood in the doorway shaking her fist at her fleeing, would-be victims.

One traveler, convinced he had been marked for

murder, told his harrowing story to a local newspaper after the Benders' grisly graveyard was discovered.

Father Paul Ponziglione, a Catholic priest, born into Italian nobility, had given up his family titles to become a missionary to the Indian tribes in the American West. Father Ponziglione was stationed at the Osage Mission and assigned to a vast territory ranging from Wyoming all the way down to the Indian Nations. It was during one of his many trips into the Indian Territory that Father Ponziglione found himself at the Benders' doorstep with night rapidly approaching.

"On a windy day toward dusk," according to the newspaper account, "Father Paul arrived at the Bender place and decided to put up there for the night. His suspicions were aroused when he happened to see old man Bender place a heavy hammer on the other side of the curtain, just back of the supper table. Later he observed the old man and Kate holding a low, whispered conversation. The hard and forbidding features of the Benders, the lonely surroundings, and the moaning of the wind had a far from soothing effect on the priest's mind.

"He remembered reading about the strange disappearance of persons in that part of the state, of whom no trace had ever been found. The more he studied over the matter, the more uneasy he became. Some warning voice within seemed to urge his immediate departure. Finally, under pretext of looking after his horses, he left the house, hurriedly hitched his team to the spring wagon and drove rapidly away."

Eventually, Father Ponziglione became an historian at St. Ignatius College in Chicago. He lived to be eighty-two years old, but as long as he lived, the priest shuddered each time he retold the story of his near brush with death at the hands of the Benders.

* * *

While there is no doubt that the Benders' weapons of choice in their bloody business were the hammer and knife, some of their victims may have been slain even when they weren't seated with their backs to the curtain. For instance, one of the Benders' closest neighbors, M.E. Sparkes, believed that the family killed ". . . anywhere and at any time they found an opportunity—always within the house of course, but just as circumstances dictated.

"You must remember that at that time the country was so new and so thinly populated that they could count on few interruptions in their business.

"One of the men who took part in the investigation of the murder farm told of his visit to the place, when, he believed, he had escaped death only because the Benders learned that he lived not far away. He had recently settled a few miles farther west, and on the first occasion when his stock of provisions ran low he had concluded to go to the Bender store to see if he might replenish his larder there . . .

"Presently the old man emerged from behind the curtain which screened the back part of the house. Bender carried a hammer such as a blacksmith uses and as he came in he looked the man over and inquired abruptly, 'Where did you come from?' He was apparently not satisfied with my friend's reply, for a few minutes later he asked again: 'Where did you say you live?'

"Still a third time Bender asked a similar question before my friend left the place. He was afterwards confident that, had he told Bender he was a stranger in the country he would have received a blow from the hammer . . .

"No, the Benders didn't take the trouble to place all

their victims against the curtain in the dirty little back room where they cooked and ate, for there was no occasion to."

William Pickering was another visitor who claimed he escaped with his head and throat intact after dropping by the Bender Tavern for a meal and made the mistake of flashing some gold coins when he paid Kate for his dinner.

As she dished up his plate, Kate invited the young man to sit at the table with his back to the curtain. Pickering, however, noticed dark stains on the canvas and, not wanting to soil a fancy shirt he was wearing, took a seat on the opposite side of the table instead.

As with Wetzell and Gordon, Kate's personality instantly changed from seductive femme fatale to snarling harpy.

"Get up," she shouted. "That's Pa's place."

Startled, Pickering shouted back that it was the only clean seat in the house and if he couldn't sit there, then he'd take his money and leave.

At that, Kate snatched up a large butcher knife and hissed that she'd chop him to pieces before refunding his money. Suddenly, the edge of the curtain was flung back, just as the terrified young visitor dashed out the door. Pickering leapt to his horse and galloped away—unfed, but still alive. Only later, when he returned to the Tavern to help exhume corpses, did he realize just how close he'd come to joining them in the Benders' backyard boneyard.

But many others were not as fortunate. And the Benders might have continued with their nearly foolproof scheme for robbing and murdering travelers had they not picked on the wrong man to kill.

* * *

Dr. William York was not only one of the leading citizens of Independence, Kansas, but a member of one of the most powerful, high-profile families in the state. One brother, the Colonel, lived in Fort Scott and was considered one of the wealthiest men in the territory. Another brother was state senator with strong political ties that reached all the way to Washington.

Dr. York had been visiting the Colonel in Fort Scott and left for home on March 9, 1873. The thoroughbred he rode, one of the finest in southeastern Kansas, carried an expensive, hand-tooled saddle. An expensive gold watch was in one vest pocket, and several hundred dollars were in the doctor's leather wallet. One estimate placed the amount at $1,500. All told, Dr. William York presented a tempting target for would-be robbers and murderers.

A few miles from the Bender place, Dr. York passed some acquaintances on the road and paused to chat. He remarked that he intended to stop at the Tavern for a plate of stew, tipped his hat, and rode away.

It was the last time anyone, other than the killers, ever saw Dr. William York alive.

Several days passed, and when the doctor failed to appear in Independence, the other York brothers were notified and search parties were organized. The Yorks hired a dozen mercenaries to scour the hilly woods between Fort Scott and Independence.

The missing man was traced as far as the Bender's wayside inn near Cherryvale where his trail vanished. On April 3, 1873, one of the search parties rode up to the Tavern, hoping that the doctor might have mentioned his travel plans to the Benders.

The family insisted they'd never set eyes on the doctor. Discouraged, the search party moved on, but the longer they searched and the more questions they asked, the more they were convinced that Dr. York's trail had ended on the Benders' doorstep.

On April 14, the searchers returned to the Bender Tavern. This time, Colonel York himself led the party of a dozen heavily armed men.

At the inn, Kate now admitted that Dr. York had, indeed, stopped by for stew, but that she'd simply forgotten the visit when questioned by the first search party. Yes, she said, she had set a plate for the doctor, but he had gone on his way after finishing the meal. Kate was so cooperative that she even offered to hold a seance in an attempt to locate the missing doctor.

"Maybe some of them outlaws hereabouts got him," John Bender, Jr., suddenly volunteered. "I been shot at by them myself. Maybe they robbed and killed your brother."

Bender's suggestion was taken seriously. This was, after all, the era of the outlaw. The James and Younger gangs were at their peak, raiding banks and railroads all along the Kansas-Missouri border. And these famous desperadoes often used the Osage Mission road on their sorties into the Indian Territory when the Pinkertons made things too hot for them back home.

Young Bender's story seemed plausible enough, so after filling up on Bender stew, York and his private posse rode off in search of murdering outlaws . . . and swallowed John Bender's red herring hook, line, and sinker.

After more weary days spent following a false trail, Colonel York and his manhunters returned to Cherryvale and resumed the search around the Bender Tavern.

On May 5, a neighbor riding by the Tavern noticed

something peculiar. The few livestock the Benders kept were crying pitifully from the corral behind the Tavern. Investigating, the man found dead and dying cows and hogs. It was obvious the animals had been without food or water for days. Moreover, the door to the inn was locked tight. The neighbor galloped into Cherryvale and spread the alarm.

News of strange findings at the Bender place quickly reached Colonel York who hurried to the Tavern along with his posse and several townspeople.

York took charge of the milling crowd, ordering some of the bystanders to break down the locked door. The sickening stench that rolled like a tidal wave from the sealed and shuttered cabin sent the men at the front of the crowd reeling and retching into the front yard. After the cabin had aired out, the searchers entered and traced the putrid odor to a trapdoor in the floor toward the rear of the building.

In the pit beneath the door, lanterns cast flickering shadows over a thick, congealing pool of what proved to be human blood. The pit itself was empty but the cabin floor was littered with scraps of clothing and other debris indicating that the Benders had left in a rush.

Under a pile of rubbish in one corner, the searchers came across an extraordinarily heavy blacksmith's hammer, a find that proved significant only later when the bodies were pulled from their graves.

While some of the Colonel's men searched the cabin and its nauseating pit, others went tramping through the orchard and the fields leading down to Drum Creek in search of more evidence. The ground they covered showed signs of frequent plowing, but there were no crops to show for the effort. Since most of the members of the search party were farmers themselves, the absence of crops immediately struck them as curious.

When the oddity was pointed out to Colonel York, he and a couple of his men climbed to the roof of the Tavern for a better view. From that higher vantage point, the distinctive oblong scars on the earth that the plowing was meant to disguise stood out clearly.

"Boys," gasped the Colonel. "Those are graves down there!"

A cry for picks and shovels went out, and while the men waited for the tools to arrive they prodded the grave sites with a long metal rod. Time and again, the rod was withdrawn with what appeared to be bits of flesh clinging to the points.

Soon, a dozen men were digging furiously. It didn't take them long, since nearly all the bodies had been hastily buried under just a few feet of dirt.

As each body was pulled from the ground, the shattered skulls made it unmistakably clear how the victims had died. Someone remembered the discarded hammer in the Tavern and raced to retrieve it. In at least half the cases, the hammerhead fit perfectly into the gaping holes in the victims' skulls.

One of the first bodies uncovered was the missing Dr. York. He had been stripped of clothing and boots and thrown facedown in the shallow grave with only a foot or two of soil covering the corpse. In addition to the vicious hammer blow, Dr. York's throat had also been cut so deeply that he was nearly decapitated.

One after another, seven more graves gave up their gruesome secrets. Some of the victims who were still identifiable included W.F. McCrotty, a Cedarville resident who had disappeared months earlier and who may have been one of the Bender's first victims; the body of Benjamin M. Brown, a horse trader from Howard County, was too badly decomposed to be identified, but someone in the crowd recognized a small silver ring they knew belonged to Brown and that the killers had overlooked; and Henry F. McKenzie, a native of Indiana, who had disappeared in December 1872, en route to Independence to visit his sister.

When the grave holding the remains of George Loucher and his tiny daughter was opened, a loud moan of outrage and despair went up from the crowd. Loucher had been a well-liked neighbor to many who now stood beside his grave. The previous fall he had buried his own wife in Cherryvale after she and an infant died in childbirth. Afterwards, Loucher said goodbye and left with his only child to return to his family's home in Iowa. The first night on the road, Loucher told his friends that he planned to stop at the Bender Tavern.

The *Springfield Times,* with its correspondent on the scene, gave this spine-chilling eyewitness account of the mass exhumation:

"After boring or prodding for nearly an hour, the rod was withdrawn with something that looked like matter adhered to the point . . . in a few minutes a corpse was uncovered. It had been buried upon its face. The flesh had dropped away from the legs. There was no coffin, no winding sheet, no preparation for the grave, nothing upon the body but an old shirt, torn in places and thick with damp and decay. The corpse was tenderly disinterred and laid upon its back in the soft April sun. One look of horror into the ghastly face, festering and swollen, and a dozen voices cried out in terror: 'My God, it is Dr. York!'

"He had been buried in a shallow hole, with scarcely two feet of dirt over him. They examined him closely. Upon the back of his head . . . a terrible blow had been given with a hammer. The skull had been driven into the brain. And from the battered and broken crevices a dull stream of blood had oozed, plastering his hair with a clammy paste and running down his shoulders. Strong men turned away from the sickening sight with a shudder. Others wept. Some even had to leave the garden and remain a ways from the shambles of the butchers.

"In an hour all the town was at the scene of the discovery. A coffin was procured for Dr. York's body, and his brother, utterly overwhelmed, sat by the ghastly remains as one upon whom the hand of death had been laid . . .

"The scene was horrible beyond description. The search went on unabated. . . . A fascination impossible to define held the spectators to the spot. The spirit of murder was there and it kept them in spite of the night and the horror of the surroundings. The crowd increased instead of diminished. Coffins were provided and the search renewed.

"Six butchered human beings were brought forth from their bloody graves and three others are yet to be uncovered. . . . The pit under the trapdoor was made to receive the body when first struck down by the murderer's hammer. All the skulls were crushed in, and all at nearly the same place . . ."

Only sundown ended the horror show. But at dawn the following day, May 6, 1873, the digging resumed. More graves were located, including the one holding the mutilated remains of the child who was never identified. Other than the two children and the lone woman, the bodies unearthed and positively identified seemed to point unmistakably to robbery as primary motive, with murder merely an expedient tool to hide the evidence.

Two of the men who had disappeared in the neighborhood, Ben Brown and W. F. McCrotty, were said to be carrying $1,500 and $3,000 each. McCrotty may have had $2,000 with him as a settlement for his land dispute case, and relatives of another victim, William Boyle, said he had $1,900 with him when he left home.

Most of the victims were known to own expensive rings, diamond stickpins, or gold watches, none of which was ever recovered. There was also the matter of the horses, wagons, saddles, harnesses, weapons, and other pieces of equipment the victims had with them when they arrived at the Bender Tavern . . . and that were never seen again.

Just how the Benders managed to dispose of possessions such as horses or buggies that neighbors of the victims would surely recognize if they spotted them on the road has never been answered. Lawmen assumed that the Benders somehow managed to spirit the stolen property out of the vicinity under cover of darkness, most likely to the nearby and lawless Indian Territory, where it was sold and the loot added to the Bender's booty.

Meanwhile, there was the small but steady income from the sale of food and accommodations at the Tavern (the Benders didn't kill *all* their guests), and the high fees Kate collected for her healing and fortune-telling work. So it's quite possible that the Benders, living as frugally as they did, fled with a sizeable fortune to finance their escape.

Now, as the truth and the full horror of the massacre began to emerge, it appeared that the Benders had not only gotten away with multiple murders, but also escaped scot-free with thousands of dollars in blood money. But the enraged Kansans weren't about to let them off so easily. Legal posses, vigilante committees, and free-lance bounty hunters galloped off to hunt down the murderous fiends. But the Benders were never found—at least not that any of the manhunters would ever admit.

They left only a single clue behind them. It turned out that as soon as Colonel York and his search party had ridden away from the Tavern, the Benders had grabbed a few things, tossed them in a wagon, and hightailed it up to the road to Thayer. A couple of days later, the team of horses was found hitched in a grove of cottonwoods just outside of town. A subsequent investigation revealed that the Benders had purchased tickets for the northbound 5 A.M. train.

From there, the trail trickled out. Some reports said that the family split up at Chanute (then known as New Chicago), the older half heading east, the younger south to Texas. Another version was the train ticket purchase was really a diversion and that the Benders had a second wagon team stashed and made a run for the safety of the Indian Territory.

It was as if the family had vanished in a cloud of Kansas dust. From the moment they hurriedly packed up and fled, the fate of the Benders dissolves into wild conjecture, rumors of violent vengeance, and a deep mystery that remains unsolved. There are just as many fantastic tales attached to the disappearance and possible demise of the Bender family as there were surrounding its origins and early days at play in the fields of black magic.

The stories that the family headed south for the dubious haven of the Indian Territory seems the most plausible. Most accounts that vigilantes caught up with the Benders and administered quick and brutal frontier justice focus on this supposed flight southward to the Nations.

In later years, some who claimed to be members of the posse that ran the Benders to ground hinted that the end came in a cornfield on what is now the Oklahoma-Kansas line. In the gunfight that ensued, Pa and John Bender were killed outright. Ma Bender was wounded and slowly bled to death. Kate, meanwhile, leapt from the Bender wagon, dashed into the cornfield, and hid behind a shock of corn.

As the posse closed in, Kate battled back with an old Navy Colt revolver until she was out of ammunition. The pursuers shredded the corn shock with gunfire. When the smoke cleared, Kate Bender was dead, her body riddled with twenty-four bullet holes. Afterwards, the four corpses where piled up on a creek bank, set on fire, and burned until only ashes remained. The manhunters then surrounded the smoldering pyre and kicked the ashes into the creek waters.

That story was never verified, nor was the one that said Kate Bender was captured, lashed to a tree, and burned alive like a witch, screaming curses at the executioners while the flames consumed her.

For years, men who claimed they rode with the vigilantes whispered tales purporting to be the truth about the gruesome end to the Benders, but all had sworn blood oaths never to reveal what happened. Many of those stories were passed down from father to son like some terrible, but treasured, family fable.

In 1910, for example, J.N. Kramer, Cherryvale's chief of police, told an historian that his father-in-law's farm had adjoined the Bender property. "I often tried to find out from him what became of the Benders, but he only gave me a knowing look and said he guessed they would not bother anyone else," said Kramer. "There was a Vigilance Committee formed to locate the Benders, and shortly afterward old man Bender's wagon was found by the roadside riddled with bullets. You will have to guess the rest."

With no Bender bodies as proof, the rumors persisted for decades that the fiendish family had escaped to resume its bloodthirsty business somewhere else on the frontier. One of those convinced that the Benders, or at least Kate and her mother, had survived the Kansas manhunt was a self-styled clairvoyant and medium named Frances McCann.

A nineteenth century version of "America's Most Wanted," the paranoid Mrs. McCann kept an eye peeled for felons whenever she ventured out of her gloomy home in McPherson, Kansas. Her dreams, she claimed, revealed to her the startling secrets about which of her friends and neighbors were wanted for various crimes and were hiding out in central Kansas under assumed identities.

In 1888, Mrs. McCann's suspicions focused on the woman who did her laundry, Sarah Eliza Davis, and her elderly mother. McCann's spirits whispered in her ear that the women were really the murderous Bender women in disguise.

Mrs. McCann pestered local authorities endlessly until they finally agreed to bring the two women in for questioning just to get the busybody spiritualist off their backs.

Sarah Davis didn't help herself by refusing to talk about her background. As a result, in November 1889, sixteen years after the ghastly murders were discovered, Sarah Davis and her mother, Almira Griffith, were hauled back to Cherryvale to stand trial for the Benders' atrocities—even though several eyewitnesses, including the judge himself who had once dined at the Bender Tavern, instantly recognized these women were not Kate and Ma Bender.

But before the trial began, papers arrived from Michigan that proved Sarah Davis and Almira Griffith were exactly who they claimed to be. The women were set free, and Mrs. McCann went back to her soothsaying.

But even that tale, like most of the Bender history, has a bizarre twist. Another version holds that it was Mrs. Frances E. McCann herself and a Mrs. L. Davis who were fingered as the Bender women and brought back from Michigan to Kansas in 1889. Of the sixteen witnesses who supposedly knew the Benders, seven identified the defendants as Kate and Ma Bender; seven insisted they weren't; two were not sure. The court eventually ruled that the women were not the Benders and set them free.

One of the most bizarre reports concerned a murder case in Idaho in 1884 in which the victim died from a mighty hammer blow to the back of the head. Besides the curiously similar "MO," the suspect charged with the slaying bore a slight resemblance to Pa Bender.

Word suddenly circulated that the infamous Kansas monster was chained to a wall in the local lockup and crowds began to gather. Grumblings of a lynching were in the air. But the terrified prisoner, who was never positively identified, got his hands on a knife and tried to cut off his shackled foot in a desperate attempt to escape the lynch mob. He failed, but bled to death nevertheless.

For decades, stories about such and such a Bender

popping up alive in this or that city abounded. Even into the twentieth century, people were still claiming to have bumped into Kate on the streets of Kansas City, New York, New Orleans, Mexico City, Havana, and even Paris. According to other "sightings" and "true histories" of the family, Pa Bender killed himself in Michigan; Ma Bender went insane and died in Texas in 1883; John, Jr., died a peaceful death in 1925 as a businessman in Amarillo, Texas; Kate supposedly married a marshal who had been tracking her all those years and lived happily ever after.

One fascinating—and quite probable—version of the Benders' fate surfaced as late as 1967. In its March 12 edition, *The Houston Post* reported:

"A confession written in 1922 has been uncovered in Houston that solves one of the most bizarre and brutal tales of murder and mystery in the history of American crime.

"The confession makes known for the first time the fate of the infamous Bender family of Kansas, which disappeared in the spring of 1873 shortly after the bodies of eight persons who had met horrible deaths were found buried in the Bender orchard.

"The confession was found among the personal effects of the late William Hiram McDaniel, of Gainesville, Texas, who died twelve years ago. At the request of a lodge brother, the confession was given in 1922 by the man who wished McDaniel to record his words.

"The identity of the Kansas man who made the confession to McDaniel was known to McDaniel and is known to *The Houston Post,* but to protect innocent persons related to the confessor, his name will not be revealed . . .

"The confession was as follows: 'You being a native

of Kansas no doubt have heard about the Bender family and the different versions of what became of them and where they are now.

" 'A posse of citizens of which I was a member went to the Bender house at night, took them captive and made them confess, killed them, split their abdomens to prevent gas bloat, weighted the bodies and sank them in the Verdigris River. The younger man and Miss Kate both were suffering from gonorrhea and confessed that [they] were living as man and wife.

" 'The members of the posse agreed that this lynching would not be told until after the death of all but one who was privileged to tell it. They are all dead but me and I am old and in bad health so I want to tell you with the understanding that you will not relate the incident until after my death.' "

If this was, in fact, the end of the Benders, the silent, muddy Verdigris River has never given up its vile and shameful secret.

TWO
THE "TERRIBLE GENNAS"

Tony "the Gent" had one ironclad rule when it came to killing.

"You go to rub out a guy," he ordered his five brothers and their pack of bloodthirsty gunners, "make sure you smear the bullets with garlic first. If the slugs don't kill him, the poison will."

It was an ancient recipe concocted in their native Sicily, one the Gennas brought with them when they left home for a ruthless life of crime in Chicago. The idea was that the mixture of garlic, onion juice, and gunpowder would induce gangrene which would slowly, agonizingly ravage any victim who miraculously survived a shredding by the Genna machine-gun, pistol, and shotgun shells packed with shrapnel-like slugs. The garlic really didn't work. But the fact that the Gennas fanatically believed that it did helps to explain why these scabrous brothers, as savage a brood of cutthroats as ever existed, were so dreaded by friends and enemies alike that they came to be called—the "Terrible Gennas."

* * *

There were six Genna brothers: Jim, Tony "the Gentleman" (or Tony the Gent), "Bloody" Angelo, Mike "the Devil," Pete, and Sam. Each was small and stocky with a swarthy handsomeness that disguised an iceberg-cold meanness glinting in each brother's eyes, the eyes of predators for whom murder was a necessary survival tool amidst the ruthless gangs that prowled Chicago's street jungles.

Fanatically loyal to each other, suspicious to the point of paranoia of outsiders, the Genna brothers shaped their own perverted version of the American dream: poor, uneducated immigrants who found wealth, success, and infamy in America by clawing their way to the top of the criminal heap over the bodies of countless murder victims.

In their climb to the top, the Genna family evolved into a deadly efficient murder machine with each brother a cog that made the machine mesh. Jim, the oldest, called the shots; Bloody Angelo and Mike the Devil were the family's main enforcers and executioners; Tony was the brains of the bunch who did most of the planning, but whose front as an opera-loving philanthropist couldn't totally mask his savagery; Sam ran the gambling interests; Pete handled the prostitution rackets.

Each brother, regardless of the public role he played, relished indulging in cold-blooded murder. Their reputation was enhanced by the way they often tortured and toyed with their victims before finally killing them. It's impossible to know how many died at the hands of the Gennas during their careers as street thugs, Black Hand extortionists, and Prohibition kingpins. Scores, at the very least; more likely hundreds if you count all those butchered by hired guns on direct orders from the Terrible Gennas.

This was, after all, the era of bloody mobocracy in America, a time when the gangs ruled by violence and the Chicago streets ran red with the blood of crooks, cops, and innocent bystanders. And none, not even Al Capone, was bloodier or more fearsome than the Terrible Gennas. There was a Niagara of money for anyone tough enough, heartless enough, or crazy enough to grab it.

Millions of gallons of potent rotgut cranked out by thousands of mom-and-pop stills; beer brewed up in gang-owned breweries; the "real stuff" smuggled in from Canada or trucked overland from East Coast rum runners.

Plus, there were the enormous profits from gambling and prostitution that went hand in glove with illegal booze.

"There's $30 million dollars worth of beer sold in Chicago every month," chortled North Side gang lord Dion O'Banion, just before Genna guns cut down the crazed Irish gangster in his beloved flower shop.

That $30 million a month came from beer sales alone—an astonishing fortune for anyone ruthless enough to seize it, especially since $1 in the 1920s would be worth about $20 today! Violent gang lords who, like the Gennas, began as mulish street thugs, were raking in as much as $100 million a year at the height of Prohibition. (About $1 million a month ended up in the pockets of dirty politicians and cops on the take.) The times produced the likes of "Scarface" Al Capone, "Machine Gun" Jack McGurn, George "Bugs" Moran, Dion O'Banion, Frank Nitti, and others whose hired guns accounted for a murder a day during one period.

Of those, Capone is the one that history (and Hollywood) remembers today. But in their day, no family was more feared than the Terrible Gennas who killed and bribed their way to power in the most corrupt and kill-crazy city in America at the time. The Gennas were the first of the ruthless Chicago gangs to seize control of the immensely profitable bootleg trade and back it up with their ferocious reputations as merciless killers and urban terrorists.

For example, one Genna innovation, as terrifying as it was effective, involved reloading their favored sawed-off shotguns with metal slugs rather than the usual buckshot. The slugs were designed to do maximum damage, literally shredding the victim into a mass of flesh resembling hamburger meat. A secondary effect of the bloody destruction was the shattering impact it had on others. Death by shotgun slugs at point-blank range was a horrifying object lesson that numbed the senses with its incomprehensible barbarity.

One of their slayings became legendary for its cruelty. Bloody Angelo, Mike the Devil, and Jim Genna took a gangland rival for a ride. On a lonely rural road, the brothers told the terrified mobster that if he prayed sincerely they might let him live. The man fell to his knees and raised his clasped hands. As he begged and prayed for his life, Mike pulled the trigger on his sawed-off shotgun and blew away the man's hands. The victim writhed and screamed in agony until Angelo finally put a bullet in his brain—not because the Gennas felt sorry for the wretch and wanted to put him out of his misery, but because the spurting blood from his flailing stumps was splattering their suits.

Even before illegal booze became the business of choice, the Genna boys had already made their bones as Chicago's most vicious band of Black Hand extortionists who preyed on fellow Sicilian and Italian immigrants.

On December 8, 1922, the Chicago papers carried an item that few outside of "Little Italy" paid much attention to. In that inner city enclave, however, the news was momentous since it meant that a new breed of remorseless killers and extortionists, even bloodier than the old, had arrived. That news item, headlined "King of Black Hand Killed in Chicago," read:

"Joseph Maggio, known throughout the Italian colony here as the 'King of the Black Hand,' was shot from behind and killed tonight as he walked near his home, 245 East Twenty-fourth Street. He is the last of three brothers to meet death in a strange vendetta.

"The body of Maggio was found in front of Haines School. Four bullcts had been fired into the back of his head, apparently at a range of only a few inches. In his pocket was an automatic pistol."

With Maggio's murder, the Gennas became Chicago's ruling Black Hand criminals, an astonishing ascension considering the tight-knit clan had landed on American shores only a dozen years earlier.

The six Genna brothers were all born in Marsala, Sicily. They settled in Chicago in 1910 where their father worked as a railroad section hand. The boys' mother died when they were still young, leaving the unruly brood to grow up on the mean streets of Chicago's Little Italy, where murder was a routine event and crime a way of life.

To survive the Gennas developed into cold-blooded, treacherous street fighters and killers. As devoutly religious as they were resolutely evil, each brother carried a rosary in one pocket, a pistol in the other when they went out to kill. The only exception was Tony the Gent, a pompous patron of the opera who studied architecture and lived regally in an expensive hotel suite. After climbing out of the gutter, Tony disdained killing himself, preferring to leave the bloody business to his more brutal brothers. However, Tony continued to sit in on all family councils and enthusiastically helped plot who and how the Gennas would kill next.

While still in their teens, their father died leaving the boys to make it on their own. But the violence-prone brothers who enjoyed standing back to back and taking on other neighborhood gangs with fists, clubs, and chains, had already caught the eye of "Diamond" Joe Esposito, a Black Hand boss. The brutality of the Gennas made them ideal enforcers, so the boys went to work for Diamond Joe as head thumpers, back stabbers, bombers, and willing assassins. The Gennas learned their trade well, adding their own sadistic innovations to the crude Black Hand racket that transformed it into a sophisticated form of terrorism. For the Gennas, the pot of gold at the end of the American rainbow was smudged with the menacing prints of the Black Hand.

The Black Hand was not necessarily the forerunner of the modern Mafia/*La Cosa Nostra,* although both indulged in murder and intimidation. But instead of a brotherhood of blood-oath criminals, Black Hand extortionists ranged from single free-lancers to organized gangs such as the Gennas.

The targets of Black Hand extortionists were primarily the superstitious Italian and Sicilian immigrants who crowded into Little Italy ghettos of New York, Chicago, New Orleans, Kansas City, and other large cities.

The pay-or-die shakedown artists didn't hesitate to kill if necessary, although maimings and bombings were preferred since the dead couldn't pay up. The Gennas, for example, developed an especially heinous method for enforcing their demands: When a victim refused to pay, they often snatched one of his children, chopped off a finger, and sent the mutilated child home. Faced with such horror in their own homes, most victims begged to pay the extortion demands.

However, most people who received the extortion note with the characteristic black hand imprint signature at the bottom paid off instantly, so ingrained was the fear of Black Hand retaliation. The Gennas were known for couching their outrageous demands in elaborately contrived politeness. A frequently quoted extortion note typical of their style read:

> Most gentle Mr. Silvani: Hoping that the present will not impress you much, you will be so good as to send me $2,000 if your life is dear to you. So I beg you warmly to put them on your door within four days. But if not, I swear this week's time not even the dust of your family will exist. With regards, believe me to be your friends.

The Gennas carved out a turf between Oak and Taylor Streets and Grand and Wentworth Avenues in the heart of Chicago's Little Italy section. The violence the Gennas inflicted on this relatively small area was appalling. If a beating, a knifing, or even a murder didn't get their point across, the brothers weren't above dynamiting entire buildings, families and all.

The Gennas delighted in gunning down victims in broad daylight, on busy streets, and calmly strolling away knowing that the scores of eyewitnesses would suffer sudden attacks of amnesia when questioned by cops. During one fourteen-month stretch, no less than thirty-eight Black Hand casualties were shot to pieces at Oak and Milton Streets, an intersection so bloody that it came to be known as "Death Corner." And at least half of those died at the hands of a mysterious and blood-drenched Black Hand assassin known only as "Shotgun Man."

For years, while the Gennas held power, Shotgun Man walked the streets of Little Italy openly, spreading horror and death wherever he went. He was never arrested, never charged with any of the twenty or thirty Black Hand murders police credited him with. Not much was known about Shotgun Man other than he was Sicilian (as were many of his victims), was a merciless hired gun who pursued his target relentlessly, and whose trademark was a sawed-off, slug-loaded shotgun. At one point, so goes local legend, Shotgun Man returned to Death Corner four times in three days to wipe out four different victims.

The terrified whispers on the street hinted that Shotgun Man was one of the Terrible Gennas, probably Bloody Angelo, the most violent and kill-crazy of the bunch. Lending credence to the theory was the fact that, like Shotgun Man, Angelo and his brothers happily endorsed that slaughterhouse method of murder and loved to watch the victims' bodies splatter when double loads of buckshot slugs tore into them from point-blank range.

Gangsters everywhere—and especially the Genna family—celebrated wildly on January 16, 1920, the day the Eighteenth Amendment to the U.S. Constitution went into effect, outlawing booze in America. At least, that was its intent, but the misguided new law created a monster. Organized crime, as we now know it, was born that day, and the Terrible Gennas plunged right in with their gore-stained hands and gleefully midwifed the unnatural birth.

Overnight, hundreds of thousands of illegal speakeasies opened for business. In Chicago alone, for every legal saloon closed by Prohibition, two illegal joints began serving beer and booze. A new class of violent criminals leapt into the void to satisfy a suddenly thirsty public: the Purple Gang in Detroit, New York's Broadway Mob, the Mayfield Road Gang in Cleveland, and, in Chicago, the Gennas, the Torrio-Capone combination, and the Irish thugs of Dion O'Banion.

With their Black Hand organization already in place, the Gennas instantly became the dominant force in Little Italy. Bootleggers required vast quantities of alcohol to produce their bathtub gin. Most of the legal alcohol-producing plants were closed, but the resourceful Gennas devised an ingenious plan to fill that bottomless need for raw alcohol.

Instead of a few factory-sized stills, the Gennas set up thousands of small mom-and-pop operations throughout Little Italy. In nearly every kitchen or spare room throughout the tenement-packed section of central Chicago, tiny stills bubbled away night and day extracting alcohol from corn sugar. The Gennas' network of stills flooded the city with thousands of gallons of alcohol and, in turn, made the brothers rich, powerful, and more bloodthirsty than ever.

Still operators were paid $15 a day, far more than the poverty-oppressed immigrants could earn for an entire day of backbreaking labor. Families who refused to turn their kitchens into smelly stills seldom held out long. To bring resisters in line, the Gennas resorted to their first love: Black Hand extortion methods suggesting that the reluctant comply or die.

The Gennas' homegrown bootleg operation was so extensive that the heavy stench of fermenting mash hung over Little Italy like a cloud. Tons of corn sugar were trucked in; barrels of alcohol trucked out. A single still could produce 350 gallons of raw alcohol, which cost the Gennas roughly forty cents per gallon. After additional processing in their Taylor Street warehouse, the Gennas peddled the alcohol at $6 a gallon wholesale.

Of course, the illegal activity, not to mention the sickening smell that permeated Little Italy, attracted the attention of cops assigned to the Maxwell Street station only four blocks from the Genna processing plant. Where the cops were concerned, the Gennas learned quickly that it was easier, and better for business, to bribe instead of kill, especially now that everyone had a hand out for a piece of that Prohibition bonanza. So along with their taste for murder, the Gennas became masters of corruption.

The public got a rare peek into just how deep that corruption went when Mike Genna's "little black book" fell into the hands of reporters. An item in the Chicago papers noted:

"The Genna gang's 'black book,' the book that escaped unread from the courtroom of Judge William Brothers and from the presence of State's Attorney Robert E. Crowe last Monday, was shown to an afternoon newspaper today and then taken away to be hidden.

"These are some of the things the list is said to record concerning bootlegging liquor and graft:

"1. More than 250 Chicago policemen were on the Genna payroll at monthly 'salaries' averaging from $10 to $125.

"2. A squad from State's Attorney Crowe's office was collecting from the bootlegging Gennas.

"3. Three squads from the Detective Bureau were on the payroll at $400 to $800 a month each.

"4. The policemen drawing pay from the gang collected at 1022 West Taylor Street monthly, between the twenty-fifth of one month and the tenth of the next month.

"5. The payroll for May totaled $6,926. Much of the payoff list was asserted to be in Mike Genna's handwriting."

But even these were lowball figures.

At their peak, the Gennas had about four-hundred cops on the pad, from foot patrolmen to station captains. On pay days, so many badges trooped through the Gennas' warehouse to fill their pockets that neighbors referred to the gang's headquarters as "The Police Station."

The Gennas were even given the badge numbers of cops assigned to the Maxwell Street station house, a system designed to prevent cops from other precincts from chiseling in on the Maxwell Street operation and grabbing a few drippings off the Genna gravy train. In exchange, the Gennas gave police a list of their stills. When an independent operation was uncovered, squads of cops raided the competition and put it out of business. Occasionally, Genna trucks making deliveries outside Little Italy were stopped by police not on the Genna payroll. To prevent such slowdowns, the Maxwell Street commanders started sending off-duty officers along to escort the trucks and protect the cargoes from other cops.

Early on the Gennas also had discovered that political corruption was as necessary as police corruption if they hoped to stay in business. At the time, Chicago's Nineteenth Ward (which became the Twenty-fifth in a

1920 redistricting), that encompassed Little Italy, was already known as the "Bloody Ward" for the often bloody political battles fought over its turf.

The Gennas made it even bloodier by aligning with Tony D'Andrea, a disgraced priest, former pimp, and convicted counterfeiter. D'Andrea was president of the powerful *Unione Siciliane* when he decided to challenge incumbent John "Johnny de Pow" Powers, the longtime Irish boss of the Bloody Ward, for the office of alderman from the Nineteenth.

In exchange for his political clout, the Gennas offered D'Andrea muscle and blood.

One of the Gennas' first chores was to bomb the front porch off Johnny Powers' house. They missed killing the alderman, but the attack enraged Powers' supporters, who struck back with their own bombs, and the battle was joined. Over the next year, at least thirty people died in the Alderman War, with the Gennas claiming most of the victims.

As experienced Black Hand extortionists, the Gennas knew that intimidation and the threat of violence were powerful weapons. Bloody Angelo, a terrorist at heart, came up with a new gimmick designed to strike fear into the hearts of even his most fearless enemies. He brazenly posted the names of those he intended to kill on a wormy old poplar tree on Loomis Street in Little Italy . . . and then went out and shot them dead. The site came to be known as "Dead Man's Tree," and before long both sides were using it to publicly announce who was marked for death.

The murder of Paul Labriola was a typical Genna killing.

Labriola was a municipal court bailiff and Powers precinct captain who refused to switch sides in the conflict. When he found his name tacked to Dead Man's Tree, Labriola refused to go into hiding as his friends urged, a brave but foolish stand on his part.

The morning of March 8, 1921, Labriola left his home in the middle of the block on West Congress Street and set out for work. Bloody Angelo and Mike the Devil Genna stood on one corner; three of their hired hoods, Salvatore "Samoots" Amatuna, Frank Gambino, and John Gaudino, waited at the opposite end of the block.

As Labriola approached the two brothers, his eyes widened in recognition as the Gennas whipped automatics from their overcoat pockets and opened fire.

Labriola crumpled to the sidewalk with nine bullets in his body. Alerted by the gunfire, Labriola's wife ran screaming to her husband's side, just in time to see Bloody Angelo straddle the already fatally wounded man.

"He ain't done yet," Angelo snarled. Then, in what became a Genna trademark, bent over and fired three more shots, blowing away most of Labriola's face and head.

Genna spat the toothpick he'd been chewing on Labriola's still twitching body. As the horror-stricken woman sank to her knees in the spreading pool of her husband's blood, Genna grinned, "Now he's done," and calmly strode away.

Only four hours later, the murder team struck again. This time the victim was Harry Raimondi, a Little Italy cigar store owner and Johnny Powers' supporter. The Genna brothers walked in and purchased a couple of cigars. When Raimondi handed them over, out came the guns. By nightfall, Harry Raimondi's name had been crossed off the list posted on Dead Man's Tree.

But Powers' boys got in their licks as well. About

2:00 A.M. on May 11, Tony D'Andrea cashed in his poker chips following an all-night game at Amato's restaurant, a popular Genna hangout. When he arrived home and mounted the steps of his apartment building, an assassin lying in wait in an empty room adjacent to the stairs opened fire through the apartment's bay window. D'Andrea tumbled down the steps and died on the sidewalk, his body shredded by thirteen slugs from a double-barreled shotgun.

The killer fled to a waiting car. He left behind the sawed-off shotgun, a fedora with a $20 bill stuck in the lining, and a note that said "For Flowers."

A month later, the Gennas avenged the murder by slaying D'Andrea's bodyguard, Joseph Laspisa, whom they suspected of setting up his boss for the hit by Powers' gunners. To make sure the opposition got the point, Laspisa was cut to pieces on his own doorstep in a carbon copy of the D'Andrea killing.

No one was ever charged with any of the thirty deaths in the D'Andrea-Powers war, although the name of every murder victim was posted in advance on Dead Man's Tree for all to read.

As the enormous profits from Prohibition mounted, the need for some kind of organization became obvious, otherwise the half-dozen warring gangs, motivated by greed, were in danger of wiping each other out. Some seven-hundred-plus Chicagoans were, in fact, slaughtered in gang-related murders during the Prohibition years.

To stem the carnage, Johnny Torrio, the leader of one of the factions and Al Capone's mentor, convinced the various gang leaders to divvy up Chicago into separate territories. There was more than enough booze money to go around without the constant threat of bloody shoot-outs and the inconvenience of bodies in the street.

Unfortunately for the peace process, the Gennas' domain adjoined that of North Side boss, Dion O'Banion and his gang of safecrackers, hijackers, and killers. The Sicilians despised the North Side Irish. O'Banion hated the Gennas with equal passion.

Moreover, the Gennas' territory, concentrated in Little Italy, wasn't big enough to contain their expanding ambitions since their cottage industry was producing more alcohol than they could handle. Squeezed between Dion O'Banion's Irish gang on the North Side and the growing Torrio-Capone combine on the South Side, the Gennas began to edge into the forbidden territories, especially the neighboring North Side where O'Banion was peddling his low-end booze for $6 to $9 per gallon. The Gennas drastically undercut the North Siders selling their cheap rotgut for $3 a gallon.

O'Banion was enraged. O'Banion was the stereotypical Irishman: jolly and friendly, a family man whose idea of fun was an evening at home belting out Irish ballads while pumping away at his $15,000 player piano. But on the job, Dion O'Banion killed casually and without mercy. Estimates on the number of people O'Banion personally murdered range from twenty-five to sixty-three.

Incredibly, this brutal, head-bashing street thug had a soft side to him. "Deanie" (as his friends called him) loved flowers. He loved them so much that he bought a half interest in the Schofield Flower Shop at 738 North State Street, across the street from Holy Name Cathedral. Here, amongst the mums and roses, this multiple murderer spent hours puttering over his beloved blossoms. O'Banion delighted in creating the outlandishly gaudy floral tributes to slain gangsters that became a bizarre idiosyncrasy of Chicago's gang wars. Under O'Banion, Schofield's became the unofficial florist to the mobsters.

Meanwhile, over in Little Italy, the Gennas, whose reputation as killers was bad enough, also surrounded themselves with a cast of cold-blooded triggermen seldom equalled in the history of gangdom.

Among them were Orazio "the Scourge" Tropea; Giuseppe "the Cavalier" Nerone, a university graduate and math teacher turned killer; and Salvatore (Samoots) Amatuna, a music lover known to weep openly over a sad opera aria, but shed not a tear over the victims he enjoyed slowly and torturously killing. Tropea fancied himself as a black magic sorcerer and had the superstitious residents of Little Italy so convinced he possessed "the evil eye" that he rarely had to pull his gun to enforce his demands. Ecola "the Eagle" Baldelli, Tony Finalli, Felipe Gnolfo, and Vito Bascone strutted the streets of Little Italy with pistols stuck in waistbands and sawed-off shotguns swinging at their sides.

But none was more fearsome or more closely matched the Gennas in temperament than the deadly duo, John Scalise and Albert Anselmi.

Scalise and Anselmi were boyhood chums who grew up in Marsala, Sicily, where their roots had been deeply entwined with the Gennas' for generations. The pair fled to the United States to avoid arrest on a murder charge and headed straight for the Gennas. The brothers gladly sheltered them as kin. Scalise and Anselmi thus became extended members of the Terrible Genna family.

While the Gennas preached the garlic bullet theory, it was Scalise and Anselmi who spread the gospel. And while the Gennas invented the "handshake" execution, Scalise and Anselmi perfected the treacherous technique and made it a part of their murderous repertoire. Feigning good fellowship, the short, powerfully built Anselmi approached the intended prey to shake hands. As Anselmi locked the victim's gun hand in a viselike grip, the taller Scalise quickly stepped up and delivered the fatal head shot.

These two kill-happy shooters became infamous for spraying crowded streets with indiscriminate machine-gun fire if it meant hitting the target they were after. During one assassination on a busy street in the middle of the Loop, Scalise and Anselmi were running to their getaway car, when one looked back and saw the victim raise his head. Annoyed that he was still alive, the two rushed back, pushed through the crowd of shocked spectators gathering around the victim, and pumped several more rounds into the body.

In the end, the treacherous pair turned traitor. Instead of hitting Al Capone as the Gennas ordered, Scalise and Anselmi sold out to Scarface and played a major role in finally exterminating the Gennas. But that came later.

In November 1924, Scalise and Anselmi were still the top gunners in the Genna camp—which is when Dion O'Banion stuck his foot in his mouth, a move that not only signed his own death warrant, but also brought down the wrath of the Gennas on his North Side mob and touched off a bloody war that climaxed with the St. Valentine's Day Massacre.

O'Banion's irritation with the Gennas' crowding into his North Side territory boiled over when he learned that Angelo Genna had recently lost a bundle in one of the gambling joints in which O'Banion had an interest and then refused to pay up. O'Banion's lieutenants suggested that he forget the debt to preserve the peace and as a professional courtesy from one gangster to another. But O'Banion was in no mood to be generous.

"To hell with them fucking Sicilians!" he raged. O'Banion got Angelo on the phone and angrily demanded that the marker be paid immediately. The ethnic slurs O'Banion flung at Angelo inflamed the savage Gennas, especially coming from "the Irish pig" the brothers detested above all others. The insult to the family honor could not go unchallenged. The six brothers sat down to plot O'Banion's death. Considering the importance of their target, the Gennas knew this hit had to be meticulously planned and flawlessly executed. Once the decision was made to rub out Dion O'Banion, the Irishman was as good as dead. Now all the Gennas had to do was wait and watch for the ideal opportunity. It came sooner than they expected.

Mike Merlo, the president of *Unione Siciliane,* died suddenly of natural causes; a rare and unnatural event among "the Windy City's" mobster set. All of gangdom turned out for Merlo's funeral, including the mayor and chief of police who served as honorary pallbearers. More than ten thousand mourners trailed the 266-car cortege to Mount Carmel Cemetery to lay Merlo to rest. It was the funeral event of the year, and Schofield's was swamped with orders for $10,000 arrangements.

By unspoken tradition, funerals were a time of truce, so when Jim Genna showed up at Schofield's to look at the flowers, Deanie O'Banion didn't think too much of the fact that his sworn enemy was in the shop; although, as usual, O'Banion kept one hand stuck in his pants pocket that had been specially tailored to hold a .38 pistol.

Jim Genna was actually on a reconnaissance mission to case the joint. He reported back to his waiting brothers that with the funeral truce on, the North Sider wouldn't expect killers to come calling. To insure the set up, Jim Genna phoned in an additional $2,000 order for a Merlo wreath and told O'Banion his men would be in to pick it up at noon the next day, Monday, November 10, 1924.

The newspapers that hit the streets the morning of November 11 screamed out the news:

BEER-RUNNING "KING" IS SLAIN
IN CHICAGO

DION O'BANION IS MURDERED IN HIS
FLORIST SHOP BY THREE GUNMEN,
WHO ESCAPE

THEIR AIDS BLOCK TRAFFIC
SIX CARS USED TO PREVENT PURSUIT
WHILE SLAYERS' CAR DASHES
SAFELY AWAY

CHICAGO, NOV. 10—Dion O'Banion, gunman and gang chief, often called "King of the Beer Runners," was shot to death today in his florist's shop at 738 North State Street. His body, pierced by six bullets, lay crumpled on the floor amid the American Beauties and chrysanthemums which he had used as a blanket of respectability to cover his underworld activities.

Two days ago, O'Banion had a new suit made with three special pockets in the trousers—two in front, one behind. Usually each held an automatic. One pocket also had an extra clip, inasmuch as O'Banion seldom moved without enough ammunition to kill forty-five men if handled with accuracy.

But today he carried only one gun, and it was useless. His right hand, which had been cordially shaking that of one of the three murderers who shot him down, reached vainly for it. From the other hand clattered a pair of shears, for the underworld leader had been following his daylight calling just before death—snipping stems from chrysanthemums to make funeral wreaths. . . .

A sidebar to the story reported that the Chicago Police Department ". . . fearful that the slaying of Dion O'Banion may mark the beginning of one of the bitterest gang feuds this city has ever experienced, tonight began a roundup of underworld characters, determined to nip any concerted gang action in the bud.

"The powerful Genna brothers, Alphonse Caponi (sic), alias 'Big Al' Brown, Vincent Drucci, Earl Weiss, and Louis Alterie, all involved at various times in bootlegging and beer-running activities were taken to the State's Attorney's office tonight for questioning, while police squads toured the city in a search for others who they believe may have information about the slaying."

The newspaper had the straight scoop on the spectacular O'Banion hit. Later, more details on the shooting emerged.

O'Banion was busy putting together the rush orders for Merlo's funeral when three men strolled into Schofield's about 11:30 A.M. The crime boss, expecting someone to pick up the Genna wreath, came from the rear of the shop with his right hand extended in friendship, his left holding a pair of trimming shears.

"Hello, boys," he called out. "Are you here for Mike

Merlo's?"

Porter Bill Critchfield was sweeping up the trimmings and glanced up as the trio entered. He later described one as tall, dark-complected, clean-shaven, and well-dressed. His companions were short and stocky and rough-looking.

The shooter in the middle was either a Genna brother or Frankie Yale, a New York killer imported specifically for this job. The other two were John Scalise and Albert Anselmi, the last people in the world an enemy of the Gennas would want to see.

"Yes," replied the gunman, taking O'Banion's hand and gripping it tightly. At that moment, the Irishman realized what was happening and tried to jerk his hand free to go for the gun in his pants pocket. But Scalise and Anselmi were faster. They whipped out their own .38s and opened fire on the doomed crime boss. Critchfield later recalled an explosion of five shots. Two struck O'Banion on the right side of his chest. Two more ripped gaping holes in his throat. The fifth shot splintered his right jaw. O'Banion was hurled against the glass-fronted showcase and crashed to the floor. O'Banion was probably dead before he hit the floor, but, in typical Genna fashion, one of the killers leaned over the body, shoved the muzzle of his .38 against Dion's left cheek and blasted O'Banion's head to smithereens.

The killers sprinted out of the shop to where a dark blue, nickel-trimmed Jewett automobile waited with Mike Genna at the wheel and the motor running.

As the killers piled in, Genna hit the gas. Instantly, six other cars peeled away from the curbs on either side of the street blocking traffic. As soon as the Jewett turned the corner headed south on Dearborn, Angelo Genna, driving the lead blocker, tooted his horn a couple of times. At the signal, all six cars merged back into the traffic lanes and disappeared in different directions.

Later, the *New York Times* grudgingly praised the flawless getaway maneuver in which ". . . the existence of a mastermind was revealed."

The newspapers predicted that blood would stain Chicago streets as a result of O'Banion's slaying. They were right. Hymie Weiss, Bugs Moran, Schemer Drucci, and Two-Gun Alterie knew exactly who'd knocked off their boss and swore "to get them goddamn nigger wops." They moved faster than even the paranoid Gennas anticipated.

Angelo was the first to go.

With Merlo dead, Angelo Genna seized the presidency of the politically powerful, forty thousand member *Unione,* leaving Al Capone grinding his teeth in frustration. Capone lusted after the *Unione.* As a Neapolitan, Scarface couldn't belong himself, but with one of his handpicked Sicilians at the helm, he would command the muscle necessary to take over all of Chicago's multimillion dollar bootlegging/prostitution/gambling rackets.

From that moment, Torrio and Capone, who had backed the Gennas in the O'Banion hit, switched allegiances. By throwing their weight to the vengeful North Siders, Capone and Torrio saw a chance to tip the balance of power and rid themselves of the dreaded Gennas without bloodying their own hands.

Angelo Genna had recently married Lucille Spingola, the beautiful, eighteen-year-old daughter of political heavyweight Henry Spingola. (Their wedding was an A-list social event that featured a twelve-foot-tall, one-ton wedding cake.) The couple was living temporarily at the luxurious Belmont Hotel. On May

25, 1925, Angelo Genna stuffed $25,000 in cash in his pockets, hopped into his $6,000 roadster, and set out for suburban Oak Park to buy a new home for his bride.

As Genna pulled away, a long black sedan fell in behind him. At the wheel was Frank Gusenberg, an O'Banion hood who was destined to die in the St. Valentine's Day Massacre. With him, each cradling tommy guns with their one-hundred-round drums primed to fire, were Moran, Drucci, and Weiss.

A few blocks down Ogden Street, the sedan suddenly accelerated and pulled alongside Genna's roadster. Bloody Angelo instantly sensed the danger. He whipped out one of the automatic pistols he habitually carried and opened fire. Machine guns barked back, and the two automobiles roared side by side down the busy street at sixty miles per hour with bullets flying wildly between them.

At Hudson Street, Angelo screeched into a sharp turn. The roadster skidded out of control on two wheels and smashed broadside into a lamp pole. Stunned by the impact and out of ammunition, Angelo watched helplessly as three men leapt from the pursuing sedan, surrounded his car, and began blasting away. Hundreds of machine-gun bullets ripped through the roadster and tore the gangster to pieces.

The five surviving Gennas sorrowfully laid brother Angelo to rest in a funeral panoply that left even gangster-calloused Chicagoans gaping. Besides the obligatory truckloads of flowers, Angelo was buried in an enormous, ornate, bronze coffin that pointedly cost $1,000 more than Dion O'Banion's. And the miles-long procession to Mount Carmel included a flatbed truck carrying the bullet-riddled, bloodstained, crepe-draped roadster in which Angelo Genna took his next-to-last ride.

After a suitable grieving period, the Gennas armed themselves and hit the streets looking for North Siders to kill.

Less than three weeks later, on the morning of June 13, 1925, Mike the Devil, Scalise, Anselmi and Giuseppe the Cavalier Nerone (who was using the alias "Tony Spano" at the time) were cruising the street along the border between the North Side and Little Italy looking for Bugs Moran and Schemer Drucci. Each was armed with pistols and sawed-off shotguns loaded with the Gennas' patented lead slugs.

One of the bloodiest episodes in the long and savage history of the Terrible Gennas was about to erupt.

Crime reporters across the country revelled in graphic, on-the-scene accounts of the astonishing, cops-and-robbers gun battle that unfolded. *The New York Times* reported:

2 CHICAGO OFFICERS SLAIN
FIGHTING GANG
A THIRD POLICEMAN IS
BADLY WOUNDED
AND ONE OF THE GENNAS
SHOT TO DEATH

BATTLE ON BUSY STREET

TWO GANGSTERS USING SHOTGUNS
LOADED WITH SLUGS ARRESTED—
AUTHORITIES AROUSED

CHICAGO, JUNE 13—Two policemen were riddled with slugs from sawed-off shotguns and killed, a third policeman was probably fatally wounded and a notorious gunman was slain today when four policemen interfered with the Genna Gang in its activities of rum running and avenging the death of Angelo Genna, assassinated May 26.

State's Attorney Crowe, Chief of Police Collins and Chief of Detectives Shoemaker, aroused by the slaying, took personal charge of the case and declared that every effort would be made to send the two gunmen, captured during the battle, to the gallows as speedily as the law would permit.

The dead policemen are Charles B. Walsh, father of three small children, and Harold F. Olson, 25, single, living with a widowed mother and four young brothers.

The wounded policeman is Sergeant Michael J. Conway, married, the father of one child. All three policemen were attached to the Detective Bureau, from which they were sent to do duty as an automobile zone squad in the Chicago lawn district.

The dead gunman was identified as Mike Genna, youngest of the Genna brothers. The two in custody gave their names as John Scalise, 25, arrested recently with Al Capone, so-called "vice lord," and a silent partner with "Samoots" Amatuna in the ownership of Citro's Cafe, and Albert Anselmi, 41.

The Genna group, three men, were first sighted in an automobile traveling south on Western Avenue at Forty-seventh Street. The policemen, Conway, Olson, Walsh and John Sweeney also in automobiles, recognized the men in it as members of the Genna gang and set out to halt them.

The gunmen put on speed and dashed south in Western Avenue. Before they had gone far, they started shooting with two repeating shotguns and four sawed-off shotguns, which later were found in their possession.

At West Sixtieth Street, the gunmen's car swerved and crashed into the curb. As it did so the occupants jumped to the ground. In front of a garage the battle went on. Walsh, Olson and Conway fell under a fusillade of slugs. Sweeney alone was left standing. He set out in pursuit of Genna.

It was at this moment that Patrolman Albert Richert of the Brighton Park Station appeared. He was off duty and was riding on the Western Avenue streetcar when he came upon the battle and saw Genna and his two companions running with Patrolman Sweeney in pursuit.

At an alley Genna broke from his companions. Turning, he fired his shotgun at Sweeney, who returned the fire and wounded Genna, the bullet severing an artery in his leg. Genna ran into a passageway and hurled himself through a basement window in the home of Mrs. Eleanor Knoblauch.

Patrolman Richert had jumped from the streetcar and taken up the pursuit. Breaking in the basement door, he found Genna with a drawn revolver. Covering him with his pistol, the patrolman took the wounded gunman into custody. Genna died later at the Bridewell Hospital.

The killing of the policemen, coming as the climax to a long string of bootleg murders, set official wheels moving as never before.

The reckless, senseless cop killings and blazing gun

battle that endangered hundreds of innocent bystanders (typical of the Gennas' indiscriminate gunplay) aroused public outrage and maddened police, most of whom were paid toadies of the killers they now hunted. The newspapers continued to inflame the shrill, anti-gang sentiment:

TAKE 400 SUSPECTS IN
CHICAGO ROUND-UP
POLICE IN FIFTY-HOUR DRIVE
AGAINST GANGSTERS CLAIM A
CLEAN-UP

ARMORED CARS IN RAID

STATE'S ATTORNEY CROWE
PROMISES INCESSANT
WARFARE ON ALL CLASSES
OF CRIMINALS

Chicago, June 15—Gangland is on the run, municipal and county authorities asserted confidently tonight after a fifty-hour broadside against the gangster and his gun. Simultaneously, it was declared that the drive against terrorism which began Saturday would continue with unabated vigor "until the underworld is licked to a frazzle."

More than 400 suspects had been placed under arrest at 6 o'clock this evening.

State's Attorney Robert E. Crowe after a conference with Chief of Police Morgan A. Collins and Sheriff Peter M. Hoffman, asserted vehemently, "We will not let down in our efforts until we have sent to jail every gangster, beer runner, criminal and lawbreaker we are able to apprehend."

The newspapers had most of the facts straight, but the real story behind the shoot-out in the street was stranger than anything the most imaginative reporter might have dreamed. Rather than riding shotgun for Mike the Devil as loyal avengers, Scalise and Anselmi, unbeknownst to Genna, had already sold out to Scarface Al Capone and were taking the boss who trusted them like his own brothers for a typical gangland ride. Mike the Devil, in fact, was doomed even before the Chicago cops intervened.

It was just before 9:30 A.M. when the big Lincoln, traveling south on Western Avenue, attracted the attention of a squad of Chicago detectives who recognized that a carload of known gangsters on the prowl meant trouble. Squad commander Michael J. Conway ordered his driver, Detective Harold F. Olson, to follow the Genna car.

As the unmarked detective's sedan fell in behind the Lincoln, the Genna driver, Nerone, stepped on the gas. In seconds, the chase was on with both high-powered automobiles hitting speeds of seventy miles per hour, dodging through the morning traffic, and scattering pedestrians in their wake.

A dozen blocks into the high-speed chase, a delivery truck suddenly pulled in front of the Genna car. Nerone hit the brakes to avoid a collision, but the heavy Lincoln fishtailed on the street still slick from a morning shower, jumped a curb, and slammed into a pole. Detective Olson skidded to a stop in the street, but the few seconds lead time was all the gunmen needed. Nerone jumped out and disappeared around a corner. When the cops piled out in the middle of the street, Mike the Devil, Scalise, and Anselmi had already taken cover on the opposite side of the Lincoln and opened fire on the exposed cops.

Shotgun slugs tore into the squad car (investigators later counted more than seventy holes in the vehicle) and ripped into the detectives as they hit the street. Olson still had one foot on the running board when a shotgun blast nearly took his head off. He died instantly. Another load caught Detective Charles B. Walsh in the side as he jumped from the rear seat. Walsh crumpled to the pavement mortally wounded. Commander Conway and the fourth officer, Detective Sweeney, crouched on the floorboards of the car. As Conway rose up to return fire, a load of slugs smashed into his chest. Although severely wounded, Conway survived.

But that left only Detective Sweeney to face the trio of desperatc killers. Sweeney ducked out of the car and, in an awesome display of courage, charged the gangsters' car, blazing away with a pair of revolvers. His timing was on the mark. The gunmen were out of shotgun ammunition, and, now with a bellowing, pistol-waving cop charging at them, the three panicked, threw down their empty shotguns, and fled across a vacant lot.

Scalise and Anselmi ducked between a row of houses, while Mike Genna headed for a nearby alley with Sweeney not far behind. At the mouth of the alley, Genna drew his own revolver and turned to fire at the cop, but Sweeney was faster. He capped off a quick shot that struck Genna just above the left knee. The shot knocked Genna off his feet, but he recovered and dragged himself deeper into the alley. Unable to run and with no cover in the alley, Mike the Devil smashed a nearby basement window and tumbled headfirst into the dark cellar.

As Sweeney paused to catch his breath, two off-duty cops, George Oakey and Albert Richert, rushed up. They had witnessed the frenzied gun battle, grabbed their own guns, and rushed to aid their fellow officers. Backed by the reinforcements, Sweeney kicked in the basement door.

Genna was sprawled across a coal pile. He raised his .38 and got off one wild shot before the three cops overpowered the cursing, struggling gangster and dragged him outside. A police ambulance arrived within minutes. As Mike the Devil was being loaded onto a stretcher, he raised his good leg and viciously kicked the attendant, who was trying to help him, square in the jaw. The man toppled over out cold.

"Take that, you lousy son of a bitch!" Genna snarled.

It was the last violent act of a thug who had lived by violence. Sweeney's bullet had severed an artery in Genna's leg. Within minutes, Mike the Devil was dead.

While Genna was bleeding to death in the grimy alley, Scalise and Anselmi were still running. Several blocks away, sweating, hatless, out of breath, they leapt aboard a trolley just as a patrolman heading for the scene of the shooting drove by. The suspicious cop followed and boarded the trolley at the next stop. Unarmed, two of the bloodthirstiest killers in Chicago history gave up meekly. However, as they arrived in cuffs at the local precinct station, word spread that the cop killers had been caught. When Scalise and Anselmi finally were transferred to police headquarters they showed up badly beaten with injuries suffered while "resisting arrest." It was about the only punishment ever meted out for gunning down the three cops. Scalise and Anselmi were charged with the murders of Olson and Walsh but spent only a few months in jail.

After years of legal shenanigans, payoffs, threatened witnesses, and jury tampering, the two killers went free on the incredible grounds that they were merely resisting "excessive police aggression" when they opened fire with sawed-off shotguns.

Meanwhile, Nerone, who had bolted from the wrecked car when the shooting started, dashed for cover down a hole in the ground and into a vast tunnel system that snaked its way beneath the streets of the Loop. Years earlier, as street urchins, the Genna brothers had discovered the underground highway and later used it to move booze and broads far from the prying eyes of corrupt cops and rival gangsters.

Days later, the papers were still reporting on the dramatic, subterranean manhunt:

HUMBOLD GANGSTER IN
CHICAGO SUBWAY

250 POLICEMEN ENGAGE IN SEARCH FOR
MAN WHO TRIED TO SHOOT
A DETECTIVE

SOME CARRYING TEAR BOMBS

OTHERS WILL TRY TO DISLODGE
FUGITIVE HIDDEN SOMEWHERE
IN 63 MILES OF TUNNELS

CHICAGO, June 17—Forty feet under the surface of the Loop District 250 policemen late tonight started a manhunt through the sixty-three miles of underground highways owned by the Illinois Tunnel Company. They had instructions to bring out their man—thought to be Tony Spano, missing fourth member of the Genna murder squad—by morning, dead or alive.

Tear bombs and smudge fires were being employed in the effort to drive the fugitive from the tunnel.

The shooter in the tunnel was never caught. Giuseppe the Cavalier Nerone (alias Tony Spano) escaped to kill again. And his next victim was the brains of the Genna family, Tony the Gent himself, betrayed, like Mike the Devil, by the very gunmen the Gennas had embraced as family.

With the murder of Mike the Devil, coming on the heels of Angelo's slaying, the message to the rest of the Genna clan was unmistakable: They were all marked for death.

It made sense to hit Angelo and Mike before the others. They were the fiercest of the Terrible Gennas and by destroying the family's main firepower first, the remaining brothers would be easier prey. The next logical target was Jim Genna, the titular head of the family; then Tony the Gent, the brains of the outfit and a cunning executioner who enjoyed plotting details of the Genna murders.

But Jim Genna was visiting the family's ancestral home in Sicily at the time, so Tony the Gent figured he had to be next in line for liquidation. Along with brothers Sam and Pete, Tony scrambled for cover. Tony barricaded himself in the Congress Hotel, converting his lush suite to a fortress with guns everywhere. He sent his mistress, Gladys Bagwell, out for supplies, and conversed with his brothers only by phone from their own private bunkers. The Terrible Gennas might have held out until Jim returned and the family could marshall a counterassault—but Tony the Gent, always the coolheaded conniver, panicked and schemed his last scheme.

One of those Tony kept in close touch with by phone was Giuseppe the Cavalier Nerone, who he still believed was his trusted lieutenant. The devious Nerone stoked his former boss's raging fear of assassination by claiming that Bloody Angelo had been the victim of a Capone-police inspired plot and that Scarface had ordered the hit on Mike the Devil. What Nerone failed to mention was that he had also sold out to Capone along with Scalise and Anselmi.

"I've got to get out of town," Tony the Gent told Nerone.

Nerone agreed to help Tony flee, but insisted that they meet first to hammer out plans for killing Capone, Torrio, Bugs Moran, and all the other Genna foes.

"Then you and the boys can come back and take over everything," urged the Cavalier. The plot appealed to Tony's greedy nature and his vow to avenge his brothers' murders. Stuffing his pockets with spare pistols, Tony the Gent set out the morning of July 8, 1925, to meet Nerone at the rendezvous spot—in front of a grocery near the intersection of Oak and Milton, the Gennas' nefarious Death Corner.

About 10:30 A.M., Tony parked in front of Charlie Capella's market, an old-time Genna front operation. The Cavalier waved from the doorway of the grocery and stepped out on the sidewalk to meet Genna. Wearing dark glasses and a hat pulled low over his eyes, Tony the Gent carefully studied the street in both directions searching for any hint of a trap. Satisfied that he was safe, Tony climbed out of the car and reached to take Nerone's outstretched hand.

At the last second, Tony the Gent must have sensed the trap he'd fallen into. As Nerone locked his right hand in an iron grip, Tony Genna tried to jerk away, fumbling with his left hand to pull a pistol from his coat pocket. As he struggled to free himself, Scalise and Anselmi dashed from the storefront next door to the grocery where they had hidden.

"You bastards! You bastards!" screamed Tony, but his shouts were drowned out by the roar of gunfire as the two gunmen opened fire with .38s.

Tony crumpled to the sidewalk, blood spurting from half a dozen holes in his body. His three assassins bolted to a waiting getaway car and sped away.

But Scalise and Anselmi, who prided themselves on certain death, made their first mistake. In their rush to escape, they failed to make sure Tony the Gent was dead. Incredibly, the gang leader was still alive. Leaving a trail of blood across the sidewalk, Tony dragged himself to the door of the grocery. An ambulance arrived and rushed Tony to County Hospital where he clung to life for several hours.

Conscious throughout his ordeal, Tony refused to talk to cops who tried to question him about his assailants. Informed of the assassination attempt, brother Sam broke cover and hurried to Tony's side. There he was joined by Gladys Bagwell, Tony's weeping mistress. At their urging, Tony the Gent croaked out a name, gasped, and died. To the non-Sicilian cops, the name sounded like "Cavallerc" and they were off on a futile search for a gunman by that name. By the time police realized who they were really looking for, Giuseppe the Cavalier Nerone was already a corpse himself.

And for the third time in as many months, the Chicago papers feasted on Genna blood flowing in the streets:

3RD GENNA GUNMAN SLAIN

IN CHICAGO

LATEST VICTIM OF BOOTLEGGING
FEUD IS
SHOT AS HE SHAKES HAND
WITH SLAYER

O'BANION MURDER SEQUEL

CHICAGO, JULY 8 – Tony Genna, member of a family of gunmen, was shot fatally today in an ambush that the police attributed to followers of Dion O'Banion still seeking vengeance for the murder of that gang leader.

Genna died this afternoon in the county hospital, while police officers questioned him about the men who had shot him. Three times Genna responded "Cavallere," as the police understood it. Officers at the Detective Bureau said they had no record of a "Cavallere."

There was a delicious irony in the murder of Tony the Gent – cozened by the handshake ploy he and his treacherous brothers had invented to trap so many of their prey; and then gunned down at Death Corner, the very site the Gennas had stained forever with the bloody corpses of so many victims. Wherever he was, Dion O'Banion must have been dancing an Irish jig over the death of Tony the Gent. Had he lived, Deanie would have been celebrating his thirty-third birthday that very day.

Two months earlier, almost all of Little Italy had turned out for the elaborate funeral of Bloody Angelo, his flower bedecked hearse escorted by a phalanx of stone-faced torpedoes, their tuxedos bulging with guns. But when it came time to plant Tony the

Gent, only cops and reporters followed his cheap, unadorned coffin to the cemetery. Not a mourner appeared, not his mistress, Gladys Bagwell, not even his brothers, Sam and Pete.

Expecting to be blasted to pieces at any second, Sam and Pete had sneaked out of Chicago in the dead of night to join brother Jim in Sicily. There they hid out in the rugged hills for the next two years, petrified that Chicago triggermen were hiding in every shadow. Meanwhile, Jim went to jail for stealing the jewels from a religious statue in a Marsala cathedral. It was such a clumsy, amateurish heist that many believed Jim Genna wanted to be caught, figuring he was safe in prison where Chicago gunners were less likely to reach him.

Years later, Jim, Sam, and Pete, the tattered remnants of the once fearsome Terrible Gennas, crept back to Chicago after most of their enemies were dead or in prison. They started an olive oil importing business and died in obscurity.

But the massacre that the Gennas had set in motion with the murder of Dion O'Banion didn't end with the death of Tony the Gent. The remaining Genna hoods were hunted down and exterminated by Scalise and Anselmi, whose cold-blooded lust for murder had been welcomed with open arms by Al Capone. Even the Cavalier had to go. Scalise and Anselmi caught Nerone in his favorite barber chair and pumped him full of machine-gun bullets. Henry Spingola, Angelo's father-in-law and the Genna family lawyer, was gunned down on January 10, 1926, by Orazio the Scourge Tropea, who had also jumped ship. But Tropea paid for his betrayal with his life. Blasts from a double-barreled, sawed-off shotgun nearly cut the

Scourge in two pieces as he strolled along Halsted Street a month later.

On January 24, 1926, Anselmi and Scalise ran the fierce Ecola the Eagle Baldelli to the ground. Baldelli fought for his life, wounding several gunmen backing up Scalise and Anselmi. The battle so infuriated the pair that when the Eagle finally ran out of ammunition, he was taken alive and hacked to pieces on the spot. Scalise and Anselmi then distributed the body parts around Chicago garbage dumps.

As late as 1929 Scalise and Anselmi were still killing. That year they were arrested as the shooters in the bloody St. Valentine's Day Massacre, which was one more attempt to annihilate Bugs Moran and what was left of Dion O'Banion's North Side gang. But justice of a sort was about to catch up with the murderous duo. Before the year was out, Scalise and Anselmi themselves were gruesomely murdered at the hands of Al Capone himself.

Capone's network of spies informed him that the two were plotting with Joseph "Hop Toad" Giunta, then president of *Unione Siciliane,* to butcher Capone and his top henchmen in one bloody coup and take over the entire Chicago operation.

A fictionalized version of Capone's revenge was a highlight of the hit movie *The Untouchables,* in which Capone, played by Robert DeNiro, used a baseball bat to bash out the brains of a gang member during an elaborate banquet.

The truth is this. Upon learning that Scalise, Anselmi, and Hop Toad Giunta were plotting against him, Capone countered with a scheme of his own. He threw a party with the three traitors as guests of honor at The Plantation, a roadhouse near Hammond, Indiana. After a heavy meal, washed down by gallons of red wine, Capone attacked the three victims. Some accounts say he used a sawed-off baseball bat; others insist that Capone swung a weighted Indian club. Whatever the weapon, Scarface flailed away at the trio until they were bloody pulps. Sweating and puffing from the effort, Capone then pulled out two pistols and pumped the bodies full of holes.

Early the next morning, police found the mangled remains of Hop Toad and the most dreaded killers of their time stuffed in the back seat of a stolen car abandoned on a lonely lovers' lane. The shocked pathologist who performed autopsies on the victims told reporters that in all his experience he had never encountered such badly beaten bodies.

In the end, the Genna brothers might have won the battle for Chicago and gone down in history as the Windy City's bloodiest gang lords, except that the family ran out of brothers before Capone ran out of guns.

The final Genna story may be apocryphal, but it's become part of gangland lore and it says a lot about the nature of the Terrible Gennas.

It seems that a Chicago cop, standing by to prevent trouble at Tony the Gent's funeral, glanced around at the other grave markers in Mount Carmel Cemetery. Only a few yards away from the plot where Tony, Mike the Devil, and Bloody Angelo lay, reposed the remains of Dion O'Banion, the Gennas' bitterest enemy whose murder eventually led to their own downfall. The officer shook his head. "When Judgement Day comes and them graves are open," he sighed, "there'll be hell to pay in this cemetery."

THREE
"MA" BARKER AND HER BLOODY BOYS

The time was the Dirty Thirties.

Prohibition was out. Depression was in. Millions in illegal booze bucks had dried up.

A new and bloody era of crime in America was beginning, characterized by bands of highly mobile, heavily armed outlaws who took to the open roads in search of money and excitement to relieve the grinding boredom of poverty. Midwesterners mainly, they had bitterly watched the banks gobble up the family farm and their meager hopes blow away with the Dust Bowl winds. They were angry. They were out to get even. And they did it by attacking the banks and shooting anyone who stood in their way.

Since the banks were almost universally viewed as villains, the gangs were transformed overnight into romantic Robin Hoods whose blazing guns, brazen bank robberies, and daring escapes were matched only by their colorful, marquee nicknames: "Pretty Boy" Floyd . . . "Machine Gun" Kelly . . . "Handsome Johnny" Dillinger . . . "Baby Face" Nelson . . . Bonnie and Clyde.

And the worst of the lot were "Ma" Barker and her Bloody Boys.

Social scientists hoping to prove the "Bad Seed" theory of human behavior need look no further than the Barker brood of misfits, thieves, robbers, kidnappers, and killers: Ma and her boys, Herman, Lloyd, "Doc," and Fred. Each lived by the gun. Each died violently by the gun. They killed even when they didn't have to. Freddie, especially, loved to kill cops with his beloved Thompson submachine guns. Doc was just as lethal, but in a quieter way. And Ma didn't hesitate to kill if murder was the best solution.

In *Murder USA: The Ways We Kill Each Other,* John Godwin wrote: "The shrewd, autocratic Donnie Clark, better known as Ma Barker, was a product of the Missouri Ozarks. A fat, frumpish shrew with the brain of a business executive, she led her near-moronic sons, plus Alvin Karpis, on a robbery-and-kidnapping campaign that cost ten lives before, her favorite boy dead beside her, she died shooting it out with the law, a machine gun in her fist."

Ma Barker, christened Arizona Donnie Clark, was born in 1872 near Springfield, Missouri. She grew up on hardscrabble sharecropper farms in the stubby Ozark Mountains. When she was twenty years old, "Arrie" Clark married George Barker and started having babies.

Herman the oldest of the Barkers, typified the murderous insanity that polluted the entire Barker family. During a gunfight in Newton, Kansas, Herman killed a cop, but was wounded himself. To avoid capture he stuck the barrel of his Luger in his mouth and blew his brains out.

Arthur (Doc) Barker was the fiercest of the bloody brothers. He killed a night watchman in Tulsa; murdered two cops during a bank robbery in Minneapolis; and butchered two kidnap victims when the plot was botched. Eventually, Doc was sentenced to life on

Alcatraz.

Lloyd Barker missed most of the family's notorious crime wave. Caught robbing a post office in Oklahoma, Lloyd spent the next twenty-five years in Leavenworth. When he was released in 1947, the Bloody Barkers were history.

Fred Barker the baby of the ruthless clan and Ma's favorite, died at her side. It was a fitting end to the maniacal mother and her homicidal son who were unnaturally addicted to one another in life.

Although she never spent a day in jail herself, Ma was the brains behind one of the most brutal gangs of the 1930s that drove police crazy with its unpredictable pattern: a $250,000 bank robbery one day, a jewelry store heist two states away the next, or a high-profile kidnapping a week later.

Once Ma even plotted to kidnap the sixteen-year-old daughter of Kansas Governor Alf Landon, the Republican party's 1936 presidential candidate. Freddie and Doc Barker were to deliver pieces of the teenager to the governor's mansion in Topeka until Landon freed imprisoned gang members. Incredibly, the ugly scheme might have worked if it hadn't been for a prison snitch, who squealed in exchange for an early release.

Eventually some of the hardest of the Thirties' hard cases would be drawn into the Barker's extended family, hoodlums such as the murderous Verne Miller, a former sheriff turned professional killer; Harvey Bailey, dean of the Midwestern bank robbers; Frank "Jelly" Nash; Wilbur Underhill, "The Tri-State Terror"; "Shotgun Ziegler"; Thomas Holden and Francis Keating, the "Evergreen Bandits"; and Alvin "Creepy" Karpis, Freddie's onetime cell mate and full-time gay lover.

FBI memo IC X7-576 dated November 19, 1936, described the gang as dedicated criminals who left ". . . a trail of victims and death in their wake. . . . Their unpredictability continually baffled law enforcement and made it difficult to link them to specific crimes. The members of the gang accumulated at least $3 million in their collective criminal careers . . . 'Ma' Barker, an intuitive criminal, with her shrewd thinking and meticulous planning, was responsible for the gang's 'success.' "

J. Edgar Hoover depicted Ma Barker as "an animal mother of the she-wolf type" and "a veritable beast of prey."

As this new breed of outlaws began making headlines, the public avidly followed the exploits of the Barkers, Bonnie and Clyde, Pretty Boy Floyd, and John Dillinger like they were Saturday afternoon serials at the Bijou.

But then things turned ugly. Too much blood being spilled turned the public against the gangs. This brief, but violent, era reached its zenith in a thundering machine-gun battle between cops and crooks on a bright, summer morning in Kansas City. When the smoke cleared, Ma Barker and her boys were exposed for what they really were—ruthless, bloodthirsty cutthroats.

The bloodbath was instantly dubbed the Kansas City Massacre, and the backlash doomed the Barkers.

But all that came later. It was an end that Barker, who nicknamed herself Kate because she thought it was lady-like, couldn't have foreseen when her boys were growing up in Webb City, Missouri, and Tulsa, Oklahoma, making names for themselves as vicious juvenile thugs and strong-arm muggers. As far as Ma was concerned, the lads could do no wrong. Anytime one of them got in trouble, Ma stormed police headquarters, screaming that the cops were mistreating the boys again. She also learned how to spot a corrupt cop or judge. Bribery became one of Ma's most effective weapons when the family graduated to the big leagues of murder, kidnapping, and bank robbery.

Just as Ma doted on her boys, they were as strongly attached to the frumpy, shrill woman who refused to let them cut the apron strings. George Barker was a minor factor in the boys' lives. Ma browbeat her weaker husband and soon walked out, taking the boys with her.

Ma moved to Tulsa where the diminutive Barker boys (they were all under five-feet, seven-inches) established themselves as street-tough incorrigible kids. They joined the wild Central Park Gang that specialized in burglaries, muggings, and hijackings. Cops, who dealt with the wild Barker boys on an almost daily basis, predicted that it was only a matter of time before they started killing.

The cops were right. While the Barker boys were still in their teens, each tasted blood for the first time. Ma not only exulted in it, but goaded the murderous strain that ran through her brood.

As soon as the boys were big enough to see over a steering wheel the Barkers hit the road and, except for jail time, never really left it. They roamed through Oklahoma, Arkansas, Kansas, and Missouri pulling stickups that grew increasingly violent as the young thugs flexed their muscles.

After a string of stickups, the boys ducked back to Tulsa where Ma waited to shelter them, count the loot, and point them down the road to their next raid on the country stores that the young Barkers specialized in robbing.

The crooks and killers the boys met on their travels

began dropping by Ma's place when they were passing through Tulsa. The Barker home became a clearinghouse for some of the Midwest's top thieves and bank robbers to make contacts and set up scores. The Barkers hooked right into this criminal network of corrupt officials, safe houses and "safe" cities, tipsters, and guns for hire. That networking contributed to the family's later successes. As word of Ma's ability to plan big scores filtered through the underworld, some of the deadliest killers and most cunning thieves of the day signed on with the Barker gang.

But still, trouble loomed.

Lloyd was the first to go down. In 1922, he successfully stuck up a post office in central Oklahoma, but flubbed the getaway. The countryside was awash in spring rainstorms and Lloyd's car became mired in the muddy back roads. A pursuing posse closed in and Lloyd went to jail.

Since he had robbed a post office, the weight of the U.S. government fell on Lloyd like a rock: twenty-five years of hard time in Leavenworth. The feds, unlike state authorities, ignored Ma's tirades, petitions, and bribes. Also, Lloyd's family name was a handicap since no one wanted him back on the streets adding to the Barker crime wave. Consequently, Lloyd became one of the rare cons to flatten his sentence: the entire twenty-five years without parole.

Lloyd was barely behind bars when it came Doc's turn to fall.

The pint-sized Doc was known as a vicious brawler who used steel pipes, broken bottles, knives, and guns to compensate for his small stature. Along with a record for burglary, robbery, and car theft, Doc picked up a morphine habit, and it was this addiction that led to his first murder.

Doc had staked out a Tulsa hospital and was in the middle of robbing a courier carrying a drug shipment when a night watchman showed up. The watchman, an off-duty Tulsa cop, went for his gun, but Doc was faster. He wheeled and pumped three shots into the guard, then straddled the dying man and emptied his revolver into the watchman's head. The description the courier provided was so accurate that Tulsa cops knew right where to look. Within hours of the robbery-murder, police were knocking on Ma Barker's door. A squad of angry cops burst in, dragged Doc outside, and beat him all the way to the police station.

It was the bloody Barkers' first cop killing. It wouldn't be the last.

The family was embittered over the brutal police beating. Depression-era gangsters harbored a hatred of police and the authority they represented. Many were cop killers who considered murder the necessary price of doing business as an outlaw. But with the Barkers, it was entirely personal. They loved to kill cops. It was a savage vendetta all the Barkers carried to their graves.

The wanton murder of the night watchman infuriated Tulsans. Doc was quickly convicted of the crime and sentenced to life in the Oklahoma State Prison.

Meanwhile, Freddie was adding to the family's growing reputation as dangerously demented gunmen. Cops throughout Oklahoma and Missouri were familiar with the boyish bandit and snagged him off the street whenever he showed his face. With each arrest, Ma was close behind with bonds or bribes to bail him out. In 1926, the young lunatic crossed over into Kansas to rob the bank in Winfield. He walked out carrying a gun in one hand, the sack of loot in the other—and right into a ring of shotguns pointed at his head. Winfield police had spotted Freddie driving through town and were waiting for him.

This time, Ma's wildest tantrums couldn't save her boy from the slammer. Fred drew ten to fifteen in the state prison at Lansing. Like generations of other budding hoods, prison was graduate school for Fred Barker. And like brother Doc in the Oklahoma pen, Freddie used the time behind bars to learn how to be a better criminal and to forge underworld links that would last for years.

Foremost among these was a young thug who had been on the road stealing cars, pulling burglaries and armed robberies, and escaping from jails since he was ten years old. Born Alvin Karpowicz in Montreal, he changed his name to Karpis after moving to Kansas as a child. There are two versions of how Karpis came by his moniker of Old Creepy. Some said it was because of his cold, dead-eyed stare, and sinister expression. Others claimed that Fred Barker dubbed Karpis Old Creepy after underworld surgeon Doc Moran botched an operation meant to give Karpis a new face.

Karpis and Fred Barker shared a cell and became lovers. Later, Karpis also kept mistresses, but his homosexual relationship with Fred Barker linked the two gangsters in a lifelong bond that they anointed with the blood of their murder victims.

One hood who ran with the gang claimed that all the Barkers, except Doc, were homosexuals who often killed in sexual rages.

"There's nothing worse than a homosexual bank robber and killer," said James "Blackie" Audett. "They would shoot to kill to protect their lovers. Freddie killed a lot of people to save Karpis. It was the same way with Karpis. I saw him do it when I was with that gang for a short time. They were all kill-crazy lovers."

Moreover, the boys may have been encouraged in their sexual attraction by Ma who often preferred young girls to Arthur Dunlop, the aging lover she took in after throwing Pa Barker out.

"When Freddie and Creepy Karpis weren't knocking over banks, they spent most of their time rounding up girls for the old lady," Audett continued. "This was when the family was hiding out in a hunting lodge in Minnesota. The boys would bring the girls there for a party and turn them over to Ma. When she was through with them, the boys killed the girls and dumped their bodies into some lake. They must have pulled bodies of young girls out of lakes all over Minnesota because of that crazy old woman."

(It may be true that Fred and Creepy procured girls for Ma's pleasures and then slit their bellies so the bodies would sink in the icy waters of Minnesota's lakes, but there's no hard evidence. Audett was a braggart who also claimed he witnessed the bloodbath at the Kansas City Union Station.)

In any event, with Lloyd, Doc, and Fred all behind bars at the same time, Ma had only her oldest son, Herman, to rely on. For a time, Herman ran with the Kimes-Terrill bank robbery gang. But after a few close calls, a disgruntled Herman headed back to Tulsa to confer with Ma.

"We can do better than that," Ma said. She began scouting out likely targets to rob, often hundreds of miles apart to confuse cops. Herman hit the road again, this time as a lone wolf bandit directed by Ma's cunning schemes. All went well until the night of September 18, 1927, when Herman rolled into Newton, Kansas.

As he cruised through the darkened streets in a stolen car, Herman attracted the attention of police officer J.E. Marshall. When Marshall drove alongside Barker's car and signaled him to pull over, the only thing Herman saw was the hated badge. The outlaw whipped out a pistol and blazed away. Slugs ripped into Marshall's neck and chest and tore away his lower jaw. Although mortally wounded, the cop managed to draw his gun and return fire. At least one round shattered Barker's shoulder. As the wounded gangster roared out of town, Marshall slumped over and bled to death.

Herman Barker, bleeding badly himself, sped south toward Wichita where he could get help through his underworld connections. But he never made it. Herman pulled off the main highway a few miles north of Wichita. Maybe he knew he was dying or was afraid of being captured as a cop killer. For whatever reason, Herman Barker stuck the barrel of his Luger in his mouth and pulled the trigger. It was his last bullet. A posse found the body the next day and the coroner ruled death by suicide.

When told how Herman died, Ma vehemently denied it was suicide: "The cops executed him," she screamed. "Barkers don't do things like that."

Nevertheless, with one dead and three locked up, Ma was without her boys for the first time in her life. She turned her home into a hideout for escaped cons, armed robbers, and killers on the run. Ma needed cash to get her boys out of jail and the hideout raised tens of thousands of dollars for payoff money.

Ma hounded parole boards, wardens, governors, and anyone who would listen with tearful pleas that she was a poor old woman who would die of starvation if her boys weren't set free to provide for her.

But it was the cash under the table, more than her tears, that finally paid off. In the spring of 1931, Fred Barker walked out of the Kansas pen. Creepy Karpis was paroled a few months later and joined the family in Tulsa. Ma took to Creepy like he was one of her own, and, within days, the Barker-Karpis crime wave which stole millions and cost scores of lives roared into action.

Freddie and Creepy started with burglaries, hauling the booty home to Ma who fenced it through her growing underworld contacts. But it wasn't enough to satisfy either Ma's greed or Freddie's lust for blood. Equipped with an arsenal ranging from automatic pistols to machine guns to grenades, the lovers switched to armed robbery. Within weeks, things were so hot around Tulsa that Ma, Arthur Dunlop, Freddie, and Creepy headed for the hills, back to the Ozarks of southern Missouri and a rustic cabin between Thayer and Koskonong, a few miles from the Missouri-Arkansas state line.

From there, the boys made sorties throughout Missouri, Arkansas, Kansas, and Oklahoma. The raids might have continued indefinitely except that Fred and Creepy suddenly got lazy. The pair wandered into West Plains, only a few miles across a mountain ridge from the hideout, and stuck up a grocery store. Ma often drove to West Plains to shop in the same distinctive new car, a 1931 DeSoto, that the boys used in the robbery.

Someone was bound to recognize them.

That someone was West Plains Sheriff C.R. Kelly who spotted both men parked on a side road just outside of town counting the loot from the robbery. Unfortunately for Kelly, the badge he wore was like a red flag waved in cop-hater Freddie Barker's face.

As the sheriff approached Karpis sitting in the driver's seat, Barker jacked a round into the chamber of his .45 automatic. "Keep him talking," Barker whispered. "I'm gonna plug the son of a bitch." He slipped out the passenger's door, strolled around behind the DeSoto while Kelly studied the fake ID Karpis had presented, and shot the lawman in the back of the head.

Barker and Karpis sped away, leaving Kelly's body sprawled in the middle of the road. They rushed back to the hideout, bundled Ma and Arthur Dunlop into the DeSoto and lit out for Kansas City.

Kansas City, at the time, was ruled by the powerful Pendergast political machine, and was a well-known safe city among underworld characters. Within a few weeks, Barker and Karpis were back in the armed robbery business, but Ma scoffed at the handful of cash they brought home from sticking up grocery stores and filling stations.

"It's just as easy to rob a bank," she scolded. "Go get some real money for a change." While holed up in the southern Missouri hideout, Ma had often visited the bank at nearby Mountain View. "There's nobody guarding it and it's full of money," Ma told the boys. Fred and Creepy drove all night; were on hand when the Mountain View bank opened in the morning; and drove back to Kansas City that night, their pockets stuffed with over $7,000.

"That's more like it!" Ma gloated. "From now on, we go after the banks."

She used the loot from the robbery to move the

family again, this time to St. Paul, Minnesota, another popular safe city, and paid the required tribute for protection to St. Paul's crime bosses and fixers, Jack Peifer and Harry Sawyer.

The Pendergast machine in Kansas City and Sawyer in St. Paul acted as switchboards for all sorts of thieves and robbers looking for work. It was a *Who's Who of Crime* and Ma skillfully used it to pick extra gunmen to fill out a crew.

There was, for example, Harvey "Old Harve" Bailey, the dean of the Midwestern bank robbers. Bailey was an architect of the spectacular robbery of the Denver Mint in 1922. The year before he joined Ma Barker, Bailey and others looted the Lincoln National Bank in Lincoln, Nebraska, of a staggering $2,654,700, the biggest haul in U.S. history up to that time.

Fred Goetz, alias Shotgun Ziegler, rumored to be a shooter in the 1929 St. Valentine's Day Massacre, worked with the Barkers. The scion of a wealthy Chicago family, Shotgun served heroically in World War I, studied engineering at the University of Illinois, played football and championship golf . . . and raped a seven-year-old child. Ziegler helped the Barkers kidnap Edward Bremer in 1934. Doc and Freddie Barker, on orders from Ma, murdered Shotgun the same year, appropriately with four shotgun blasts that vaporized the gangster's head.

Francis Keating and Thomas Holden, known as the Evergreen Bandits, got their name after planting a bomb beneath the tracks of the Grand Trunk Railway in Evergreen Park, Illinois. The explosion derailed a mail train, and the bandits got away with more than $133,000. But a confederate squealed and the pair was shipped off to Leavenworth to spend the next twenty-five years.

They stayed only one year. With the help of George Barnes, a clerk in the prison's front office, Holden and Keating obtained fake passes and walked out the front door. George Barnes later gained infamy as the maniacal Machine Gun Kelly. With Federal manhunters hot on their trail, the Evergreen Bandits hooked up with Ma's gang in Kansas City.

Several ex-lawmen jumped on the Barker bandwagon, including such turncoats as Verne Miller, a former South Dakota sheriff who became one of the most savage killers of the Thirties and the only gunman ever identified in the Kansas City Massacre; an ex-motorcycle cop named Phil Courtney; and Bernard Phillips, a retired policeman turned robber.

Larry DeVol, a vicious gunman later killed in a holdup, enlisted, as did Earl Christman who was fatally wounded in the Barker raid on the Fairbury, Nebraska, bank in 1933 and was secretly buried by the Barkers. Frank (Jelly) Nash, a wanted fugitive and escapee from Leavenworth, became part of the gang. It was Jelly's arrest in 1933 that triggered the infamous Kansas City Massacre. Other members of Ma's gang included Volney Davis, Doc Barker's partner in the murder of the night watchman, and William "Lapland Willie" Weaver, an Arkansas gunman who had celled next to Freddie and Creepy in the Kansas prison.

All in all, it was a ruthless, bloodthirsty crew that took their marching orders from Ma Barker and her bloody boys.

With the nucleus of the murderous gang established, the Barker family closed out 1931 with another big score—and a couple more murders—that set the tone for the Barkers' reign of terror that gripped the Midwest over the next three years.

In November, Ma sent Freddie, Creepy, Lapland Willie Weaver, and Larry DeVol over to Minneapolis to rob a branch of the Northwestern Bank. The quartet came home with $81,000 in cash and $185,000 in bonds.

Later the same month, Freddie and Creepy were scouting potential robberies when they rolled into Pocahontas, Arkansas, to check out the bank. The flashy gangsters in their brand new touring car caught the eye of Chief of Police Manley Jackson. The chief followed the boys out of town before signaling them to pull over. It was a replay of the West Plains killing, and Freddie couldn't have been happier.

With automatics tucked into the back of their pants, the two bandits cooperatively stepped from the car with their hands up. As Chief Jackson turned to check the backseat of their car, Barker and Karpis whipped out their weapons and shot the cop five times in the back. By the time passersby found Jackson's body, the killers were already into southern Missouri and laughing all the way back to St. Paul.

The next murder was close to home. Ma had wearied of her lover, Arthur Dunlop, and his whining over the family's constant moves. Also, when he was drinking, which was most of the time, Dunlop tended to brag about the "big scores" Ma was plotting.

When Fred and Creepy rolled in, their hands still bloody with the cop killing in Arkansas, Ma pulled them aside. "Get rid of the old bastard," she growled.

It was a chore that delighted the boys who had come to detest the old man as a useless fifth wheel who talked too much. While Ma packed for a return trip to Kansas City, Freddie and Creepy took Arthur Dunlop for a ride. His body was found several days later, nude, spread-eagle on a frozen lake north of St. Paul. The old man had been stripped and then shot as he lay facedown on the ice. The bullets hadn't killed him—he died of exposure—but the blood from Dunlop's body had frozen to the icy surface and the remains had to be, literally, scraped up.

With the new year, Ma focused on planning bigger jobs and getting her other two boys out of prison. Lloyd's was a hopeless cause. The Feds controlled Leavenworth and all of Ma's tears, threats, or bribery attempts were in vain.

Not so in Oklahoma, where flamboyant Governor William H. "Alfalfa Bill" Murray was willing to listen to a poor mother's entreaties . . . especially when those pleas were green and untraceable. Despite his reputation as a vicious, unrepentant cop killer, Doc was paroled on September 27, 1932, less than ten years into his life sentence.

Even without Doc's gun, the Barker gang had rolled up an astonishing record of bank robberies and electrifying shoot-outs that made them the darlings of the headline writers.

During the first months of 1932, the Barker gang hit a dozen or more banks, primarily small-town institutions in rural areas that Ma knew would be lightly guarded, if at all. The crazy-quilt pattern drove cops batty. A typical week might see the Barkers hitting banks in Redwood Falls, Minnesota; Flandreau, South Dakota; Beloit, Wisconsin . . . and the following week raiding south into Arkansas or Oklahoma.

Bank robbery still wasn't a federal offense, so the gang skipped from state to state without fear of pursuit. Meanwhile, the country was sinking deeper into the Depression. Poverty was everywhere—except in the Barker gang whose members lived high, spent big, and when they ran low on funds merely went out and robbed another bank.

In the spring, Ma moved her headquarters back to the Missouri Ozarks to be close to the next operation she was planning, the Fort Scott, Kansas, bank raid. Ma recruited Harvey Bailey, Keating and Holden, ex-cop Phil Courtney and the homicidal Larry DeVol to accompany Fred and Karpis.

On June 17, Thomas Holden parked a long, black Hudson down the street from the bank and waited behind the wheel. The others marched into the bank, but the instant a teller saw machine guns coming through the door, she hit an alarm button.

Fred Barker went berserk. Firing a burst into the ceiling, Freddie screamed, "I'm gonna kill everybody in here!" While the other bandits scooped $47,000 out of the teller cages, the enraged Barker herded the handful of employees to the front door, stepped into the street, and waved for Holden to bring the getaway car. When the powerful Hudson car screeched to a stop in front of the bank, the gangsters, lugging sacks of loot, piled inside.

At the last second, a shot rang out. Freddie peeked out from the bank door and saw several Fort Scott policemen, guns drawn, racing down the street.

"Grab these girls!" Barker shouted, pointing at the bank employees. Karpis and DeVol dragged three hysterical females outside and forced them to stand on the running boards as human shields. As the Hudson roared away, Freddie and DeVol leaned out the windows and opened up on the cops. The barrage of machine-gun fire ended the pursuit and the traumatized women were set free when the gangsters were safely across the Missouri state line, only a mile or two from Fort Scott.

After that, the human shield became a cruel, contemptible, but effective technique the Barkers often used to protect themselves as they fled from robberies. Several months after the Fort Scott robbery, the gang swooped down on a bank in Hays in western Kansas. According to newspaper accounts:

> Four machine gunners held up the Farmers State Bank here, abducted twelve persons for a wild flight southward in stolen motor cars and escaped across the Oklahoma line after freeing the last of their hostages near Holyrood, Kan., tonight.
>
> Eight hostages, including Miss Hilaria Schmidt, 22-year-old bookkeeper, were marched out of the bank to the bandit car, but two stepped off as the machine left the curb, fired on three times by Professor James Rouse of Fort Hays State College, from across the street.
>
> Machine gun bullets rattled from the rear window of the bandit car in response, but the shots were wild.
>
> S.W. Arnold, cashier, one of the hostages, was wounded in the leg, apparently by a bullet from the professor's rifle. With four other prisoners, he escaped when the robbers' machine crashed into another near the city limits.

After fleeing Fort Scott, the gang hustled back to Kansas City to split up the loot.

On July 7, Bailey, Holden, Keating, and Jelly Nash, all avid golfers, fenced several thousand dollars worth of negotiable bonds taken in the Fort Scott heist, and headed for the links.

Just as the foursome teed off at the Old Mission Golf Course, a squad of Federal agents led by Raymond Caffrey closed in. Jelly Nash dashed for the woods, but the other three bandits were surrounded and arrested.

As escapees, Holden and Keating went straight to Leavenworth to finish serving their sentences. Ma hired J. Earl Smith, one of the top defense attorneys in the area, to defend Harvey Bailey at his trial for the Fort Scott robbery. But Bailey was convicted and drew a stiff ten to twenty years sentence in the Kansas prison at Lansing. A few days later, Fred Barker called Smith and asked the lawyer to come to Tulsa to help with the family's attempts to win Doc's freedom. The call was a sham. The attorney's bullet-riddled body turned up on the ninth hole of a Tulsa golf course, his mouth stuffed with sand from a nearby trap. It was a clear signal to the underworld that Ma and her bloody brood wouldn't abide such failures.

And no sooner had the prison gate clanged shut behind Old Harve, than Ma began rebuilding the gang and plotting ways to spring Bailey. He was too valuable a bank robber to leave rotting in jail.

On July 26, the revamped gang pulled a daring daylight holdup of the Cloud County Bank at Concordia, Kansas. They got away with an incredible haul—$250,000—and left behind an enduring legend.

Weeks earlier, a conservatively dressed matron had approached bank officers and introduced herself as a wealthy Oklahoma oil widow. She claimed she was moving to Concordia and would be making substantial deposits in the bank. But first, she wanted to be sure her money would be safe from the terrible bank robbers terrorizing the Midwest. Anxious to get their hands on the old lady's cash, the accommodating bankers happily detailed the bank's security measures, showed her the location of guards, and explained how alarms were wired directly into the local police station. When the gang showed up to rob the bank, they immediately cut that alarm, disarmed the guards, and vanished with the bank's assets.

A big chunk of the Concordia bank money paid for Doc's "parole" from the Oklahoma pen. Doc Barker was released in September and sent home to Ma with the governor's blessing. By December, Doc was packing a gun and back robbing banks.

Doc's first big score was the holdup of the Third Northwestern Bank of Minneapolis on December 16, 1932. It turned out to be a bloody affair in which all of Doc's pent-up rage against lawmen erupted in a violent shoot-out. Fred Barker, Alvin Karpis, Verne Miller, Lapland Willie Weaver, and Larry DeVol were the other gunmen on the raid. Jess Doyle, disguised as a chauffeur, waited in the getaway car parked in front of the bank.

As the gang ran from the bank with $112,000 stuffed in bags, Minneapolis policemen Leo Gorski and Ira Evans arrived on the scene.

Doc signalled the other gang members to stand aside. "I've been waiting a long time for this," Doc said. "These guys are mine." Doc opened up with his machine gun and splattered the two officers all over the sidewalk. But the killing wasn't over. The gang had stashed a second getaway car across the river in St. Paul's Como Park. As they were making the switch, twenty-nine-year-old St. Paul resident Oscar Erickson, out walking his dog, stopped to watch the excitement. Freddie grabbed the man and shoved a .45

under his chin. "You didn't see nothing, did ya," Barker snarled.

Before the terrified man could answer, Barker pulled the trigger and blew the victim's head off. "Now you won't tell nothin' neither," he laughed.

The slayings of the two police officers and the senseless murder of an innocent bystander inflamed the community and the state. With the heat on as never before, Ma decided it was best to get far away. She moved the boys all the way to Reno and settled in to plot her next moves.

As it turned out, 1933 would be the Barkers' busiest and bloodiest year yet. A series of gunfights, prison breaks, holdups, kidnappings, and murders—peaking with the horrifying Kansas City Massacre—all carried the imprint of Ma Barker's bloodstained hand.

The Barkers' first major strike in 1933 was against the Fairbury, Nebraska, bank. The gang got away with more than $150,000, but the caper ended in bloodshed and death . . . this time one of their own was among the dead.

Doc, Fred, Creepy Karpis, and Earl Christman, waving shotguns, machine guns, and pistols, stormed into the bank building just before noon on April 4. Freddie grabbed the bank president by the tie and yanked him to the vault. "Open the goddamn safe," the outlaw ordered.

Even with Barker's gun pointed at his head, the bank official showed incredible courage. "No, sir," he shook his head. "You're not taking our money."

The defiance dumbfounded the always unstable outlaw. "All of a sudden he just seemed to go crazy," recalled the banker. "He started shooting into the ceiling and screaming that he would kill us all. Then he shot me in the leg."

Convinced now that Barker meant to carry through on his threats, the banker stumbled to the vault door and twirled the combination. Meanwhile, in the confusion created by Freddie's outburst, the lone bank guard dove behind the teller's counter and grabbed a pistol hidden on a shelf.

He got off one shot before the outlaw guns opened up turning the guard into hamburger meat. But his shot found its mark. The bullet struck Earl Christman, burrowing deep into his gut and lodging in an intestine.

The gang grabbed the money sacks from the vault, shouldered the wounded Christman, and dashed for their waiting car. Speeding along back roads, the bandits crossed into Kansas and turned east toward Kansas City. By nightfall, they had made it to gangster Verne Miller's hideout. But it was too late for Christman. Without treatment, he died before morning. The gang, with Ma reading from a worn, family Bible, conducted its own funeral service and buried Christman in the wooded bluffs above the Missouri River.

Part of the loot from the Fairbury robbery helped finance one of Ma Barker's biggest operations yet, a brilliantly executed mass prison break that stunned the nation with its audacity. On Wednesday, May 31, 1933, headlines from coast to coast blared out the news:

CONVICTS KIDNAP WARDEN
AND 2 GUARDS IN KANSAS;
HOLD 3 WOMEN HOSTAGES

11 FLEE IN PRISON BREAK

USE PRISONERS AS SHIELDS
Partly Paralyzed Woman and
Two Girls, Borne Off.

All those who went over the wall were hard-core cons. Eight were convicted murderers. The ringleaders were the Barkers' old bank robbing chum, Harvey Bailey, who Ma had vowed to set free, and Wilbur Underhill, a ferocious killer known as the Tri-State Terror.

The thirty-three-year-old Underhill had previously escaped from the Oklahoma state penitentiary, where he was doing time for three murders. While on the run, Underhill gunned down Wichita policeman Merle Colver. He was captured and drew life without parole in the Kansas pen.

For days, Warden Prather had been hearing rumors of an escape attempt, but didn't take them seriously. He should have listened, since the scheme was a carbon copy of an elaborate plot to spring Freddie Barker, Alvin Karpis, Wilbur Underhill, and others before Barker and Karpis were paroled in 1931. Had it worked, the Lansing prison yard would have become a carnage house.

The 1931 plan was to use smuggled guns to kill the three guards and three trusties guarding the prison gates. Following this wholesale slaughter, the convicts intended to scale the wall with rope ladders, seize the guard tower, and turn the machine guns and other firearms stored there on the rest of the guards.

On the eve of the attempt, prison officials were

tipped off and seized three shotguns, a machine gun, a rifle, a revolver, and ammunition that had been smuggled into the prison. Underhill was fingered as a ringleader and tossed into solitary confinement. He remained there for three years. Underhill finally convinced Warden Kirk Prather he would behave himself and was released from solitary. A few weeks later, he went over the wall . . . and took the Warden with him.

The Memorial Day break occurred while the 1,861 inmates watched a baseball game on the prison diamond. The convicts in on the plot were armed with six new automatic pistols that had been smuggled into the prison in bales of sisal used to make twine.

On a signal, Underhill seized Warden Prather; Bailey and the others took two guards hostage. Using grappling hooks and a rope ladder made in the prison twine shop, they scaled to the top of the wall, shot a guard, grabbed the machine guns and rifles from the tower, and climbed down the outside wall to freedom.

Commandeering cars and taking more hostages, including the three women, the convicts eluded a massive manhunt involving the state militia and disappeared into Oklahoma's rugged Cookson Hills, a hostile territory that had traditionally sheltered renegades and badmen.

The prison break stirred up so much heat that the Barkers scurried back to their Minnesota sanctuary. There, Ma summoned Shotgun Ziegler to join the family near Bald Eagle Lake. She had a new caper in mind, one that would be less risky than sticking up banks and promised to be more profitable: kidnapping.

The gang's first target, Ma decreed, would be William A. Hamm, Jr., the wealthy St. Paul beer baron. On June 15, 1933, Hamm was yanked off the street, blindfolded, and driven to Bensenville, Illinois. Ransom negotiations moved along smoothly. Four days later, Hamm was released unharmed on a country road forty miles from St. Paul, and the Barker gang drove off with $100,000.

However, even as the ransom was being delivered, other elements of the Barker gang were coordinating one of the blackest episodes ever to stain American law enforcement: The Kansas City Massacre.

The blood spilled that day forever changed federal law enforcement, placed incredible power in the hands of J. Edgar Hoover, and triggered a juggernaut that steamrolled Ma Barker and her reign of terror.

For years, Barker associate Frank (Jelly) Nash had been high on the government's most wanted list. In 1930, while a trustee at Leavenworth, Jelly had embarrassed federal authorities by strolling out the front door of the warden's house and vanishing. He became an important cog in Ma Barker's crime machine and played a role in smuggling the guns into Lansing.

In mid-June, Federal Agents Frank C. Smith and F. Joseph Lackey, assigned to the Oklahoma City office of the Bureau of Investigation, heard scuttlebutt that Nash was living it up in Hot Springs, Arkansas, another favorite safe city.

Smith and Lackey set out to nail Jelly to the wall. They recruited McAlester, Oklahoma, Police Chief Otto Reed. Reed's purpose was two-fold: He knew Nash well and could identify him despite the disguise snitches said Jelly had adopted. Second, Reed rode shotgun for the federal agents who had neither the power to arrest nor the authority to carry firearms.

The usually bald Nash sported a bright red wig when he was nabbed sauntering into a Hot Springs hangout. Nash was cuffed, tossed in the backseat of a waiting car, and hustled out of town before he knew what hit him. The posse with its fugitive made a dash for Fort Smith to connect with a Kansas City-bound train.

"You guys are nuts," Nash snorted. "None of us are never gonna make it back to Leavenworth alive."

The lawmen didn't know how right Jelly was. Even before they cleared the Hot Springs city limits, the news of Jelly's capture was flashing over the criminal grapevine. When word reached Kansas City, panic gripped the Barkers and others. Nash knew too much. Something had to be done. A murder squad gathered and money was spread around in the right places. Before sundown, the killers knew which train Jelly was on, what time it would arrive, who would be there to meet it, and the make of the car that would take Nash to Leavenworth.

When the 7:15 A.M. arrived on Union Station's Track Twelve the next morning, two welcoming parties were on hand. One consisted of Bureau agents Reed E. Vetterli and Raymond J. Caffrey, along with Kansas City detectives, W.J. "Red" Grooms and Frank Hermanson.

The second was made up of three, possibly four or more, hired guns, all armed to the teeth with brand new, fully loaded tommy guns. One member of this second group was the Barker gang's Verne Miller, the disgraced sheriff who had made a new name for himself as one of the underworld's most pitiless killers.

The others were never positively identified. Two of the shooters may have been Doc and Fred Barker. Both were in the Kansas City area at the time. Both worked closely with Verne Miller. And both of the cop-hating brothers would have jumped at the chance to gun down lawmen and get a shot at Jelly at the same time. There was dark talk that Jelly had turned rat because he'd escaped so easily from the trap that snared Bailey, Holden, and Keating on the golf course. Ma suspected that Nash had set up the others in exchange for his freedom.

J. Edgar Hoover, strong evidence to the contrary, decided the two machine gunners with Miller were Pretty Boy Floyd and his running mate, Adam Richetti. After the Massacre, the Bureau's energy was focused on getting the pair. Floyd was shot as he ran across an Ohio cornfield fleeing from Melvin Purvis. (One lingering story holds that agents actually "executed" the wounded outlaw in retaliation for the Union Station hit.) Richetti was captured nearby and convicted of the mass murder. In 1938, Richetti went to his death in the Missouri gas chamber muttering, "What did I do to deserve this?"

In any event, the seven officers escorting the handcuffed Nash walked to their car parked in front of the Union Station that Saturday morning in June while hard eyes watched from ambush. Nash was placed in the front seat. Chief Reed, Lackey, and Smith climbed in back. Suddenly, the doors of a Chevrolet sedan parked nearby burst open. Three machine-gun-toting killers leapt out and ran toward the officers.

"Up! Up! Get 'em up!" shouted Miller.

Detective Grooms reacted by reaching for his revolver, but before he could draw someone else shouted, "Let 'em have it!"

The three machine guns opened up with a deafening roar. Nash, frantically waving his distinctive red wig, was heard to scream, "No! No! For God's sake, don't shoot me!"

The barrage continued for more than a minute.

Two of the gunmen moved to one side of the car catching the lawmen in a deadly cross fire. Grooms and Hermanson were nearly cut in two with the first burst of lead. Caffrey went down with bullets in his head and later died en route to the hospital. When the firing began, Vetterli dove under the car and received only a slight wound to the arm.

The trio of shooters raked the car with wave after wave of machine-gun fire. The three officers in the backseat were hit. Reed was killed instantly. Lackey and Smith, although badly wounded, survived the attack.

Torrents of lead tore through the front windows of the car ripping Frank Nash to pieces. The barrage was so intense, in fact, that officers later concluded the killers meant to murder Nash, not free him, and the cops just happened to be in the way.

After blasting the officers' car, two of the machine gunners jumped into the waiting Chevy and sped away. One gunman lingered to spray the parking lot a final time, then ran to a second getaway car, and disappeared with the others.

They left five dead behind and the parking lot awash in blood.

The murders shocked the nation. This was no St. Valentine's Day Massacre with killer killing killer. This was an arrogant, vicious attack on the very foundation of law and order. An outraged Congress quickly passed nine major anticrime bills greatly expanding the powers of Hoover's Bureau of Investigation, which became the Federal Bureau of Investigation in 1935. Agents finally had the authority to execute warrants, arrest fugitives, and carry guns. The murder of a government agent also was made a federal offense.

George (Baby Face) Nelson was riddled by FBI machine-gun fire in a roadside ditch on November 28, 1934. Ma and Fred Barker battled the feds for six hours before they were killed in January 1935.

But the bloodletting of 1933 didn't end with the Kansas City Massacre. There was more to come before the year was over.

In August, Doc and Fred led the gang on a raid of the Swift Company payroll office in South St. Paul which netted them $30,000. As the outlaws ran to waiting vehicles, a St. Paul squad car pulled up. Fred and Creepy Karpis opened up with machine guns. One cop died in the street; a second was wounded and crippled for life.

Less than a month later, a Chicago policeman, making a routine traffic stop of a suspicious car, was machine-gunned to death. His fatal error was failing to recognize the carload of wanted killers.

But cops weren't the only ones to die at the Barkers' hands. Verne Miller was the object of a nationwide manhunt for his role in the Kansas City Massacre, and that intense heat was hurting the Barkers. On November 2, Miller shot his way out of a trap set in a Chicago hotel by federal agents. Ma decided that Miller had become a dangerous liability. If captured alive, he could bring down the whole family. Miller had to go and her boys caught up with the ex-sheriff in a Detroit hideout.

The newspapers told part of the story:

MILLER, GUNMAN
SLAIN IN DETROIT

KILLING LAID TO GANGS

> DETROIT, Nov. 29.—A nude body discovered yesterday in a ditch outside the city limits was identified today as that of Verne C. Miller, 37 years old, who was said to have handled a machine gun that mowed down five men in the Kansas City Union Station massacre on June 17. . . .
>
> Miller evidently had been beaten to death. His head was crushed. The body had been wrapped in two blankets and tied into a jack-knife position with a few yards of clothesline. . . .
>
> Miller, who was once Sheriff at Huron S.D., deserted the side of law some years ago. His technique with firearms was said to have been perfect and his courage was unquestioned. Federal authorities had been seeking him as a suspect in many of the crimes of Ma Barker. . . .

Miller's mutilated corpse was wrapped in a ratty old blanket and dumped in a drainage ditch. He had been gruesomely tortured, apparently for hours, his tongue and cheeks punctured with ice picks, his genitals scorched with hot irons, and dozens of cigarettes ground out on his body. Finally, the killers crushed his skull with a tire iron and riddled his body with .45 slugs.

With Verne Miller out of the way, Ma got back to the business of stealing. Doc, Fred, Shotgun Ziegler, and two other gunsels hijacked a federal reserve mail truck on a Chicago street. As they tossed sacks from what they thought was a money shipment into their getaway car, two policemen raced up firing their revolvers.

Shotgun and Freddie leapt onto the running board

of their car as it drove away. Holding on with one hand and laughing like maniacs, the killers cut loose with tommy guns and sawed-off shotguns. Patrolman Miles A. Cunningham was killed instantly.

But the robbery was a bust. The gang had grabbed the wrong sacks and instead of bringing a fortune home to Ma, they returned with bags of worthless mail.

Ma Barker berated the boys for taking foolish risks. She reminded them of the easy $100,000 they'd collected for snatching William Hamm. It was time for another kidnapping, Ma announced. (The Hamm kidnapping had opened the floodgates. Soon, so many wealthy citizens fell prey to kidnappers that newspapers ran box scores of who was kidnapped, released, or killed; those arrested, ransoms paid.)

In St. Paul, both the financial pages and the society pages were filled with stories about Edward George Bremer, a member of one of the city's most prominent families and president of the Commercial State Bank. Bremer ought to be worth twice what they got for Hamm, Ma mused. So in December 1933, the gang returned to the Twin Cities and began stalking Edward Bremer.

On January 17, 1934, Bremer dropped his eight-year-old daughter off at school and continued on to his bank. As he pulled up to a stop sign, masked and armed men jerked open the front doors of his Lincoln sedan.

"Don't move or I'll kill you," a gruff voice ordered. Bremer was clubbed on the head with the barrel of a shotgun, shoved to the floor, and goggles stuffed with cotton slapped over his eyes.

While Doc, Creepy Karpis, Harry Campbell, and

Lapland Willie raced off with their victim to the same Bensenville farm where they'd kept William Hamm prisoner, Ma and Freddie opened ransom negotiations with the family. Walter Magee, a close friend of Bremer's, was chosen to make the ransom exchange.

But this snatch didn't go as smoothly as the Hamm kidnapping. Ransom negotiations dragged on for weeks. Bremer was kept blindfolded most of the time and chained to his bed each night. All the while, Edward Bremer diligently memorized every possible clue that might help identify his abductors.

On the evening of February 6, 1934, Walter Magee, following the kidnappers' instructions, dropped $200,000 in $5s and $10s in a ditch outside Farmington, Minnesota. As soon as Ma had her hands on the ransom money, she sent a signal to Doc. Bremer was driven to a lonely spot near Rochester, Minnesota, and released.

Then, three days after Bremer's release, fingerprints found on a gasoline can abandoned when Bremer was dropped off were positively identified as those of Arthur (Doc) Barker. With that solid piece of evidence, plus Bremer's descriptions of sounds and names overheard, along with his estimation of distances traveled, authorities pieced together a profile of the Barker gang.

Teletypes were flashed to all Bureau offices instructing the special agents in charge to: "Pick up the Barker-Karpis Gang . . . wanted for kidnapping of Edward George Bremer . . . urgent . . ."

Soon photos of Doc and Fred Barker, Alvin Karpis, and others appeared on wanted posters from coast to coast. Their faces were splashed all over newspapers and stared out from the pages of such widely read magazines as *Liberty* and *True Detective*. Millions of amateur crime stoppers were now on the lookout for the notorious Barker boys and their sinister Ma.

Moreover, the pressure was disrupting Ma's operations and driving chinks between gang members. Suspected informants were everywhere. Loyalties, always tenuous at best, were severely tested. Shotgun Ziegler, especially, became the object of Ma's paranoia.

Most of the $200,000 Bremer ransom had been turned over to Ziegler who claimed he could fence the hot money through his Chicago underworld contacts. But first he stashed it in an in-law's garage and left it there to "cool." As the weeks went by, however, Shotgun developed a fatal case of loose lips. He started bragging about the Bremer job as though it were his own.

Ma scowled when she heard that Shotgun had been talking. On March 22, 1934, she sent Doc and Freddie to silence the gangster. As Ziegler left a lounge in Cicero, Illinois, the Barker boys stepped from the shadows, each armed with a double-barreled, sawed-off .12 gauge shotgun, and blew Shotgun away. To make identification difficult, the brothers reloaded and fired again. They left behind only a gore-covered, headless corpse still twitching on the sidewalk. It was days before cops identified Shotgun by his fingerprints.

In his pockets, police also found clues to the gang's whereabouts. Now even the usual safe cities were no longer safe enough. With wanted posters everywhere and the relentless notoriety in the press, Ma and the boys were running out of places to hide.

Doc and Freddie decided that desperate times called for desperate measures, so with Creepy Karpis they went looking for Doc Moran.

* * *

Joseph Patrick Moran was an alcoholic physician who did a stretch in Joliet in the 1920s for performing illegal abortions. Through his prison contacts, Doc Moran soon became the surgeon to the underworld, digging slugs out of wounded outlaws that legitimate doctors would have reported to police.

By the 1930s, Moran was specializing in operations that he claimed could give wanted hoods new faces and alter their fingerprints. The infamous John Dillinger was one of Moran's early experiments in plastic surgery.

The Barkers and Karpis secretly met with Moran in a seedy Chicago whorehouse where the plastic surgery was to be performed. At the last minute, Doc Barker backed out, but Freddie and Creepy went under the knife . . . and with dreadful consequences. Moran was so juiced up when he started cutting that he nearly butchered the two gangsters. After injecting them with morphine, Moran started chopping away at their noses and chins, slicing away jowls, doing a nip here and a tuck there to tighten the skin over their faces.

Next, Moran froze their fingertips with cocaine and started scraping away the telltale fingerprints with a dull scalpel.

The operations were totally botched. Rather than emerging with new faces, all that Barker and Karpis had to show for their excruciating pain was a patchwork of grotesque scars and devastating infections.

"He sharpened the ends of my fingers the way you'd sharpen a pencil," Karpis later complained.

"They're twice as ugly as when they started," Doc confided to a worried Ma, who nursed the boys back to health.

The boys' fingertips were so infected that it was

weeks before either gunman could pick up a weapon, much less fire it if he had to. The pain was so intense that everyday when Ma changed the dressing, Freddie screamed. "I'm gonna kill that son of a bitch Moran as soon as I can hold a gun!"

He would have, too, except the cagey Moran, despite his booze-fogged brain, knew a golden opportunity when it landed in his lap. He convinced the Barkers that he could help unload the red-hot Bremer ransom money for the gang. That got Ma's attention. She had easily disposed of the Hamm ransom money in Reno, and it only cost her five percent. But there was so much heat from the Bremer kidnapping that none of Ma's underworld contacts would touch the $200,000 ransom. So when Doc Moran bragged that he could wash the money, Ma listened, and kept the furious Freddie in check . . . temporarily.

Moran did, in fact, move some of the ransom money, but at a high price. He returned with only ten percent in usable cash. Moreover, the feds, who had been waiting for the ransom money to surface, pounced on Moran's money launderers. Ma, Doc, Fred, and Creepy, fearful that the authorities were just a step behind, scurried off to a new hideout in Toledo and took Doc Moran with them, still believing he could launder the rest of the ransom money.

But Doc Moran got drunker than usual in a Toledo whorehouse where he was hiding out and bragged to the madam: "I've got those Barkers in the palm of my hand. One word from me and their goose is cooked."

The madam reported the boast to the Barkers, and, in early August, Ma turned Doc and Fred loose to deal with the talkative Moran. Freddie later told Karpis that "Me and Doc shot the son of a bitch. Anybody who talks to whores is too dangerous to live. We dug a hole in Michigan and dropped him in and covered the hole with lime. Nobody's gonna see Doc Moran again." No one ever did.

Next, Ma Barker decided that the family should split up so they'd be harder to track. They had plenty of money to tide them over for awhile. Doc slipped into Chicago and holed up in a North Side apartment; Ma and Fred headed south to Florida and rented a two-story cabin in Oklawaha, overlooking Lake Weir.

Alvin Karpis headed for the East Coast, but during the holiday season, wandered down to Florida to celebrate what would be Ma's and Freddie's last Christmas and New Year's.

In the first week in January, about the same time Creepy was packing to leave Florida, federal agents were talking to an informant in Chicago and making preparations for a hush-hush raid on Doc Barker's hideout.

The night of January 8, the raiding party headed by Melvin Purvis surrounded the apartment and nabbed the unarmed outlaw as he strolled out. Barker was spirited to Bureau headquarters in downtown Chicago, manacled to a chair, and except for trips to the bathroom, was held there for the next eight days and nights. Agents grilled Doc for hours at a stretch in an interrogation bordering on the third degree. Although he sagged from exhaustion, the hardened con sneered at all of Purvis's questions and refused to reveal where Ma and Freddie were hiding.

Doc never broke, but even without his cooperation, agents got lucky. A search of Doc's apartment turned up a Florida map with the area around Oklawaha circled in red.

* * *

A squad of fourteen agents closed in on the backwoodsy, central Florida locale noted for its hunting and fishing and began asking questions. They struck pay dirt when they came across a fishing guide Freddie often employed. The guide recalled that Freddie once rolled up his shirtsleeves and revealed a distinctive tattoo on one arm—a red heart with an arrow shooting through it, emblazoned with the word "Ma."

Only Fred Barker bore such a brand. Ironically, it was this fanatical devotion to his Ma that contributed to their violent, bloody deaths.

The guide directed the hunting party to the Barker's lakeside hideout. In the predawn darkness of January 16, the federal agents, accompanied by a score of local and state cops, quietly encircled the cottage. They came bearing high-powered rifles, machine guns, and tear gas. They would need every bullet . . . and then some.

When all were in place, a voice boomed out: "You in the house! You are surrounded. Come out one by one with your hands in the air!"

For a moment there was silence. Then the command was repeated and answered this time with a snarl from Ma. "To hell with you, all of you!"

The agent in charge of the operation, E.J. Connelley gave thc Barkers one more chance to surrender. "If you don't come out," he shouted, "we'll have to use tear gas."

"All right, go ahead," Ma bellowed. "Let the bastards have it, Freddie!" With that, the Barkers opened up with machine-gun and rifle fire from the upstairs bedroom windows.

Lawmen ducked for cover as a withering fire sprayed the trees and bushes. The battle was on and raged for several hours. Thousands of rounds were fired at the house, and a dozen tear gas bombs were hurled through broken windows. But Ma and Fred fought back with nearly as much firepower as that arrayed against them. In fact, at one point when it appeared the officers might run out of ammunition, Connelley sent men to Jacksonville for more.

The gunfight blazed throughout the morning, but about 11:00 A.M. the firing stopped. Connelley waited nearly an hour before sending a handyman who had worked for the Barkers into the house.

"They're dead in there," he reported back. "They're all dead."

Inside, agents found the bodies of Ma and Freddie sprawled beneath bedroom windows. Freddie clutched a .45 automatic pistol, an empty machine gun at his side. Freddie had been hit fourteen times, but had continued fighting until he bled to death.

Ma had three bullets in her body. The fatal wound was right through the heart. A machine gun with only half of its one-hundred-round drum expended was clenched in her fist. Surrounding both was a carpet of hundreds of empty shell casings indicating the Barkers had reloaded several times during the miniwar and were determined to die fighting rather than surrender.

Connelley found more than $10,000 in cash in Ma's handbag and in a money belt around Freddie's waist.

The next day, the *New York Times* carried a front-page account of the climactic gun battle that Hollywood would imitate for decades to come:

> OKLAWAHA, Fla., Jan. 16—Federal agents trailed "Ma" Barker and her son, Fred, long sought as members of the gang that kidnapped Edward G. Bremer, St. Paul banker, to their Florida hiding place today and killed them both

after a machine gun battle lasting six hours.

Mrs. Kate (Ma) Barker who has been called the brains of the Barker-Karpis gang held responsible for the kidnapping of Mr. Bremer, died with a machine gun in her hand. Residents of this little village described the scene as "like a war." Barker was 32 and his mother 55.

The battle began soon after daylight this morning when Department of Justice agents, led by E.J. Connelley of Cincinnati, surrounded the house occupied by the Barkers on a shore of Lake Weir. Connelley approached and called to the outlaws to surrender.

Machine-gun fire was the answer. The government agents replied in kind, also using tear gas.

Rifles and machine guns would crack for fifteen minutes, then there would be a lull, followed by a renewal of firing from both sides. Most of the shooting from the besieged house came from upstairs, witnesses said. The white house was pock-marked by bullets. The agents said they had fired 1,000 rounds of ammunition.

"Ma" Barker fell holding a machine gun in her hand. A portion of the drum of ammunition had been exhausted. One shot had killed her. Her son's body was sprawled on the floor with eleven machine-gun bullets in one shoulder and three in the head. . . .

The bullet-riddled bodies of the mother and son were kept on ice for the next eight months while the curious trooped through the mortuary to view the remains. Eventually, they were shipped back to Oklahoma and buried next to Herman.

* * *

Creepy Karpis, who missed getting caught in the trap by hours, continued to rob banks and even hijack trains, although constantly on the run from Hoover's agents who had sworn to get him. After a cross-country chase, Karpis was captured in New Orleans in May 1936. He spent the next twenty-six years on Alcatraz. In 1962, Karpis was transferred to McNeil Island where he tutored a young car thief named Charles Manson on how to kill. Old Creepy Karpis was paroled and deported to his native Canada in 1969. He died there peacefully years later, the last of the flamboyant Depression Desperadoes.

While he was still at the Rock, Karpis shared a cell block with his gangster pal Doc Barker.

But not for long.

In 1939, Doc and four other inmates made a futile dash for freedom. The San Francisco papers reported that:

> "Escape-proof" Alcatraz today thwarted an attempt by five convicts who sawed their way out of a steel cell block and were making ready for a desperate swim toward freedom when armed guards captured them, wounding two.
>
> One of the wounded was Arthur (Doc) Barker, gang leader and kidnapper. He died tonight from his wounds.
>
> In one of the thickest fogs the rock prison island had experienced since it became the terror of Federal convicts in 1934, the five prisoners slipped quietly through the bars which they had severed and, in a manner yet unexplained, out of the cell building into the darkness.
>
> At 4 A.M. a guard noticed the empty cells and saw the severed bars. In a few moments the entire twelve-acre island was aglow with light. But

even powerful searchlights did not penetrate far into the fog, which Warden James A. Johnston described as "like a mass of wool."

Guards along the island's rim finally sighted the prisoners fleeing toward the waters of San Francisco Bay, stripping off their clothes as they ran toward the water. . . .

Barker was shot through the head and legs as he ignored a guard's order to halt. Dale Stamphill, 27, Oklahoma kidnapper, was shot through both legs.

The other three fugitives surrendered. . . .

Barker, a leader of the Barker-Karpis gang, was serving a life sentence for the kidnapping of Edward G. Bremer. Alvin Karpis, co-leader of the notorious gang, also is in Alcatraz.

The foolhardy break was doomed before it even started. No one had ever escaped from the Rock and lived to tell about it. The frigid, mid-January bay waters would have killed Doc in minutes if the guard's bullets hadn't gotten him first.

Besides, the superstitious killer should have known better. The date was Friday the thirteenth.

Doc soon joined Ma, Freddie, and Herman in the family plot near Welch, Oklahoma. And with the arrival of Lloyd, murdered by his wife in 1949, the Bloody Barkers were, finally, all together again.

FOUR
THE MCCRARY-TAYLOR CLAN

It was October 1971, and there were too many bodies piling up. Too many reports of unsolved murders coming in from around the country that had too much in common.

The MO was always the same: The victims, mostly young women in their teens or early twenties, working alone at night in donut shops or convenience stores, were kidnapped, raped, sexually tortured, shot, strangled, and dumped miles from where they were snatched.

Dallas County Sheriff Clarence Jones had three such murders on his hands. All had occurred within a few days of each other in Mesquite, a small Texas town about to be swallowed up by the booming Dallas-Ft. Worth metroplex. First, it was a young couple kidnapped from a mom-and-pop market. Next, a sixteen-year-old girl vanished from a Sweet Cream Donut Shop. Their mutilated bodies were discovered a few days later, dumped in separate rural locations in neighboring Hunt County.

At that point, the cops still didn't know what they were dealing with. The term "serial killer" hadn't been coined yet. But even if it had been, the murders wouldn't have fit the classic serial killer profile of a Ted Bundy or a "Green River Killer."

Texas was no stranger to violent random murder, and the three Mesquite slayings might have been written off as just more of the same. At the time, however, Sheriff Jones had at his disposal a new, but still primitive, law enforcement tool. The Traveling Criminal network was an early attempt to track a new generation of highly mobile professional criminals.

Beginning in the late 1960s, organized bands of sophisticated thieves and killers took to the roadways and airways throughout the South and Midwest. Generally known as the Dixie Mafia, these modern outlaws drove police crazy as they leapt across state and jurisdictional lines robbing and killing with impunity.

For once, the cops put aside their traditional turf battles and intra-agency jealousies to form a secret intelligence network to track the Dixie Mafia and others like them. Police intelligence units stayed in touch through Traveling Criminal Bulletins or TCBs, that reported on gang movements, major crimes, murders, and criminal connections.

Shortly after the Mesquite murders, Sheriff Jones was handed one of those TCBs that described murders with almost identical MOs in Kansas, Colorado, Utah, and elsewhere. Nearly all the victims were young women who were taken from donut shops where they were working alone, then raped and murdered. Moreover, the same types of weapons were used—.22- and .32-caliber pistols indicating there were probably two killers.

Sheriff Jones issued a call to law enforcement agencies investigating similar murders to meet in Dallas. Several homicide detectives from neighboring states showed up lugging their unsolved case files with them.

In addition to the three Mesquite murders and the suspicious disappearance of a Lubbock, Texas, waitress in September, Sheriff Jones's agenda included killings in Goodland and Elkhart, Kansas, South Salt Lake City, Utah, and Lakewood, Colorado, a suburb of Denver, plus a dozen or more from other parts of the country.

The list was pared down and a second meeting held in February 1972. By then, FBI lab reports had come back linking several of the killings to the same .32-caliber Gertsenberger pistol.

More than forty lawmen reconvened in Dallas on February 22-24. A bulletin describing the killer's MO was prepared and passed out at the meeting.

"The victim is young, white female of average or better looks, employed as the only clerk or waitress in a small grocery store, cafe, or donut shop. The location of the crime is probably cased, at least just prior to the crime. Between 8 P.M. and 10 P.M., the perpetrators enter the location, remove the cash from the cash register, and kidnap the victim. The victim's personal property is left at the scene. Some victims may be held captive for as long as 24 hours before death.

"Victim is forced at gunpoint to submit to sexual intercourse. She is then allowed to dress and is then taken to a remote area on a little used road leading off of a main highway. She is then shot in the head and upper torso and her body dumped along the road. On some occasions underwear or jewelry is missing from the body.

"A nine shot .22 caliber revolver and a German make .32 caliber revolver have been the murder weapons."

But almost at the exact moment the cops were gathering in Dallas to compare notes, another name was added to the list. On the afternoon of February 20, 1972, while most of the lawmen were still packing for their trip to Dallas, a Woodland, Washington, couple decided to take advantage of the unseasonably warm afternoon to walk their dog along an abandoned logging road near their rural home about thirty miles straight north of Portland, Oregon. The steep, rutted trail they wandered along deep in the woods was rarely used and hardly the kind of place casual outsiders were likely to visit.

Suddenly, the small dog bolted into the deep woods lining the road, barking furiously at something hidden in the thick underbrush. The couple chased after their frantic pet . . . and stumbled over a nightmare.

At their feet lay the body of a young woman, her once lovely features obscured by dried blood that caked her face and the mutilation caused by gun shots fired at point-blank range. Apparently, the body had been dragged through the underbrush and tossed behind a rotting log where it might never have been found had it not been for the freak warm weather and the curiosity of a frisky pup.

When police arrived to investigate, they followed a trail of blood from the logging trail down to where the body lay on its back in a pool of blood that had soaked into the ground. The girl wore jeans. A red blouse and blue sweater were pulled up exposing the breasts. There was no bra in sight.

A quick check revealed a gunshot wound behind her left ear and what appeared to be a second bullet wound to her right breast.

After the body was removed, police carefully searched the area. The only clue they turned up was an empty .22-caliber shell casing on the logging trail, next to scuff marks that indicated the victim had been shot on the road and then dragged into the underbrush.

Meanwhile, an autopsy was underway on the murdered girl. The findings shocked the medical examiner and the attending cops who were hardened to death in its many forms. They'd all seen their share of shooting victims, but this one was different, fiendishly different.

When the blood was cleaned from the girl's face, two more bullet holes appeared, one in her left cheek, the other almost directly under her chin.

"You know," muttered the doctor performing the autopsy, "I've heard about this kind of thing, but it's the first time I've seen it."

As investigators crowded around the coroner, he inserted a probe into the chin wound. Stepping back, he studied the trajectory of the bullet. "The only way she could have been shot from that angle is if the guy was laying on top of her when he fired," declared the examiner.

"He was probably holding the gun under her chin while he raped her and then shot her at the moment he ejaculated. It's sick, but it's happened before."

The complete autopsy did indeed confirm the young woman had been raped. The condition of her clothing also indicated that she had been disrobed, raped, and then clumsily redressed before her body was dragged into the woods and dumped.

Washington cops had a pretty good idea who the victim was even before the autopsy was finished.

Cynthia Ann Glass had been reported missing the night before from nearby Portland, Oregon. At twenty-six, Cynthia was unmarried and still living at home with her mother.

On February 19, she reported to work at the Get-

and-Go Market to start her 4:00 P.M. shift, prompt as usual. Cynthia had worked there only six months but had already demonstrated that she was dependable and trustworthy. Thus, the owners were mystified when police called that evening to report that their store was empty and money missing from the open cash register.

Foul play was immediately suspected since Cynthia's winter coat was still hanging in the back room and her car remained in the parking lot.

Either the killers were extremely lucky or they had the market staked out waiting for the opportune moment to strike, because one of the last persons known to see Cynthia Glass alive was a patrolling Portland cop. According to the officer's log, he had stopped by the market to buy some cigarettes at 8:19 P.M. The call to police reporting the unattended store came in at 8:56 P.M.

Meanwhile, the homicide seminar in Dallas broke up on an even more somber note than it began—and with a greatly heightened sense of urgency now that Cynthia Ann Glass's name had been included in the roster of possible victims. Fortunately, as it turned out, her name would be the last on the list.

The cops who were just starting to sniff out the killers' trail didn't know it at the time, but the end was near, for the network, designed to track sophisticated, traveling criminals and organized crime figures, had swept into its net a family of itinerant small-time thieves, boosters, and ignorant, but cunning, killers: the brutal McCrary-Taylor clan.

Homicide investigators from coast to coast were about to discover, to their amazement, that the killer wasn't a single sexual psychopath but, incredibly, an entire brood of parents, in-laws, children, and grandchildren.

This nomadic band of cutthroats was headed by brutish, alcoholic Sherman McCrary and his loathsome, sadistic son-in-law Carl Taylor. Together they robbed, raped, and murdered their way across country in a wandering horror spree that went undetected for three years. The McCrary-Taylor bunch admitted to ten murders. Police and the FBI believe the actual toll was more than twenty. And the motives behind their randomly ruthless murders were as mindlessly moronic as the nomads themselves.

The McCrarys and Taylors all sprouted from the same backward, hardscrabble stock of rural sharecroppers. In another time and place, they would have been the perfect models for John Steinbeck's displaced "Okies." As a matter of fact, Sherman McCrary *was* an authentic Okie. Born in Byers, Oklahoma, on December 6, 1925, he grew up in the cotton fields that turned to dust when drought and the Depression swept over the harsh Oklahoma hills in the 1930s and put a whole generation of dispossessed Sherman McCrarys on a wandering road to nowhere.

The McCrarys and Taylors were cut from the same cloth: Crude, uneducated, down-on-their-luck day laborers who drifted from odd job to odd job, living from hand to mouth, floating bad checks, hatching small-minded plots to steal enough gas money to get on down the road to the next town . . . or back to their favorite Texas haunts that drew them like a magnet, especially when the law was breathing down their necks.

Sherman McCrary was solidly built, but the chunky muscles that gave him the look of an over-the-hill wrestler were turning to puffy fat. He was only forty-six at the time of his arrest, but the effects of the fifth of booze and countless beers he put away every day, plus years of haphazard diets on the road, made him appear much older and worn-out. Work interfered with his drinking time, so Sherman limited his labor to scheming two-bit robberies or bad check scams . . . until he hooked up with Carl Taylor, and the minor crimes escalated overnight into rape and murder.

Balding and bullet-headed, the coarse, semiliterate McCrary enjoyed ravaging the helpless girls and young women that he and Taylor preyed upon like wild beasts. In fact, a psychiatric examination done during one of McCrary's stints in a Navy brig described him as ". . . a tall, unkempt individual with a dull, vacant facial expression who appears to be defectively motivated. . . . He apparently is a constitutional psychopath, emotionally unstable. Impression: Personality Disorder."

Sherman Ramon McCrary married Carolyn Elizabeth Tribble in 1943, when Liz, as she was called, was only fifteen. Always in frail health, Liz, nevertheless, possessed a tough, cunning personality that manipulated Sherman's brutish mentality like a puppet on a string.

Carl Taylor was born in Greenville, Texas, northeast of Dallas, on April 7, 1938. Taylor came into the world with an ugly, disfiguring harelip and mismatched ears that made him the butt of jokes from infancy. As he grew older, Taylor used that birth defect as an excuse for all the ills in his life and his inability to rise above them.

Taylor never knew his real father and grew up with a succession of abusive stepfathers who taught Carl to be an abuser himself. He was in the seventh grade when he first got into serious trouble—threatening to slit the throat of a classmate who teased Carl about his harelip. Kicked out of school, Taylor hit the road with a mean chip on his shoulder. From then on, Taylor relied mostly on small burglaries and hot checks to survive. Until he met Sherman McCrary.

When Taylor was seventeen years old he joined the Army, but the discipline was too tough and the ridicule over his misshapen mouth with the faulty dentures he was forced to wear drove the already angry young man over the edge. Taylor went AWOL after only five months, stole a car, was caught, and tossed out of the Army with an undesirable discharge.

For the next several years, Taylor wandered back and forth between Texas and California, pulling small crimes and doing short time. By 1969 Taylor had been in and out of jail and married so many times that Taylor himself lost track. Along the way, he fathered several children who were doomed to grow up like he did, never knowing their father. Shortly before Christmas 1969, Taylor was back in Texas and on parole from a stretch in the Washington state prison. He dropped into a Texas honky-tonk and met a skinny redhead named Ginger McCrary.

Their wedding in January 1970 was just as impulsive as Taylor's other marriages, but this union contained a deadly element all the others lacked. For reasons no one ever understood, the chemistry cooked up when the McCrary and the Taylor bloods mixed and boiled over into murder and rape. It was as though each had something the other lacked and, once merged, the two were transformed from petty thugs into merciless killers.

Liz and Ginger were mother-daughter look-alikes, blocky, square jaws sliced by razor-thin lips; both scrawny, flat-chested, chicken-necked, and sickly looking. Their plain homeliness was topped by stringy hair usually chopped short. Thick horn-rimmed glasses conveyed a mousey appearance that concealed tough-as-nails, shrewish interiors.

Eighteen-year-old Danny McCrary was the oddball of the bunch in that he was almost good-looking, with reddish-blond hair tumbling over his eyes, and a "Leave-It-to-Beaver" demeanor that contrasted sharply with the drooling Tobacco Roadish image of the others. But up close, the all-American boy facade disintegrated. Behind the flat, vacant, almost cruel eyes, one sensed that nobody was home inside.

Accompanying the adults on their rootless rambles were three youngsters, two of Ginger's girls nearing adolescence, and a boy who was just a toddler. Authorities believe the youngsters often were crowded to the side in the family's cars while terrified kidnap victims were being raped and brutalized. The children themselves were incest victims. "We had reason to believe that Ginger's two girls were really fathered by Sherman, her own father," recalled one investigator. "In fact, Sherman came close to killing Carl one time when he caught him fooling around with one of those girls who was retarded. The whole family was one big inbred, incest mess."

In late 1972, after the family was in jail, a "CONFIDENTIAL" Traveling Criminal Bulletin was issued updating lawmen on the McCrary-Taylor clan. It stated in part that:

"Sherman Ramon McCrary, white male, dob 12-6-25, FBI #11 674E, has been indicted in the kidnap-slayings of Sherri Lee Martin, age 17, who disappeared from a doughnut shop in Kearns, Utah on August 12, 1971 and whose body was found September 4, 1971 in Elko County, Nevada and Leeora Looney, age 20, who disappeared from a doughnut shop in Lakewood, Colorado on August 20, 1971 and whose body was found August 23, 1971 in Weld County, Colorado.

"Carl Robert Taylor, white male, dob 4-7-38, FBI #818 488B, has also been indicted in the kidnap-slayings of Sherri Lee Martin and Leeora Looney. Taylor is the son-in-law of Sherman McCrary.

"Carolyn Elizabeth McCrary, white female, dob 3-12-27, has been indicted in the murder of Leeora Looney. Carolyn McCrary is the wife of Sherman McCrary.

"Danny Sherman McCrary, white male, dob 11-18-52, FBI #715 768H, has been charged in the kidnap-slayings of Mrs. Jena Covey, age 19, and her husband, Forrest Covey, age 22, who disappeared from a drive-in grocery in Mesquite, Texas on October 17, 1971 and whose bodies were discovered in Hunt County, Texas on October 24, 1971. Danny McCrary is the son of Sherman and Carolyn McCrary.

"Ginger McCrary Taylor, white female, dob 3-30-49, wife of Carl Robert Taylor and daughter of Sherman and Carolyn McCrary, has not been charged in the kidnap-slayings but is being held in Colorado on bad check charges. Ginger Taylor has been granted immunity in the Colorado kidnap-slaying to be a States witness.

"The men involved worked as itinerant ranch hands, odd jobs and carnival workers, while the women in cafes or restaurants. Armed robbery charges are pending against family members in numerous cities in Texas and in Boise, Idaho and Omaha, Nebraska."

According to the same TCB: "The following kidnap-slayings are believed connected to the McCrary-Taylor clan but formal charges have not been filed: Susan Darlene Shaw, age 16, kidnapped from a doughnut shop in Mesquite, Texas on October 20,

1971 shot several times and the body thrown into a lake east of Mesquite.

"Elizabeth Perryman, age 24, kidnapped from a cafe in Lubbock, Texas on September 28, 1971 shot and killed and the body left on a ranch near Amarillo, Texas.

"Cynthia Ann Glass, age 25, kidnapped in Portland, Oregon on February 19, 1972 shot and killed and her body found near Woodland, Washington.

"The following kidnap-slayings have a similar pattern and may be connected to the McCrary-Taylor clan: Patricia Marr, age 22, and Bobbie Turner, age 37, kidnapped from a beauty shop in Starke, Florida, on November 30, 1971, shot and killed and bodies found near Melrose, Florida." (Actually, Mrs. Marr and Mrs. Turner were murdered, sexually molested, and their nude bodies left in the back room of the beauty shop. Mrs. Turner's sixteen-year-old daughter, Valerie, was abducted. Her skeletal remains were found six months later in a pine swamp near Jacksonville. Carl Taylor later was convicted of these murders.)

Other killings that fit the McCrary-Taylor pattern, itinerary, and time schedule included those of a Las Vegas, Nevada, couple Florence and Robert Lemmon, who were abducted, murdered, and their bodies dumped in the desert on August 31, 1970; the slaying of sixty-two-year-old Wallace Newton Patton, a service station attendant in Goodland, Kansas, on November 8, 1970; Mabel Manley, sixty-eight, and Jake Green, sixty-nine, shot and killed on March 1, 1971, after being kidnapped from the Bigger Jigger Tavern near Kansas City.

But that all came out later.

First came the killings . . . and the first of these, at least the first any family members admitted to, was that of Sherri Lee Martin, who had the misfortune to be working alone in Winchell's Donut Shop in South Salt Lake City the night of August 12, 1971, when a dark blue Ford Galaxie with a white top and bearing Nebraska license plates rolled into the deserted parking lot.

A battered Volkswagen van, whose occupants included several sleepy children, may have followed the Ford, according to some witnesses.

Sherman and Carl always maintained they were alone during their murderous forays. But authorities who prosecuted the clan believe otherwise. A few vague eyewitness reports and a couple of ambiguous statements by family members themselves indicate that Elizabeth, Ginger, Danny, and even the little kids were right in the middle of the robberies, kidnappings, murders, and even the sexual assaults from start to finish.

Carl Taylor almost admitted as much when, describing the Sherri Lee Martin kidnap-murder, he let it slip that "Ginger knew that she was in the car, because we went by the house and Sherman left the money there (after robbing the donut shop)." And of the Cynthia Glass murder, Taylor commented, "I come in with blood on my hands. She (Ginger) knew it wasn't my blood and it wasn't Sherman's blood. It had to be somebody else's blood."

Moreover, several cops believed that the waitress uniforms, stripped from the murdered women, were given to Liz and Ginger for the occasions when they picked up part-time jobs waiting tables in greasy spoons and truck stops.

Robert N. Miller, the Weld County, Colorado, D.A., who prosecuted the clan for the Leeora Rose Looney murder and who lived with their bloody deeds for years, believes that Sherman and Carl were covering up for the women when they claimed only the two of them were involved in the rapes and murders.

"The hideous part," said Miller, "is not only that they kidnapped and killed people, but the sexual brutality they inflicted on those young girls.

"I believe the whole clan participated in those acts. In one of the cases in Texas two or three acres of grass and brush had been mashed down around where they found the victim's body, which sure indicated that more than two people were participating.

"The first story Ginger gave out was that all of them, including the young children, were all in the car when the men went in to get Leeora Rose Looney, and that the kids were put into the front seat with Ginger and Elizabeth while Sherman and Carl crawled in the backseat and raped her all the way up to Wyoming.

"As far as I'm concerned the women were involved in everything—the robberies, the kidnappings, the murders, the sexual molestations and rapes, and Carl and Sherman were just covering up for their wives. The women condoned, if not encouraged, everything. In fact, Sherman was pretty much of a drunken dullard who wasn't bright enough to plan their crimes himself. Liz was the real power. She called the shots and Ginger had just about as much influence over Carl," Miller said.

At any rate, Carl Taylor insisted that he was behind the wheel of the Ford Galaxie and Sherman McCrary, half-drunk as usual, was at his side when they pulled up to Winchell's Donut Shop on State Street about 9:45 P.M. and noted with satisfaction that the counter girl was by herself.

Sherri Martin, seventeen, had just graduated from Kearns High School that spring. A part-time Sunday school teacher, Sherri, like most of her Mormon friends and relatives, was looking forward to a life devoted to serving her church and raising a family. She wanted to take some college courses in the fall, but her real sights were on the lifelong role of wife and mother to a houseful of healthy, happy children she envisioned for herself.

The McCrary-Taylor clan had other plans, plans that would soon see Sherri Lee Martin's torn and ravaged body rotting in the desert sun. Even in death, Carl Taylor brutalized her memory. "Ugly girl," was all he could recall about the Martin girl. "About sixteen or seventeen. Claimed she was still a virgin," he snorted.

The donut shop stood alone on a small parking lot on South State Street, one of Salt Lake City's main north-south thoroughfares. Police officer Bill Ralphs, cruising by on routine patrol about 9:45 P.M. noticed that the lights were out at the donut shop. That's not right, Ralphs thought, wheeling his car into a U-turn. The shop stayed open twenty-four-hours a day and late nighters, like Ralphs, could always find a warm smile there to go with a fresh cup of coffee.

Sherri Martin's locked car was parked behind the shop. The door to the shop was unlocked, and the cash register was open and empty. Later, investigators determined that the entire take in the robbery was a measly $83.

Bulletins on the robbery and apparent kidnapping went out immediately to all surrounding police agencies. The news media was given descriptions of Sherri Lee Martin in hopes that some citizen would recall seeing her. The FBI was called in, but could do nothing. It was as though the earth had opened up and swallowed Sherri Martin. And, in a sense, it had. Even as the cops searched Salt Lake City for the missing girl, a pair of demons named Sherman and Carl was scraping out a shallow grave in the desert sands of Nevada more than one hundred miles away to dispose of Sherri Lee's raped and mutilated body.

That night, Taylor later claimed in his confession, he and Sherman had set out to rob a state-owned liquor store during one of the clan's brief stopovers in Salt Lake City en route to California. Instead, they pulled into the donut shop.

"She (Martin) was in there by herself," said Taylor. "We were sitting there drinking coffee and Sherman leaned over and told me, 'I'm going to rob this goddamned place.'

"I thought he was bullshitting me. And he just got up, and she was around behind this little old partition. So, hell, I just got up, locked the doors, dropped the blinds on them, opened the cash register, and got the money."

Taylor left by the back door and found Sherman holding Sherri Martin at gunpoint in the backseat of their car.

"We'll take her out of town. Drop her off out in the country someplace," McCrary said.

With Taylor at the wheel, the kidnappers headed west out of town on U.S. Highway 40. As the new Ford Galaxie skirted the tip of the Great Salt Lake and sped through the night across the Salt Flats toward Nevada, Sherman chugged down cheap wine and pawed at the terrified, sobbing girl in the backseat.

As Sherman tore at her clothes, the Martin girl pleaded for him to stop. "Please don't," she begged. "I've never been with a boy before. I'm a good Christian."

But that only seemed to incite Sherman more. He threw his sweaty, alcohol-soaked body across the girl and tore off her panty hose. Soon, the only sounds coming from the backseat were Sherman's animallike grunts and the moans of pain from Sherri Lee Martin.

Crossing into Nevada at Wendover, Taylor turned left down U.S. 93, an alternate highway cutting southwest into the desolate badlands. He drove another fourteen or fifteen miles before pulling off into a dry wash. The car bumped along another mile and then stopped. When Carl switched off the headlights, only the stars in the bright desert night lit the death scene.

McCrary staggered from the backseat, hitching up his pants, his part in the brutal rape finished. While Sherman stood by, belching and fiddling with his .32-caliber pistol, Carl Taylor climbed in back to take his turn at the helpless girl.

When he was done, Taylor ripped up the panty hose, tied Sherri Lee's hands and feet, and dragged her out of the car.

"It was dark out there," Taylor later recalled. "I start around the damn car and the first thing that I know is BOOM! BOOM! BOOM! BOOM! The goddamn gun starts going off. And she was moaning and groaning. I knew he'd (Sherman) shot her. . . ."

Sherman reloaded and continued firing. Although he wouldn't admit it, cops are sure that Carl Taylor pulled his own .22 pistol and joined his father-in-law in the shooting.

When it was over, they dragged Sherri Lee Martin's body several yards off the trail and scraped out a shallow grave in the sand.

But there was one more horrifying scene yet to unfold in this heinous drama. Despite her multiple gunshot wounds and the savage sexual attack she had suffered, Sherri Lee Martin still clung to life. Before they kicked sand over her to hide the body, one of the men bent over the dying girl and, in a final outburst of sexual rage, shoved the barrel of the .32 pistol into her vagina and pulled the trigger.

Sherri Lee Martin's decomposed remains were found on September 9 by a family on a desert outing. But by then, it was already too late to save Leeora Rose Looney.

August 20, 1971, was a warm, muggy Friday, and Leeora Rose Looney arrived for work at the Mister Donut Shop on busy Colfax Avenue in Lakewood, Colorado. Most of Denver, it seemed, was streaming past her, headed for a weekend among the cool Rocky Mountain peaks.

But Leeora's thoughts were more on the parched flatland of Kansas than on refreshing mountain meadows. On the way to work that day, she'd stopped by the bank to withdraw $100 for a trip she was planning to Salina, Kansas, to visit her fiance. His birthday was coming up, and this would be Leeora's surprise to her childhood sweetheart.

Barely twenty years old, Leeora had graduated from Mapleton High School near Denver in 1969 as an honor student and one of the most popular kids in school. Like the victim before her, Leeora came from a deeply religious background and a family whose bonds among themselves and their church were strong; their commitments, once made, were for a lifetime.

Leeora Looney attended Western Bible Institute in Morrison, Colorado, while also putting in service as a missionary for her church, the Mountain States Baptist Church. Leeora regularly taught Sunday school, and, based on the strong work ethic her parents had taught her, was now earning her own way in the world.

And, like Sherri Lee Martin, Leeora Rose Looney had caught the eye of the murderous McCrary-Taylor bunch. Even as the pretty girl with the dark, shoulder-length hair mopped the counter and chatted gaily with the regulars from the neighborhood, unseen eyes, like a grinning death's-head, were stalking her from a blue and white Ford Galaxie parked across the street.

The eyes waited until all the customers had left the donut shop and then made their move. It was 9:30 P.M.

The call from some unknown citizen that something was amiss at the Mister Donut shop on West Colfax came into the Lakewood police dispatcher at 10:15 P.M. Within minutes, several officers, who were fond of dropping in at the donut shop during breaks and when their tours ended, converged on the scene.

Close behind came the department's new chief, or director as he preferred to be called, Pierce Brooks. It was Brooks, a former Los Angeles homicide detective, who gained fame as the cop who finally brought the Onion Field killers to justice, a case immortalized in Joseph Wambaugh's book and movie of the same name.

One glance at the scene at the donut shop and Brooks's instincts told him this was no routine case of a disgruntled employee walking off the job. Brooks immediately ordered that the disappearance of Leeora Rose Looney be treated as a probable kidnapping, a possible murder.

With that professional, experienced hand on the tiller, Lakewood police (a relatively new department with few seasoned homicide officers) went to work. Their careful, systematic collecting of evidence and canvasing of possible eyewitnesses put together a solid case that bound the McCrary-Taylor clan to the murder of Leeora Rose Looney with an unbreakable chain of evidence. It was that evidence gathered by the Colorado investigators that finally took the nomadic family of killers off the road and put them behind bars.

For example, Lab Technician Gerald S. Cole carefully noted the items found on the Mister Donut counter and dusted everything in sight for prints. One of those items was, according to Cole's report, ". . . a Mr. Donut coffee cup from atop the east counter, positioned above extreme north stool. Cup contained small amount of liquid resembling that of coffee with cream added. Also collected were metal cream container, teaspoon and moistened napkin inside coffee cup."

A single fingerprint Cole found on that porcelain cup belonged to Carl Taylor. It was that damning piece of evidence that helped establish Colorado's case against the killers as the strongest of all the states and was a major factor in the McCrary-Taylor murder convictions.

There was another piece of eyewitness evidence that wasn't presented in court, but that convinced Miller and others involved in the investigation that Liz and Ginger were much more deeply involved in the family's crimes than Sherman and Carl wanted them to believe.

Lakewood police took statements from a Denver couple who had been in the donut shop shortly before Leeora Looney was reported missing. As the couple drove away, they noticed two women crossing Colfax headed toward Mister Donut. One was in her forties, about five-foot, two-inches tall with her red hair up in curlers. The second woman was about twenty-six years old, five-feet, five-inches tall, and wearing tan slacks.

The description fit Liz and Ginger perfectly. In fact, added the witnesses, they had the distinct impression they were mother and daughter since they looked so much alike.

However, even as the Lakewood cops were swarming over the crime scene on Colfax, the Ford Galaxie with its three occupants was speeding through the night on the Valley Highway, headed north toward Wyoming.

Again, Carl Taylor was driving and Sherman McCrary was in the backseat, holding a pistol to the head of Leeora Rose Looney and already beginning to molest the terrified young woman.

"What are you going to do?" the woman sobbed. "You already got all the money. Where are you taking me?"

"Shut up," Sherman growled, slapping the girl with the barrel of the pistol that he waved menacingly. "And get them clothes off," he ordered.

"Wait a minute," Carl protested from the front seat. "That Utah girl was yours. Save this one for me."

"You just keep driving," Sherman answered. "You'll get yours when I'm done."

This time, Sherman and Carl had come prepared for dealing with struggling young women who fought desperately against being gang raped by a pair of animals. Sherman reached for a rope he'd earlier stashed on the floor of the backseat, looped it around the Looney girl's neck, and jerked it tight.

With the girl now gasping and moaning under the weight of Sherman's beefy, smelly body, the Ford continued north past Greeley and onto the flat plains, sloping up to the Wyoming border and the city of Cheyenne.

A mile or two south of the state line, the headlights picked up a gravel road leading off into the darkness. Taylor braked sharply and swung the Ford onto the side road that trickled off into the prairie vastness.

Carl Taylor switched off the engine and climbed in the backseat to take his turn.

For a long time, the only sounds in the night were the wracking sobs of a young woman being brutally violated. Gathering the last ounce of strength in her ravaged body, Leeora Rose Looney screamed and shoved a sated Carl Taylor aside. She pushed open the car door and jumped out, her naked body glowing white in the moonlight, the rope trailing from around her neck as she tried to run.

One of the men chased the girl, grabbed the rope, and yanked her to her knees. Choking for breath, the woman still tried to crawl away from the rapists she knew would never let her go alive.

Now the second man joined in. Together the killers yanked and pulled on the rope, dragging the dying woman through the prairie grass to the top of a small mound. Each drew pistols and began firing into the twitching body of Leeora Rose Looney until the guns were empty and the girl was dead.

The first news of the donut shop robbery-kidnapping appeared in the Sunday edition of *The Rocky Mountain News*. A photo of the missing girl accompanied the story that was headlined "Disappearance Baffles Lakewood Police."

While admitting they had no solid leads, the Lakewood investigators did say they were checking into a similar case in South Salt Lake City, Utah, that occurred a week earlier.

The next day, the *News* reported that ". . . Lakewood officials were exchanging information with Salt Lake City police because of a nearly identical case there a few weeks ago when a Salt Lake City girl disappeared from a Winchell's Donut Shop there and shop's cash register was emptied. . . ."

Investigators later determined that the $100 Leeora

had withdrawn for her trip to Kansas was missing from her purse. That, plus a handful of bills and change stolen from the cash register, was the price McCrary and Taylor put on the young woman's life.

The Denver newspapers with the donut shop story had barely hit the streets when an urgent teletype landed on Pierce Brooks's desk at Lakewood Police Headquarters. Time-stamped 2:30 P.M., the teletype advised that officers from the Weld County Sheriff's Office in Greeley had ". . . located the nude body of a white female, partially decomposed and lying in a field some distance north of the city."

That same morning, Brooks learned, the manager of the Lazy "D" Ranch was out at dawn's light checking a water pump when he came across the corpse about one hundred feet off a narrow dirt trail that cut across the pasture.

The manager notified the Weld County Sheriff's office and later guided deputies to the lonely, windswept killing ground. Unfortunately, it had rained heavily since the body was dumped, possibly destroying valuable pieces of evidence. However, deputies did find an expended .32-caliber slug that eventually helped convict Sherman McCrary of the murder.

Leeora Rose Looney's body was facedown, her right arm extended and her left drawn back in a crawling position. Even in death, she looked like she was still trying to escape. The body had lain exposed to the fierce August weather for more than sixty hours. Decomposition was advanced, making it impossible to identify the body visually. Lakewood technicians were able to positively identify the remains only after comparing fingerprints taken from the body with those on the Looney girl's driver's license application.

There were gunshot wounds under her left shoulder

and behind her left ear, and ugly discoloration marks around her throat indicating strangulation. Swarms of huge black flies and ants covered the body.

And, as if to demean Leeora Looney even after death, her body had been discarded facedown on a pile of cow dung.

Later that day, Dr. Lewis A. Kidder performed an autopsy in Greeley. He ruled that the cause of death was a combination of strangulation and gunshot wound to the head. Either one could have been fatal.

The autopsy also found sperm cells in the girl's vagina.

After leaving Leeora Rose Looney's strangled, raped, and bullet-riddled body spread-eagled on the manure heap, Sherman and Carl continued on to Cheyenne, where the rest of the family was waiting in a seedy motel at the edge of town.

Taylor didn't waste any time.

"Come on," he prodded Ginger and the sleepy kids. "Load up the stuff. We're gettin' outta here."

"Where to?" Ginger asked, already gathering up scattered belongings. Long accustomed to the life of a nomad, when it came time to move, Ginger simply moved, rarely questioning the reason why.

"I dunno," Carl shrugged. "Back to Texas maybe. Amarillo, I guess. Let's just get on down the road."

At least, that's the version of the Looney slaying that Sherman and Carl stuck to in an apparent attempt to shield their women from murder charges.

However, Ginger's story didn't jibe with her husband's. During an interview with several Colorado and California cops while she was still in jail in Santa Barbara after the whole family was rounded up, Ginger said that she, Carl, Liz, and Sherman were all involved in the death of the young waitress.

According to that statement, the four were in the donut shop when Carl ordered Ginger and Liz to move the car around to the back door. They did, and minutes later Carl and Sherman emerged with Leeora Looney at gunpoint. Carl pushed the girl, who was crying uncontrollably, into the backseat while Sherman took the wheel and headed north.

"Carl then raped Miss Looney in the backseat of the car," the police report continued. "When Carl was unable to silence her screams by slapping her, he strangled her with a cord or similar item, possibly the apron strings of her uniform.

"The four then drove to a secluded field not far from their motel . . . Miss Looney was then shot to insure death. The four then returned to their motel, located in Cheyenne."

September 28, 1971. A month after the Leeora Rose Looney murder. The sky glows blood-red in a dusty, west Texas sundown.

It's a Tuesday evening. Carl and Sherman have shifted their attention from donut shops to the Toddie House chain of restaurants. But their intentions remain the same: robbery, rape, murder. Like the donut shops, the Toddie House coffee shops, with their late hours and lonely waitresses, were prime pickings for predators like the McCrary-Taylor clan.

The family had come to roost, temporarily as usual, in Amarillo. But the killers foraged far afield and this night Carl and Sherman pulled into Lubbock, nearly 150 miles straight south of Amarillo on U.S. 87.

The hunters had already checked out several possible targets in the Lubbock area without success when they drove along a street fronting the sprawling Texas Tech University campus. A roadside Toddie House restaurant sign with its trademark crooked letters loomed ahead of them. Cruising slowly past the restaurant several times, Carl and Sherman checked to make sure the waitress was alone. She appeared to be cleaning up and getting ready to close as Carl swung the Ford into the alley behind the short-order cafe, parked, and got out.

"I'll go in the front," he instructed McCrary. "You cover the back door."

The lone waitress on duty, twenty-six-year-old Elizabeth Perryman, was anxiously eyeing the clock, counting the minutes before closing time so she could head home where her husband, Van Perryman, would be waiting. The young couple was saving their pennies for a new home they planned to fill with babies, and they needed the income from Elizabeth's waitressing job even if it meant she had to work night hours alone.

Elizabeth Perryman never made it home that night. Her disappearance and ultimate fate remained a mystery for the next three months until December 19, 1971, when a farmer discovered human skeletal remains scattered over a wide area of pastureland several miles northeast of Amarillo. A pile of woman's faded undergarments was found nearby along with a pair of man's shorts, later identified as belonging to Sherman McCrary.

A check of dental records confirmed the remains were those of Elizabeth Perryman. Ballistic evidence uncovered at the scene showed she had been murdered with the same .32-caliber revolver that was used in the slayings in Colorado and Utah.

The only record of what happened after Carl Taylor and Sherman McCrary entered the Toddie House that fateful night is found in Carl's own confession, most of which lawmen took with a large grain of salt. As always, Taylor (or McCrary, depending on who was talking) tried to portray his actions in the best light possible, as though he were an innocent bystander trying to protect the poor victims from Sherman's evil deeds. In the Perryman murder, for example, Taylor, in his blatantly self-serving confession, admitted he planned to rob the Toddie House, but intended to leave the waitress tied up. Sherman, as usual, screwed up his plans.

"I come in the front; he comes in the back," Taylor related. "There wasn't nobody in there but her. Hell, I don't need no help. So, he comes in. Uh, right away, uh, I get the impression from her the minute she seen that gun it didn't shake her up any at all.

"She was kinda grinning about the whole damned thing. And, she said, 'Well, I suppose you're going to take me with you.' Just like that. Sherman said, 'You got the idea.' So she said, 'All right,' just like that.

". . . So all the way from Lubbock to Amarillo, I don't believe that she'd ever opened her mouth. She was just too hung up on the whole damn thing . . . Sherman was talking about wasting her . . .

"So we left her out there outside of Amarillo. I came back into town and Ginger asked me, 'Where we going?' And I told her, 'We're fixin' to go back to Dallas.' And that's when we got back down there."

Taylor also claimed that the Perryman woman (and some of the other victims) freely offered herself to the killers—sex in exchange for life—but he, fine fellow that he was, gallantly refused. Carl and Sherman both were reluctant to admit they were ruthless rapists, preferring instead to see themselves as romantic road warriors irresistible to women, a distorted image they expected others to accept. And again, the take in the Lubbock robbery was hardly worth the effort, much less the price of a human life. The killers got only $125.

The area around Dallas was home stomping ground for the family and represented a haven, even though there were warrants out for their arrests on bad check charges. Carl's mother still lived in Athens, not far from Dallas, and the clan made her home their first stop.

Also, during this foray back to Dallas, Sherman began to include eighteen-year-old Danny in the family's criminal business, particularly the armed robberies.

Danny apparently rode shotgun for the older men for the first time the night of October 17, 1971, and again on October 20, when Sherman and Carl went shopping for more victims. Both times their hunting ground was Mesquite, Texas.

October 17 was a Sunday. Sherman, Carl, and Danny had been in Dallas most of the day and were meandering back through Mesquite looking for likely prospects. Sherman pointed at a small, Mr. M Store, one of the many mom-and-pop operations that stayed open late and rarely had more than a couple of customers at a time.

"Pull in there," Sherman ordered Danny, who was driving. "We'll get you a crack at this one."

Inside the small convenience market, Forrest Covey, twenty-two, was waiting for his nineteen-year-old wife, Jena, to check out and close up for the night before the pair headed home to their two small children, one just an infant.

A few months earlier, Covey had hurt his foot and Jena had taken the part-time job to help out. This evening, just as he had been doing for the past several nights, Forrest had left the kids with a relative and brought Jena her dinner. Now he was waiting to take her home. Because the McCrary-Taylor killers just happened to drive by about then, the Coveys never saw their babies again.

After looting the Mr. M cash register, the three killers forced the young couple into the backseat and headed east into neighboring Hunt County. With Sherman and Danny holding the Coveys at gunpoint, Carl Taylor drove since he knew this part of the country better than the others. He had practically grown up in Hunt County, and, as he twisted and turned along the Texas back roads, Taylor thought of the ideal spot for this kind of nasty business.

His grandparents once farmed near the small town of Quinlan. Taylor remembered there was an old barn on the farm that was isolated from the rest of the property. Since it was late at night, he figured they could get in and out without being spotted by the neighbors.

The way Taylor later told it, "He (Forrest Covey) stepped out of the car and he tried to run. I shot him right in the back of the head.

"Danny helped me pick him up and carry him in that barn.

"Sherman brought her in then, and he shot her. And I think the first time he shot her was right up over the eye or somewhere right up in the forehead.

"Sherman asked me if I was sure Forrest was dead. I thought he was, 'cause I shot him in the back of the head with a .22 with a hollow point on it. It done pretty good damage," Taylor recalled with a smirk. "But I went over there and I shot him four or five more times."

Three days after the Coveys disappeared, and only two blocks from the Mr. M market, Carl and Sherman dropped into a Sweet Cream Donut Shop on Main Street, the main east-west thoroughfare running through Mesquite. They were the only customers and the single waitress on duty smilingly stepped up to take their orders.

"I got to admit," Carl Taylor later said. "She was a pretty little girl. I noticed Sherman was watching every move she made. And, uh, I asked him, 'Are you thinking what I think you're thinking?' He says, 'Um-hum.' "

The "pretty little girl" was a sixteen-year-old high school beauty, Susan Darlene Shaw. Like most of the other McCrary-Taylor victims, Susan was working the hazardous, late-night job to earn money for college and to better her life. But once Sherman McCrary and Carl Taylor walked into her donut shop, the young girl's future ended.

The time was 10:00 P.M. Soon after, Susan's mother arrived to take her daughter home. But she was fifteen minutes too late.

A Mesquite police report later boiled down the sudden, tragic death of Susan Darlene Shaw into a few terse, unemotional comments:

Victim: Female Caucasian Age 16

Clothing: Partially Clothed (Bra and Pants) Rest Not Found

Place of Abduction: Sweet Cream Donut Shop—Main Highway—Commercial Area (Within Shopping Center) Mesquite, Texas

Time: 2200 Hours (10:00 P.M.), October 20, 1971, Wednesday

Suspect Vehicle: Chevrolet

Weapon: .22 caliber pistol and .32 caliber pistol

Wounds: Raped Shot in Head (Multiple) and

Back Two .32-caliber, Plus Four Fragments One .22 Caliber

Of Defendants: Two Males, Possibly Three

Disposal Of Body: In A Water Filled Ditch Running Into Lake Ray Hubbard, in Dallas County

Travel: Five Miles North of Scene of Abduction, Mesquite, Texas

Discovery of Body: October 24,1971

Time Of Death: October 23, 1971

Other Crime: Robbery—$95.00

The only thing missing in the report was an explanation of a mysterious time gap that investigators could never account for. What happened to Susan Darlene Shaw during the three days that elapsed between the time she was abducted and the time the coroner estimated she was killed? Carl Taylor insisted she was shot within an hour after she was taken from the donut shop, but that obviously was a lie.

Cops picked up tips that Danny McCrary knew the victim before she was murdered. And one witness reported seeing someone matching Danny's description throw what appeared to be a body into the canal. Some believe that the McCrary-Taylor clan held the girl prisoner those three days, repeatedly raping and sexually abusing her. But not even this collection of conscienceless killers would admit to such barbaric behavior, and the missing three days remain a mystery.

Almost at the same hour that passersby spotted Susan Shaw's body floating in the cold and muddy Lake Ray Hubbard canal on October 24, a farmhand pushed back the dilapidated door of a barn in Hunt County and found the bloody remains of Forrest and Jena Covey lying side by side.

The fully clothed bodies were bound with discarded lengths of bailing wire. Forrest Covey had been shot in the head nine times with a .22 caliber. There also were four .32-caliber slugs in his back. Jena Covey had been shot in the back at least six times with a .32-caliber. Three more slugs from a .22 had blown her face to bits. Ballistics experts later matched the .32-caliber slugs with those that killed Sherri Lee Martin, Leeora Rose Looney, and Elizabeth Perryman.

The killers got less than $100 in the Mr. M robbery.

With a gruesome triple murder—and a panicky public—on their hands, Texas lawmen turned up the heat. A door-shaking manhunt was on to track down the killers. The McCrary-Taylor family responded as they always did when things got too hot. They hit the road again, this time bound for the Pacific Northwest.

With the latest move, the clan also moved up a notch or two on the armed robbery scale. Except when they reverted to form by kidnapping, raping, and murdering Cynthia Ann Glass on February 19, Sherman and Carl started concentrating on large supermarkets, instead of late-night convenience stores or donut shops where the pickings were slim—but the sexual bonuses were high, even if the sex was taken by brute force.

By March, the McCrary-Taylor family had settled in Boise, Idaho, as their temporary base of operations. Now driving a rented brown Rambler Ambassador, Sherman and Carl made lightning raids from the Portland-Vancouver area on the west to as far east as Iowa and south to Denver.

They robbed at least three stores around Portland. In one, they planned to kill all fourteen employees until they discovered that they didn't have enough bullets to do the job. So instead they herded the group into a walk-in cooler and left them there to freeze to death. Fortunately, the employees managed to open the door from the inside and escape.

On March 23, Sherman and Carl stuck up the Foodland Supermarket in Boise and got away with about $4,000—big-time bucks for a group used to nickel-and-dime hauls. Figuring it was an easy mark, the two hit the same supermarket again on April 9, for another three or four grand. By now, Boise police were on the alert and putting in overtime in the search for the bandits . . . who had already packed up and left town.

The clan's next and final destination—before prison—was Santa Maria, California, a small city up the coast from Santa Barbara, where the unruly, bickering bunch suddenly descended on shocked relatives they hadn't seen for years.

On April 22, the McCrarys and Taylors finally rented a house of their own. A week later, Sherman and Carl stuck up the Williams Brothers Market in Santa Maria. They got more than enough to pay the rent—$16,000.

But Carl had been growing restless and was seething over Sherman's constant boozing and the heavy-handed way he ordered Carl around. Also, there was the growing friction between the two men over the incestuous attention Carl was paying to Ginger's (and Sherman's?) ripening daughters. Carl convinced Ginger to move to Santa Barbara, but within days the McCrarys followed the Taylors down the coast, taking a place in Goleta, a small seafront community just outside Santa Barbara.

On May 31, Carl Taylor struck out on his own by robbing a Jordanos Supermarket of over $11,000.

The score went off so smoothly that by June 16, Taylor was ready to try again. His target was another

Jordanos Supermarket that he had cased close to the house he and Ginger were renting.

(A favorite ploy of the outlaw clan was to rent houses close to the places they intended to stick up so they could be off the streets and out of sight before cops arrived at the scene of the robbery.)

Shortly before 5 P.M., Carl parked the Toyota he was now driving close to the exit of the Jordanos parking lot, left the engine running, and walked into the store.

Inside, he pulled a .38 revolver and stuck it in the manager's face, and ordered him to open the office safe. To Taylor's dismay, the safe that he expected to be stuffed with cash for Friday afternoon paychecks was nearly empty.

Taylor pushed the manager to the front of the store. "Now," he ordered. "Open all the fucking cash registers and give me the money." Unseen, one clerk slipped away and sounded a silent alarm. Meanwhile, the store manager stalled for time by fumbling to open each cash register.

Carl Taylor knew he was running out of time. He finally grabbed the cash-filled paper bag from the manager and dashed out the door. But he'd waited too long. A Santa Barbara cop, responding to the alarm, was coming around the corner of the store, shotgun in hand, and was between Taylor and his waiting Toyota.

In a panic, Taylor ran in the opposite direction, across a street, and into an alley. But he'd run into a dead end, and the only escape in sight was a flight of stairs leading to some second-floor apartments. Taylor scurried up the stairs, only to find the door at the top was locked.

Taylor started back down the stairs just as the officer entered the alley. Carl spotted him first and realized, with a shock, the cop was Dennis Huddle, the son of the Taylor's landlord and the same man who had even helped the couple get settled.

Taylor knew he was dead meat for sure. Even if he got away, Huddle would know who he was and come after him. Instinctively, Carl raised the .38 and fired almost point-blank at the young officer. The bullet hit Huddle in the head. The officer went down in a heap, blood spurting from the wound, but incredibly still alive and still conscious.

By now, bystanders and store employees were rushing to the alley, shouting for help.

Taylor pulled Huddle to his feet. Holding the wounded officer as a human shield, Carl pushed Huddle ahead of him back across the street toward the Jordanos parking lot, where a customer was just pulling in. Carl jerked the car door open and motioned the driver to get out. Shoving the officer to the ground, Taylor jumped into the commandeered car and sped away.

Instead of running to his own rented house which was closer, Carl made a beeline for the McCrarys' place in Goleta, parked the stolen car in the garage, and dashed into the house to hide in the bedroom.

The clan held a frantic powwow. All of them realized that shooting a cop was bad news. Now every badge in California would be hunting them relentlessly.

Sherman, Liz, and Ginger hurried back to the robbery scene. Despite the army of cops swarming over the neighborhood, they managed to retrieve the Toyota without notice.

Within hours of the robbery and shooting, Carl, Ginger, and the kids were on the run again, back to Texas where they naively imagined things would be safe. Sherman and Liz stayed behind, a bad decision on their part for a second bizarre coincidence was about to bring them down.

Carl Taylor shot Dennis Huddle in a panic, knowing the officer would recognize him. Now, as the Jordanos manager described the harelipped robber to his brother-in-law, the man, a power company employee, immediately recognized the bandit as the same one whose electricity he had turned on a few weeks earlier.

Police quickly raided Taylor's home. Carl and Ginger were long gone, but clues they left behind led the cops directly to the McCrarys. When a raiding party swept down on the house in Goleta, they uncovered a cache of weapons and arrested Sherman, Liz, and Danny.

Someone in the family talked and on the morning of June 24, heavily armed Texas lawmen gathered at the Athens police station and laid plans to take down the Taylors, who were staying with Carl's mother and stepfather. Officers on stakeout followed and arrested Ginger in downtown Athens as she was taking the kids in for haircuts. Carl gave up quietly minutes later when cops surrounded his mother's home and ordered him to come out with his hands in the air.

The deadly rampages of the nomadic McCrary-Taylor family were finally over.

Sherman and Carl both went to trial in Colorado for the Looney murder, were convicted, and sentenced to life in the state prison at Canon City.

Prosecutor Robert Miller, who lived with the Mccrary-Taylor degradations night and day for more than two years, still recalls that experience with a shudder. "I've dealt with a lot of bad, mean criminals, but those two were the worst," Miller said. "Carl Taylor was downright scary. I hate to think what those poor victims must have gone through with him looming over them in the backseat of some dark car speeding down the highway. It's an awful thought."

To avoid facing the death penalty in Texas, the pair worked out a plea bargain in which they received life sentences to be served in the Lone Star State if, and when, they were ever paroled in Colorado.

As part of that complicated plea bargain, Carl Taylor also was shipped back to Florida to face murder charges there after he failed a lie detector exam.

That case, involving a triple homicide, began shortly before 9 A.M., on November 30, 1971, when three women were surprised by an intruder at Nell's Beauty Shop, on the outskirts of Melrose, Florida, just down the road from the state penitentiary at Starke.

Bobbie Turner, thirty-eight, and Patricia Marr, twenty-two, had just opened the shop for business. With them was Bobbie Turner's sixteen-year old daughter, Valerie, who had stopped by on her way to school.

When the bodies of the two older women were found in the back room of the shop later that morning, both had been stripped naked and shot repeatedly. Bobbie Turner was hit in the head, eye, chest, and back. Patricia Marr was shot in the head, hands, chest, and back.

The weapons used were a .38-caliber revolver and a .25-caliber automatic. The .25 automatic was one Bobbie Turner carried in her purse for protection.

Valerie Turner's remains were not found until six months later, on June 25, 1972, in a swamp sixteen miles north of the beauty shop. The girl had been shot twice in the head and back with the .25. The killers also had shot her twice in the body with the .38, and, in what appeared to be a coup de grace, finished her off with a .38-caliber shot fired into her eye.

During the investigation that followed the discovery of the bodies in the beauty shop, one witness reported seeing two men push the Turner girl into the backseat of a Chevrolet and drive off. Another eyewitness, under hypnosis, recalled the number of the Tennessee license tag on the car. That plate later was found among Carl Taylor's effects when he was arrested in Athens.

The money taken in the robbery was only $12.00.

On September 22, 1975, Carl Taylor was tried in the Bradford County Court House in Starke on a charge of first degree murder in the death of Patricia Marr. After the prosecution presented its case, Circuit Court Judge R.A. Green directed a verdict of acquittal.

The next day, a second trial in the death of Valerie Turner got underway. This time the case went to the jury which was out only two hours before coming back with a verdict of guilty of murder in the first degree. Carl Robert Taylor was sentenced to life imprisonment and ordered to begin serving his sentence upon completion of the life terms imposed in Texas and Colorado.

The McCrary-Taylor killing clan finally was off the road for good, but the evil they set in motion didn't end at the prison gates.

Across the country, a dozen or more families of victims, who may have been murdered by the clan and whose killers were never brought to justice, were left in that painful limbo of never knowing for certain who destroyed their loved ones or why.

Dennis Huddle, the Santa Barbara police officer shot in the head by Carl Taylor, never recovered from the brain damage he suffered in the attack. In 1978, unable to cope any longer with the constant pain he suffered, Huddle took his own life.

Van Perryman, the husband of Elizabeth Perryman, the Lubbock victim, later became a police officer, partly as a means of avenging his wife's murder. Frustrated that the two killers had escaped Texas-style justice, Perryman pressured state officials to renew efforts to extradite the pair to Texas where a possible execution—rather than a life sentence—awaited them.

Terrified of the possibility of facing the fierce, vengeance-minded Texans, Sherman McCrary, on October 9, 1988, took the easy way out. His death certificate on file at the Colorado penitentiary in Canon City reads: "Strangulation—Hung By The Neck. Electrical Cord."

After serving only ten years of his life sentence for the Covey murders, Danny McCrary was paroled in 1983. He returned to the Dallas area and soon moved in with a woman and her young daughter.

In 1986, the eight-year-old girl fled to her aunt in terror and with a horrifying story to relate. Danny and her mother were forcing her to watch sex videos and join them in their sexual romps in bed. Danny repeatedly molested the child, she reported, forcing her to perform oral sex, masturbation, and other depravities. Based on the child's complaint, Danny was charged with "Sexual assault by mouth on a child under 14 years of age." He pleaded guilty, was sentenced to an additional twelve years in prison, and his parole revoked.

In October 1992, Danny was back before the Texas parole board. This time his request for parole was denied. But he will be eligible again in 1994.

* * *

Carl Taylor is still serving out his life sentence in the Colorado state prison at Canon City. When he finishes that sentence, Taylor owes two more life sentences to the states of Texas and Florida.

Elizabeth McCrary did two years in the Jefferson County, Colorado, lockup on a plea-bargained charge of accessory after the fact of murder. Sickly and frail most of her life, Liz lived only a few years after her release from jail. She died of natural causes at a relative's home in California.

Ginger McCrary Taylor cut a deal that gave her immunity on murder charges in exchange for her testimony in the Looney homicide. The judge, however, threw the book at her on felony check charges: a maximum sentence of seven-ten years in the Colorado prison. She served eight years and returned to Texas following her release.

"The last I heard," said Colorado investigator Joe Fanciulli, who continues to track the remnants of the murderous clan, "Ginger was in Dallas working as a waitress . . . in a donut shop!"

FIVE
THE LEWINGDONS: "THE .22-CALIBER KILLERS"

They were just a couple of colorless nobodies. A matched pair of mousey wimps you'd overlook in a crowd of three. Just two meek, mild, working-class stiffs who spent their weekends . . . butchering people.

In their pale hands, thc brothers Lewingdon held central Ohio in a grip of terror for more than a year in the 1970s, while competing with one another to see who could pump the most slugs into the bodies of their victims.

Operating as a team, Thaddeus Charles and Gary James Lewingdon brutally gunned down ten people in a senseless. year-long bloodbath. The rampage, with its characteristic massive overkill, came to be known as "the .22-caliber killings," a series of apparently senseless, random murders that created a near panic over a three-county area that included Columbus, the home of Ohio State University. No one knew where "the .22-caliber killers" might strike next. No one felt safe even in their own homes.

True, robbery appeared to be a motive for the killings, but from the beginning, the randomness of the attacks baffled investigators. So did the execution-style slayings. The multiple gunshot wounds just didn't make sense, especially since so many slugs were fired into victims' heads at point-blank range. What are we missing here? the cops asked themselves. Where is the pattern we're overlooking? Drug murders? Some deranged cult? Organized crime hits? After all, hadn't the papers been full of stories lately about how the Mob's preferred weapon was a .22-caliber handgun—simple, quiet, and, at close range, almost always deadly? At one point in the investigation, *The Columbus Dispatch* quoted a police source who speculated that since the murders took place on a Saturday or Sunday, the .22-caliber killings might be a ritual ceremony or some kind of hideous initiation rite.

The first hint the world outside Columbus had that something deadly was afoot in the Ohio heartland was this item that appeared in the June 3, 1978, edition of the *New York Times.*

> Nine Central Ohio killings in the last six months have been traced to one gun, with two murders last year being added to the list yesterday.
>
> All the victims, who came from widely varying backgrounds and were apparently selected at random, were shot at close range, always on a weekend, in what people are beginning to call "the .22-caliber killings." All were shot 10 to 17 times in the head and face.
>
> "I don't want to panic people," Detective Paul Short of the Licking County sheriff's office said, "but what we are dealing with here is a cold-blooded, sadistic killer."

What Detective Paul Short did do, in fact, was to panic the hell out of hundreds of thousand of Ohioans, who upon hearing a murderer was loose in their midst, turned much of Columbus and the small communities surrounding the university city into armed camps.

Nor did it help that the newspapers pinned the sobriquet, .22-caliber killer, on the monster, since it immediately evoked images of another fiendish serial murderer the police first labeled "the .44-caliber killer," but whom the world came to know more intimately as "Son of Sam."

Adding to the confusion was the fact that the killings involved half a dozen different jurisdictions. The bureaucratic sniping and in-fighting among the various law enforcement agencies hampered the investigation from start to finish. Jealous cops and prosecutors, motivated by narrow political ambitions, gave only token lip service to interagency cooperation at best; at worst, they deliberately withheld vital information from one another, information that might have led to the Lewingdons before they killed more.

"The Lewingdons," commented one disgruntled prosecutor long after the case was closed, "got away with murder simply because the authorities made it so easy for them to go on killing. The police were more interested in covering their own ass than in stopping those guys."

In fact, the investigation was so bogged down in official squabbling and pettiness that the first two Lewingdon murder cases sat on a shelf, overlooked until after the sixth and seventh victims were butchered in their home.

It began early one December morning in 1977, right in the middle of a record cold snap when only mad dogs and murderers go out in the freezing night.

Joyce Vermillion, thirty-seven, was at work at her waitressing job at Forker's Cafe, a combination restaurant-beer joint and neighborhood hangout in Newark, a community of forty-one thousand and the county seat of Licking County, about thirty miles due east of Columbus.

She usually worked three nights a week to help out

with the family's bills. About 10:00 P.M. on December 10, a Friday night, she phoned home to tell her husband, Larry Vermillion, that she had a ride home after work so he wouldn't have to go out in the biting cold to pick her up. Larry asked her to bring some sandwiches home for his lunch the next day and went to bed.

The next morning, Vermillion awoke to find his wife hadn't come home. He drove over to Forker's about 8:00 A.M. and walked into a scene of bloody carnage.

Joyce Vermillion's body lay sprawled on the cafe's back porch a sack of sandwiches still clutched in her hand. Beside her was the body of another Forker's waitress, thirty-three-year old Karen Dodrill. Friday had been Karen's night off, but she'd stopped by the cafe to cash her paycheck and offered to stick around and drive Joyce home after closing.

The bodies were caked with gore. The cafe's normal closing time was 2:30 A.M., and it appeared from the frozen blood that the women had been killed about that time. Ned Ashton, the Newark police department's chief of detectives, didn't have to deal with many homicides in this small city, but even his limited experience told him there was something terribly out of synch about this double killing.

The multiple bullet wounds and the number of empty shell casings surrounding the bodies told him that this was something other than your run-of-the-mill robbery that maybe escalated into murder when a victim resisted. Each woman had been shot several times in the body and at least once in the head at close range. Powder burns indicated the killer or killers had deliberately leaned over the fallen women and fired the fatal shots into their heads to make sure they died.

Agents of the State Bureau of Criminal Identification were called to the scene to help Newark cops. The bodies were taken to Cincinnati for autopsies. Joyce Vermillion had bullet holes in her left chest, her left shoulder, her head, and her face. Karen Dodrill had been shot in her left breast, stomach, and several times in her face.

Police didn't know, or wouldn't say, whether Mrs. Vermillion left the cafe with the day's receipts or whether the women's personal money and valuables were missing.

One theory that popped up almost immediately was that this was a crime of passion, otherwise how to explain why the women were shot so many times. One woman probably was the primary target of a jealous or spurned lover, according to the theory, and the other victim was killed just because she was there and could identify the murderer. The multiple gunshots to the face was a pretty good sign of a rage killing or someone out to punish the victims.

Larry Vermillion scoffed at the lovers' triangle theory, calling the killings a "senseless, senseless thing." And even though Karen Dodrill was a divorcee, investigators couldn't find any men in her life with either the motive or the opportunity to kill her.

But the nine bullet holes in the victims had already sidetracked the investigation, sending cops off pursuing false leads. Nor would it be the last time before the .22-caliber killers were caught. Actually, the truth was much simpler. The motive was robbery, although the crime netted the killers a paltry $38. And, as it turned out, the solution was as close as their own backyard, if only the Newark cops had looked.

Early that frosty morning, just four blocks west of Forker's Cafe, in a plain white frame house at 62 North Pine Street, "Dee" Grumman waited up for her lover, Gary Lewingdon, to get home. It was highly probable, cops later surmised, that Gary and Dee were familiar with the routine at the nearby El Dorado bar. Both were habitual barflies; Gary as customer, Dee as combination barmaid-topless dancer, although many later found it astonishing that anyone could find anything remotely sexy about the scrawny, horse-faced, street-hardened hag. However, lurking behind the homeliness was a conniving, steel-trap mind and a survivalist mentality. The oft-married (at least four husbands before Gary Lewingdon came along) Delaine survived on toughness and by hustling her way around society's underbelly. Said a Columbus detective who knew her well, "In street smarts, old Dee's got a PhD."

Much later, during the brothers' trials, defense attorneys accused Delaine of masterminding the crime spree; pointing out that neither of the Lewingdons showed any inclination to rob and kill until she entered the picture; intimating that her greedy demands were the motivation behind the murder orgy. In his confession, Thaddeus Charles, in fact, fingered Delaine as the brains of the family.

Moreover, cops who worked the complex investigation observed that the string of robbery-homicides didn't begin until Gary took up with Dee. They met while she was dancing topless in a dive owned by one of the victims of the .22-caliber killers.

Delaine Lewingdon admitted, even testified, that she knew her husband and brother-in-law were killers. But she stoutly maintained that it was Thaddeus who planned the robbery-murder scheme and then forced his weaker brother to go along. Delaine kept quiet about the murders, she claimed, because Thaddeus Charles repeatedly threatened her with a gun to her head that if she talked, she died.

In any event, the chemistry within the Lewingdon family hit critical mass once Delaine was tossed into the mix. The once bland combination suddenly boiled over into a volatile, unstable concoction ready to explode.

* * *

Shortly after the Newark homicides, Gary and Delaine made it legal and got married. Within days, the Lewingdon brothers were tracking their next victim; one who Delaine, the newest member of the family, knew firsthand habitually carried huge wads of untraceable cash.

As the case of the .22-caliber killings unfolded, cops became mighty curious about the convoluted connections linking Delaine, Gary, and murder victim "Mickey" McCann. The point where all those crooked tracks intersected was McCann's raucous Eldorado Club on Sullivant Avenue, a centerpiece of the sleazy west side section of town known as the Bottoms.

Columbus police and the Franklin County Sheriff's Office both had thick files on Mickey's Eldorado Club and its shady owner who for years had skirted the fringes of Ohio's organized crime scene, the kind of guy reporters like to describe cryptically as an "associate." The chunky McCann had a rap sheet dating back to 1959 and included charges of assault and gambling.

The previous year, McCann and three of his girls were busted in a raid by state liquor agents and charged with eleven counts of unlawful conduct, four counts of permitting public gaming, and twenty-nine counts of liquor violations. McCann had run out of appeals, and the Eldorado Club was about to be padlocked for six months for violating ordinances against allowing nude dancing in a bar where liquor was sold.

The street talk was you could find a high-stakes poker game in Mickey's back room and that women and dope were available, if you knew who to ask and carried the cash. Although McCann wasn't directly involved in prostitution as far as cops could determine, the Eldorado Club and other joints McCann had owned in the past were favorite hangouts for hookers. Among Columbus police, Mickey's clubs had the reputation as tough places and were frequently the scenes of barroom brawls and occasional shootings.

Considering the players involved, there appeared to be no shortage of motives for murdering Mickey McCann.

Sunday night. December 12, 1977. Mickey McCann, fifty-two, locked the door of the club, counted the day's profits (considerable), turned out the lights, and patted his latest squeeze on her tight, shapely ass as she slid into the passenger's seat of Mickey's prized red Cadillac Eldorado with the white top. Under her winter coat, twenty-seven-year-old Christine Herdman still had on the sequined bottom of her go-go outfit she wore while dancing topless, or, depending on the clientele, entirely nude.

Mickey climbed behind the wheel, and the pair headed west along Interstate 70 toward his home in the secluded development of luxury ranch houses west of Columbus in unincorporated Franklin County, where he still lived with his seventy-seven-year-old mother, Dorothy Marie McCann.

At 4187 Ongaro Drive, McCann steered the Caddy up the driveway, pushed the button on his remote control to open the garage door, and drove inside. As they stepped out of the car, Mickey and Christine were confronted by two gunmen who had been waiting in the shadows of the two-car garage, shivering against the subfreezing cold. Neither man spoke as they both opened fire.

The next day, bar manager Keith Walker opened the Eldorado for business. Everything seemed normal, until early evening when Mickey hadn't shown up as usual. Walker tried calling Mickey at home. After a couple of hours without an answer, Walker became worried. It wasn't like Mickey. The club was Mickey's life, and he was always there from the time it opened until well past closing time. Walker finally called the Franklin County Sheriff's Office and asked them to send a deputy out to

Ongaro Drive to check on his boss.

Deputy George Nance took the call. When he arrived, Nance trudged through the deep snowdrifts surrounding the home and rang the front doorbell. When he got no response, the officer peered through a side window and spotted what appeared to be the body of a woman lying on the floor. Nance ran back to his patrol car and radioed for backup. Without waiting for help to arrive, Nance returned to the house. Maybe the woman had passed out and needed help. He found a side door that had been forced open and entered slowly, flashlight in hand and revolver at the ready.

The gray-haired, grandmotherly woman, clad in nightgown and bathrobe, was beyond help. She'd been shot several times, mostly in the head. Her face and hair were matted with dried blood, and the smell of death was beginning to permeate the room. From the smell, Nance figured the woman had been dead at least a day or two. The heat was turned up full blast which sped up the decomposition. Several .22-caliber casings were scattered near the body.

Nance moved quickly through the rest of the house, noting that bureau drawers were turned upside down and mattresses pushed aside. Wall and ceiling paneling had been ripped off in the finished basement. Even the stereo speakers were torn open. Whoever was here, Nance observed, had done a damn good job of tossing the house for valuables.

The last place Nance checked was the garage. As he switched on the light, he saw a second body sprawled on the frigid cement floor. The dark-haired, young woman probably had been pretty in life, but in death her face was contorted by the blood frozen on her features and mutilated by the slugs that had ripped into her forehead and right cheek.

The woman's rust-colored slacks, ripped at the crotch,

had been jerked down to her knees. The white-and-blue spangle dancer's panties were pulled down to mid thigh. More .22-caliber casings surrounded the body like tiny tombstones.

Before he could search further, Nance's backup began arriving. Soon, a host of uniformed officers, homicide detectives, and forensic technicians were swarming over the McCann home. Among the first to arrive was Franklin County Sheriff's Detective Sergeant Howard Champ, who took charge of the crime scene.

He made a quick tour of the house with Nance as guide, then set detectives to work photographing the crime scene, and marking the shell casings so they wouldn't be disturbed. Champ knew the house belonged to Mickey McCann, but since the nightclub owner wasn't found, the detective suspected that McCann may have fled after shooting the two women, who by then had been identified as Dorothy McCann and Christine Herdman. Rather than broadcast a bulletin to pick up McCann over the police frequency that was monitored by the news media, Champ tried to telephone headquarters. It was then that he discovered the phone lines outside the house had been cut.

Champ went to a neighbor's to borrow their phone, but while he was still conferring with superiors about a warrant for McCann, a detective interrupted him. McCann's body had been found in the garage, squeezed between the wall and the driver's side of the car where it had been overlooked during Nance's initial search.

Shit! Champ muttered to himself as he hurried back to the McCann house. Two homicides were bad enough, but a triple was brutal. It meant he had a real big-league case on his hands, the biggest in Franklin County history, as far as Champ knew. And anything this big could only mean long nights and big trouble.

The corpse was lying faceup. Like the woman in the garage, Mickey's trousers had been pulled down around his calves and, curiously, the knee sock on his right leg was also pulled down. McCann's topcoat, suit jacket, and blue silk shirt were ripped open and pulled aside. Evidently, the killer had searched the body, probably checking for a money belt.

The body bore an appalling number of bullet holes, Champ noted, enough to kill Mickey McCann several times over. He'd been hit in the right knee; the shot that apparently brought him down and made him an easy target for the two shots in the back and the five shots to the head that followed: two in the forehead, two in the back of the head, and, as if for good measure, one in the mouth. All the holes in Mickey McCann were made by .22-caliber slugs.

Piecing together the bits of evidence, the Police Crime Scene Search Unit determined that the amount of shooting inside that death house had been truly amazing. In addition to the dozen or more bullets in the three victims, the investigators found that one tire on the Cadillac had been flattened by a .22 slug. Another left a dent in the passenger's door. A stray bullet, apparently meant for Christine Herdman, had shattered the handle of her purse. Another slug had gone through the living-room picture window. All told, the cops collected sixteen empty .22-caliber casings and two live bullets that the killers had left in the wake of their slaughter.

The next day, Tuesday, December 14, the story of the triple homicide was splashed across the front pages of the city's two newspapers, was the lead story on every television newscast, and was the main topic of conversation at every bar in town since Mickey McCann was one of the area's most colorful characters.

Champ told a crowded news conference that ". . . this

wasn't your ordinary burglary. This was planned. I believe the shootings grew out of an armed robbery. Mickey McCann was known to carry large amounts of money with him. The mother was apparently killed first. Then the killers waited for McCann to return home. He and his girlfriend, Christine Herdman, were ambushed in the garage between four and five-thirty Sunday morning, February twelfth."

Another "source close to the investigation" hinted that McCann was slain over a $50,000 debt he owed to Las Vegas gamblers. A third "source" claimed that gangsters from the Cincinnati-Dayton organized crime family had whacked Mickey as part of a move to take over his nightclub and gambling games.

In its first story on the murders, *The Columbus Dispatch* reported these sharp differences of opinion among cops that splintered and hampered the investigation from the moment the bullet-riddled bodies were found:

"Despite the opinion of other investigators that the slayings were the work of a hired killer, Champ said deputies officially are operating on the theory the three people were killed by a burglar or burglars who were surprised in the act," the *Dispatch* stated, adding:

> Other officials close to the investigation, however, said the shootings were the work of at least one professional killer.
>
> "This wasn't some jealous husband," said one officer who did not want to be identified.
>
> "It wasn't someone mad at him (McCann), 'cause no one man could have taken Mickey," the officer continued. "For some reason it was a professional job."
>
> Other investigators voiced a similar sentiment.

Within a day or two, the news media was referring to

the murders as "execution-style killings," while adding the obvious contradiction, that "Investigators are discounting earlier information that the bar owner's death was 'a professional killing,' saying that 'hate or intense dislike' may account for the cold-blooded style of the killings."

Friends and acquaintances of McCann spoke of his fondness for carrying large amounts of cash. Flashing a bankroll of five or six grand made him feel like a big man. Some fellow gamblers claimed they'd often seen Mickey pull out a roll of $20,000 or more to pay a bar tab. And one of McCann's ex-dancers, who was also one of his many mistresses, later told an interviewer that her lover-boss kept piles of money squirreled away in secret caches throughout the Eldorado Club: ". . . in the back room, over the furnace in the basement, in the beer coolers. The money he kept on him, he went to bed with. He slept with it under his pillow—all hundred-dollar bills—$40,000 or $50,000 . . . he also kept large amounts of money in a sock, which he then stuck into one of the stockings he was wearing. Thousands of dollars kept on his person at all times."

As the investigation dragged on through the winter and into early spring without results, the newspapers reported that ". . . investigators have not completely discounted the 'street talk,' (that robbery was the motive) but say now that the killings point to a person who hated or had an intense dislike of McCann. . . . The killer hated McCann and went berserk during the shootings."

As it turned out, investigators were both right and wrong in their suppositions about the motives for the murders. And while the Columbus cops and Franklin County deputies became bogged down in a murder probe that seemed headed for a dead end, the .22-caliber killers were busy stalking their next prey.

Just before 1:00 A.M. on April 8—a Saturday—John and Doris Williams returned to the semi-rural home they shared with Mrs. Williams's father, Jenkin L. Jones. The house was on an isolated stretch of Route 37, running north and south just a few miles west of the Newark city limits.

The minute they stepped out of the car the Williamses sensed something was wrong. The whole family loved dogs and owned five frisky hounds who never failed to set up a clamor when someone drove into the yard, especially if it was late at night.

Tonight, it was quiet as a tomb.

As they stepped up on the front porch, the floor lamp shining from the living room revealed the spidery cracks radiating from the small, round hole in the glass storm door. Suddenly gripped by panic, Doris Williams jerked open the door and ran inside screaming, "Dad! Dad! Where are you?"

As she recalled later, "The lights were on, the doors were open, and our little dogs were gone."

Mrs. Williams found the body of her seventy-seven-year-old father on the floor of a back bedroom. He had been shot numerous times in the head. Jones's trousers had been pulled down around his legs. Several .22-caliber shells were scattered about the living room and bedroom.

Telephone lines outside the house had been cut, so the Williamses leapt in their car and sped to a neighbor to summon help. Licking County Sheriff Max Marston and his homicide detectives responded to the call.

When they searched the farmhouse and outbuildings, they found two of the family's dogs had been lured into the basement and shot in the head. Two other pets were shot to death in an outside pen. One was found alive, but wounded, cowering under a shed. It appeared to grim-faced investigators that the perps had gone out of their way to cruelly massacre the family's pets while just as casually slaughtering their owner.

As investigators reconstructed the crime, it appeared that the first shot was fired through the front-door glass and struck Jones as he lay on the couch, reading a magazine. The killers then broke in, shot him once more in the back. He was then dragged to the bedroom and executed with four shots to the head.

The rooms throughout the house, as well as a cluttered shop out back where Jones loved to tinker with machinery, had been thoroughly ransacked. "Whoever was here, took their time searching the place," said Sheriff Marston. "Obviously, they were looking for old Jenk's money cans."

Jones, a lifelong resident of the small farming community, was known throughout Central Ohio for his genius at fixing things and jerry-rigging parts from cannibalized pieces of machinery. Anyone who knew Jenk Jones knew how he loved to prowl around garage and equipment sales buying up tools, old motors, and other mechanical oddities. It was also well-known that he kept large amounts of cash on hand for such spur-of-the-moment purchases. He often flashed a roll of $3,000 or $4,000 when he was on a buying spree.

Guided by Mrs. Williams, Licking County deputies found several thousand dollars hidden in Jones's home that the killers, for all their searching, had missed. She didn't know how much cash her father may have had on him when the murderers broke in.

Marston routinely sent the .22-caliber shells to the Bureau of Criminal Identification and Investigation (BCII) in London, Ohio.

Oddly, with three rather spectacular and mysterious homicide cases involving six victims—the two women in nearby Newark, the three victims west of Columbus, and now Jones—no one seemed to notice the frightening pattern that was emerging, especially with the multiple gunshots, all from .22-caliber weapons.

In fact, the murder of Jenkin Jones was barely noted in the Columbus press. Only the following obit appeared with nary a word that the popular handyman had been shot to pieces, just like the McCann victims:

> Jenkin T. Jones, Sr., age 77, of 3014 Lancaster Rd., Granville. Died Saturday evening at his residencc. He was a self-employed general contractor. Surviving are 1 son, 4 daughters, 8 grandchildren and 8 great-grandchildren.

Only later was it learned that both Lewingdon brothers lived within fifteen miles of Jones and that they also haunted the same kinds of auctions and equipment sales that Jones frequented. While the Jones homicide was largely overlooked by officials, the next killing about two weeks later attracted a ton of press and—finally—a grudging admission by authorities that they were facing a serial killer or killers.

The Monday, May 1, edition of the *Columbus Citizen Journal* informed its horrified readers that:

> A dedicated man of the cloth, who carried a gun one night a wcek, was brutally gunned down. . . .

The murder victim was the Reverend Gerald Fields, the thirty-five-year-old pastor of the Berean Baptist Church, located in Pickerington, a tiny Fairfield County village just across the county lines south of Licking County and southeast of Franklin County.

The previous Saturday night, Fields was working as a substitute night watchman at the Wigwam, a one hundred-acre wooded retreat and club owned by Wolfe Industries for use by employees of the corporation's many subsidiaries. Fields had taken the job so that the full-time security officer, one of his parishioners, could have a night off to spend with his family. Although he carried a .38-caliber revolver, Fields was there more to watch for accidental fires than to ride shotgun over the property. Even pointing a gun at another human being was inconceivable to this man of peace.

When Virginia Fields awoke early to find her husband of fourteen years hadn't returned home to begin preparing for his Sunday morning service, a suffocating sense of foreboding rolled over her like a black, wet blanket. "I knew something was wrong," she said, explaining why she called the Sheriff's Office for help and rushed off to search for her husband. "I didn't know if he'd be there at the Wigwam or lying along the road somewhere, but I knew he was in trouble."

The Fairfield County deputy who responded to Mrs. Fields's call for help searched the Wigwam property while she waited at the front gate. It took him about an hour to find the body. The deputy took one quick look and then ran to call Sheriff Dan Berry.

The death of any murder victim is a loss to be mourned, but the slaying of Gerald Fields seemed especially heinous to the folks who made up the small and neighborly farm communities. First, a beloved minister, who had dedicated his life to helping others had been slain. "They didn't need to kill him," mourned a parishioner. "Jerry would have happily given them everything he had. All they had to do was ask."

Second, the way Reverend Fields was murdered was shockingly brutal. The killers literally shot him to pieces. And then intentionally executed the preacher as he lay wounded.

As Sheriff Berry studied the crime scene, he pictured

the minister's last horrifying moments of life. It appeared that Fields probably surprised the intruders near the Wigwam's maintenance barn around 12:30 A.M.

There was a bullet hole in the left window of a dump truck; a second bullet was lodged in the truck's windshield; and there were bloodstains on the side of the truck as if the wounded man had slumped against it.

Berry speculated that after Fields was shot he staggered three hundred yards to a bunkhouse before the shooters caught up with him and ". . . where they really cut loose on him," said the sheriff. Nine slugs had ripped into the minister's legs and chest. Then the gunmen had dragged Fields around behind the bunkhouse to conceal the body. There, at least one—maybe both—of the killers straddled the wounded man and pumped six more slugs into his head. Tests indicated that the shots were fired at ranges varying from twenty feet away down to four feet. The final head shots were from only 2½ feet away.

Deputies found eighteen casings between where Fields first encountered his killers and where his body was found. All were .22 caliber. Berry told the news media he believed at least two shooters were involved. "I don't see how one guy could shoot that many times," the sheriff explained.

The .38-caliber Colt revolver Fields carried was missing. His pockets had been turned inside out. Later that day, deputies found Fields's billfold, credit cards, and driver's license tossed in a ditch almost within the shadow of the humble church he had built with his own hands and where he should have been preaching his Sunday sermon.

Six of the slugs recovered from Fields's body were sent to BCII to be compared with those taken from the other murder victims in adjoining Franklin County and Licking County. Somebody had finally glommed on to the possibility that the killings—at least five people shot in the head multiple times with a .22-caliber weapon—just might be connected.

On Saturday, May 6, a week after the Fields murder, the *Citizen Journal* ran a big black headline across the top of the front page dubbing the case: " 'The .22-caliber slayings.' "

The story that followed reported:

> A "group" of at least two and possibly more persons is believed responsible for five Central Ohio area slayings which have strikingly similar patterns and law enforcement agencies are fearful the killing will continue.
>
> It was revealed Friday that one of the guns used in killing a Licking County man in April and a Pickerington minister last weekend also was used in a triple slaying in Franklin County in February.
>
> All the victims were shot several times in the head, execution-style, at close range.
>
> "Apparently there is somebody kill-crazy running around," Franklin County Sheriff Harry Berkemer said Friday. "I'm afraid we're going to have some more murders.
>
> "These people aren't just burglars. They are making sure they leave no witnesses because each victim was shot three or four times in the head.
>
> "There is no hurry because they stay and tear up the place. They are cool or they are spaced out on drugs."

Three more weeks passed and then, exactly as police feared and predicted, the .22-caliber killers struck again.

Family and friends were planning to gather at Jerry and Martha "Marty" Martin's rustic home in north Columbus, Sunday afternoon, May 21, for a cookout to celebrate Marty's fifty-first birthday. That morning, when the popular, gregarious couple didn't answer their phone, Jerry's nephew, Albert Martin, drove over to the comfortable, tree-shrouded house on Morse Road to check up.

He found his uncle's body facedown next to a couch in a family room in the north end of the one-story brick house. Mrs. Martin's body was in a hallway connecting the family room with the rest of the house.

In a copycat of the Jones murder, investigators discovered two bullet holes in a window screen of the family room where Martin was found. Empty .22 casings were picked up on the ground outside the window. Several more were scattered throughout the house. As in the previous murders, police also found live cartridges among the empty shells—nine were found in the Martin home—a clear sign that the same automatic weapons, which occasionally misfired, had been used in each case.

"Bullet-riddled" had become an overused cliche in reporting the .22-caliber murders, but in the case of the Martin slayings it was deadly accurate. Dr. Nobuhisa Baba performed the autopsies on the couple and confirmed that Martin, forty-seven, was shot three times in the head, four times in the chest, once in the left leg, and twice in the left arm. His wife was shot once in the neck and twice in the head, including one shot fired from point-blank range into the back of her head, apparently as she lay facedown on the floor.

There were no signs of a struggle. Evidently, Martin, a large, powerful man, had been shot through the window as he stretched out on the couch in the family room. The killers then broke in and finished off the wounded man. Mrs. Martin was gunned down when shc rushed to help her husband. Unlike the other crime scenes, however, the killers had ransacked only two bedrooms. Martin's wallet and Mrs. Martin's purse containing $30 dollars were undisturbed.

Sergeant William Steckman of the Columbus Police Department's homicide squad took charge of the investigation. He learned from neighbors that Jerry Martin had just recently been promoted to general manager and vice president of the Perma Stone Company. Marty was a loan officer at the City National Bank where she had worked for thirteen years. The couple had been married eight years, the second marriage for both of them. Each had a multitude of friends; neither had any known enemies.

With the Martin murders added to the list, cops from five different jurisdictions in three counties and two cities were now chasing the same leads, bumping into one another as they tromped back and forth across the killers' trail. Despite the overwhelming evidence authorities still resisted connecting the .22-caliber killings. The Columbus newspapers weren't so hesitant. They told their readers that all the shootings occurred in remote or fairly secluded areas, but with quick access to freeways; victims were shot numerous times and always more than once in the head; live rounds of ammunition were found, including the misfires due to a defective firing pin; rooms were ransacked in search of valuables; all the slayings occurred late on weekends, usually on a Saturday night or early Sunday morning.

Sergeant Steckman added one more item to the list: "While there appears to be no connection among the victims, the most striking similarity is the brutality involved."

The remoteness of the Martin home also puzzled police. It was only one of a handful of residences in the neighborhood accessible by a gravel drive and surrounded by empty lots and thick stands of trees. The closest house, about seventy-five yards away, belonged to

Mr. and Mrs. Charles R. "Ron" Schremser. The couple helped Steckman pinpoint the time of the murders at between 1:00 A.M. and 2:00 A.M. The Schremsers were playing cards with guests when they heard four "very faint cracks" about that time which may have been gunshots. The family dog also began barking excitedly at the same time.

"It's difficult to understand why the killers picked them (the Martins)," Steckman wondered aloud.

(Months later he got his answer. And the Schremsers learned to their horror that the late-night card game saved their lives. One of the Lewingdons used to drive through the isolated neighborhood on his way to work and observed how easy it would be to get in and out of the homes there without being spotted. The night the brothers arrived to rob and kill, the home they intended to hit was the Schremsers. But all the card players made it too risky, so the brothers improvised and went next door searching for an easier target. Unfortunately for the Martins, they were home alone.)

Within a week, the *Citizen Journal*'s front page story confirmed everyone's worst fears:

> Ballistics tests in last Sunday's slayings of a Morse Road couple confirmed Friday what homicide detectives have suspected—the two were the latest victims of the ".22-caliber" killers.
>
> Sgt. Tom Aurentz said the bullets . . . were fired from one of the weapons used in the slayings of five other persons . . . two .22-caliber weapons were used in the Martin slayings. Two guns were used in the Fairfield County slaying.
>
> Police think the killers will probably continue striking and believe they may stay on the three-week interval pattern. But, police don't know where they will strike again. Consequently, authorities don't

know where to increase their patrols in hopes of catching the killers in the act.

BCII ballistics tests verified that the same gun had been used to kill the Martins, Fields, Jones, and the three victims at the McCann home. The weapon was identified as a semiautomatic .22-caliber Stoeger Luger manufactured in West Germany. Firearms experts label the Stoeger Luger a "junk gun" because it often misfired and jammed. The weapon had been a popular mail-order item until 1968 when a federal law was passed prohibiting selling handguns through the mail.

Now that the cops had officially acknowledged that the murders were indeed related, they braced themselves for the next round of killings. If the .22-caliber killer(s) held true to form there would be another murder on a weekend three weeks after the Martin slayings.

It never happened.

But it was like waiting for the next grenade to drop. Police throughout the three-county area were sure they hadn't heard the last of the .22-caliber killers, but when three weeks went by and no murder, then three more and three more weeks after that, cops began to breathe a little easier. Maybe the serial murderers had had enough and the killing binge had run its course. Maybe the publicity had scared off the .22-caliber killers. *Maybe.*

Gradually the terror that had nearly paralyzed the city and surrounding areas lost its grip. Although people still kept loaded guns handy and continued to double-lock their doors, life slowly reverted to normal.

The lull lasted about six months before another barrage of fire shattered the peace and left the tenth—and final—victim in the string of .22-caliber murders sprawled facedown in a pool of blood.

About 10:45 P.M., Monday, December 4, 1978, Joseph

Kate Bender.
(*Courtesy of the Kansas State Historical Society*)

John Bender, Sr.
(*Courtesy of the Kansas State Historical Society*)

The Bender Tavern in Labette County, Kansas, circa 1873.
(*Courtesy of the Kansas State Historical Society*)

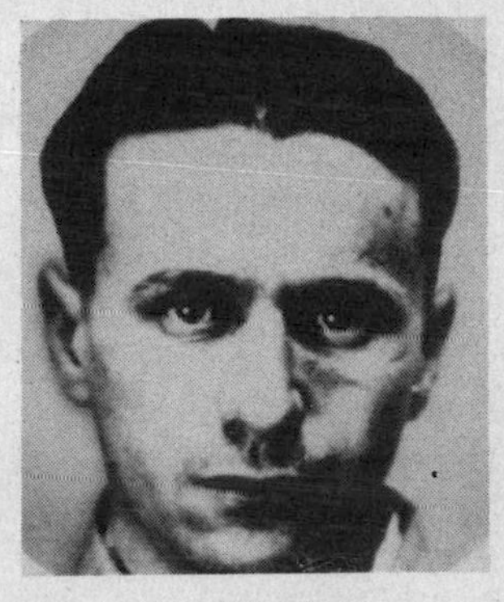

Fred Barker.

Arizona Donnie Barker
a.k.a. Ma Barker.

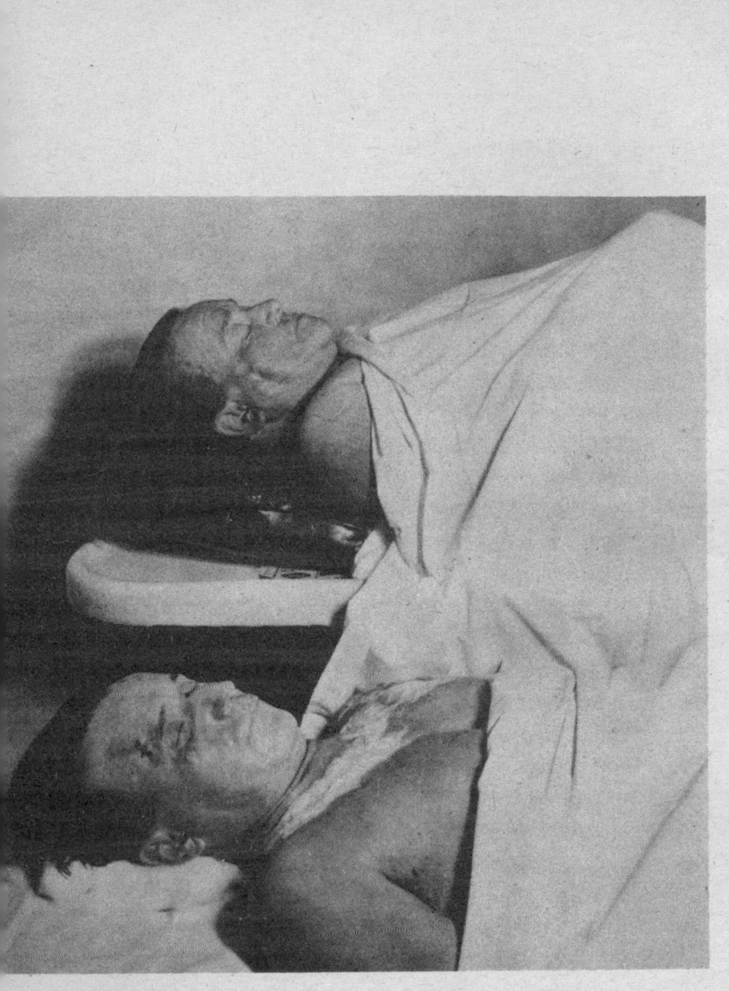

The bodies of Ma Barker (*top*) and her son Fred in the coroner's office shortly after their fatal shootout at Oklawaha, Florida on January 16, 1935.

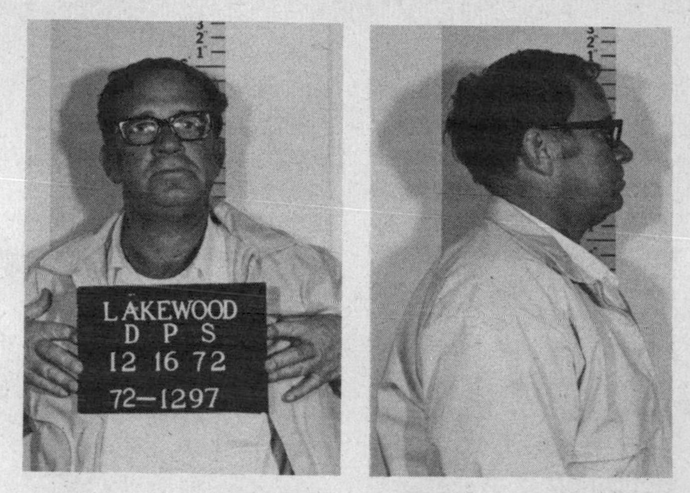

Sherman Ramon McCrary.

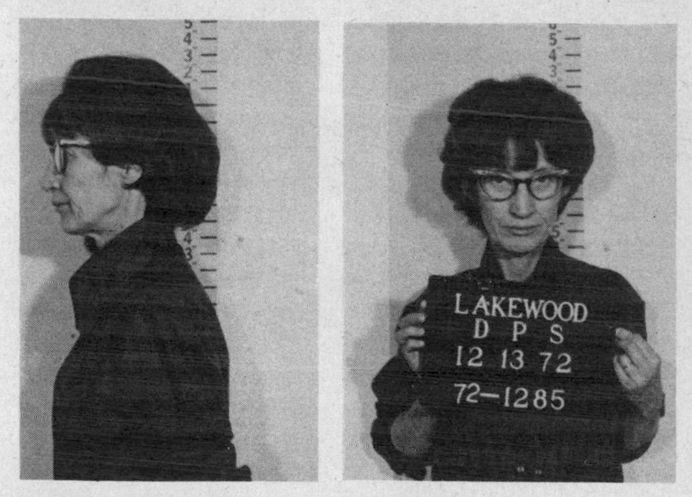

Carolyn Elizabeth McCrary.

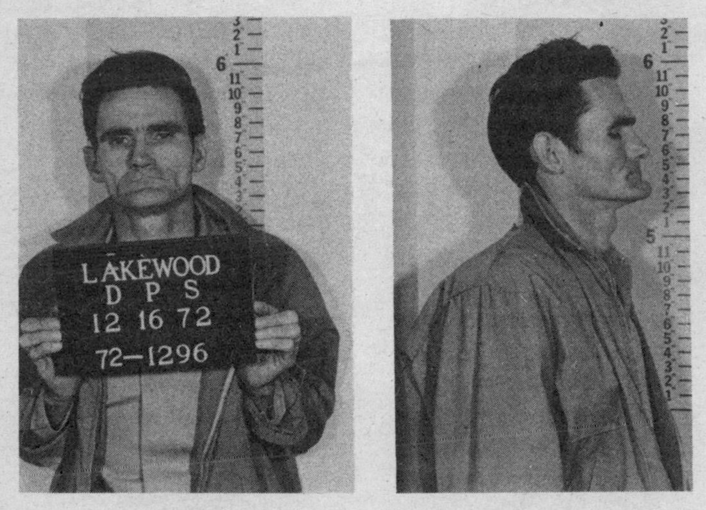

Carl Robert Taylor.

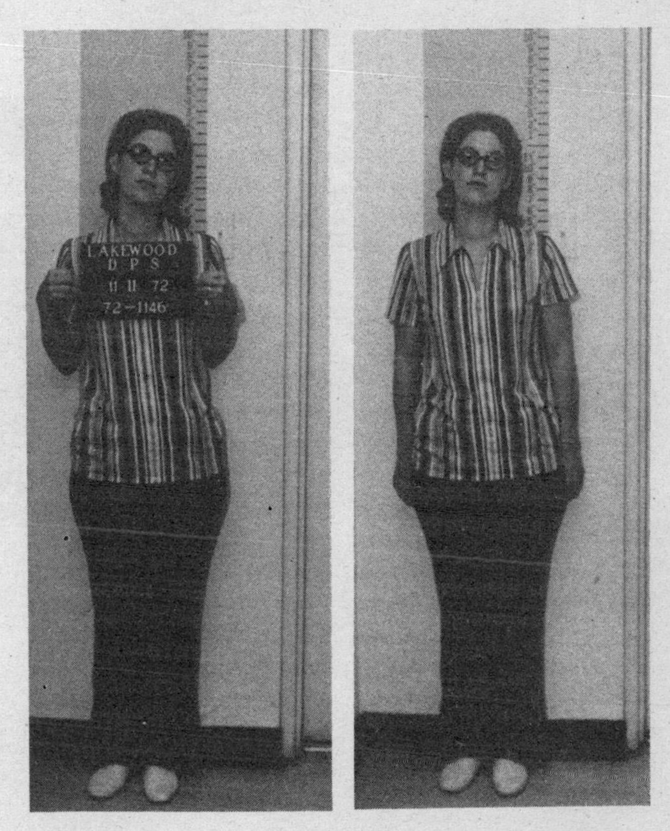

Ginger McCrary Taylor.

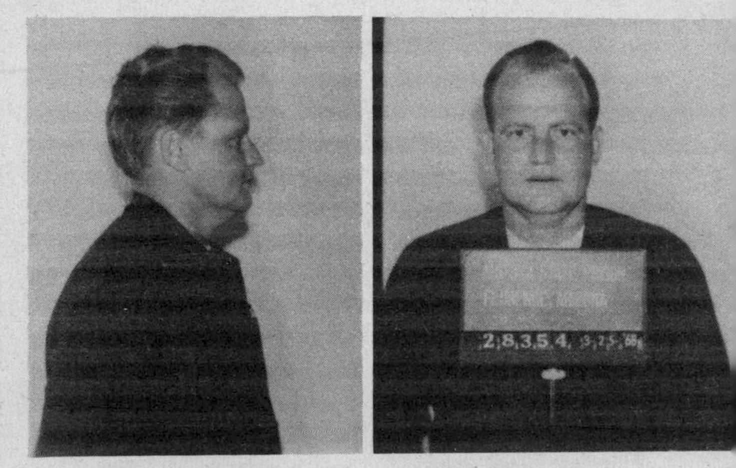

Gary Gene Tison.

Ricky Tison.

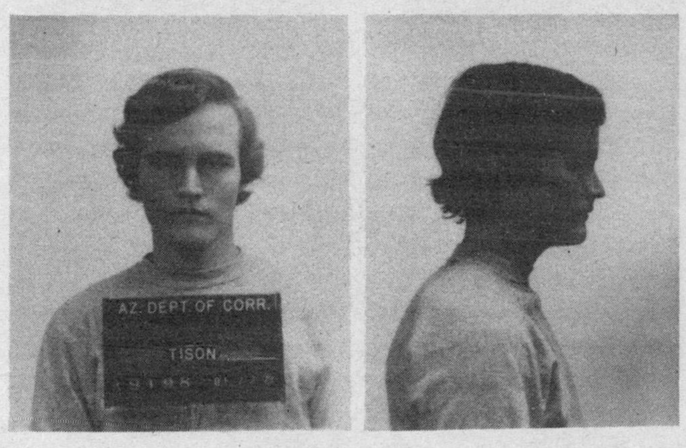

Raymond Tison.

Gerald and Charlene Gallego.

Mrs. Alice Lundgren, her son Damon, and Jeffrey Lundgren, father and cult leader. (*Courtesy of San Diego Union/John McCutchen*)

Joseph Kallinger (*left*), his wife, Elizabeth, and their son, Joseph, Jr. (*Courtesy of the Urban Archives, Temple University*)

Annick, the fifty-six-year-old assistant adjutant of the Ohio Department of the American Legion, parked his tan sedan in the garage he rented across the street from his Euclaire Avenue home on Columbus's east side.

Annick was a native of Cleveland, but had lived most of his life in Columbus. A lifelong bachelor, Annick lived with his sister, Anna Annick, and devoted nearly all his time to his American Legion duties as the activities director responsible for the Ohio state convention, social activities, and special Legion functions. This night, he had been visiting friends and told his sister to expect him home at 11:30 P.M.

Outside the garage, waiting in the deep shadows for Annick to arrive home, stood a figure dressed in dark clothing: Ski mask pulled down over his face; hooded parka buttoned up to his neck. In one hand, the killer carried a leather satchel; in the other, he fingered a silencer-equipped .22-caliber automatic pistol.

When Annick switched off the engine and stepped from the car, the killer emerged from the shadows and opened fire while the surprised victim stood between the driver's side door and the wall of the garage.

Annick's startled cries and grunts as the slugs tore into him drowned out the faint putt-putt-putt of the muted gunshots. The killer fired the entire clip of nine bullets as Annick bounced against the wall and slid to the garage floor. Four shots went wild. Five found their mark.

The gunman slipped a new clip into the automatic before lowering the garage door and switching on a flashlight he removed from the satchel. The killer quickly rummaged through Annick's pockets, removing a billfold that held about $300, credit cards, driver's license, and the usual papers. He jerked the dead man's pants down to his knees and ran his hands around Annick's waist, searching for a money belt. Finding none, the man cautiously raised the garage door and peeked up and down the dark, deserted street. No one had seen or heard a thing. Satisfied he was in the clear, the killer walked briskly to the corner where he'd parked a new blue Omni, got in, and calmly drove away.

Anna Annick waited until after midnight for her brother to return. It wasn't like the religiously punctual bachelor to be late, so about 12:15 A.M., she threw a coat over her shoulders and went down to the garage to check if Joseph's car was there.

Anna switched on the garage light. Her anguished screams of horror brought neighbors running.

The police investigation that followed determined that Annick had died almost instantly from the five gunshot wounds to the chest and stomach. Several .22-caliber shell casings littered the floor of the garage.

Although Annick had been slain in the same brutal manner as the other victims of the .22-caliber killer, Columbus cops were reluctant to pin this murder on the same serial killers.

After all, it had been over six months since the last killing. And there were a couple of major differences in the Annick slaying. Foremost was that Annick hadn't been shot multiple times in the head which investigators had come to expect as the signature of the .22-caliber killers. Also, unlike all the other weekend killings, Annick was gunned down on Monday. Furthermore, ballistics evidence indicated that only one weapon was used in this killing, indicating a single armed robber may have been watching Annick and had sized him up as an easy score.

Despite those deviations, investigators from the five jurisdictions were still worried. Was this the other shoe that had been waiting to drop? Reluctantly, the cops geared up for a new round of .22-caliber killings.

Five days later, Gary and Delaine Lewingdon went

Christmas shopping.

It was a busy Saturday night at the Woolco Department Store in Columbus's Great Southern Shopping Center. The skinny, little guy with the goatee and the black; horn-rimmed glasses ordinarily wouldn't have drawn a second look when he handed clerk Cheryl Young a Visa card to pay for a shopping cart filled with toys.

The young clerk routinely checked her list of stolen credit card numbers . . . and the one she was holding in her hand jumped out at her. It was Cheryl's first catch, and she excitedly alerted her supervisor who called the Visa credit center to double-check.

Rather than wait around, the couple scurried out the door. Store security officers and an off-duty Columbus police officer caught up with the pair as they were climbing into a Chrysler station wagon. Officers insisted the man return to the store to settle the matter of the stolen credit card. The woman, however, jumped in the vehicle and drove off.

In addition to the Visa card, the man was carrying other credit cards, Social Security, and insurance documents made out to Joseph Annick. Gary James Lewingdon was arrested for possession of the stolen credit cards. At the Columbus Police Department, Homicide Detective Jerry McMenemy, who had been working the Annick killing, was eager to sit down and talk to the timid-looking man who carried property belonging to the murder victim.

Lewingdon said he worked at Rockwell International in Columbus and had lived in Kirkersville, between Columbus and Newark, with his wife, Delaine, and her three kids from two of her four previous marriages, before that they lived in Newark. Police records revealed Gary had been arrested on charges of petty larceny, possession of criminal tools, carrying a concealed weapon, and indecent exposure, but had no convictions. Lewingdon said he found the credit cards by the side of a road when he stopped to fix a flat tire.

McMenemy checked Lewingdon's wallet and came across a receipt made out to Delaine Lee Grumman for a .22-caliber semiautomatic Sturm Ruger and some ammunition purchased at the Cartridge Case Store in Newark.

"My wife bought it for my birthday present," Lewingdon explained.

McMenemy studied the fidgety prisoner and decided to play a hunch based on years of dealing with murder suspects.

"How come you pulled Mr. Annick's pants down?" McMenemy suddenly shouted, jabbing his finger in Lewingdon's face. "You got some weird sex thing wrong with you?"

The unexpected accusation totally unnerved Lewingdon. "No, no! I ain't a homo! That wasn't it," he protested.

McMenemy settled back in his chair. "Okay, Gary," he said softly. "Then how about telling me how it really was."

It was as if the detective had pulled the plug on a dam. The confessions came pouring out of Gary Lewingdon as fast as the stunned officers in the stuffy interrogation room could take them down.

Lewingdon told how he'd murdered Annick and where they could find the .22 Sturm Ruger he'd used, along with Annick's wallet and driver's license. He also told officers where to look in his house for a couple of .38 revolvers, three other .22 handguns, a Glenfield rifle, a 410 shotgun, and a 30-30 rifle.

While Lewingdon continued to spill his guts, Columbus and Franklin County detectives got a search warrant and headed east to rendezvous with counterparts from Licking County and Newark. At Lewingdon's home they recovered most of the guns, homemade silencers, and a stockpile of ammunition. They also found a well-used target range in the basement.

One of the .38s was the one taken from Reverend Fields in the Fairfield County murder. The other belonged to Mickey McCann.

But they didn't get the .22 that killed Annick. Delaine beat them to it. She had rushed home from the shopping center, cleaned out that evidence, and hidden it at Gary's mother's house.

Late that afternoon Delaine telephoned police, demanding to know why her husband was being held. She told officers she was at her mother-in-law's home and gave them the address. While one detective kept her on the phone, another checked her record and learned that Delaine Lewingdon/Dee Grumman was wanted for passing bad checks. A patrol car was dispatched, and Delaine was picked up while she was still on the phone.

For a while, she denied any knowledge of the Annick killing. But when told that Gary had already confessed, Delaine broke down and told cops where to find the incriminating evidence.

"I didn't want the police to find them," she admitted. "I guessed you would search the house, so I took them out."

Meanwhile, BCII technicians called Columbus to report that a .22-caliber casing taken from Lewingdon's firing range matched one recovered at the Jenkin Jones murder scene. That, with the two .38 revolvers, gave cops enough hard evidence to charge Lewingdon as the .22-caliber killer. Now they wanted the second shooter.

Cops were convinced that Delaine was in it up to her bumpy nose and frizzy hair, although she insisted that Gary's brother, Thaddeus Charles, was the main man behind the killings. So to get to Charles, police decided to make a smelly deal: Give up both brothers, they offered Delaine, and we won't charge you as an accessory or a co-conspirator. You talk, you walk.

One of the detectives involved in the negotiations was convinced that Delaine had been programmed ahead of time by some cagey criminal lawyer for just such an offer. "When she started talking, she knew exactly what kind of deal to ask for. It was like she had everything rehearsed," said the officer.

"Gary told me that Charles killed the girls at Forker's Cafe in Newark," Delaine began. "Gary was with him, but Charles did the killings."

The motive?

"I don't know about that one, but Gary killed Mickey McCann to revenge me, because Mickey forced me into prostitution," she said.

Down the hall, meanwhile, Gary was still confessing for all he was worth.

The slayings at Forker's Cafe, like all the others, took place on a weekend because he and Charles worked during the week and didn't have time to get out to kill on weeknights. Robbery was the motive, although they netted just a few dollars and a nail clipper from the two women.

Before the McCann job, Gary said he and Charles cased the house three times over a two-week period.

The night of the murders they wore boots, ski masks, and heavy parkas with hoods. Charles pried open the side door with a tire iron while Gary cut the phone lines. They knew from casing the house that McCann's mother would be there, but figured one little old lady wouldn't be much trouble.

Mrs. McCann was coming down the hallway to check the noise when Thaddeus popped the door open. Gary charged in and started firing wildly with the .22 Stoeger. A couple of shots missed, but at least one hit the woman and she fell almost at Gary's feet.

"Then," Gary claimed, "Charles took the gun, put in another clip, and shot her in the head, two or three times."

The brothers took their time searching the house but found only loose change. They then settled down to wait for McCann and Christine Herdman to get home.

As soon as McCann parked the Caddy in the garage, the two killers rushed out and began firing. Christine Herdman went down screaming as Thaddeus fired nearly a full clip at her. Gary said he shot McCann twice, but the bar owner got to his feet and staggered out the open garage door into the deep snow.

Together the brothers chased the wounded man, shot him in the back two more times, dragged him back into the garage, and closed the door.

"He's still not dead yet," Gary's confession continued. "He looks up at us and begs, 'Please don't kill me.' Then Charles finishes him with another clip."

The killers searched the car and found $2,000 in bar receipts wrapped in newspapers behind the driver's seat. As they searched McCann's body, Gary said he felt a bulge at the back of his leg. A money-filled sock tucked inside Mickey's knee sock held $5,800.

One of the brothers also pocketed the .38 that McCann always carried for protection.

They also searched Christine's body, and while they suspected she carried drugs and wore expensive jewelry, the only thing they were interested in was cash.

Gary's rambling confession continued for hours. For each murder, he provided investigators with an abundance of details on how the killings went down and the loot from each one.

Finally, one of the cops had to ask the question that was on all their minds, "Gary, why did you shoot those people so many times? Why did you have to kill them?"

Lewingdon shrugged and answered as blandly as if commenting on the weather, "No witnesses."

Shortly before 11:00 P.M. that same night, a well-armed raiding party quietly surrounded Thaddeus Charles Lewingdon's house in Glenford. A Licking County deputy telephoned the house, told Lewingdon he was wanted for murder and to come out with his hands in the air. Minutes later, Lewingdon walked out the back door and surrendered.

Police found the Stoeger Luger used in nine of the .22-caliber killings hidden in a utility trailer parked behind the house. They also recovered a .22-caliber Derringer, a homemade silencer, ten live rounds of .38-caliber ammunition, nearly one hundred rounds of .22-caliber ammunition, and several fully loaded clips.

The brothers quickly proved that neither was a hard-case, stand-up guy. By 12:13 A.M., less than two hours after cops hauled him in, Thaddeus Charles signed a waiver of his constitutional rights and started singing.

For the next four hours, Charles spit out details on the killings—all except Annick's since Gary did that one alone. Most of what he said was generally consistent with Gary's versions of the murders.

The major difference, according to Charles, was that Delaine was the one who planned the murders. He refused to budge on that point. For example, Delaine had thoroughly briefed them on the layout of Mickey McCann's house because she had spent time there when she worked for the bar owner, Charles explained.

When the brothers returned from McCann's and told Delaine about the horrible bloodletting, "She was just happier than hell," Lewingdon said.

In 1979, before the .22-caliber killers went to trial, Delaine Lewingdon granted a remarkable newspaper interview, a wild ramble in which she left a mile-wide trail of red herrings in a desperate attempt to deflect suspicions from herself and, only incidentally, to help husband Gary's cause.

According to the newspaper:

> •She believes Robert "Mickey" McCann, his mother, Dorothy, and his girlfriend Christine Herdman . . . were victims of killings for hire. She believes the same is true of Joyce Vermillion and Karen Dodrill killed in Newark . . . and Joseph Annick, killed here. . . .
>
> •She feels that Thaddeus Charles killed nine of ten victims. . . . She said . . . Gary was forced to do whatever he did.
>
> •Driven to desperation by what she called a "year of nightmares," she urged her husband (Gary) to kill the brother (Thaddeus Charles).
>
> •She believes the slayings of the two women killed in Newark were drug related. She believes McCann's enemies in what she called "the Cincinnati syndicate," paid to have him killed.

On January 29, 1979, Thaddeus' trial started in Newark for the murders of Jenkin Jones, Joyce Vermillion, and Karen Dodrill. Columbus defense attorney Gary Tyack represented the accused killer.

During most of the trial, the defense tactic was to shift the blame to Delaine Lewingdon, portraying Gary's wife as a nude dancer in trashy bars who "hired out her body to men." Tyack implied Delaine was wired into underworld connections and big-time drug smugglers. Finally, Tyack tried to paint Delaine as the mastermind of the robbery-murder foray: "She did admit that she bought

Gary a gun, using a fraudulent name," Tyack told the jury. "She admits trying to hide evidence. She admits having possession of a gun taken in one of the robberies, and having property taken from a robbery in which Gary is charged."

Wearing a demure nurse's uniform to court, Delaine testified that Charles was the triggerman and forced Gary to help him. She admitted that the brothers recounted the murders in horrifying detail when they came home from killing, but denied she had anything to do in setting up the crimes.

The jury found Thaddeus Charles Lewingdon "guilty on all counts" on February 19, 1979. Judge Winston C. Allen quickly sentenced him to three consecutive terms of life imprisonment, plus seven to twenty-five years for armed robbery.

Charles's second trial in March was moved to Mansfield, Ohio. Fairfield County authorities agreed to consolidate their charges in the Reverend Fields murder with the five Franklin County slayings (the McCann deaths and the Martins).

Gary Tyack again hammered away at his theme that Delaine Lewingdon concocted and directed the .22-caliber murder spree. And once again, a jury didn't buy it. Thaddeus Charles was found guilty on twenty counts of robbery, theft, and aggravated murder. Judge J. Craig Wright added another six consecutive life sentences to Lewingdon's rap sheet.

After judges in the three counties agreed to consolidate all ten of the .22-caliber murder charges facing Gary James Lewingdon, his trial opened on May 14, 1979, following a motion for change of venue.

Franklin County Prosecutor Daniel Hunt told the jury and the packed courtroom: "They left no witnesses. They killed everyone."

Pointing at Gary Lewingdon, scrunched down at the defense table, Hunt thundered: "There's a direct tie-in of the defendant to that (Eldorado) bar. He'd been there. He knew Robert 'Mickey' McCann had gone to bed with his wife. He knew that she had prostituted for him. He had all kinds of motives and revenge against that man. But the overriding thirst was for money. So what did he and Thaddeus do? Act like two insane men and run out and shoot him on the street? That isn't what they did. They carefully planned. They went to that house not once, not twice, but three times."

Public Defender James Kura conceded that Gary had accompanied his brother during the murders, but insisted that Thaddeus was the lone triggerman during those barrages of gunfire. Thaddeus bullied Gary, dominated him, Kura said, and when he needed someone to help him rob, he forced his shy, withdrawn brother to pick up a gun and go with him. Moreover, Thaddeus threatened to kill Delaine and her three kids if Gary didn't participate, argued Kura.

Delaine Lewingdon testified that she was terrified of Thaddeus Charles. "On several occasions," she told the court, "Charles held a gun to my head and threatened that if I ever told anybody what was going on, he'd kill me. And I knew he would."

She added that when the brothers came home after the murders, Charles ordered her to fix something to eat. "He always had a ferocious appetite after he killed somebody. But Gary would usually cry."

On May 26, 1979, the jury found Gary guilty of eight of the ten murders. They couldn't decide on the Jones and Annick slayings.

Moments after the verdicts were announced, Gary Lewingdon stood up and asked the judge to give him three hundred-cubic centimeters of sodium pentothal so he could kill himself.

"Justice was not done by the jury," Gary read from a statement. "I ask to go beyond the bonds of punishment . . . and relieve the court of any obligation."

The motion was denied. Judge George Marshall then sentenced Lewingdon to serve eight consecutive life sentences.

For a time, Gary James Lewingdon was housed at the Lima State Hospital for the Criminally Insane. In February 1983, he was retried on the Joseph Annick slaying, was found guilty, and another consecutive life term was tacked onto his sentences. He's now doing time at the Mansfield Correctional Institution.

Thaddeus Charles developed into a jailhouse lawyer. He made headlines in 1985 when he claimed he'd discovered a loophole in the law big enough to drive a fleet of trucks through. He argued that, thanks to some weird wording in the state's constitution, Ohio might not legally be a state, so the laws it had passed over the years didn't count. Therefore, Lewingdon contended, he and all other cons in Ohio should be set free.

Even if Lewingdon had won his screwy appeal and walked out the prison gates, he wouldn't have had long to enjoy his freedom. Thaddeus Charles died on April 16, 1989, at the Southern Ohio Correctional Institution.

Lung cancer got him.

SIX
THE TISONS: HONOR THY FATHER THE MURDERER

The smell of death hung heavy around the Papago Chemical Company field office, growing worse by the day.

Dead critters were normal around this company outpost where agricultural fertilizers are made, especially this time of year when the fierce August sun baked the desert dry. In this well-cooked Arizona setting, about six miles south of Casa Grande near White Horse Pass, dead things got dead a whole lot faster than usual.

Ray Thomas, the plant supervisor, was bothered by the buzzing swarms of large, green flies around the cinder block building. That, plus the lack of any breeze to stir the stifling heat and blow away the nauseating stench was making working conditions intolerable, so Thomas decided to take a look.

The date was August 22, 1978, a Tuesday, eleven days since a spectacular shoot-out between prison escapees and cops manning a roadblock just a mile or so from the Papago plant. One outlaw was killed and two others arrested. A fourth got away.

Since then, hundreds of manhunters on foot with trained bloodhounds, others on horseback, in four-wheel drives and in helicopters equipped with infrared sensors for night searches had been combing a ten-square-mile expanse of unforgiving desert and the rugged arroyos of the Sawtooth Mountains. Teams of searchers tossed tear gas grenades into scores of caves and crevices hoping to flush out the fugitive killer.

Despite all that manpower and high technology, Gary Gene Tison still beat the manhunters. But he couldn't escape nature. Tison, who'd spent his life playing the tough guy role, had died a tough and terrible death of thirst and exposure.

Thomas found the body a short distance from the plant, squeezed into a narrow furrow Tison had scraped out in some thick brush surrounding a scrawny mesquite tree. What remained of the man's features, blackened by the sun and decay, were contorted into an ugly grimace. Flies and maggots crawled in and out of the black hole of a mouth, wide open in a silent, death-throes scream. His body had bloated in the heat and split open in place like, recalled one observer, "an overcooked sausage." A husky, barrel-chested 250-pounder when he broke out of the state penitentiary at Florence on July 30, now all that was left of Gary Tison after the summer sun finished cooking him was a putrid lump of rancid meat weighing a mere 138 pounds.

From the way the ground was torn up around him, the dying man must have writhed and kicked violently in his final agony. The heels of his cowboy boots had gouged out deep trenches in the ground. A cocked .45-caliber pistol, the kind of macho, Wild West gun Tison thought made him look mean and tough, had slipped from the claw-like fingers contracted in death.

Officers from the Arizona Department of Public Safety and the Pinal County Sheriff's Office rushed to the site in response to Thomas's call. Sheriff Frank Reyes studied the grisly corpse and confirmed it was indeed all that remained of Gary Gene Tison. "We must've walked by him a half a dozen times when we were out here looking for him," said Reyes, kicking sand into the makeshift cave where Tison crawled and died.

Lab technicians performed their rituals over the corpse. Police photographers gagged while they snapped their close-ups. Gary Tison was then slipped into a rubberized body bag and hauled off to the morgue. Lawmen, who had been observing the scene, strolled over to the Papago plant building three hundred feet away and leaned over a flowing, outdoor spigot.

Gary Gene Tison had come that close to a long, cool drink of water.

The gruesome discovery of the rotting carcass rang down the curtain on a savage family melodrama that had begun three weeks earlier. In its July 31, 1978, edition, the *New York Times* reported the bare bones of a bizarre prison break out West:

> FLORENCE, Ariz., July 30 (AP) – Three brothers who showed up for visiting day today with sawed-off shotguns hidden in an ice chest freed their father and another convicted murderer from Arizona State Prison, corrections officials said . . .
>
> No shots were fired and no one was injured as the sons held guards at bay while the prisoners were being brought from their cells for visits . . .
>
> The prisoners, who escaped in an automobile, were being sought by air and ground police forces today. A relative of one of the convicts was believed to be a pilot, Department of Public Safety officials said.

After that brief mention, the eastern press generally ignored the story. But a continent away, spread across hundreds of desolate miles of Arizona's burning, life-sucking desert landscape, a monstrously cold-blooded tragedy was unfolding.

Self-styled bad man Gary Tison,who had been in and out of Arizona prisons most of his life, was on the run again.

The spectacular jailbreak spawned the largest and most furious manhunt in the state's long history of posses chasing outlaws across Arizona's godforsaken deserts and grim, desolate mountains. Embarrassed and angry cops from a dozen law enforcement agencies pursued the fugitives. Hindering the search was the support the escapees received from family and friends along the way, some of whom ended up in jail for aiding and abetting.

For three weeks, the chase wound across Arizona, through New Mexico, up into Colorado, and back to a sun-baked Arizona crossroads near Chuichu.

But it was the maniacal murders they committed on the run that rank the Tisons as among America's most merciless and nightmarish family killers.

The way *Time* magazine told it: "There wasn't much good that anyone could say about Gary Tison except that he inspired a remarkable loyalty from his family." Unfortunately, that fealty led his family down a dead-end road to early graves: either holes in the ground or buried alive in hard-time cells.

Between stretches in jail, Gary Gene Tison fathered three boys, Donald, Raymond, and Ricky. Indoctrinated by their mother that Daddy always came first, the boys grew up blindly loyal to their psychopathic old man. His three sons affirmed that allegiance by engineering the jailbreak that sprang their Dad. And now they were running with him.

Accompanying the Tison family on its latest and most ill-fated dash for freedom was Randy Greenawalt, a cherub-faced, roly-poly, myopic homicidal maniac who thought it great fun to shoot and kill truck drivers from ambush.

Arizona lawmen who had skirmished with Tison for years could have predicted the daring prison break and the flight into the wasteland. He tried it before, many times. Tison's prison rep was that of a high-risk, murderous escapee who should have been stuck in a hole deep enough to pump light to. Instead, Tison sweet-talked his way into a plum prison assignment that was practically an open-door invitation for someone with Tison's penchant for busting out.

As a result, six innocent people were ruthlessly slain. In the end, Gary Gene Tison, a victim of the relentless desert sun, also was among the dead . . . which Arizona cops applauded with a hearty "Good riddance!"

Gary Gene Tison was born in 1936 and grew up in Kern County in the heart of the San Joaquin Valley where the Tison family had settled, more unwashed members of the Great Dust Bowl migration out of Oklahoma and into the promised land of California.

Like his father, Curt Tison, who'd done time for a string of armed robberies in Oklahoma and Texas, Gary grew up shunning honest work in favor of the easy buck. Gary was in the tenth grade when he dropped out of school in 1951 and took up the store-robbing trade.

He was caught breaking into a store, but sent home on probation because he was a juvenile. In 1954, eighteen-year-old Gary stole a car, drove to Arizona, and was caught after sticking up a grocery store. Gary drew seven to fifteen years hard time, but he did only two years and was released on parole.

Gary met Dorothy Stanford, a strict Pentacostalist, and the couple was hurriedly married in October 1957, just in time to beat the stork which arrived January 1,

1958, with little Donny. Ricky was born December of the same year, and Raymond eleven months after that.

With all those kids coming one right after the other, Gary needed to find more work to pay the bills. So he fell back on his first love: armed robbery. After a series of nickel-and-dime stickups around the family's hometown of Casa Grande, Gary went for the big time—the wholesale looting of guns from the National Guard armory that he planned to smuggle across the border and resell in Mexico.

Tison was caught in the act, but while waiting trial he broke out of the Pinal County Jail, the first, but not the last escape of his career. Instead of hightailing it out of town, Tison hot-wired a car and went off to burglarize a Casa Grande store. Forty-eight hours later, he was back in the same old Pinal County Jail cell. Sticking close to home may have demonstrated incredible stupidity on his part, but it was a pattern Tison would repeat until his death.

A psychiatrist, assigned by the court, reported that Tison ". . . is impressed with being dangerous. His self-image is that he is dangerous . . ." and concluded that Gary Tison was ". . . a sociopathic personality whose abiding rage and poor judgment made him capable of pronounced moral perversity . . ."

Dorothy came to court with the three Tison tots to plead for mercy for Gary. Their tears didn't sway the judge who shipped Gary to the state penitentiary in nearby Florence for twenty-five to thirty years.

But Dorothy Tison, raised with the strict belief that the man of the house was supreme on earth, wasn't giving up so easily. She bombarded the parole board and every other state official she could think of with pleas and petitions to release poor, misunderstood Gary to the bosom of his loving family.

Apparently it worked, because Gary was granted an early parole and on July 1, 1966, was back home after serving only five years of the long sentence.

But born with a crooked streak, Gary Tison was incapable of walking a straight line for more than ten months. He started papering his hometown with bad checks, became involved in an outlandish embezzlement scam to peddle used tractors in Mexico, and was arrested again.

On September 18, 1967, Judge E. D. McBryde revoked Gary's parole and ordered him returned to prison to finish serving his armed robbery sentence, plus five more on the embezzlement charge.

Prison guard Jim Stiner cuffed Tison and started the drive to Florence. They hadn't gone a mile when the prisoner pulled a gun someone had smuggled to him, and ordered Stiner to head for the desert. Near Coolidge, Tison had the guard park alongside an irrigation ditch and get out. Tison told Stiner to go sit down on an upturned washtub and not to move until he was out of sight. Then, just when Stiner thought he was safe, Tison raised the gun and shot the guard three times square in the heart.

Once more, Tison might have gotten away, at least for a while, but, true to form, he drove right back to Casa Grande and to an abandoned house where a change of clothes and food had been stashed for him. The next morning he hijacked a station wagon from a woman with a baby and minutes later was spotted by cops as he cruised through town. Gary jumped from the car and took cover behind a wall and started shooting. Tison shouted that the cops wouldn't take him alive, but he threw down his gun and surrendered when a shotgun blast blew his Stetson off his head.

The cold-blooded cop killing aroused such anti-Tison sentiment that Gary's brother, Joe, changed the spelling of his name to "Tyson" to avoid being painted with the same tar brush.

On March 25, 1968, Gary Tison was tried, found guilty of killing Jim Stiner, and sentenced to two consecutive life terms at the Florence prison.

Through it all, Dorothy remained unswervingly loyal to her violent husband, even though it now appeared he might die an old man in prison. Daily she drummed the same lesson into the three impressionable boys that they must do the same. Thanks to Dorothy's single-minded zeal, the Tison boys grew up believing their Dad was a hero who'd been railroaded into prison. They idolized the old man and, in their longing to have him home again and brainwashed by their mom, vowed to do whatever it took to bring him home.

Every weekend, Dorothy faithfully trucked out to the prison, dragging the boys along so the Tison family could spend a few hours together in the visitors' outdoor compound. Every weekend, witnesses said, the boys sat at a picnic table and held up newspapers to hide the action from guards and other families while Mom faithfully hunched over and gave Dad blow jobs.

Besides getting Daddy off, they also schemed to get Daddy out.

The first escape attempt in September 1972, desperate though it was, nearly succeeded. With two other inmates, Gary invaded the guards' office on the main yard, produced guns that had been smuggled into the prison, and took four hostages. They forced the men to disrobe and locked them into a storage closet.

The three inmates donned the guards' uniforms, then calmly strolled over to an industrial yard, where they planned to scale a fence and hop into a car supposedly waiting on the other side. But the wall was too much for them and when the alarm was sounded they took refuge in the prison laundry. The other two cons surrendered, but it took two volleys of tear gas to flush Tison out of his hole. A search of the laundry produced another pistol, and while a subsequent investigation couldn't prove it, prison officials strongly suspected that Dorothy somehow had smuggled the weapons to Gary.

Following the failed attempt, Tison was locked down in maximum security. Over the next few years, Gary applied repeatedly to be moved to medium security. His applications coincided with a prison reform lawsuit in which a federal court judge ordered a twenty percent reduction of the maximum security population. Thus, in September 1977, despite his vows to escape and kill more cops, Tison was among the cons transferred out of the main prison and moved across the road to the lightly guarded medium security Trusty Annex. From there, with the help of Dorothy and the three Tison boys, it was a cakewalk to freedom.

Through the spring and into early summer of 1978, the Tison family visits to the prison concentrated less on oral sex and more on the plot to bust Gary out.

In May, the family contacted a Casa Grande gunsmith with underworld ties and placed a custom order based on Gary's specifications: a .16-gauge sawed-off shotgun and a .45 revolver with thirty rounds of ammunition. They added those pieces to a small arsenal already accumulated—.38 silencer-equipped revolver, .380 Erma-Werke automatic rifle, and three more sawed-off shotguns, two .12 gauges and a .20-gauge Magnum. Gary insisted on the sawed-off shotguns for their power to intimidate anyone who got in their way and for their capacity to make hamburger out of human flesh.

In June, the Tisons picked up a couple of used cars: a green 1970 Ford Galaxie and a 1969 cream-colored Lincoln Continental. Big cars for carrying big loads. They packed the trunk of the Lincoln with a hoard of camping gear, prepared foods, beer, soft drinks, bottled water, and other survivalist stuff, but only enough for the short run. After all, the way Gary had it planned, they'd be laying on the beach in Mexico, maybe even Costa Rica, forty-eight hours after busting out of Florence.

In July, they waited.

Dorothy got the call from Gary on Friday night, July 28. In between the "hellos" and "how-are-yous," Gary muttered, "See you Sunday morning." The escape was a go. The boys spent Saturday cleaning and reloading the weapons, checking their equipment, gassing up the cars. Nobody slept much that night.

Just after sunrise that Sunday morning, July 30, Donny, Ricky, and Raymond lined up to kiss their mom goodbye. "Be careful," she cautioned. "Call as soon as you can."

Ricky and Raymond drove the Galaxie. With Donny following in the Lincoln, they headed for Florence. The boys drove to the Pinal General Hospital, parked the Lincoln, and Donny climbed in the Galaxie with his brothers.

The trio arrived at the prison parking lot about 8:30 A.M. Even that early, the temperature was already racing toward ninety. The day promised to be another scorcher, high of 107, according to the weather report, and no relief in sight. Although most Arizonians were accustomed to the blistering heat, they still respected it and took pains to avoid its dangers. Gary Gene Tison was preparing to flee into that furnace that would soon cook him alive.

Eighteen-year-old Raymond, dressed in the usual black T-shirt and jeans, got out and walked to the Trusty Annex building. Originally built as a women's prison, the Annex had been converted to hold men classified as medium security risks. Its low wall and chain-link fence, opposed to the high walls and threatening concertina wire at the high security prison across the road, made the Annex look like a luxury hotel compared to the main joint. Inmates housed in the Annex lived in dorms rather than cell blocks and because of their status were given the choicest work assignments.

Raymond Tison routinely signed in at the Annex registration window and made the same request the family had made for years—to see inmate 28354, Gary Gene Tison. For the guards on duty that morning in the office, Lieutenant George Goswick, Sergeant Marquis Hodo, and Ed Barry, the Tisons were a familiar sight, almost family themselves. Over the past eleven years, the Tisons' weekly visits had been observed as strictly as a religious ritual. Most of the guards, while still wary, had grown to like the shy, friendly Tison boys with their toothy grins and short haircuts (Dad despised hippies and hated longhairs).

After a casual body search, Raymond was buzzed through a security door and entered the open-air courtyard where inmates and visitors met. The gate across the compound, leading to the confinement area, opened and Gary Tison joined his son. They sat together at a picnic table and waited tensely for the next step in the plot to unfold.

Minutes later, the same gate opened and Randy Greenawalt waddled into the compound. The twenty-nine-year-old convict didn't match the Hollywood image of a serial killer. Carrying 240 pounds of blubber on his five-foot, nine-inch frame, the soft, puffy Greenawalt looked more like the Pillsbury Doughboy than a sadistic, remorseless monster for whom murder came as easy as crushing cockroaches. Thick, horn-rimmed glasses bounced on his chubby chipmunk cheeks as he lumbered across the courtyard to the Annex office door.

Greenawalt arrived at Florence in 1974 following a

first degree murder conviction in Flagstaff. He was doing life for the cold-blooded slaying of a sleeping truck driver at a rest stop. However, authorities believed—and Randy slyly hinted—that as many as four other drivers had been gunned down in similar ambushes at truck stops in other Western states.

In fact, Randy enjoyed playing the role of mad-dog assassin who specialized in offing drivers of those huge eighteen-wheelers simply because no other serial killers targeted them. It was a mind-fuck game and with an IQ in the genius range, Randy Greenawalt had the brains to play it out.

What he lacked was a conscience.

As he explained to prison shrinks, Randy hated truck drivers because one had shoved him around when he worked at a Denver warehouse. He also knew that cross-country drivers often were loaded with money and their practice of stopping to sleep at highway rest stops made them easy prey.

Randy Greenawalt was born in Hannibal, Missouri, in 1949, the second of four kids. But only he and brother Jim grew up to be killers. Randy studied for a year at Missouri Baptist College, thinking he might be a preacher . . . until he discovered sex. From then on it was all downhill to hell: couple of busted marriages, less than honorable discharge from the Navy, robberies, and finally murder.

In January 1974, he and brother Jim pulled into an I-40 rest stop near Flagstaff. They badly needed cash to make it on to California and were looking to rob a trucker, Randy's favorite MO. They soon found their target asleep in the cab of his truck. Randy crept up and drew an "X" in the grime on the side of the door in line with the sleeping man's head, returned to his car and took aim with a .243-caliber rifle. The slug slammed through the door of the truck and blew the driver's skull to smithereens.

Randy and Jim got the driver's money, but they also got caught. Jim shrugged off the murder telling an investigator, "Randy just feels good when he kills."

And a veteran Arizona lawman told an interviewer that Randy Greenawalt was ". . . a cold-blooded killer—the worst I've ever seen. I worked eight homicides on that son of a bitch. At least eight innocent people died because of him, which is why I'm going to be there when they execute him."

Once at Florence, Greenawalt teamed up with Gary Tison in the escape plot. He also conned the prison administrators into moving him to the Annex and making him a clerk-typist, the kind of assignment usually reserved for model prisoners. In hindsight, considering his record, it's a mystery why this vicious, unrepentant thrill killer was let loose from his chains and, like Gary Tison, placed in a position where the potential for escape was so high.

This Sunday morning, Randy Greenawalt barely nodded to the Tisons as he crossed the compound and entered the Annex office to begin his weekly chore of typing up work assignments.

He had just started to type when Donny and Ricky Tison entered the Annex waiting room. Greenawalt glanced up at the clock. It was 9:00 A.M. Right on schedule.

Donny set a cardboard box labeled "Salem Cigarettes" on a table as Ricky stepped to the registration window. Sgt. Hodo glanced up from his paperwork and looked right down the barrel of the sawed-off .12 gauge that Ricky had leveled at him.

Behind Ricky, Donny reached into the box, pulled out a .38, and used it to cover the half-dozen other visitors in the lobby waiting to register. "Behave and nobody gets hurt," Donny warned. "We don't want to hurt anyone."

At Hodo's gasp of surprise, guard Ed Barry turned from his desk and found himself covered by the menacing shotgun held by a grinning Ricky Tison. Guards stationed in the Annex were unarmed so there never was a question of resisting.

Randy Greenawalt moved quickly to the window and grabbed a second sawed-off shotgun and a pistol that Ricky handed to him. "Get on the floor," he snarled at the two guards as he unlocked the door and let Ricky and Donny into the office. Greenawalt then pressed the button that electronically opened the inner door to the visitation area.

Meanwhile, Gary Tison had strolled casually across the compound and when the door opened, Donny slipped him the .45 pistol. Tison concealed the weapon beneath his shirt, walked over to where two other guards were lounging in the shade of the building, took them hostage, and, at gunpoint, forced them to walk slowly into the Annex office.

Other on-duty guards were rounded up from other offices in the building, and, in a matter of minutes, the Tisons and Greenawalt had seven guards and six visitors stretched out on the control room floor. The room was air-conditioned but Randy Greenawalt broke out in a heavy, nervous sweat as he swung the shotgun back and forth and went to work disabling the prison's phone and alarm systems, one of the skills, aside from being a ruthless killer, that won him a spot on the Tison escape team.

Next, Gary Tison pulled two sets of clothes and two pairs of boots out of the box the boys carried in. After he and Greenawalt had changed out of their prison garb, Gary Tison pointed the .45 at the seven guards and told them to get up. "Okay," he growled. "You guys first and no quick moves or I'll blow you all away." He directed the guards across a hallway and into a large storage closet. The civilian hostages followed and Tison used a key taken from Lt. Goswick to lock them inside.

The boys returned the shotguns to the Salem box, picked up an ice chest another visitor had brought in, and followed Gary out the front door. They had one more obstacle to pass, the guard in a tower. But when he saw the five men emerge carrying a cooler and stroll slowly across to the parking lot, the guard barely noted their passing. Visitors were coming and going all weekend, and there was nothing suspicious about these guys.

A mere twenty minutes after Ricky first shoved the shotgun in the astonished face of Marquis Hodo, the Tisons and Randy Greenawalt were speeding away from the Arizona State Prison in the overloaded, green Galaxie.

The second phase of the escape began with the fugitives switching to the Lincoln parked at the hospital and turning west, speeding along secondary roads across the Gila Indian Reservation. Three hours and 140 miles after the spectacular jailbreak, the five fugitives arrived at Hyder, a speck of a town smack in the middle of Arizona's baddest badlands, where daytime temperatures of 120 degrees and more are common and where even the shade can't stand the heat.

But for men on the run, Hyder's remote and hostile environment was perfect. None of the few desert rats who clung to its venomous surroundings cared enough to report the airplanes that occasionally landed and took off and banked for the Mexican border fifty miles away just beyond the wild and treacherous Cabeza Prieta mountainous desert. Dope smugglers were known to use the wide gravel road leading to Hyder as a clandestine runway. Gary's brother Joe was a pilot and often bragged about making the moonless flights over the Cabeza Prieta to Sonoma and back. Nothing to it.

The Lincoln pulled up to an abandoned house. The men quickly concealed the big car in a dilapidated shed, hauled the food and drinks into the house, and settled down for what Gary Tison predicted would be a short wait. Everything was going even better than he planned as radio newscasts reported that authorities were searching for the escapees east of the prison, in the opposite direction from Hyder.

Only Dorothy knew her family was hunkered down in the harsh desert hideout, waiting for her to send a plane.

But the fugitives waited through the night and all the next day without sight of a plane. By nightfall on July 31, everyone was half crazed by the relentless heat and boiling mad that Dorothy hadn't come up with a plane and pilot. This called for a hasty change of plans, so an angry and increasingly edgy Gary Tison ordered the Lincoln reloaded. They'd go north toward Flagstaff. Maybe get a plane there.

About 11:30 P.M., along U.S. 95, a lonely stretch of highway between Yuma and Quartzsite, the Lincoln had a blowout. But the spare, they discovered, was also flat, leaving the fugitives stranded in the middle of the night with no transportation. Come daylight, they'd be sitting ducks for any search party that happened by.

"Here's what we'll do," Gary told the others. "Donny and Ricky will hide on one side of the road, me and Randy on the other. Raymond will stay with the car. Folks around here don't leave other people stranded in the desert, especially a kid by himself. Soon as a car stops to help, we'll jump em." They waited only half an hour before headlights appeared on the southern horizon headed toward them.

John Lyons was taking his family home.

Lyons had spent the last two years stationed at the Marine Corps Air Station in Yuma. Now that his discharge had come through, Lyons, twenty-four, was eager to get back home to Omaha, Nebraska, where he'd already enrolled at Creighton University to study law. With him were his wife Donnelda (everybody called her "Donna"), also twenty-four, and son, Christopher, only a month shy of his second birthday. The Lyonses' fifteen-year-old niece was with them. By a twist of fate, the girl's name was Terri Jo Tyson.

The headlights of the orange Mazda washed over the boy waving beside the disabled car near the turnoff leading to Palm Canyon, part of the Kofa National Wildlife Refuge. Lyons braked and got out to offer his help, only to find himself surrounded by armed and dangerous men.

The Lyonses and Terri Jo were crowded into the backseat of the Lincoln. Donna held a softly whimpering Christopher and Terri Jo clutched her pet Chihuahua. With Gary Tison covering the hostages with a sawed-off shotgun, Greenawalt turned the Lincoln around, bouncing along on the rim back to the Palm Canyon Road. It made it a few hundred yards along a gas line maintenance road before bogging down in the gravel.

The Tison boys, riding in the commandeered Mazda, followed and parked a short distance away.

What happened in the next few minutes was later pieced together from evidence found at the scene and from statements provided by Ricky and Raymond Tison. Con-wise Randy Greenawalt only alluded to his role in the horror.

Gary Tison ordered everyone out of the Lincoln while the boys transferred their weapons and supplies to the Mazda. As that was being done, Tison paced back and forth smoking and fiddling with the .12-gauge shotgun and listening as John Lyons pleaded with his captors.

"Don't hurt us," the young ex-Marine begged. "We don't know you guys. Just leave us some water and you'll be long gone before anyone finds us."

Suddenly, Gary Tison turned his shotgun on the front of the Lincoln and blasted volley after volley into the grill and engine block. Double 00 buckshot shattered the headlights and ripped apart the radiator. When the firing abruptly ceased, everyone's ears rang and the only sounds in the dark night were the hissing of coolant escaping from the ruined radiator and little Christopher's hysterical sobbing.

When the Mazda was packed and ready to roll, Tison told his prisoners to get back in the Lincoln's rear seat and called Randy Greenawalt to one side. The two killers conversed in whispers, then Greenawalt, armed with the sawed-off .20 gauge, went to stand by the front passengers' door. Gary Tison took up a stance beside the open rear door on the driver's side.

The last thing Ricky Tison remembers hearing before the shooting resumed was John Lyons's mournful cry, "Jesus, please don't kill us!"

"My dad was on one side and Randy was on the other," Ricky recalled. "They raised the shotguns and started firing. I seen the flashes from each weapon . . ."

Eight or nine shotgun explosions again shattered the quiet. The killers paused, reloaded, and resumed firing into the backseat of the Lincoln; the buckshot disintegrated windows, tore through upholstery, and ripped into the four screaming victims, twisting and jerking convulsively with each shotgun blast as the muzzle flashes lit up the darkness like strobe lights.

John and Donna Lyons and Terri Jo Tyson were practically shredded by the gunfire. Donna, who was holding Christopher between her legs, bent over him in a feeble attempt to shield her baby with her own body. She was hit the worst, first in the chest and then repeatedly in the back of the head and her back. John and Terri Jo were both riddled with buckshot and immediately lost consciousness.

Finally, the shooting stopped. Sixteen empty shotgun shells littered the desert sands on either side of the Lincoln. Randy Greenawalt shouldered his weapon and strolled back to the Mazda. Gary, meanwhile, reloaded and paused to check that all were dead.

Almost miraculously, little Christopher, protected by his mother's body, had survived with only minor wounds. When Tison heard the child whimper, he leaned in the open door for a closer look. He poked at the toddler with the barrel of the shotgun, and then, with the muzzle only two feet from Christopher's head, Gary Tison fired once and then twice. When he was sure there was no more movement amidst the carnage, Tison calmly walked away, lighting a cigarette.

The Mazda returned to the highway and headed north. But while the killers sped away and the desert darkness closed in on the nightmarish death scene, incredibly, sparks of life returned.

John Lyons, critically injured with chunks of flesh torn from his body and bleeding profusely from his many wounds, stumbled from the car, collapsed, and dragged himself about twenty-five feet before rolling over on his back and dying.

Terri Jo, who had been sitting on the opposite side, also regained consciousness. Donna's body had absorbed most of the shots intended for Terri Jo so her only major wound was to her left hip. Still holding on to her little pet that also had survived the terrible fusillade, Terri Jo pushed open the door, rolled to the ground, and started crawling down a dry wash toward the highway.

A beautiful young woman with long, lustrous brown hair flowing past her shoulders, Terri Jo Tyson had been an honors student in high school. Until the Tisons came along, she was awaiting her almost certain acceptance as a cadet in the Air Force Academy. Now she was desperately hurt and dying in the desert. Fighting for every inch, the severely wounded girl managed to crawl one thousand feet away from the Lincoln before she could go no farther. Then she did something remarkable for someone in her condition. She removed the Chihuahua's collar with the Lyonses' name and address on it and fastened it around her own ankle so whoever found her would be able to identify her. Then, curled on her left side, with her hands beneath her head as if going to sleep, Terri Jo closed her eyes and died. The little dog never left her. A few days later, it died of exposure, still huddled against the girl's body.

And there the dead rested, the heat and the desert insects rapidly going to work on the remains.

Nearly a week passed before Arizona game warden Tom Peeples drove into Palm Canyon for a routine inspection of the area. It was Sunday, August 6, when he spotted the car bogged down in the sand and exposed to the searing heat. When Peeples parked and stepped from his air-conditioned car, the stench hit him like a sledgehammer between the eyes.

Immediately, Peeples knew that he'd discovered more than an abandoned car. He'd stumbled onto a field of gore.

A bloated, decomposing corpse that appeared to be that of a woman sat upright in the backseat covered by swarms of flies. Another swarm nearby attracted his attention to the second body, a man wearing red shorts and T-shirt.

Peeples didn't bother looking farther. He radioed for help and within the hour, deputies from the Yuma County Sheriff's Office were on the scene. Choking back their nausea and stunned by the violence of the murders, the deputies were even more horrified when a closer inspection revealed a third body of a child, still tightly held between the legs of the dead woman. One deputy vomited when he got close enough to see that the baby's head had been blown off. Only shreds of tissue remained.

Among the evidence collected was a prescription medicine bottle bearing the name of Christopher Lyons, indicating it had been filled at the Marine Corps dispensary in Yuma. With that information, investigators were able to identify the Lyons family.

As deputies wrapped up their investigation at the murder scene, Yuma County Sheriff's Captain Cecil Crowe was sickened by what he saw and called it the worst slaughter in his twenty years as a cop. Had he searched a little farther, Crowe would have been even more appalled. The body of Terri Jo Tyson still lay by itself one thousand feet away, unnoticed in the desert scrub brush.

By Tuesday, August 8, authorities had tied the murders to the escapees. Governor Bruce Babbitt offered a $10,000 reward for information leading to the capture and conviction of the killers. The atrocious slaying of the young family so shocked and outraged the people of Arizona that Governor Babbitt, a liberal Democrat not known for his support of the death penalty, angrily commented, "This is a classic illustration of why we must have the death penalty, and why we must apply it."

Meanwhile, the Tisons and Greenawalt were far away. After reaching Flagstaff, they convinced an acquaintance of Randy's to buy them a half-ton 1970 Chevrolet pickup with four-wheel drive. They hid the Mazda beside a riverbed, piled into the truck, and headed for New Mexico.

Along the way, Gary Tison kept in touch by phone with Dorothy and his brother, Joe. That's how manhunters learned where the fugitives were bound—Clovis, New Mexico, and its little-used municipal airport. Gary still thought he could get away to Mexico and he demanded that Joe get a plane and pick him up in Clovis, even if it meant throwing Randy Greenawalt and his own sons to the wolves.

Arrangements were made to meet August 6, about the same time Tom Peeples was making his ghastly discovery in Palm Canyon. But Gary didn't count on brother Joe ratting him out to the cops. Arizona police rushed to set a trap at Clovis, but somehow word leaked out, and, when the Tisons and Greenawalt drove by the airport on a reconnaissance, they found the place overrun by cops and the news media.

With his second flight plan shot down, Gary Tison, growing more desperate by the hour, turned north and raced for Colorado with the vague idea of maybe hiding out in the Rockies.

August 6 was also an important day in the lives of James and Margene Judge since it marked their first full day as husband and wife. The Judges were married Saturday evening in Amarillo and spent their wedding night in Texline, Texas. The young couple planned a few leisurely days of camping and fishing along the Rio Grande River in southern Colorado before driving on to Denver in their new Ford van to take in an NFL preseason game between the Broncos and Dallas Cowboys.

On Tuesday, while the couple honeymooned, the Tison party was moving slowly westward along U.S. 160 . . . slowly because the Chevy pickup was falling apart and because the fugitives were on the lookout for another vehicle to steal. They'd heard on the radio that the bodies of the Lyonses had been found, and Gary figured it was only a matter of time until cops followed their trail to the pickup truck. They badly needed new wheels, he told the others.

On Wednesday, the Judges and the Tisons crossed paths.

The Judges were driving west on U.S. 160 en route to Shaw Lake when they were halted at a construction road project on the steep grade up to Wolf Creek Pass. The vehicle in line behind them was a dark blue, grime-covered pickup with a noisy transmission.

"That," declared an exultant Gary Tison, pointing at the roomy, well-equipped van, "is just what we're looking for." He and Randy walked up to either side of the van, jerked open the doors and, with guns drawn, forced their way inside. Randy shoved James and Margene to the floor in the back of the van and sat over them with his .357 pointed at their heads. Minutes later, the flagman signalled the line of vehicles forward and the procession moved out.

With Gary leading in the van, the two-vehicle caravan crossed the mountain and descended into the San Juan Valley. As he approached monument-like Chimney Rock, Tison turned and followed a dirt road a couple of miles into Cabison Creek Canyon and parked. While the three Tison boys waited in the pickup, their old man and Randy Greenawalt ordered the Judges out of the van.

Gary pressed his revolver into Margene Judge's back and pushed her toward a nest of trees and bushes growing along the banks of Cabison Creek. He gestured in the opposite direction. "Take him over there," he told Greenawalt.

About seventy-five yards north of the road, Greenawalt muttered, "That's far enough," and shot James Judge in the back of the head. A second, nearly simultaneous shot echoed through the narrow canyon. Gary Tison also shot Margene Judge, but cruelly he first made her turn to face her executioner before he blew the top of her head off with a single slug from the powerful .45-caliber handgun.

Margene toppled against the base of a tree. Tison hurriedly tossed loose branches over her body and rushed back to the van that the boys were busy reloading with their arsenal. Randy took a little more time to scrape out a shallow grave for his victim. He rolled James Judge's body into it faceup, rummaged through the dead man's pockets, and even pulled the brand-new gold wedding band off the man's finger. Greenawalt kicked a few inches of dirt over the body and trotted back to the van where the others waited.

Six people were now dead and the killers had their new set of wheels. They could go anywhere, but, true to form, Gary Tison was going home. On Thursday morning, August 10, the day after the Judges were murdered, he shocked the others when he cut south on U.S. 666, straight into the teeth of the dragnet spread out to snare them.

Gary had guessed that Joe betrayed him. "We're gonna stop in Casa Grande and kill the cocksucker," he raged. "Then we'll head for Mexico and shoot our way across the border if we have to." Twelve hours later, their van rolled into the outskirts of the one place in America where every cop in town with an itchy trigger finger knew Gary Tison by sight. For the next three hours, the killers roamed around unnoticed despite the high state of alert. Fortunately for Joe Tyson, he wasn't at home when Gary came to call or else he probably would have been added to the list of victims.

By coincidence, there had been a burglary reported at the Border Patrol Armory in Gila Bend earlier that night, and lawmen in Maricopa, Yuma, and Pinal counties were notified to be on the lookout for a gray or silver vehicle spotted leaving the scene.

There was good reason to believe, the report continued, that the Tison gang might be involved. Tison's inclination to head for home when he was in trouble was well-known and the fact that he had looted weapons from an armory once before made the Tison gang the logical suspects.

Roadblocks were set up on all major highways leading to the Mexican border, including one at the intersection of Battaglia and Chuichu Roads, a few miles south of Casa Grande, at the point where Arizona Highway 15 entered the Papago Indian Reservation. There were seven officers on duty, but somehow word hadn't reached these Pinal County deputies that the statewide alert had been called off and the other roadblocks lifted about midnight. The communications glitch proved fateful.

Moreover, about 2:00 A.M., Captain Minor Stephens ordered a second roadblock be set up about seven miles south of the first on Chuichu Road, just in case the fugitives bypassed Casa Grande en route to Mexico. Four deputies went to man the second roadblock; Sergeant Armando Valenzuela and deputies Wade Williams, Steve Greb, and Billy Jewel remained at the first.

About 2:30 A.M., headlights approached from the north, then slowed and coasted up to the roadblock with high beams still on. Sergeant Valenzuela stepped toward the center of the road, his hand up signaling the driver to stop. But at a distance of about six feet, someone leaned out the passenger's window and opened fire with a high-caliber weapon. At the same time, the driver hit the gas. Tires howling and guns blazing, the van roared past the roadblock as the passenger continued shooting.

Valenzuela dropped to the ground with the slugs tearing up shards of asphalt only inches from his head. The van was rapidly disappearing down the dark highway before the deputies, taken completely by surprise, could recover and take up the chase, lights flashing and sirens screaming, ignoring the furious gunfire now directed at them from the rear window of the van.

At speeds hitting one hundred mph, the chase bore

down on the second roadblock where three heavily armed deputies waited, alerted by Valenzuela's frantic radio call that a van loaded with gunmen was coming toward them. They stood alongside the two pickups that formed the roadblock and listened as the deadly chase came closer and closer.

When the headlights of the van burst around a corner, one of the deputies shouted, "Okay, open fire!" Dozens of slugs smashed into the speeding van, shattering side windows and crashing through the windshield. For a moment, the van slowed, then brushed between the two pickups, apparently unfazed by the rapid-fire fusillade, like a charging bull shrugging off biting flies.

But just beyond the roadblock, the van seemed to shudder and suddenly lose momentum. It veered to the left and then to the right, lurched into a broad drainage ditch beside the highway and skidded to a stop in a shower of dust and gravel. The engine coughed and died. Seconds later, the pursuit cars screeched to a stop on the road, headlights aimed at the bullet-pocked van.

Inside, Donny Tison, who had been driving when the fugitives ran the roadblock, was dying, his brains and blood splattered about the interior and covering Ricky Tison, who was crouched on the floorboard next to the driver's seat. The slug from a high-powered rifle had shattered Donny's skull. Amazingly, the boy wasn't killed instantly. But he was as good as dead; his body twitched and spurted blood and gore.

As the bullet-scarred van rocked to a stop in a cloud of dust, Arizona tough guy Gary Tison suddenly turned yellow. He climbed over Raymond's back, shoved Randy Greenawalt away from the sliding side door, and leapt to the ground. "Every man for himself," he yelled, disappearing into the pitch-black desert. Gary Tison left behind one son dying with a bullet through the head and two more terrified that any second now they'd be cut to pieces by lawmen's lead.

Rather than risk casualties by rushing the van carrying desperate men who were obviously armed to the teeth and willing to shoot to kill, the Pinal County deputies trained their headlights on the van and called for reinforcements, including a chopper from the Arizona Department of Public Safety.

While the cops waited, Ricky Tison squirmed out from under Donny's nearly lifeless body. With Ray's help, the two eased their dying brother onto the seat and left him there, then followed Randy Greenawalt, who scrambled out the side door and dashed toward the desert.

Greenawalt was barely clear of the van's protection when a deputy spotted him making a break and fired his shotgun. The fleeing figure hit the ground and didn't move.

Minutes later, when the helicopter arrived and trained its powerful searchlight on the scene, two more motionless figures were seen nearby. Like Greenawalt, Ricky and Raymond had dropped to the ground when the deputy fired. However, none of the trio was wounded. All three remained pressed to the gravelly ground until the growing posse surrounded them and ordered them, one by one, to stand and walk backwards toward the highway. The three were strip searched, wrists and ankles shackled, and each was made to lie on his back in the beds of separate pickup trucks.

When the officers cautiously inspected the van, they found the still-warm body of Donald Tison. After photographing the remains, and before the body was shoved into an ambulance for a trip to the morgue, a Pinal County deputy, who was acquainted with Donny Tison and knew he wasn't married, noticed a gold wedding ring on his left hand. The ring was removed and remained sealed in an evidence locker until months later when grieving relatives identified it as James Judge's wedding band, the one he'd worn for only two days.

Ever since the ghastly discovery in the Palm Canyon slaughter pen, authorities had feared that Terri Jo Tyson was a hostage of the Tison gang, forced to accompany them for their sexual amusement. When they found she wasn't in the van, there was a great sense of urgency to learn where she was. If alive, maybe there was still time to save her.

But Ricky and Raymond refused outright to even acknowledge they'd been at the murder scene. They knew nothing about a missing girl, they claimed. Randy Greenawalt was a different matter, however. A cop, who had arrested Greenawalt for the murder of the truck driver and who knew how to appeal to the serial killer's ego and braggadocio, conned the pudgy murderer into admitting there had been a teenage girl with the Lyonses. But Randy denied she had been kidnapped and raped.

"You're goddamn right she was shot," the sadistic killer finally blurted out. "Maybe she walked away, but she sure as hell couldn't have gotten far the way she was shot up."

The Yuma County sheriff was notified and told that it was likely there was another body still out there in Palm Canyon that had been missed the first time.

Scores of deputies and volunteers immediately rushed to the murder site and began scouring the surrounding desert in an organized grid search. Half an hour later, Ken Lewis of the Yuma County Search and Rescue Team and Game Warden Larry Young found what they were looking for and dreaded finding.

Terri Jo's badly decomposed body was lying curled up on its side in a shallow depression, the remains of her pet Chihuahua pressed against her stomach. The corpse was impossible to identify on sight, but the tiny collar Terri Jo had clasped around her ankle, probably as her last act, told who she was.

Finding Terri Jo Tyson ended one mystery, but another remained and there were more bodies to be accounted for. When the Tison boys and Greenawalt were captured, the ownership of the van was immediately traced to the Judges. But where were they and what had happened to them? The three prisoners resisted relentless grilling and cajoling by the cops and refused to reveal the location of the honeymooning couple now presumed to be dead. Months passed while the Judges lay rotting in their shallow, unmarked graves deep in Cabison Canyon. Finally, when the Tison boys saw it might be their only chance to beat the gas chamber, they struck a deal to save their own skins and described where searchers should look for the bodies in Colorado.

There was snow in the air the morning of November 15, 1978, when a search party gathered at a highway cutoff west of Pagosa Springs, Colorado. They had a huge expanse of rugged country to cover since the Tisons couldn't remember the exact location of the graves, only that they were a couple of miles up a canyon just south of Chimney Rock.

Charles Kalbacher, an investigator with the Archuleta County District Attorney's Office, led the parade of off-road vehicles into Cabison Canyon. Picturing the killers in his mind, Kalbacher figured that neither one was apt to drag a body very far, so the search was concentrated along either side of the narrow canyon road. His hunch was on the money. Two hours later, searchers uncovered a skull on the creek bank, then some scattered bones chewed by animals along with a pair of feminine sunglasses and a woman's wedding ring. Shortly afterwards, the skeletal remains of James Judge were found on the opposite side of the road.

(The Tisons and Greenawalt were never charged with the murders of James and Margene Judge after Colorado authorities decided that Arizona's death penalties would be enough to kill the killers.)

Later that same month, on November 29, 1978, Ricky Tison tried to carry on where the old man left off, keeping alive the Tison family tradition of busting out. Along with two other inmates, Ricky jumped a guard and escaped from the Pinal County Jail. He was on the run for fourteen hours, and once more the countryside around Casa Grande was aroused with a Tison on the loose. But Ricky was cornered in a cornfield about a mile from the jail and gave up without a fight.

Long trials and retrials, sentencings and resentencings followed . . . and that continues into the foreseeable future. But they are all epilogues to the drama in the desert.

In January 1979, Ricky and Ray Tison and Randy Greenawalt were tried together in Pinal County for the escape and routinely found guilty. Each was sentenced to thirty years to life for assault with a deadly weapon.

The next month, Randy Greenawalt was tried in Yuma for the murders of the Lyons family and Terri Jo Tyson. Trials for Ricky and Raymond Tison followed. In each case, to no one's surprise, the defendants were convicted and sentenced to death. Under Arizona law it didn't matter that Ricky and Raymond Tison hadn't actually pulled the trigger. They were still parties to a savage multiple murder that they did nothing to prevent which earned them a seat in the gas chamber.

However, in April 1987, the U.S. Supreme Court ruled that in order to apply the death penalty, Arizona had to show that Ricky and Raymond Tison had exhibited ". . . reckless indifference to the value of human life . . ." when they helped spring two convicted killers from prison and gave them weapons. The boys went back to court and were resentenced to die under that proviso.

Not good enough, said the Supreme Court five years later when the Tisons again appealed "for relief of death sentence" on the grounds that they were just walking down the road when Daddy and Randy Greenawalt butchered the Lyons family. The Tisons won the second round and in 1992 were given four life sentences, each without parole for twenty-five years—two of those sentences were to run consecutively, two to run concurrently.

Also in 1992, Arizona voters decided at the polls that the state's method of execution should be changed to lethal injection. About the same time, the governor signed a death warrant ordering prison officials to put Randy Greenawalt to death on February 17, 1993. The order meant that Greenawalt would be the first killer executed under the new method.

But Randy busied himself in the prison library and created a new legal loophole to leap through. Assistant Attorney General Bruce Ferg said Greenawalt filed an appeal claiming "ineffectual counsel" at his murder trial. Since it was the first time that issue had been raised on appeal, the Arizona courts decided to hear Greenawalt's argument. Consequently, a different killer won the dubious distinction as the first to be needled to death in Arizona.

A decade and a half after he was first sentenced to die for the Quartzsite bloodbath, Randy Greenawalt still has several more years in which to dream up more appeals while the wheels of justice grind ponderously along.

On August 23, 1979, a year after Gary Tison's scorched remains turned up, Dorothy Tison and Joe Tyson were charged with conspiracy for their parts in the prison break. Dorothy pleaded no contest and received a thirty-month jail sentence. She was released on parole in

1981.

Joe Tyson got four years in the slammer, but a plea bargain allowed him to serve that sentence concurrently with jail time he owed on a previous drug conviction.

Every weekend, Dorothy Tison still goes visiting at the Arizona State Prison in Florence. No contact visits allowed, however, like when Gary ruled the roost. Now thick, bulletproof glass and steel bars separate Dorothy Tison from her boys.

"Rick and Ray are all I have left," she once said. "I'll be here for them when they get out."

She may have a long wait. The Tison boys won't be eligible for parole until sometime around 2042.

SEVEN
THE GALLEGOS: SEX SLAVES AND SERIAL KILLERS

The first two "sex slaves" Mr. and Mrs. Gallego butchered were just kids. Bouncy, bubbly teenagers teetering on the breath-thin threshold between girlhood and womanhood. Each a woman-child: souls of innocents prancing around in the kind of bodies that detonate a thousand wet dream eruptions.

The time: September 11, 1978, the waning days of summer vacation. The place: the enormous, and enormously busy, Country Club Plaza Mall on the outskirts of Sacramento, California. The victims: Rhonda Scheffler, seventeen, and Kippi Vaught, sixteen, excitedly running through the Mall for the latest in cool to complete their back-to-school wardrobes.

Lustful, lecherous eyes watched from aside as the two giggling girls danced from store to store, vibrantly alive.

The next time anyone saw Rhonda and Kippi, their raped, tortured, and mutilated remains had been tossed like garbage bags in a roadside drainage ditch. Meanwhile, in a charming little picket-fenced house on Bluebird Lane, Gerald and Charlene Gallego were luxuriating in the sexual afterglow of a nightlong orgy of gutter-level sex and murder. Their mutual fantasy of sexual slaves to rape and torture were, for the moment, fulfilled and their demon sex gods appeased.

The beastly atrocities inflicted on their victims by the Gallegos were bad enough by themselves, but what makes this family murder spree even more revolting is the combination of husband and wife hunting together and killing together to gratify their raging sexual perversions.

Gerald and Charlene Gallego comprised a couples-only family unit: husband and wife going it alone without the kids once deemed necessary to define the traditional American nuclear family. The Gallegos were a family of two, and, so far, that makes the Gallegos—Mr. and Mrs. Murderer—one of a kind.

When author Eric van Hoffman chronicled the Gallegos' rampages in *Venom in the Blood,* he observed that:

"According to the 1987 FBI Task Force statistics on multiple homicides in the United States, there are at least five hundred active serial killers operating around the country at any given time. . . . Nowhere in the mass of statistics is there a single reference to a husband-and-wife serial killer team. . . . The unprecedented and bizarre fact that a wife would not only actively condone, but would use herself as bait to lure the victims, then willingly and vigorously aid and abet her husband in a series of violent sex crimes was a first . . . a documented sex-murder team comprised of a husband and wife . . . one in which the wife was an equally active sexual aggressor."

Gerald Gallego is another of those Bad Seed characters whose very existence begs for abortion. Whatever Bad Seed was planted in the Gallego family produced a bumper crop of criminals, killers, and assorted sociopaths.

Where many sons follow their father into the family business, generation succeeding generation, building on the family honor and tradition, Gallego followed in his father's footsteps straight to Death Row and a state-ordered execution. When (not if) the State of Nevada sticks its death needle in Gerald Gallego's arm, it may be one of the few times that a father and son have both been executed for murder in America.

Few have deserved it more.

Gerald Armond Gallego was born in the Sacramento County Hospital on July 17, 1946. His mother's name was Lorraine. His father's San Quentin prison number wasn't recorded.

Gallego grew up mean and out of control, with his first felony arrest coming just before his tenth birthday. In March 1956, the kid who was already known as the neighborhood bully broke into a neighbor's home in the Oak Park section of Sacramento. The woman resident returned unexpectedly, just as Gerald was running out the door with a portable television set and a diamond ring. When the woman tried to stop him, the young hood pulled a knife and threatened to cut off her breasts.

Gerald was charged with burglary, carrying a dangerous weapon, and assault with intent to kill. A judge shipped him off to reform school, but ninety days later he was back in Sacramento. Within twenty-four hours, the woman's house burned down. Fire inspectors ruled arson, but no one was charged.

Gerald grew up on the streets where he studied pimping, panhandling, and pickpocketing. For exercise, he rolled drunks; for lunch money, he burglarized stores. When he was twelve years old, Gallego lured a six-year-old child into a basement and raped her, an offense that shocked the community, but that cost the young thug only a few months in the slammer.

Before he was thirty, Gallego had been married

seven times . . . most of them bigamous. For as vile as his sexual tastes may have been, it's undeniable that Gerald Gallego possessed an animal magnetism that some women found irresistible. He wasn't tall, maybe five-eight or five-nine, but was strong as a bull and women loved to run their fingers through the thick, curly black hair covering his powerful barrel chest. More than one woman fell under Gallego's spell when he turned on his "stare," a technique he'd practiced in front of mirrors, in which he focused his deep, dark hypnotic eyes, wide and unblinking, on the object of his choice and made her believe she was the only woman in the world.

Gallego cleverly manipulated that attraction to marry for money—often. It was the old marriage scam of "love em and leave 'em . . . after you've cleaned out their bank accounts." Few marriage scam artists are ever caught; fewer convicted because the victims are usually too ashamed to press charges. Gallego spotted that weakness and exploited it to his advantage.

All told, Gallego had been picked up twenty-seven times on such felony charges as burglary, grand theft auto, assault with intent to commit murder, assault and battery with intent to cause great bodily harm, felonious assault upon a person over sixty-five during a strong-arm robbery, and escape. When he was arrested for the string of sex murders, Gallego was also wanted on outstanding warrants charging him with incest, rape, and sodomy on his own daughter, whom he molested from the time she was six years old until her early teens.

Whenever he went to jail, which wasn't often enough (thanks to California loopholes, he spent less than six years behind bars for all those felony arrests and convictions), Gallego had a whole tribe of relatives to keep him company. Two or three uncles and some cousins on his mother's side were doing time for murder. One of his half brothers was knocking down fifteen to life for shooting a clerk during an armed robbery.

Doing the crime and dodging the time was a way of life among the clannish Gallegos. You weren't a man until you had a record, preferably a violent one.

It was, as they say, in the blood.

About the same time Gerald was threatening to knife his next-door neighbor, his father achieved lasting notoriety when he became the first killer to be executed in Mississippi's brand-new gas chamber for the barbaric and cold-blooded slayings of two cops.

Gerald Albert Gallego was a native Californian and a dedicated criminal whose career ran the gamut from petty theft to murder. He was doing another of his frequent stretches in "Q" when his son and namesake was born.

In May 1954, on the bricks again, Gallego was passing through Ocean Springs, Mississippi, and paused long enough to kick in the window of a store in the Gulf resort town. He was caught before he'd gone a block by Ernest "Red" Beauquez, the thirty-two-year old night marshal, a part-time, small-town cop with no experience dealing with a hard-core con like Gerald Albert Gallego.

Before he could cuff his prisoner, Gallego turned on the startled officer, knocked him to the ground, and grabbed his revolver. For the next fifteen minutes, Gallego held the gun to the cop's head, inviting Beauquez to beg for his life.

Then he shot him in the face.

(In a diary Gallego kept while on Death Row, he wrote: "I don't think I ever felt so good in my life as when that cop was telling me how much his wife and kids needed him. When he asked for five minutes to pray, I gave him thirty seconds, then let him have it right in the head." Years later, Gerald Armond Gallego treasured those last words from his old man.)

Gallego was caught still carrying the dead cop's gun. Two weeks later, he and another convicted killer concocted a scalding, acid-like mixture of disinfectant, detergent, urine, and feces, and threw it in the face of their lone guard, Jack C. Landrum. Before fleeing, Gallego lingered long enough to brutally beat the blinded and helpless man to death with his fists.

A posse ran Gallego to ground in the Mississippi swamps. To no one's surprise considering Mississippi's swift brand of justice (especially for dark, foreign-sounding cop killers from California which most Mississippians regarded as the asshole of the world), the elder Gallego was sentenced to die. He became the first man to take a seat in Mississippi's new, untested gas chamber. State officials were pleased that it worked so well.

Gerald Armond Gallego was proud of his old man. He wanted to be just like him.

On the other hand, Charlene Adelle Williams wasn't at all like her prosperous, upright, upper-middle-class family, and lived her life as though trying to prove she'd been switched at birth. After Charlene, they broke the mold on rich-bitch-spoiled-rotten.

Her father was a top executive with a supermarket chain, so Charlene was born into a socially prominent and affluent lifestyle on October 10, 1956. Always a precocious, China-doll child, she grew into a strikingly beautiful young woman: a pixieish five-feet tall and one hundred pounds with long, honey-blond hair, sky-blue eyes, and a sensuous, pouty mouth

Her IQ tested out at a whopping 160, which easily

qualified her as a genius. As a child, Charlene mastered the complexities of the classical violin as naturally as other little girls learned to play dolls. At one point, her talents earned Charlene an invitation to study at the distinguished San Francisco Conservatory of Music.

Charlene also possessed the remarkable ability to recall minutia of places and events with astonishing accuracy, a feat that constantly amazed officials who later spent long hours listening in fascination as Charlene reeled off precise details of each horrendous murder, rape, or mutilation and the remote spots where the bodies were buried.

Charlene had it all: All-American cheerleader looks, outstanding mind, social position, money to burn, and a family that indulged her every whim. In fact, she probably had too much. By age twelve, Charlene was already into drugs; by fourteen, she was a confirmed teenage booze hound.

She also had a reputation as a liar, a phony, and a promiscuous slut; a druggie who bragged about her weird sex escapades; a girl who regaled her ex-boyfriends with fantasies about being raped by another woman and her longings for sweaty, all-night rounds of ménage à trois.

These two extremes of society collided in September 1977, when tiny, pampered Charlene Adelle Williams, she of the privileged gentility, went on the prowl for drugs in South Sacramento, the lair of the bestial Gerald Armond Gallego, he of the gutter side of humanity. Within a week, the two had set up housekeeping in a love nest on Bluebird Lane. A year to the day after bumping into one another in the South Sacramento dive and getting married, Mr. and Mrs. Gallego began killing.

Poles apart doesn't begin to define the differences between Gerald and Charlene Williams Gallego. Their only common ground was a gluttonous, piggish lust for sex, the kinkier the better. They instantly bonded in a depraved sexual dance, almost as if their sex organs were powerful magnets drawing one irresistibly to the other. For instance, each craved oral and anal sex until their mouths turned raw and their organs bled. Their bizarre sexual fantasies meshed perfectly. They called each other by pet names. She called him "Daddy." He called her "Cunt."

Gerald's obsessions extended to young girls who reminded him of the daughter he had been having incestuous relations with since she was six years old. Charlene thrived on risky sex—she once had a blazing affair with a married man in which her favorite interludes were fucking in the garage while the man's wife slept in the next room—and then peeking through the window to watch while the man returned to bed and had sex with his wife.

Charlene also had a taste for lesbian sex and spent hours with girlfriends binging on cunnilingus or romping the night away with monstrous dildos while Gerald watched and masturbated.

Because these two beasts in heat somehow sniffed each other out and went to rut, ten innocent people were slaughtered to satisfy their sadistic needs.

The notion of sex slaves as platforms on whom they could act out their grotesque sexual fantasies was hatched in the summer of 1978 when the Gallegos invited Gerald's daughter and her best friend—both fourteen years old—to help Daddy celebrate his birthday. Charlene wasn't yet aware that Gallego had a long-standing sexual relationship with his daughter and that he performed best when his sex partners resembled the child, but she learned some amazing things about the man she'd married during the birthday party that became a sex orgy.

She already knew, for example, that while Gerald's mad craving for sex never flagged, the flesh sometimes rose only to half-mast. But never if the sex partner was his daughter—or someone who looked like her. (Charlene even shaved her pubic hair and dressed and behaved like a fourteen-year-old to excite Daddy Gerald's kinky libido.)

During the four-way sex party, (which was confirmed in an affidavit Gallego's daughter gave during his murder trials), Gerald, Charlene, and the two teenagers spent the night in a writhing jumble of naked bodies that began with Gerald sodomizing his daughter, and Charlene and the girlfriend tangled in a "69."

After the party, the Gallegos had a long talk. With a couple of teenage sex toys to play with whenever they wanted, Gerald could always get it up and Charlene could always get off. The problem would be getting them to freely submit to rape, sodomy, and bisexual torture, which included having their nipples bitten off. The answer for the Gallegos was simple: take what they want, use it, abuse it, and lose it. Everything else in society was thrown away, so why not disposable sex slaves?

The first step in their sex slave plot was the purchase of a 1973 gold and white Dodge van that they converted into a combination prison cell and sex playpen on wheels. Gerald installed a cot, camp stove, and ice chest, tinted the rear windows so no one could see in, hung a curtain behind the seats to further isolate the rear of the van, and outfitted it with ropes to bind their sex slaves.

It was a Tuesday, September 12, 1978, when Gerald

pocketed his favorite .25-caliber semiautomatic pistol and told Charlene to go get dressed. For the occasion, Charlene squeezed into short blue jean cutoffs, tight enough so the cheeks of her ass pumped up like a pair of balloons about to pop. She donned a blue tank top without a bra that let her firm breasts bounce free and her hard nipples poke out like fresh-plucked grapes. In fact, everything about Charlene oozed the ripe look of a sexy fifteen-year-old.

Then the Gallegos went shopping.

Their first stop was the Country Club Plaza Mall crowded with hoards of back-to-school shoppers. Charlene, in her teenybopper apparel, blended right into the crowd. Like a wolf on the prowl, she spotted her prey standing in front of a food court, smoothly cut Rhonda and Kippi out from the rest of the flock, and set them up for the kill.

Charlene disarmed them with her looks—one of their own—and baited the trap with the offer of a party and free drugs. In minutes, the two teens were traipsing along behind Charlene to where Gerald waited in the parking lot.

As soon as Rhonda and Kippi settled into the back of the van, Gerald pushed his way through the curtain partition and pounced on the startled victims. The Gallegos quickly hog-tied the girls and gagged them with layers of sticky gray duct tape plastered over their mouths.

The van, with its cargo of terrified sex slaves, sobs muffled beneath their gags, headed northwest out of Sacramento on I-80. At Baxter, just before the Interstate bends east for the climb to Donner Pass high in the Sierras, Gerald turned off onto a web of side roads, winding through the pastoral meadows fronting the Eldorado National Forest.

Stopping in a grove of pine trees, Gallego turned to

his passengers. "This is the place," he said. "Get undressed," he told Charlene as he began ripping the clothing off the two girls.

It was close to midnight before the van rolled back along I-80 approaching the outskirts of Sacramento. Rhonda and Kippi, raped repeatedly, brutally sodomized, their bodies a patchwork of human bite marks, lay in the back, stupefied by the violence of the past six hours.

Charlene was driving and at Gerald's direction turned off on a rural side road toward an area of rich farm fields and migrant worker camps known as Sloughouse. Charlene drove until they were beyond the lights of any farm building and parked at the side of a dirt road.

Gerald dragged the two girls out of the van, their eyes wide with horror, their bound bodies trembling in terror. He pushed them off the side of the road and across an irrigation ditch. There, Gallego raised a jack handle he carried and with a single blow shattered the skull of the shorter of the two girls, whirled and smashed the taller girl across the temple.

Both girls crumpled without a sound. Gallego bent over one girl and fired a round from the .25 automatic into her head. He straddled the second victim and put three slugs into the back of her head.

As Gallego turned to leave, Charlene shouted, "That one's still moving!" Gallego ran back and shot the dying girl three more times in the head.

"That oughta do it," he grunted.

On the way home, the Gallegos stopped long enough to clean out the van and dump the victims' belongings into a Dumpster behind a supermarket. Back at their cozy little love pad on Bluebird Lane, Gerald and Charlene showered, fell into bed, and, adrenaline gushing with the thrill of the kill, fucked till dawn.

About the time they finally dozed off, two migrant farm workers stumbled over the ravaged remains of Rhonda Scheffler and Kippi Vaught by the side of the farm-to-market road.

The autopsies performed that same day on the murdered girls revealed in chillingly graphic details all the appalling sexual suffering they'd endured before they died. With minor variations, the report filed that September 14 by the Sacramento County coroner could have been duplicated for most of the killings that followed. It read in part:

> #91478-13-04: Jane Doe One is a well-nourished normally developed white female, 15-18 years of age, 5 feet 2 inches tall, weighing 135 lbs. . . . Victim was having menstrual cycle at time of death with a Tampax-type sanitary pad inserted in vagina. . . . No traces of semen were found in or around vagina. . . . Severe trauma around anus arca . . . 1.2 ml of semen found in rectum and mouth of victim . . . not sufficient quantity of semen here to indicate a normal ejaculation . . . perpetrator's blood type "O". . . .
>
> Deep human bite wound 1 cm below victim's left breast and nipple of same has been almost severed, indicating another probable human bite . . . deep trauma wound on left side of victim's head near temple area indicating a blow from a solid rounded instrument . . . three 6mm-sized (probably a .25 caliber) bullet wounds in victim's head, any one of which could have caused death. . . .
>
> Cause of death is probably due to one or all three bullet wounds to head. Victim was probably

unconscious at time of death, possibly due to blow on head. Victim was sodomized and apparently performed fellatio on perpetrator sometime prior to death.

#91478-13-05: Jane Doe Two is a well-nourished normally developed white female, 16-24 years of age, 5 feet 7 inches tall, weighing 110 lbs . . . 3 ml of semen in victim's vagina . . . 4.5 ml of semen in victim's rectum. Traces of seminal fluid also found in mouth and left ear. The 1.5 ml difference between amounts of semen in vagina and rectum would indicate the probability that victim was sodomized before vaginal penetration.

Judging from the grossly differing amounts of semen in rectum and mouth of Jane Doe One and Jane Doe Two, it is probably indicative that Jane Doe Two was sexually molested first. Semen samples from Jane Doe Two indicate the perpetrator's blood type to be "O".

There is a deep human bite wound on victim's left buttock, 2 cm left of anus opening . . . a marked difference in teeth size in comparison to bite on Jane Doe One and possibly indicates two perpetrators . . . massive trauma to victim's right breast nipple, indicating probable chewing from human teeth . . .

"Grazing" type, nonfatal bullet wound behind victim's left ear . . . massive trauma wound on top of victim's head, indicating a blow from a rounded metal instrument . . . three 6mm-size bullet wounds in victim's head, indicating Jane Doe One and Jane Doe Two were shot with same weapon, probably a .25 caliber handgun . . . Despite blow to head and "grazing" type bullet wound, victim was probably conscious when fatal shots fired.

Cause of death probably came from any or all of three bullet wounds to head . . . massive trauma of the genitalia and anus area indicate victim was probably sodomized then raped via vaginal penetration with ejaculation occurring in both body cavities. Victim probably performed fellatio on perpetrator sometime prior to death and ejaculation may or may not have occurred in victim's mouth . . .

The autopsy findings left no doubt that an extremely dangerous and sadistic sex killer had surfaced in Sacramento. Only a psycho in a sexual rage bites like that. One such crazy on a killing rampage was almost too terrible to imagine, but the teeth marks indicated that more than one person gnawed and chewed on the bodies of the two girls while raping and sodomizing them. Veteran homicide detectives shuddered to think what other horrors awaited them with a pair of sexual psychopaths working as a team.

A few days later, a homicide detective from the Sacramento County Sheriff's Office met with a juvenile officer to compare notes on missing or runaway teenagers. One report of two missing girls matched the descriptions of the Jane Does lying in the morgue. By nightfall, the bodies of Rhonda Scheffler and Kippi Vaught had been identified.

Meanwhile, their experiment with their sex slaves overwhelmed Mr. and Mrs. Gallego and left them glutted for weeks. Replaying the memory of the orgy for each other provided nightly stimulation for months. But the time came when the memories failed to excite and their sex together lagged. Then the craving resurfaced.

Before sunup on June 24, 1978, Gerald Gallego rousted his young wife out of bed. Time for her teeny-bopper act. Time to go hunting again. Daddy Gerald had read in the paper that the Nevada State Fair was playing in Reno, about one hundred miles east of Sacramento across the Sierra Nevada Mountains.

A state fair with its carnival rides and giddy crowds was the perfect hunting ground. Daddy Gerald had dreamed of hoards of tight teenage cunts strolling the midway—a smorgasbord of sex slaves to choose from. And Reno was far enough away from the Sacramento scene that cops wouldn't likely make the connection with Rhonda and Kippi.

To the Gallegos' delight, the next set of sex slaves were even younger and more nubile than the first. Brenda Judd was fourteen and Sandra Colley only thirteen that Father's Day Sunday when they strolled through the gate at the Washoe County fairgrounds. Both were dressed in tight jeans and body-hugging shirts, and when Gerald Gallego saw them coming, a vision of his fourteen-year-old daughter flashed before his eyes.

"They're the ones," he pointed out to Charlene. "Go get 'em."

Charlene was wearing her hair in pigtails and with her shorts and T-shirt looked enough like the two girls to be a schoolmate. So when she asked Brenda and Sandra if they wanted to make $20 helping her place advertising flyers on cars in the parking lots, the pair had no reason to suspect a trap. When their mamas told them not to talk to strangers, they didn't mean a girl like Charlene.

At the van, instead of flyers, Gerald waited with a cocked .357 Magnum. "Get in, girls," he ordered. "This is a kidnapping."

After gagging the girls, Charlene took the wheel and

drove northeast out of Reno on I-80. Gerald remained in the back of the van and for the next one hundred miles repeatedly raped the two young girls both anally and vaginally. Charlene tried to keep one eye on the road and one on the rearview mirror. The sight of Daddy Gerald ramming into the tiny, helpless bodies kept Charlene squirming in her seat. By the time she turned off the highway, Charlene felt like she'd already come a dozen times without even touching her sopping wet crotch.

The area where Charlene finally parked to take her turn was a desolate stretch of desert known as Humbolt Sink. About the only visitors to this 130-degree hellhole were lizards and snakes and Gallegos, predators all.

For the next couple of hours, while Gerald rested and watched, Charlene forced the sex slaves to do things neither had ever imagined . . . and had they lived, would never forget. Charlene shrieked and squealed and moaned her way through orgasm after orgasm. Once, an agonized scream ripped the night as Charlene viciously bit the thirteen-year-old's nipple and blood poured down her breast.

Finally, when Mr. and Mrs. Gallego were drained and sated, it came time to discard their disposable love slaves.

Gerald took a folding Army-surplus shovel from under the seat, pulled Sandra Colley out of the van, and marched her off into the dark toward a dry creek bed. A few minutes later, he called for Charlene to bring Brenda Judd. At the creek bank, the starlight was bright enough to illuminate the body of Sandra Colley, stretched out on the sand; wide, unseeing eyes staring back at the stars, the pooling blood spreading in a darkening halo around her bashed-in head.

Gerald stepped behind Brenda Judd, lifted the

shovel over his head, and swung at the girl's head like he was swinging a sledgehammer to break a boulder. When she described the scene later, Charlene said there was a loud splat like a flat rock hitting mud and the girl sank to her knees and slowly toppled over on her face.

Gallego went to work digging a single grave. It took him an hour to hollow out a hole in the rough, rocky ground large enough to hold two dead girls. He neatly folded the naked bodies into the hole, spoon-like, stomach to back, covered them up, and wrestled a big black rock over the grave.

On the way home, the Gallegos stopped for coffee and donuts, paid for with $3 they took from Sandra's purse. The shovel and the girls' purses went into the swift waters of the American River as they rolled back into Sacramento; their clothing was tossed in a Dumpster and the sex slavemobile washed and vacuumed to remove any traces of Brenda Judd and Sandra Colley.

For the next four years, the teenagers were listed as runaways. It wasn't until Charlene Gallego started confessing in 1982 that the girls' families learned the horrifying truth.

A full ten months passed before the Gallegos felt the urge to go hunting again for sex slaves to jump start Gerald's drooping libido and satisfy Charlene's rapacious hunger. On April 24, 1980, the couple parked at the Sunrise Mall in Citrus Heights, a recently developed bedroom community just north of Sacramento.

For half an hour, Gerald and Charlene strolled through the open-air mall or sat on the benches shaded by olive trees and watched a pair of giggly teens window-shop. With their long blond and brownish hair, both looked a little like Gerald Gallego's daughter. The slight resemblance was enough to doom them.

Karen Chipman-Twiggs and Stacey Redican were

both seventeen years old. They wore fashionably faded jeans and baggy gray sweatshirts. They should have been in school, but this soft spring day they'd decided on a lark to skip and mess around at the mall. Both turned when they heard a friendly "Hi!" The smiling girl walking up to them, also wore tight faded jeans and a thin T-shirt. She looked about fifteen, maybe another hooky player looking for some company.

For a reason they never explained, the Gallegos decided to return to the Nevada desert once they had their latest sex slaves trussed up in the back of the van, bound and gagged with the usual duct tape. They drove for over three hundred miles with their hostages, out onto the high plateau of the Humbolt Range. About 5:00 P.M., just beyond Lovelock, at a wide spot in the road called Oreana, they turned off onto a gravel road and followed the rusty signs to an old campground named Limerick Canyon.

It was after 3:00 A.M. when the Gallegos finally had their fill. This time, Gerald used a brand-new claw hammer to shatter their skulls, and even though he was exhausted with a sore, raw penis to remind him of the nonstop sex, Gallego took time to dig a grave. Deep this time. Down to maybe five feet, he figured, and then shoved rocks and a couple of old tree logs on top so the coyotes wouldn't dig up the bodies.

It kept the coyotes out, but not somebody's pet. On July 1, 1980, while on an outing in Limerick Canyon, the family pooch started barking and digging furiously under a large log. As the owners wandered over to check on the commotion, the dog uncovered a decaying human arm, pulled it out of the sand, and proudly dragged it over to his master's feet.

Pershing County officials dug up the rest. Eventually, they identified Karen Chipman-Twiggs through her dental records. Since the girls had disappeared together, the second

By then, the Gal
ready killed again.

Soon after the
Charlene discovere
feared Gerald woul
prise he was thrille
Gerald Gallego to
tion. To celebrate,
honeymoon, a camp
Oregon Coast.

That's where the ... Mexican
hitchhiker stuck out her thumb on the remote logging road twisting through the pine forest. Linda Aguilar was 21 years old and six months pregnant. She just needed a lift home to Port Orford, a few miles down the road.

Ordinarily, Gerald would have passed her by. Not his type. Didn't look at all like his daughter. But this day he was horny and the blood lust was rising. Besides, he was curious to see how it would feel to ass fuck (his favorite term) a pregnant woman, especially now that Charlene was beginning to show.

Later, in her confessions, Charlene recalled how she helped Gerald undress their expecting sex slave after they tied her up and how she straddled the sobbing woman, ran her fingers through Linda's pubic hair, and studied her swollen belly.

Charlene also remembered that this one begged more than the others. "I'll do whatever you want," she cried. "For God's sake, don't hurt me or my baby." Although she was pregnant herself, Charlene was unmoved. Linda Aguilar's pleas for her unborn baby had about as much impact on Charlene Gallego as a snowflake on a desert rock.

Gerald were finished, the softly but no longer begging. ing down when the van stopped tretch of wild and rocky coastline at the mouth of the Rogue River.

s hadn't planned this sex slave escapade, so Gerald had to improvise a murder. They dragged the still hog-tied woman down beach where Gerald picked up a heavy rock and ashed Linda over the head. He then fell on the woman and choked her until he felt the bones in her neck snap and she went limp. He scooped out a shallow grave in the soft sand, shoved the body in, and hastily covered it.

Linda Aguilar's badly decomposed body and that of the unborn fetus were discovered by tourists on June 22. Her hands and feet were still tied with nylon cord. Her skull was fractured but that wasn't what killed her. According to the autopsy's finding, there was sand in her throat and lungs. Linda Aguilar had been buried alive. The pathologist also estimated that the fetus was over six months along and probably would have survived outside the mother's womb.

The lack of planning in the Aguilar murder was an indication that Mr. and Mrs. Gallego were getting sloppy. They didn't stick to the rigid requirement that the sex slaves be carbon copies of Gallego's daughter. And they were getting careless about covering their tracks.

Victim number eight, in fact, didn't come close to matching the Gallego girl. She just happened to be convenient.

Virginia Mochel was a thirty-four-year-old barmaid who the Gallegos grabbed from the parking lot of a West Sacramento beer joint where she worked. She vanished after closing the Boat Inn the night of July 17, 1980. But it was months later, on October 30, before her skeletal remains, still bound with fishing line, were fished out of the Sacramento River near Clarksburg, about ten miles downstream from the city. There wasn't much left. Authorities could only guess that Virginia Mochel had been garroted with a length of the fishing line.

Had they seen the condition of her body before the Gallegos deep-sixed it, they would have been shocked by the wanton brutality inflicted on the woman before she, mercifully, died.

The Gallegos had stopped at the Boat Inn before closing to celebrate Gerald's birthday. For weeks, they'd been searching for more sex slaves, but every young girl they approached slipped through their fingers. Both Gerald and Charlene were about to explode in frustration.

At the Boat Inn, Gerald got into a pool game while Charlene struck up a conversation with the barmaid. ("Everybody calls me Gennie.") The longer they talked the better the woman looked. She was much older than all the other sex slaves, but she still had a great body and, Charlene convinced herself, if the light was just right, Gennie did look a little like Gerald's daughter.

Charlene sauntered over to the pool table and nudged Gallego. She tilted her head toward the barmaid. "You like her, Daddy?" she asked in her best little-girl voice.

Gerald studied Gennie Mochel and nodded. "Yeah," he grinned. "I think I could use some of that."

At 2:00 A.M., Virginia Mochel turned out the lights, locked the doors, and walked to her beat-up Pinto in the parking lot. There was a shiny Dodge van parked next to it, and Mr. and Mrs. Gallego waited in the dark with their .357 Magnum and roll of sticky duct tape.

Three hours later, Gennie Mochel lay panting in agony on the bedroom floor of the little house on Bluebird Lane. All the frustration and pent-up sexual frenzy came rushing out of the Gallegos and washed over the barmaid like scalding lava from an erupting volcano. Every sexual indignity in the S&M book had been inflicted on her. Brutal rape by the animalistic Gerald Gallego was the least of it. She was also repeatedly sodomized—at least three times by the man and forced to perform cunnilingus on the woman at the same time. Then they switched around. She had to suck the man until he climaxed in her mouth while the woman ravaged her anus with an enormous dildo. She was tied to a hook on the wall and lashed with a rope until her body was crisscrossed with raw welts. Both tormentors, but especially the woman, had chewed and bitten her breasts and nipples.

There may have been more, but her body and mind could no longer distinguish one pain, one indignity from another.

And now it was time to die. For Mr. and Mrs. Gallego, it merely meant that playtime was over; for Virginia Mochel, it was blessed relief. Gerald shouldered her battered body and lugged her outside to the van and strangled her. When they threw her body in the Sacramento River, Gallego predicted it would be carried downstream to be devoured by sharks in San Francisco Bay. Virginia Mochel's body didn't make it that far, but it vanished as if lost in the belly of the beast.

The Gallegos didn't have long to wallow in the euphoria that had kept them floating on a dreamy high for weeks after their earlier sex slayings. A few days after the Virginia Mochel murder, news hit the papers that the bodies of Karen Chipman-Twiggs and Stacey Redican had been recovered from their Limerick Canyon grave.

The news panicked the killers. They hurriedly packed their camping gear and hit the road. For the next few months, they roamed throughout the West, living in cheap motels or holing up in campgrounds.

But by October 1980, Charlene was seven months pregnant, and life on the road was getting her down, so the couple returned to Sacramento. Fearing that cops might be looking for the van, Gerald sold it and bought a 1977 Oldsmobile Cutlass that was registered in Charlene's parents' names since Gallego was a convicted felon and still wanted on the incest rap.

Saturday, November 1, 1980, was a cold, damp, and foggy night in Sacramento, a Halloween kind of night, when ghouls like the Gallegos prowled the eerily misty gloom in search of sex slaves.

Charlene, no longer the lithe and limber sexual acrobat, had pleaded with Gallego for one more sex slave run before the baby came. In truth, Charlene feared Daddy Gerald would lose interest as her pregnancy advanced. The slaves kept Charlene involved in Gerald's sex life, and the murders kept them bonded in blood. This might be their last hunt together for a while, maybe forever, and both were feverishly desperate to wallow in at least one more slave orgy to tide them over.

Maybe it was the weather that kept people off the streets, but after prowling the malls and usual teen hangouts for six hours, the Gallegos were still without a slave. Angry and more frustrated than ever, they drove through Arden Park, an upscale enclave of North Sacramento. It was about 1:00 A.M. when the couple cruised past the popular Carousel Restaurant. Surprisingly, lights still blazed and the parking lot remained crowded. Inside, members of the Sigma Phi Epsilon fraternity from California State University at

Sacramento were partying.

The Gallegos parked in the shadows to watch the tuxedoed and begowned couples drift in and out of the restaurant. After a half-hour wait, they spotted their targets: Craig Miller, twenty-two, and his twenty-one-year-old fiancee, Mary Beth Sowers. The girl, dressed in an expensive, silky blue gown, caught their attention. Small and slim with long blond hair, she looked to be in her early teens. More to the point, in the dim light, she might have passed for Gerald's daughter.

As the young man started to unlock the door of his Honda Civic, a silver-gray Oldsmobile screeched to a stop beside him, and a young woman, her pregnancy covered by a loose-fitting ski jacket, leapt out and pointed a .25 automatic at the startled pair.

The male driver leaned out, a huge, menacing .357 Magnum revolver in his hand and snarled, "Get in the fucking car." Too shocked to resist, the couple climbed in the backseat of the Olds, just as another young man, tall and built like an NFL linebacker, ran up to the car. "Hey, wait a minute," he called.

The tiny woman in the parka blocked his way. "What the fuck do you want?" she demanded.

The man pointed to the Olds. "I want to talk to Craig," he replied. "He's my frat brother."

Charlene, who had never had much use for Joe College-types, and now burning to feast on her sex slave, angrily grabbed the young man's shirtfront. "Get outta here, you cocksucker," Charlene screeched and, rearing back, punched him in the mouth. Small though she was, the blow had the power of a mule kick and knocked the big guy on his butt.

Charlene then crawled behind the wheel and, with Daddy Gerald keeping the prisoners covered, burned rubber out of the parking lot.

The fraternity man, although stunned and surprised

by the powerful punch, recovered in time to memorize the license plate—ROV 240—on the Olds as it raced off into the darkness.

The Oldsmobile sped across the American River bridge into Sacramento, and headed east on Highway 50, past foreboding Folsom Prison off in the darkness, until it reached the Bass Lake recreation area. Charlene drove through the park to an empty, grassy meadow and stopped.

"Get out," Gerald told the young man. Craig Miller pulled himself free of his sobbing girlfriend's grasp and climbed out of the car. On Gerald's order, he walked to the front of the car and stood in the glare of the headlights.

Without warning, Gallego lifted the .25 and fired three rapid shots. Craig Miller spun around and fell flat on his face, dead before he hit the ground. (The coroner's report later commented on the amazing accuracy of the shooter. All three slugs were in a tight grouping directly over Craig Miller's heart.)

The sudden fury of the attack and the thunderous gunshots in the still, foggy night ripped through Mary Beth Sowers like she'd been shot herself. "Oh God! Oh God!" she babbled hysterically and collapsed in a dead faint in a corner of the backseat.

The Gallegos drove back to Sacramento, arriving home on Bluebird Lane around 2:30 A.M. The ferocious sexual assault on the Sowers girl that followed was as savage and predatory as any that had gone before.

When the Gallegos finally had had enough, they dressed the ravished victim in the tatters of her Alice-blue-gown and loaded her into the backseat of the Olds. They caught I-80 and drove about fifteen miles to the Loomis turnoff. From there they followed a deserted county road another twenty miles into the heart of '49er gold rush country where the land was still deeply scarred by hoards of prospectors who had frantically gouged into the earth in search of riches.

Too dazed to struggle any longer, Mary Beth Sowers had slipped into an almost catatonic state, her senses shutting down to shield her mind from the violent, gut-wrenching insanity of the last few hours: her anus ripped and torn by the sodomizing Gallegos; her breasts and nipples oozing blood from the raw, open wounds left by Charlene's ferret-like teeth. Gerald dragged the limp girl from the backseat and carried her several yards to an old dredging ditch. He let her drop like a sack of rotten potatoes, jacked a live round into the chamber of the .25 automatic, and shot Mary Beth three times in the head.

(A hunter came across Miller's body the day after the murder, but Mary Beth Sowers was not found until November 22.)

An officer who worked the case later commented that "If anyone was ever in the wrong place at the wrong time, it was Craig Miller and Mary Beth Sowers." But the same could be said for Gerald and Charlene Gallego. Their judgment clouded by an uncontrollable lust that drove them over the edge of a sexual abyss, the killers made the mistake of snatching the wrong people.

Craig Miller was a senior honor student, vice president of his fraternity, and Sigma Phi Epsilon's 1979 Man of the Year. He was due to graduate in seven months and already had accepted a full partnership in one of California's leading advertising/marketing firms. Craig came from Old California stock. The mere mention of the Miller name opened doors throughout the capital city.

In short, Craig Miller was the All-American kid who

seemed to have everything—including the blond and beautiful Mary Beth Sowers, runner-up for the title of Miss Shasta County.

Mary Beth's family was also prominent, her father an eminent nuclear scientist. She and Craig made the perfect match; both intelligent, ambitious, and attractive. An honor student and a finance major, Mary Beth, like Craig, had been offered an important management position with a top financial firm following graduation.

Thus, Craig Miller and Mary Beth Sowers were nothing like the Gallegos' previous victims, all members of the underclass or overlooked segments of society. Craig and Mary Beth came from high-profile, influential families capable of marshalling the full powers of the state, inciting the press, and calling down the wrath of "decent" society on the heads of the killers.

In other words, once the slime slid over into the "nice part of town," soiling proper folks of good breeding, political pull and economic clout, Mr. and Mrs. Gallego didn't stand a chance.

The day following the abduction, cops traced the tag number supplied by Craig Miller's frat brother to Charlene's parents and went knocking on the Williamses' door. The Williamses said the car was indeed registered in their name, but admitted that their daughter and her husband were using it. As soon as the police left, the Williamses, protective as always and convinced their baby girl could do no wrong, got word to the Gallegos to beat it.

Investigators routinely ran Gallego's name through the computer, but the instant his rap sheet came back, with its astonishing record of violence, police interest in Gerald and Charlene Gallego zoomed into the red zone. They fit the descriptions of the kidnappers; they were driving the Olds used in the abduction; and when cops rushed to search the little house on Bluebird Lane they uncovered the disgusting hoard of S&M gear, plus a small arsenal: .357 Magnum revolver, .25 automatic pistol, and an AR15 assault rifle with a loaded, twenty-round clip.

An APB was issued for the Gallegos warning that they should be considered armed and extremely dangerous. And since it was likely the couple had high-tailed it out of California, the FBI was called in to declare the Gallegos as federal fugitives in unlawful flight to avoid prosecution.

Meanwhile, the Williamses hired a lawyer and refused to talk to the cops anymore.

But over the next several days, the Williamses received several telephone calls from Charlene that the FBI apparently monitored through court-authorized wiretaps. They learned that Gerald and Charlene had abandoned the Olds in the parking lot of a Reno casino and grabbed a bus for Salt Lake City, where some money from Charlene's family awaited them at Western Union. From there, they took another bus to Omaha, with Dallas as the ultimate destination where, Gallego was convinced, distant relatives would provide a hideout.

On Sunday morning, November 16, the Williamses left home and, apparently oblivious to the FBI car on their tail, drove all the way across the Sierra Nevadas to Sparks, Nevada. After a brief visit to the Western Union office there, the couple drove back to Sacramento.

When FBI agents flashed their badges, they were told that $500 had been wired to Charlene Williams in care of the Western Union office in Omaha. The Special Agent in charge in Omaha was alerted and plans made to pounce on the fugitives when they showed up to collect the funds.

Monday morning, Charlene Gallego sauntered into the Western Union office on Dodge Street, identified herself and asked for her money. She barely noticed the scruffy looking cowboy until he turned and said, "FBI, Charlene. You're under arrest."

Charlene's eyes rolled back in her head, and she fainted to the floor.

Loitering outside, Gerald Gallego's street-smart antenna started vibrating wildly when he noticed the two plain sedans moving slowly toward him from either end of the block. He eased toward an alley, but before he could make his break, the cars sped up, jumped the curb, and trapped Gerald between them. Six shotgun- and pistol-toting agents leapt out. When they shouted, "Get on the ground, asshole!" Gerald Armond Gallego hit the pavement like a ton of bricks.

In court later that day, the U.S. Attorney asked that the couple be held on bonds of $1 million each. The judge lowered that to $100,000, and, while federal marshals dragged them off to separate cells, the lovebirds blew kisses to one another from across the courtroom.

Back in California, the pressure was applied to Charlene to give up Daddy Gerald in exchange for a lighter sentence. She hung tough for a year and a half until shortly before the first trial when it finally dawned on her that the state had reserved a seat for her in the gas chamber at San Quentin. Charlene told her attorneys to cut the deal. For her statement outlining all the sex slave killings, and for testifying against Daddy Gerald, Charlene was handed a flat sentence of sixteen years and eight months without parole.

As expected, Gerald Gallego was outraged over Charlene's sweetheart deal. But he wasn't the only one.

Mary Beth Sowers's grieving and outraged father wrote to the judge who approved the plea bargain: "With a sentence of sixteen years, justice has not been served for her admitted part in the murders, which were so heinous, atrocious, cruel, and which manifested exceptional depravity. Her sentence is menial and grossly unfair to the victims."

Nevertheless, the deal was done, and in November 1982, Gerald Armond Gallego went on trial for killing Craig Miller and Mary Beth Sowers with an arrogant Gerald Armond Gallego acting as his own attorney.

His face-to-face confrontation with Charlene on the stand and her testimony describing the cold-blooded shooting of Craig Miller and the sexual torture and death of Mary Beth Sowers was the centerpiece of the four-month-long trial.

However, one crucial witness, fearful of facing Gallego in person, did not appear. Instead, the judge entered into the record a statement given to the prosecution by Gerald Gallego's teenage daughter. According to the judge reading from the affidavit:

"Her father's sexual molestation has left her with ambivalent feelings toward him. At times she hates her father, at times she loves him. . . . He told her that it was natural for her to allow him to commit sexual acts with her. She would protest the sexual contacts sometimes, but would usually oblige. The assaults were committed periodically, sometimes with force, from the time she was six until she was fourteen. Those acts were intercourse, oral copulation, and sodomy. Her father celebrated his thirty-third birthday by committing sodomy and other sexual acts upon her and a minor girlfriend. On occasion, Charlene Gallego was present in the same apartment when she was being abused. The sexual attacks stopped only when the witness reported them to the Butte County authorities, and formal charges were filed against Gerald Gallego on September 25, 1978."

The trial ended on June 22, 1983, with prosecutor James Morris telling the jury: "Gallego's acts are the most monstrous of crimes. The people have had enough of Gerald Armond Gallego. If anyone ever deserved to be executed, it's Gallego."

The jury, reflecting the sentiments of most of the people of California, agreed. It took them only fourteen hours to reach a verdict: guilty of murder in the first degree with the penalty fixed at death.

In explaining why he was following the jury's recommendation and sentencing Gallego to die in the gas chamber, the judge read a probation officer's report that stated: "Gerald Armond Gallego's deviance is so thoroughly ingrained, and of such long standing, that it would be utter foolishness, at best, and probably criminal, to even suggest that Gallego be released to society again. Gerald Armond Gallego is a veritable monster, cunning and devious, virtually devoid of all feelings and emotions such as empathy and compassion, and he is not fit to live in a free society.

"He has committed one of the most monstrous series of crimes that can be imagined. And his victims are forever dead because they were available when Gerald Armond Gallego felt the urge to act out his aberrant fantasies."

Now it was Nevada's turn to try Gallego for the kidnap slayings of Stacey Redican and Karen Chipman-Twiggs. To secure Charlene's testimony, Pershing County District Attorney Richard Wagner agreed to the same plea bargain her attorneys had hammered out in California.

He also worried aloud over the capacity of his sparsely populated county to pay for such a lengthy and expensive trial. Wagner's concerns reached the desk of *Sacramento Bee* columnist Stan Gilliam who wrote a piece suggesting that people who hoped to see justice done send $1 to Wagner in Lovelock, Nevada, to help pay for the cost of the trial.

The results were unprecedented. Stories of the Gallegos' astonishing depravities provoked a massive public wrath unseen since the days of vigilante, lynch-mob justice in the Old West. Thousands chipped in to support the grass roots "Hang the Bastards" campaign. Contributions eventually totaling nearly $40,000 poured in from across the country.

On May 24, 1984, Charlene again took the stand in Lovelock and described in mind-numbing detail how she and Gerald had kidnapped, tortured, and then murdered the two seventeen-year-old girls, taken as slaves to fulfill their sexual fantasy.

The jury demonstrated Nevada's reputation for swift justice by remaining out less than four hours before returning with a guilty verdict. The jury strongly recommended that Gerald Armond Gallego be executed posthaste.

But more than a decade has passed and Gerald Gallego continues to dodge both the lethal injection needle in Nevada and the gas chamber in California. In 1989, he was one of the first cons moved into the state's new maximum security prison in Ely, Nevada, where he continues to fire off appeal after appeal.

As of summer 1993, the case was headed back to the federal courts for yet another endless round of appeals. Kevin Higgins, the senior deputy attorney general handling the state's responses to Gallego's many appeals, sighed and said: "It's been more than ten years, but I'm afraid we still have a long way to go before the sentence of the court is carried out.

"The people of Nevada want to see the end of the Gallegos. They were probably the nastiest killers we ever had to prosecute," he added.

On January 17, 1981, Gerald Armond Gallego, Jr., was born in a hospital prison ward. When he was old enough, the infant was turned over to his maternal grandmother. The boy will be seventeen years old when Charlene flattens her sentence and goes free in late 1997. With her parents' wealth to support her, Charlene likely will start a comfortable new life at age forty-one.

After all the bodies were reburied in hallowed ground, after all the sentences pronounced, and after the psychologists and criminologists were done chewing over the sex slave case, the haunting question still hung in the air like the stench of decaying flesh: *Why?* Why did the horror happen in the first place?

Charlene Adelle Williams Gallego probably provided the only answer that made any sense out of the insanity when she shrugged and told an interviewer: "Well, see, we had this sexual fantasy and we just did it because it was so easy."

EIGHT
THE JOHNSTONS: ALL IN THE FAMILY

They were just kids, but they knew they were in love, passionately on fire with their sexual discovery of each other and planning to get married as soon as she turned sixteen in three more months.

They also knew they were in mortal danger.

But they had risked everything to be together and not even threats nor the ominous specter of murder hanging over them like a fog in the valley could keep them apart.

Bruce Johnston, Jr., and fifteen-year-old Robin Miller had met in February, only six months earlier. Bruce had just turned twenty-one when Robin came into his life, but folks who knew the unwanted, unloved high school dropout often remarked that "Little Bruce," as he was called, with his shoulder-length, dark, wavy hair, seemed even more like a kid than Robin.

Already the young couple had survived enough ups and downs to last most people a lifetime. Through it all, their devotion to each other and their determination to be together had grown so strong that Robin's mom had not only dropped her opposition to their dating but had actually allowed them to share a bedroom of the Miller's white, two-story farmhouse on the outskirts of Oxford.

That's where Bruce, Jr., and Robin were this muggy August 30 night, early morning actually, since it was 12:30 A.M. when Bruce turned the yellow Volkswagen Rabbit off the farm road and into the Millers' gravel driveway. The couple had spent the day at an amusement park in Hershey. They'd stayed till dark before starting for home. It was a long drive of more than one hundred miles through the rolling, Southeastern Pennsylvania farm country, and, worn out from the day at the park and the trauma of the last few weeks, Robin slept most of the way while Bruce drove. Alone with his thoughts, Bruce pondered the predicament he was in, the kind of trouble few young men his age are asked to endure, but something that a borderline career criminal who's trying to go straight had come to expect.

Bruce pulled into the driveway, turned off the engine, and gently shook Robin's shoulder. "We're home," he whispered. Although it was late, Bruce anticipated climbing into bed with Robin. With Labor Day just around the corner, Robin's mother, Linda Miller, and Robin's sixteen-year old brother had gone to Virginia to visit relatives. Robin's sister Roxanne was staying with her grandparents in Oxford. Bruce, Jr., and Robin had the big, comfortable farmhouse all to themselves. Just like an old married couple, he grinned to himself.

As Robin sat up and stretched, Bruce studied the girl he loved in the dim light of a half-moon. Weighing barely one hundred pounds, the bouncy, happy-go-lucky Robin was one of the most popular kids around the East Nottingham Township; although with a single mother working nights, she had matured quickly inside while the outside remained gamine. Everybody who knew Robin loved her, recalled a family friend in the awful days to follow. "She was just the happiest little kid there ever was. She was up all the time and made you feel better," cried the acquaintance.

But that August night all of Robin's happy days had come to an end. She reached for her purse in the backseat of the Rabbit. "I've got to feed the cats," she told Bruce.

They were her last words.

The two hulking shadows came out of the darkness at the side of the house. For four nights they'd stalked the young couple, waiting for the right moment to strike. Now, with no one else at home in the Miller house, the moment had come. One ran to Robin's side of the car, the other jerked open the driver's door. Without a word, both men opened fire on the startled lovers.

Flashes from the two .38-caliber pistols lit up the night. Thundering echoes of gunfire rolled over the hilly barley- and corn fields, while the little yellow car shook from the impact of bullets as though raked by a summer hailstorm.

Stunned by the slugs ripping into his body, Bruce, Jr., pushed the screaming girl from the car. "Run!" he yelled. "Get in the house!"

In seconds the brutal attack was all over. The gunmen melted back into the shadows, leaving behind a ghastly scene of murder and mutilation.

Somehow, Bruce and Robin stumbled to the farmhouse. Bruce grabbed the phone and called police, screaming, "Robin's been shot! They're still shooting!" Robin staggered up the stairs and collapsed. Bruce followed and found Robin clutching at Louise Miller's bed as though seeking the safety and comfort of a mother's sheltering arms.

Robin could only gurgle. She was suffocating in her own blood. Desperately wounded himself, Bruce gathered the small body in his arms and tried mouth-to-mouth resuscitation.

It was nearly thirty minutes before help arrived. Cops found Little Bruce holding Robin in his arms, both soaked in blood from the terrible wounds. She was dead from two gunshot wounds to the head. One bullet had smashed into her left cheek, turning the pretty, pixie face into a gory mess. As rescuers pried Robin's body from his arms, Little Bruce cried. "It's my fault! If it weren't for me, she wouldn't have gotten killed."

Nine .38-caliber slugs had shattered Bruce's body. He'd been hit behind his right ear and the back of his head. A third bullet creased the back of his neck. Other slugs exploded through his right shoulder, right arm, and right elbow. Surgeons spent hours digging bullets out of his back near the shoulder blade, his chest, and his stomach.

Doctors worked desperately to patch up the boy's appalling wounds, but no one expected him to live through the night. "I saw him lying on a hospital table an hour after we brought him in," recalled one cop. "It looked like they were doing an autopsy. I never saw so much blood or anyone who looked so dead."

Incredibly, none of the wounds proved fatal. Even with the massive loss of blood, Bruce, Jr., battled to stay alive to tell investigators all he could remember.

The ambush unfolded so quickly that Bruce, Jr., hadn't gotten a clear look at the killers' faces. But even in the darkness and in the midst of all that terror, he still recognized them. One was Uncle Norman. The other was Uncle Dave. Norman and David Johnston, the brothers-in-crime of gang leader Bruce Johnston, Sr. In an act of unthinkable brutality, Bruce, Sr., had put a $15,000 price tag on Little Bruce's life and then sent his brothers to murder his own son; if they got Robin Miller in the process, so much the better. Little Bruce was already talking to the cops, and Robin knew too much.

They deserved to die. But one good treachery deserves another. Bruce, Jr., beat the odds and lived to avenge Robin's murder in the only way he could – by putting his father and uncles behind bars for life.

Blood other than that of Robin Miller also stained the hands of the murderous Johnstons. This family of killers had more deaths to answer for.

Months later, New Year's celebrants who even bothered to pick up the January 1, 1979, edition of the *New York Times* probably skipped over the one-paragraph item buried on page six that carried a Chadds Ford, Pennsylvania, dateline:

> Three bodies were found in a grave in a farm area here last night and authorities said the discovery could be linked to an interstate burglary ring. The discovery brings to five the number of bodies found in the investigation of the ring, which operated for 10 years in Maryland, Delaware and Southeastern Pennsylvania. Chester County District Attorney William Lamb said that it was not known at the moment how the three died.

Except for the bullets in the head and the putrefying flesh from too long spent in a hole in the ground, albeit historic ground, the trio of long-hairs looked as if they had just come from a rock concert.

Even as the three victims were being pulled from the frozen ground of Chadds Ford, Lamb already knew that these murders and the ambush of Robin Miller and Bruce Johnston, Jr., were all part of the same horrifying package that included family betrayal, family vengeance, and family murder.

Along with the bodies, investigators unearthed a spine-chilling, Gothic tale of greed and of a family motivated to murder to protect its unique criminal enterprise that for years rode roughshod over the rural countryside of Pennsylvania, Maryland, and Delaware.

Lamb branded the Johnstons a "family of crime."

"We weren't dealing with a regular family," Lamb emphasized. "This wasn't a family of love. This was a family of crime!"

In the end, the Johnston family fell because greed drove it to kill its own. And its own rebelled.

For more than a decade, the Johnston family was one among many criminal organizations congregating in the Philadelphia-Southeastern Pennsylvania area, each with its own little empire. Angelo Bruno (and later "Little Nicki" Scarfo after Scarfo whacked Bruno) was occupied with hijacking and labor racketeering. The Gambinos stayed put in Manhattan, but their control over gambling and the heroin traffic reached deep into rural Pennsylvania. Bloodthirsty posses moving in from Jamaica were seizing control of the coke trade and about to pollute the countryside with the new and destructive crack. Black pimps ran prostitutes and pot out of their plush North Philly town houses.

And down in bucolic Chester County, the Bruce Johnston, Sr., family monopolized the hot farm machinery market.

Farm machinery. Hardly the sexy patina of drugs and whores and high rollers, but, for a generation, the traffic in tractors was just as highly organized, just as profitable, and a damn sight safer than all those other big-city rackets.

Despite their city slicker-country boy differences, the Bruce Johnstons and the Nick Scarfos shared a trait that bonded them together in a bloody brotherhood: They all murdered, quickly and viciously, to protect their turfs and expand their empires. But Bruce Johnston went them all a step better. When need be, he killed his own flesh and blood . . . mercilessly and without remorse.

Perched as it is right atop the Mason-Dixon line, Chester County has always drawn the rootless out of Appalachian hills and hollows to work its fields and factories. The Johnstons arrived on this northern migration and the cops who chased the family for years often referred to them as "Tennessee ridge runners" or, more to the point, "those fucking hillbillies." In other times and places, the Johnstons would have been branded "poor white trash." Cultural stereotypes, true, but in the case of the Johnstons they fit. The men shared similar physical traits: long, lanky bodies; protruding noses that spread out at the end to overhang recessed mouths that made them look like they'd left their false choppers soaking at home. The Johnstons were Southern hill people, the prototype *Deliverance* characters.

The importance of the family, the survival of the family, the defense of the family against outsiders—all were lessons drilled into both Louise Price and Passemore Johnston, who traced their roots to the Appalachian mountain culture of Northwest North Carolina and Tennessee.

When she was twenty years old, with two toddlers from a first broken marriage, Louise Price married Passemore Johnston. They settled near Marlboro, Pennsylvania, went to work as tenant farmers, and had more kids. Bruce, born in 1939, was one of nine brothers and half brothers who grew up dirt-poor in the rolling Pennsylvania hills.

After Passemore died, Louise took over the solo job of raising the brood of rough, rowdy boys, most of whom dropped out of school and drifted into petty crime while still in their early teens. Although no more than five-feet tall, and weighing barely one hundred pounds, Louise Johnston was the iron-fisted ruler of the clan. She demanded that the family stick together no matter what. Mother Johnston's word was law and even after some of her boys had matured into vicious killers, who bowed to no man, they still bowed to the tiny woman and stole to keep her in comfort.

This family-first mentality that the Johnstons inherited from the backwoods of Tennessee and the Carolinas—an "us-versus-them" bunker mentality—adapted very well when they settled among the horsey, snobbish, old-line blue bloods of Chester County, Pennsylvania.

Chester County, just west of Philadelphia, borders both Maryland and Delaware, with Wilmington just a few miles across the state line. It's a county of contrasts: one rich in history, art, wealth, and privileges; it's sober, piously simple Amish country; extravagant, imperious horse country, where the landed gentry ride to the hounds, raise thoroughbreds, and preserve their pedigrees that date to Colonial times.

More than anything, however, Chester County is prosperous, fruitful farm country. The Johnstons made their headquarters in Kennett Square, the center of the county's mushroom-growing industry, where they found that fleecing their affluent neighbors was vastly more profitable than plucking mushrooms. Here they set about carving a vicious new criminal empire out of staid, old-line Chester County, an empire they controlled through threats, intimidation, and, finally, murder.

Louise Johnston was the matriarch of the clan, but Bruce, Sr., called the shots when it came to the family's criminal activities. "You just knew it would be your ass if you ever crossed Bruce," recalled a former Johnston associate. "He'd look at you with those mean eyes and say, 'Don't ever try to fuck me,' and you'd know he meant it."

Bruce followed up a record as a juvenile offender with a couple of stretches in state prisons during the 1960s. By the time he hit the streets again, Bruce Johnston was a hardened criminal who had learned his lesson: Don't get caught. He vowed never to return to prison, even if it meant killing anyone who tried to put him there.

For a decade, Bruce, Sr., and the family Johnston prospered. Brothers David and Norman learned the business, and together the brothers solidified a tight circle of thieves, all recruited for their loyalty to the Johnstons and for their allegiance to the criminal code that made ratting to the cops an offense worthy of death. Utilizing the contacts he'd made in prison, Bruce, Sr., also carefully cultivated an alliance with fences throughout the tri-state area and consolidated a criminal intelligence network that became the backbone of the gang's operation.

Initially, the Johnstons and their handpicked associates concentrated on stealing Corvettes to feed a rapacious black market for the high-ticket, sporty cars. However, since there was a limited supply of Corvettes in Chester County, expansion was necessary.

When the Johnstons studied Chester County's other potentials, they noticed that everywhere sat expensive, unguarded, hard-to-trace and easy-to-peddle farm machinery, tractors, trucks, and heavy construction equipment. The tractors, hay balers, and other farm implements represented an enormous untapped reservoir for innovative criminal entrepreneurs such as the Johnston family.

The Johnstons also developed an interest in the treasured American antiques that the Brandywine Valley was famous for. The market in stolen antiques proved to be exceptional, particularly for skilled, ballsy burglars with the connections to peddle the goods quietly through an efficient network of fences and unethical middle-men antique dealers who didn't ask questions.

During the 1970s, cops say, the Johnston gang stole millions in machinery, antiques, vehicles, guns, and sporting goods. They drove expensive, customized cars and, in what became the signature of the Johnston family, flashed wads of $100 bills. For Bruce Johnston, Sr., and his brothers, the $100 bill became a symbol of their power to corrupt and a sure fix for any problem.

The Johnstons happily stole anything, but became known for their skill at ripping off farm tractors, hay balers, even bulldozers and other heavy construction equipment: the kind of loot most thieves never touched, and thus was seldom locked up. The Johnstons exploited that lack of security for years. They skipped across the countryside, pulling farm thefts and burglaries over a wide area so that no single police jurisdiction would latch onto their trail.

For obvious reasons, the Johnstons worked night hours. When they set out on a job, the Johnstons assigned gang members equipped with walkie-talkies to man key intersections a safe distance from the burglary site to warn them of approaching cars. Two or three men would then creep in before dawn, slip a tractor into neutral, and roll it silently toward the road. Meanwhile, other gang members circled the area in a (usually stolen) transport truck. When the tractor thieves were ready to load up, they tossed weeds onto the highway as a signal to the circling transport. The next time around, the truck stopped; the tractor was quickly loaded and disappeared into the night with hardly a sound . . . and nary a trace.

At times, the stolen tractors were used to tow larger equipment such as combines or balers out to the pickup site. If the target was construction equipment, the boys would hot-wire the engine and drive it away; sometimes to a waiting truck, other times parked in a confederate's barn until the coast was clear to move it out of state.

Cops and the feds discovered, to their amazement, that fencing such massive, unwieldy implements was hardly more complicated than disposing of automobiles. A thriving underground market existed for purloined tractors that was just as efficient as the nationwide stolen car network.

"And," added an FBI agent, "the markup is huge."

If they were looting a warehouse or store, the gang often stole large, eighteen-wheelers to haul off the booty. That way, they could simply walk away without a loss if interrupted by cops.

Boldness was one reason for the family's success. But the real key to the Johnstons' success was the business-like intelligence system Bruce, Sr., carefully fostered, and that often was more efficient than the police, who were fragmented into a dozen small, understaffed, and uncoordinated jurisdictions.

The system kept the Johnstons posted on police activity anywhere in the County. Courthouse workers passed on copies of such bothersome documents as arrest and search warrants; tipsters phoned to let them know when Farmer Jones over by Nottingham or Mr. Smith up around Pottstown had some new machinery. Although the Johnstons themselves weren't farmers, they knew the importance of good fertilizer spread around in the right places. The bag of $100 bills the Johnstons lugged around with them nurtured fields of friends and bought lots of silence. When that didn't work, there was always intimidation to fall back on: hints of a midnight barn burning, some poisoned livestock, maybe a sudden attack by pipe-toting head-thumpers some dark night when the farmer stepped outside to hush his dog howling at the moon.

A Chadds Ford mechanic, who often worked on the family's constantly changing roster of expensive cars and trucks, once remarked, "Sure, we know all them boys. None of 'em are too healthy for work.

"But," he grinned, "they always had them $100 bills to pass around."

Occasionally, when there were arrests, Louise Johnston showed up with a satchel full of the ubiquitous $100 bills to bail out the boys before the ink was dry on the police blotter. Indictments usually were quashed on technicalities cited by the Johnstons' high-priced lawyers. Investigative blunders also helped the Johnstons and their henchmen escape convictions; many cases against the Johnstons fell apart due to foolish technical errors or tainted evidence. The closemouthed ways of residents and a mistrust of outsiders, especially anyone wearing a badge, also worked to the Johnstons' advantage. "Around here," explained Lamb, "when people have a problem they prefer to settle it themselves."

And the brothers paid special attention to any associates who might be tempted to talk. Snitches, they repeatedly warned, would die.

The Johnstons became so arrogant that they delighted in rubbing the frustrated cops' noses in their failures. During one trial, for instance, before the case was thrown out of court on a technicality, investigators testified about the mileage shown on the odometer of a stolen U-Haul truck the gang allegedly used to carry off a load of food looted from a supermarket warehouse.

From then on, when police recovered vehicles believed used in Johnston operations, the odometers were torn from the dash.

"It was pretty obvious they were sending us a message," one chagrined cop commented.

The more embarrassed the cops became, the harder they worked at "getting" the Johnstons. The constant scrutiny got under their skin. Sometimes, Bruce, Sr., complained, he couldn't even take a piss without some asshole cop following him into the john, trying to get a peek at his pecker.

"Big Bruce" insisted he was innocent, but that the police were out to get him as part of a vendetta that started with a double cop killing in 1972.

There was a cold drizzle falling the night of November 15, 1972, when two of Kennett Square's eight-man police force parked their patrol car in front of police headquarters sometime after midnight. An hour later, when Officers William W. Davis, twenty-seven, and Richard J. Posey, thirty-eight, had failed to respond to the police dispatcher, state troopers were sent to search the borough for the missing men.

Troopers found the borough patrol car with the motor still running and the light on. The driver's window was shattered. The bodies of the two officers were on the ground beside the car. It appeared that a sniper, armed with a high-powered rifle, had picked off Davis with a single shot to the stomach as he stepped from the car. Davis may have sensed he was under attack. His unholstered and unfired revolver was on the pavement beside him.

Investigators piecing together the crime scene theorized that after Davis was hit, Posey rushed around from the passenger's side to aid his brother officer, was shot in the chest, and collapsed on top of Davis's body.

"They never had a chance," growled an angry and anguished trooper. "The son of a bitch stood out there in the dark and picked them off like ducks in a pond."

The ambush slaying of two cops in a quiet country town where murder, much less cop killings, was almost unheard of, shocked and alarmed the nation. If it could happen in sleepy, peaceful little Kennett Square, it could happen anywhere.

Early in the investigation, an anonymous tip pointed to Ancell Eugene Hamm, then twenty-eight, and high on the local cops' list of known burglars and thieves. A few months earlier, Hamm and Davis had punched it out when the officer went to arrest Hamm on a larceny charge. A search warrant of Hamm's home turned up a huge cache of weapons, including an illegal machine gun. The big break in the case came when searchers found a Belgian-made rifle in the woods not far from the ambush site. The rifle had been smashed against a tree to foil ballistics tests. A crude attempt had been made to alter the serial number, but investigators were still able to trace it back to Hamm.

In 1974, Hamm was convicted of the double slaying and went to prison for life.

The odious residue of the ambush murders lingered over Kennett Square and Chester County for years. Cops who worked on the investigation, all friends of the slain officers, were never totally satisfied with the outcome. "There was always a feeling," recalled one county detective, "that we never got all the shooters. Someone else was working with Hamm and got away with murder."

That someone, many angry cops speculated, was Bruce Johnston, Sr. Investigators fingered Hamm as the Johnston gang's safe blower, and Big Bruce even appeared at Hamm's murder trial as a character witness. The killings, officers suspected, were in retaliation for police harassment of the gang and a warning to lay off.

[A thirst for vengeance was why the cops were always on his ass, always trying to frame him, Bruce protested.] With no solid evidence to link them to the murders, however, the Johnstons went about plundering the County while police ground their teeth in frustration.

By the late 1970s, the Johnstons were the "Untouchables" of Chester County, operating with impunity and growing bolder by the day. Despite no "visible means of support," the Johnstons and their associates wheeled about the county in fancy Corvettes, Lincolns, Thunderbirds, and the most expensive pickup trucks money could buy. Their pockets bulged with rolls of $100 bills, big enough to choke a whole team of Clydesdales.

However, authorities had no idea just how lucrative the stolen tractor racket was until FBI agent Dave Richter traced some stolen farm implements across the state line into Maryland that were peddled through Baltimore-based fences with nationwide contacts. Richter, assigned to the FBI office in Newton Square, was well acquainted with the Johnston family. They were prime suspects in a $500,000 antiques theft Richter was investigating.

Curious, the agent ordered a computer check of all the tractors reported stolen in Pennsylvania, Maryland, and Delaware over the previous five years. Richter also requested a comparison of tractor thefts in the other forty-seven states. The results were a shocker. More tractors had been stolen in those three states, the home turf of the Johnston family, *than in all the other states combined!*

A handful of dedicated cops studied Richter's stunning data and decided that finally, come hell or high water, it was time to bring the Johnstons down. FBI agents, Pennsylvania troopers, and cops from Chester County and local municipalities formed a multiagency task force to target the family and hopefully catch them in the act of hauling off some farm machinery. In the past, there were plenty of witnesses to the brazen thefts, but fear of the Johnstons (and the $100 bills spread around the neighborhood) shielded the family with a conspiracy of silence. However, if the witnesses were cops, the family's usual intimidation tactics wouldn't work.

The task force turned up the heat on the Johnstons through constant, unnerving surveillance and fierce pressure on associates to inform on the gang's activities. Developing snitches, the cops believed, might be the only way to drive a wedge into the fortress-like walls the family had erected around Chester County.

It was a good idea, but unfortunately in the case of Gary Wayne Crouch it badly underestimated the Johnstons' power to terrorize and the intelligence network that kept the family a couple of jumps ahead of the cops. What happened to Gary Wayne Crouch explained precisely why insiders rarely ratted on the Johnston gang.

Crouch, thirty-one, was just another run-of-the-mill thief with a long record as an inept burglar, but with a reputation as an expert car thief. It was a talent Big Bruce valued enough to overlook Crouch's other shortcomings, not the least of which was his tendency to talk too much. For the xenophobic Johnstons, admitting the questionable outsider was totally out of character. It was a mistake they'd come to regret.

Crouch was a weak link that was already disintegrating when he joined the Johnstons. The task force cops knew that Crouch had a hard time doing hard time. Faced with the choice of jail or talking, Crouch was liable to jabber like a jaybird—which is what he did the first time the cops put the screws to him.

Overnight, Bruce, Sr., got word through his spy system that Crouch was talking to the wrong people.

In July, gang member Leslie Dale joined Bruce, Sr., at the Wooden Shoe Inn, one of the group's hangouts in Kennett Square. "Crouch's gotta go," Bruce growled. "The fucking son of a bitch's been talking to Delaware cops about some cars we got over there." Bruce reached into his pocket, pulled out the ever-present roll of $100, and began counting them off. When he reached $3,000, he pushed the pile of crisp bills across the table to Dale. "This is yours. You're coming with me."

Together, they drove to an isolated spot along one of the many dirt roads meandering through western Chester County. Johnston grabbed two shovels out of the bed of his pickup, tossed one to Dale, and pointed to a clump of woods a few yards off the road. "Dig," he said.

The next evening, July 17, 1977, Leslie Dale phoned Crouch on the pretext that he was needed to help with a burglary over in Stottsville. Crouch left his girlfriend's house across the state line in Delaware, met Bruce, Sr., and Dale at the Wooden Shoe, and the trio set off for Stottsville. Along the way, they veered off onto the dirt road leading to the grave site.

Dale later claimed he was at the wheel of the stolen car. Crouch, unaware he was being driven to his death, sat beside him in the front seat, chatting away about the upcoming burglary and how he intended to spend his share of the loot.

Bruce, Sr., rode alone in the backseat, silently caressing the .38 Special in his jacket pocket. As the trio turned off the paved highway, Johnston leaned forward, pressed the barrel of the gun to the back of Crouch's head, and pulled the trigger.

The bullet exploded through Crouch's skull, took out one of his eyes, and shattered the car windshield.

"Goddamn!" Bruce shouted. "Look at the hole in the windshield!"

Crouch slumped against the dashboard, blood spurting from the hole in his head like a garden hose leak.

Dale skidded the car into the ditch, leapt out, and jerked open the passenger's door. He and Bruce pulled Crouch to the ground. "The blood!" chortled Johnston, dancing around the pool of red rapidly puddling in the dirt road. "Look at all that fucking blood!"

"Come on," Dale urged. "Let's get rid of him."

The pair dragged Crouch into the patch of woods. "We just chucked him into the grave and covered him up and that was that," Dale related.

Not quite. First, the killers rifled their victim's pockets and found $80 that Johnston gave Dale as a bonus.

More than a year later, after Leslie Dale had flipped on the Johnstons and led cops to the grave, an autopsy was performed on what remained of Gary Wayne Crouch. Enough remained that Dr. Halbert Fillinger, an assistant medical examiner from Philadelphia, found dirt in Crouch's lungs. Incredible as it seemed, the shot to the head hadn't killed Crouch outright. He was still alive when the killers "chucked" him in the hole and shoveled dirt over him. "He was breathing for at least a few minutes, maybe a few hours, after being placed in the grave," said Fillinger. "They buried him alive."

Not that it much mattered to the Johnstons how Crouch died as long as he was no longer a threat as an informant. As far as Bruce, Sr., was concerned, it was all a big joke. When one gang member asked where Gary Crouch was, Bruce grinned and replied, "I gave him a new job. Pushing up daisies."

But disposing of the troublesome Crouch didn't stop the once impenetrable Johnston operation from continuing to unravel.

Coincidentally, about the same time the police task force stepped up pressure on the gang, the next generation of Johnstons was coming of age and eager to follow Big Bruce down the road to easy money. These younger family members were not yet con-hardened thugs like their fathers and uncles who lived by the underworld law that "if you rat, you die." The street-smart cops instantly spotted the weakness and began to exploit the immaturity of the Johnstons' "kiddie gang," as it came to be known.

In September of 1957, when eighteen-year old Bruce Johnston married Jennie Steffy, a waitress he'd met in an Avondale diner the year before, she was only fifteen-years old and four months pregnant. The son that was born five months later in February 1958 was named Bruce Alfred Johnston, Jr. Ever after, father and son were Big Bruce and Little Bruce to the rest of the family.

Before Little Bruce was a year old, Big Bruce was back in the slammer on several larceny charges. Johnston pleaded the hardship of a new young family, and a sympathetic judge let him out on probation. A few months later, Bruce, Sr., was arrested again, but there were no more second chances, and he was off to do time in a state prison. While Big Bruce was locked up, Jennie got pregnant again. Her second son was born in February 1960. She called him James and although Bruce, Sr., wasn't his real father, Jennie gave the infant Johnston's surname. Growing up, Jimmy was allowed to call Bruce, Sr., "Dad." But Big Bruce was never the daddying type, not even with his own flesh and blood, so until they were in their teens neither boy had much contact with Bruce, Sr., although both worshiped him from afar. While Jennie supported herself working in the mushroom canneries, Little Bruce was raised mainly by his maternal grandmother, Harriet Steffy; Jimmy grew up with Jennie's aunt, Sarah Martin.

Following in the Johnston family tradition, Little Bruce dropped out of school when he was fifteen, and before he was nineteen had a hefty criminal record all his own: theft, receipt of stolen property, criminal conspiracy. Like his dad, Little Bruce loved fast cars. He also developed a raging appetite for pot, LSD, speed, Quaaludes, angel dust, and just about any other chemical he could swallow or snort.

Jimmy Johnston also left school and bunked in a cramped mobile home with his great-aunt Sarah. The half brothers hung out together, getting high, and scheming how to scrounge more drugs. Both were typical drug-addled dropouts with no future, and fewer prospects, when Bruce, Sr., suddenly started taking an interest in the pair. The boys were thrilled with the unexpected attention.

"When Big Bruce came around there wasn't much I could do," Jennie Johnston shrugged. "Little Bruce just idolized him, you know, with his big money and his big cars."

Sarah Martin also complained that she had no more control over Jimmy Johnston. "Jimmy thought Big Bruce hung the moon. You'd have thought he was his real daddy," she said. "I didn't like it when Jimmy started running around with him, but that's what Jimmy wanted and I couldn't stop him."

Little Bruce and Jimmy had been weaned on the outrageous tales of the Johnstons' legendary exploits in Chester County. Among their boyhood pals, they basked in the reflected glory of the Johnston name. Naturally, both boys yearned to follow in Big Bruce's footsteps. Within a year, they were deeply involved in the gang's activities. Early on, while he was still learning the ropes, Bruce, Jr., took a load of bird shot in the face and neck when a farmer caught him trying to steal a tractor. To prove his mettle to his old man, Little Bruce refused treatment for his wounds. He gritted his teeth and used a razor blade and tweezers to pick the bird shot out himself.

Big Bruce promised to pay the boys $150 for each tractor they swiped, a pittance compared to what he resold them for, but a fortune for a couple of teenage dropouts. Little Bruce also recruited a couple of pot-smoking buddies, the Sampson brothers, James and Wayne, who'd been uprooted from their Havre de Grace, Maryland, home a few years earlier when their alcoholic father keeled over and died. Jimmy Johnston brought along another boyhood chum from a broken home, eighteen-year-old Duane Lincoln.

It never dawned on the boys that Bruce, Sr., might have an ulterior motive for cozing up to the sons he hardly knew and cared less about. The fresh blood and young legs, he reasoned, were perfect for working a new scam he'd been eyeing for a long time: the potentially rich market in small garden tractors. The riding lawn mower/tractors were a fixture at nearly every farm or semirural residence throughout Chester County—hundreds of them sat around unattended. In Big Bruce's larcenous eyes, they all wore big Day-Glo signs screaming, "Steal Me!"

So while the older gang members continued to concentrate on the large farm machinery and other big-ticket items, the youngsters went to work stealing garden tractors. Before long, they were hauling off tractors like apples at harvest time. Even the most honest citizens of Chester County, it seemed, harbored a streak of larceny when offered nearly new tractors at ridiculously low prices. The customers lined up in droves; no questions asked, none needed.

Fifty-nine tractors were stolen in the Avondale area alone in a matter of weeks and moved swiftly through the Johnstons' efficient stolen property pipeline.

As the number of small tractor thefts mounted, the task force decided to focus on this new wrinkle. They figured, rightly so, that the Johnstons were branching out. Concentrating on this fresh trail might lead back to the source. Cops started watching a couple of known fences in the area. If they could catch the fences holding the stolen tractors, maybe they could pressure them to flip against the Johnstons in exchange for lighter sentences.

It worked. Within a month, they'd recovered thirty stolen tractors. During October and November, the state trooper compounds at Lancaster overflowed with another 120 garden tractors.

In February 1978, after a Kennett Square resident lost his tractor to thieves, he installed a burglar alarm on his garage before replacing the tractor. The second time around, the thieves bypassed the alarm by breaking into the house first and stealing the garage key. As a bonus, they also took a new television set.

But the thieves left behind a telltale mark of a Johnston job. Footprints in the snow led from the woods in back of the garage to the crime scene and returned. A rare informant had reported that gang members often approached a burglary scene, tampered with a lock, and then backed off to watch if they'd tripped a silent alarm before proceeding.

The day after the first tractor was stolen, agents spotted Norman and David Johnston delivering a similar garden tractor to a Boothwyn resident, whom they had under surveillance as a fence. When the second tractor theft was reported, the agents again staked out the Boothwyn home. As expected, the Johnston brothers returned after dark with another tractor to sell.

Police surrounded their truck and left one local cop on guard while the others drove to the township office to obtain a search warrant. To justify searching the Johnstons' truck, agents described the double-dip theft in Kennett Square and added, almost incidentally, that Duane Lincoln, the younger Johnstons' teenage sidekick, had told police the Johnstons were, in fact, stealing tractors.

Armed with the search warrant, the cops recovered the second tractor and the stolen television set. But the case, like so many others involving the Johnston family, was tossed out of court on the grounds of "insufficient probable cause."

However, the search warrant had deadly repercussions. In fact, it became the death sentence that doomed the three young men to the bloody mass grave near Chadds Ford.

The instant Duane Lincoln's name appeared on the document, the Johnstons' always alert intelligence network snapped to attention. Word went out that there was a snitch in the gang's midst. Already under intense police pressure, the Johnston brothers launched a witch hunt for rats within the organization. The search naturally focused on Duane Lincoln and his fellow kiddie gang members. Here there be traitors, Bruce, Sr., concluded, and family policy decreed that traitors die. Even if their name was Johnston.

Also in February 1978, about the same time Big Bruce set out to purge the gang, Little Bruce met Robin Miller.

She was fifteen, Bruce nearly twenty-one. At first, both mothers, who had gone to school together, argued that Bruce was too old for the pretty, dark-haired ninth-grader. But Jennie was only fifteen when she met Big

Bruce, and she knew that if the young lovers were determined to be together, they'd find a way. In fact, Jennie conceded that Robin might be just what Little Bruce needed to straighten out and break away from his father's corrupting influence. Robin's divorced mother, Linda Miller, also relented. She urged Bruce, Jr., to go back to school and get a steady job so he would be in a position to marry Robin when she graduated.

Meanwhile, Big Bruce, David, and Norman continued to operate as they always had. In April 1978, the brothers and gang associate Ricky Mitchell looted a vending company warehouse of more than $30,000 worth of cigarettes that were on the way to East Coast markets before the sun came up.

In May, the same four men raided the treasured Longwood Gardens on the grounds of the old du Pont estate, which was open to the public. The lavish Gardens were a constant and painful reminder of the Johnstons' own impoverished background. Big Bruce, especially, had long coveted the wealth and respectability symbolized by the magnificent estate. Over the long Memorial Day weekend, the gang used an acetylene torch to burn through the office safe and escaped with more than $48,000.

The gang rushed back to Louise Johnston's home and there, on the kitchen table, divvied up the take. Ricky Mitchell felt he was cheated out of his full share, but knew better than to argue with the Johnston brothers who brooked no opposition. Instead, he kept his mouth shut and nursed his grudge.

By chance, Little Bruce was picked up that same night in connection with a different robbery and, based on his prior record, was ordered held at the Chester County Prison Farm.

* * *

When task force members heard Bruce, Jr., was behind bars and thus vulnerable, they huddled with local prosecutors. Keep him handy, they urged. Maybe we can get to the rest of the family through him. Bond was set at $35,000, but to the annoyance of the cops, Big Bruce immediately showed up with his $100 bills, posted the required ten percent, and took Little Bruce home with him. However, within days, the cops dug up another arrest warrant on a separate theft charge. This time bail was boosted to $100,000, and Little Bruce was hustled back to the Prison Farm.

The cops let Bruce, Jr., sit and stew for a few days, then paid him a visit and laid out a proposition. A federal grand jury in Philadelphia had been empaneled to investigate the epidemic of farm equipment thefts in the area. If Bruce, Jr., would testify about the Johnston family's involvement, they'd see what they could do about a reduced sentence. At first he refused, aware that by testifying he would be turning against his own father and violating the strict Johnston code against talking to outsiders. When the offer of a plea bargain didn't work, the cops sent in their heavy artillery: Robin. She begged him to listen to the police if it meant they could be together. She was miserable without him and terrified that he'd be sent to prison for years if he didn't go before the grand jury.

Robin's tears melted Little Bruce's resolve. The next time Jennie Johnston came to visit, he told his mother, "I've had it in here. Robin and I had a long talk. I'm going to the grand jury. It's the only chance I've got to straighten up."

Inevitably, Bruce, Sr., heard through his grapevine that Little Bruce had been transferred from the Prison Farm to the state police barracks at Avondale, where he'd be available for his appearance before the grand jury.

* * *

Bruce, Sr., was frantic. He showed up on the doorstep of Harriet Steffy, Jennie's mother, "all wild-eyed" as she described it, and waving a handful of $100 bills.

"The boy's turned on me," he told Harriet. "He's got enough stuff on me that I'll do fifty to ninety-nine years. You go see Little Bruce and tell him I'll give him $12,000 to say he was high when he testified and that it was all lies."

Then, more ominously, he added, "It's all that girl's fault. She's got a very big mouth."

Big Bruce had good reason to worry. He knew that the loyalty of the kiddie gang was more to each other than to the head of the family as it had always been in the past. If one broke and talked, the others might follow, and the whole operation would unpeel, layer by layer, like an onion.

When Little Bruce didn't respond to his father's $12,000 deal, Big Bruce decided the time had come for more drastic action. On an afternoon in late June, he and James Sampson went to see Robin Miller.

Playing the con man, Big Bruce convinced the lovestruck young girl that he only wanted to help her and Bruce, Jr., be together. To prove he was sincere, he offered to drive Robin over to the jail to visit Little Bruce. After the surprise visit, the three drove across the state line to a motel in Maryland. Robin never explained why she went along, but apparently Bruce, Sr., had won her over with his promise to post the bail money to get Little Bruce out of jail. The men were drinking and offered Robin a couple of shots to wash down a Quaalude. Doing drugs was nothing new for Robin. If you hung around with Bruce Johnston, Jr., you dropped ludes and smoked a joint. That's just the way it was.

But with Bruce, Sr., things got out of hand. Robin passed out and when she awoke hours later she was alone and nude in the motel bed. Her clothing was tossed in the corner. Still groggy from the effects of the drugs and booze, Robin recalled enough to know she'd had sex with the men. Raped, actually. She'd been having her period, and the tampon was gone.

The next day she visited Bruce, Jr., in jail and tearfully told him the whole, awful story. "Your father screwed me while I was passed out. The son of a bitch raped me." Enraged, Little Bruce beat on the walls of the visiting room and screamed loud enough to bring the guards running. The Johnston message had come through loud and clear: Keep your mouth shut or pay the price.

The same day, Little Bruce asked to see the cops on the task force. "I'll tell the grand jury everything I know, but not until you get me out of here," he offered. Robin needed him now more than ever and he'd gladly trade his father's freedom to be with her. Moreover, Bruce, Jr., called Jimmy and persuaded his half brother to testify.

On August 15, Jimmy Johnston gave his first statement to police at the Avondale barracks. He was then handed a subpoena to appear before the federal grand jury the following day. When he walked out the door, two burly cops grabbed Jimmy by each arm. "Whatever you do," one admonished, "don't tell your dad about this. Don't tell anybody."

Jimmy promised to keep quiet and ran off to catch up with Duane Lincoln. The two friends were headed for the Oxford Volunteer Fire Department's annual fundraising carnival. The boys were seen living it up at the carnival, but then vanished. Later, a friend recalled asking Jimmy where he was going when he left the carnival. His reply was chilling. "I'm either going to a motel or six feet underground," Jimmy said.

* * *

When Jimmy didn't show up for his grand jury appearance the next day, the cops were disappointed but not too concerned. Cold feet, they figured. But Jimmy's great-aunt Sarah was troubled. Jimmy had called her from the carnival to tell her he'd be home late so she wouldn't worry. "He mentioned that Big Bruce had warned him not to testify," Mrs. Martin said. "He didn't say so, but I think Jimmy was scared. That's why he called."

Days later, when Jimmy and Duane Lincoln still hadn't shown up, a missing persons report was filed. The task force cops who read the report had a sudden sinking feeling. Two other gang members, the Sampson brothers, had also been reported missing. Jimmy Johnston's car turned up in the parking lot of a Chester County motel. Several days later, James Sampson's car was found abandoned at the Philadelphia airport. It was all too much to be a coincidence, but there was no evidence the Johnston family was behind the strange disappearances. Police didn't think Bruce, Sr., would harm Jimmy, the kid he'd treated like his own son. The investigators latched onto Jimmy's last remark about the motel. That's probably where he was. Big Bruce had him tucked away in some motel so he wouldn't talk to the grand jury. As for the other boys . . . well, you know pot heads. They were probably sleeping off a high somewhere. Besides, the task force cops were busy trying to keep Little Bruce happy and on line to testify. He was yelling to get out of jail, so despite their misgivings the cops let him go if he promised to stick close to the Millers' place. With Lamb's assistance, Little Bruce's bond was lowered to $1. Robin was waiting to take him home the instant he was released.

Just past midnight on August 30, 1978, Little Bruce

and Robin drove into the driveway of the Miller home. After Bruce's long stretch in jail, the young lovers had been together only six short, but happy, days—and then the darkness exploded with gunfire.

The day after the ambush, police and FBI agents went to Big Bruce's new home on Blue Ball Road near Elkton, Maryland, and arrested him on charges of obstruction of justice for his attempts to dissuade Little Bruce from testifying. But he had an airtight alibi for the time the killers were blasting holes in Bruce, Jr., and Robin. He and Ricky Mitchell had made themselves conspicuous at a tavern far from the shooting scene. What the cops didn't learn until much later is that it was David and Norman Johnston who filled the $15,000 contract Bruce, Sr., had offered for the murder of his son and his girlfriend.

Over the next few months, the murder investigation dragged, but things had changed. The relentless pressure by the task force was getting to other gang members. If Big Bruce could put out a hit on his own son, then nobody was safe. Also, there was the matter of the missing kiddie gang. The question in everyone's mind was who would be next. Finally, the dominoes started toppling.

Gang member Leslie Dale was hauled in and, to save his hide on an old 1970 murder charge, agreed to talk about the slaying of Gary Wayne Crouch. Dale also related that the day after the ambush at the Millers, Norman Johnston had laughingly told him how the little yellow VW rocked and rolled when he and brother Dave riddled it with bullets.

Ricky Mitchell, still chafing over his short take on the Longwood Gardens job, was picked up on a larceny charge. Mitchell cut a deal with prosecutors. In exchange for a light sentence in a secure jail, he'd show them where the missing boys were buried.

* * *

Thus, on the late afternoon of December 30, Ricky Mitchell led a search party out to the Brandywine Game Preserve. The cops trailed Mitchell as he climbed a fence and followed a faint path into the dense woods. He pointed to a spot at the top of a small mound. "That's where we buried 'em," Mitchell said.

The searchers attacked the frozen ground and were still at it when darkness fell. Portable lights were set up and the digging continued. Finally, one of the shovels struck something soft, and an evil stench arose from the hole in the ground. Nauseated, the men resumed digging; this time using only spoons to laboriously scrape away the dirt so they wouldn't destroy traces of evidence. Slowly, one decomposing body was unearthed, then another below that one, and still a third beneath the first two. They were all that was left of Jimmy Johnston, eighteen; Duane Lincoln, seventeen; and Wayne Sampson, twenty. All three had died from multiple gunshots to the head fired at point-blank range. Nothing was left of their faces. Long, stringy hair, the symbol of their generation, was matted to the decaying scalps. Sadly, one body was clad in a sprightly Tweety Bird T-shirt, a sign that, whatever they might have done in life, mere children were buried here.

According to Mitchell and Dale, the three were targeted for execution and killed about two weeks before the ambush on Little Bruce and Robin. "We're going to kill them all," Dale said Big Bruce warned him. "If one talks, they'll all talk."

On August 15, 1978, the three Johnston brothers and Ricky Mitchell spent the morning scouting isolated locations for a killing ground that passersby wouldn't stumble over accidentally. They settled on the deeply wooded Brandywine Game Preserve, about 2½ miles north of the Delaware state line. The next night, the quartet put the murder plan in action.

Jimmy Johnston was the first to go. Just as the cops had suspected, Big Bruce had picked up Jimmy after he left the carnival in Oxford and deposited him in a motel on Route 30 in Lancaster County, supplied with enough beer and ludes to keep him quiet for days. In his zombie-like state, Jimmy docilely went along with the four men when they told him they needed help recovering a stolen tractor that was stuck in the sand.

When they reached the grave site, Jimmy turned to Big Bruce with a puzzled grin on his face. "Where's the tractor?" he asked. In reply, Bruce shone a bright flashlight into his stepson's eyes and fired two shots from a .22-caliber pistol into the boy's head.

Jimmy went down like a sack of cement. Mitchell and one of the Johnstons rummaged through his pockets before kicking the body into the open grave.

"He was still kind of gargling funny-like," Mitchell recalled. "Big Bruce didn't say much, but he looked like he kind of enjoyed killing the kid."

Mitchell was probably right. Killing Jimmy was easy. Not only did it eliminate a snitch, but, in Big Bruce's mind, the murder erased the one living symbol of his cuckolded past, a humiliation that all of his tough-guy posturing couldn't live down.

By now it was nearly midnight, but there was more killing to be done. The four men drove back to Louise Johnston's home in Kennett Square, where they'd stashed Duane Lincoln and Wayne Sampson, the other two suspected informers. The boys were fed the same lie about the tractor stuck in the sand, and the whole party returned to the game preserve.

Norman Johnston and Wayne Sampson remained in the car with the stereo turned up to cover the sound of gunfire while Bruce, Sr., David, and Ricky led Duane Lincoln to his death. This time, as Bruce shone the light into the victim's eyes, David Johnston stepped up from behind and shot the long-haired teenager repeatedly in the back of the head. Again, the men searched the boy and removed his pocket change before shoving the body into the grave atop Jimmy Johnston.

Next, Wayne Sampson, still suspecting nothing, was taken into the woods. In recounting the murder to police, Mitchell, who took his turn as executioner, said that the third killing didn't go quite as smoothly as the first two. "Bruce shined the light in the boy's and my eyes," said Mitchell. "My first shot missed. The boy turned around and asked if that was a real gun. Bruce moved the light from my eyes and I fired two more times. The boy fell down."

Once more, the vultures rifled the pockets of their victim looking for spare change. It was the only hard money Ricky Mitchell received for his part in the triple homicide. He told police that he agreed to help the Johnstons kill the boys in exchange for getting his car fixed: about $700 worth of repairs.

Even after the night of horror, the killings still weren't over. On August 21, James Sampson was exterminated. Naively, the twenty-four-year-old had come around asking after his younger brother. "He's over in Lancaster County setting up a score," the Johnston brothers lied. They offered to take James Sampson with them to meet Wayne. Instead, they drove to a landfill near Honey Brook. This time, Norman Johnston did the honors. After a couple of bullets to the brain, James Sampson was rolled into the landfill and vanished under a mountain of Lancaster County garbage. His body was never recovered.

Several days later, gang member Roy Meyers inquired

about the missing boys. "You don't have to worry about James Sampson any more," David Johnston muttered. "The worms will take care of him. If he wants to talk to his [brother] Wayne, maybe they can send messages by groundhog." And when asked if he'd seen Jimmy Johnston lately, Big Bruce merely shrugged. "Where Jimmy is he has friends and he doesn't need anything to eat," he said.

But it was the last bragging the Johnstons would do. Armed with the informants' testimony and the evidence from the exhumed bodies, the task force finally, after more than a decade, slapped the family with the kind of charges that would put them all away for good.

On March 18, 1980, after a five-week trial, a jury found David and Norman Johnston guilty of four counts of first degree murder in the deaths of Robin Miller, Jimmy Johnston, Duane Lincoln, and Wayne Sampson. They were acquitted of killing James Sampson only because defense attorneys convinced the jury that without a body, there could be no murder. But in November, another jury wasn't swayed by eight weeks of such arguments and concluded that Bruce Johnston, Sr., was guilty of six counts of first degree murder: Robin Miller, Jimmy Johnston, Duane Lincoln, the two Sampsons, and Gary Wayne Crouch.

Norman and David are serving four consecutive life terms; Bruce, Sr., recieved six consecutive life terms.

But the bloody saga of the Johnstons didn't end with the multiple guilty verdicts. In March 1986, Big Bruce went on trial in Allegheny County on charges of killing a fellow inmate at the Western State Correction Institute near Pittsburgh.

This time, prosecutors asked for the death penalty. Johnston was accused of the revenge killing of George Arms. Witnesses claimed that on January 28, 1985, they saw Bruce, Sr., throw a cup of flammable liquid on Arms who was locked in his cell and unable to flee. An accomplice then tossed a lit book of matches at Arms, and the cell interior erupted into an inferno.

"It was like an explosion," the witness testified. "Arms was screaming and waving his arms like a chicken on fire."

By the time guards extinguished the blaze, the prisoner had suffered burns over seventy percent of his body. Arms lived in agony for months. His feet were amputated in March in an attempt to save his life, but he finally died of massive infections on May 31.

However, despite the overwhelming evidence, and to the astonishment of the prosecutor and the presiding judge, the jury acquitted Big Bruce of the horrendous murder. "I think," said a reporter, who covered the trial, "it was a case of sleazebag killing sleazebag. So what?"

Following his father's convictions on the six murder counts, Little Bruce dropped out of the federal witness protection program and went his own way. He surfaced in January 1981, when he and his new girlfriend were nabbed breaking into a Maryland pharmacy to get drugs. Incredibly, the girl's name was Robin, and Little Bruce was identified by the multiple gunshot wounds to his body. After doing time for the burglary, Bruce Johnston, Jr., returned to Chester County and settled down.

Long after he'd helped dismantle the Johnston killing machine, District Attorney William Lamb still had nightmares over the family's cold-blooded reign of terror: "These were the worst kinds of crimes imaginable," Lamb said. "Not only was it murder, but murder for a purpose. Murder to stop people from taking the witness stand and telling the truth.

"Louise Johnston," he continued, "did not show one shred of remorse in court, despite the fact that some of the victims were her grandsons. Why not? Because Bruce, Jr., and Jimmy Johnston were snitching, and you didn't snitch on the family. What her boys did was okay.

"For the Johnston family, murder was okay."

NINE
THE LUNDGRENS: THE CULT OF MURDER

One time, when Jeffrey Lundgren was still a child, he caught a rabbit, nailed it to a board, and watched in delighted fascination as the suffering, crucified creature writhed in agony.

When he grew up, Jeffrey Lundgren put aside childish things as most men do . . . and sacrificed human beings instead.

All in the name of God.

Fast forward to a frigid January night in 1990 outside Kirtland, Ohio, where the bitter, biting winds sweeping in off Lake Erie slash at the skin like icy machetes. A crowd of quilt-coated cops is gathered in a sturdy old barn ripe with the stench of decay. Batteries of portable lights cast ghostly shadows over a macabre scene as grim grave diggers slowly unearth long-dead bodies.

More than once that dreadful night, first one digger and then another dropped his tools and bolted for the barn door to vomit outside.

These were all seasoned cops, fire fighters, and rescue personnel hardened to the realities of death, but this gory task was more than they could handle. This was horror like none had ever experienced, not even in their worst nightmares, which were many and often. It wasn't just the overpowering stench of decomposing flesh filling the dense, already putrid atmosphere of the old barn that sickened them. They'd been around such revolting scenes before.

This one was different.

This one was pure evil.

The thing that disturbed them most as body after body was uncovered—father, mother, and three young girls—-each shot point-blank and dumped one atop the other in this muddy pit, was the realization that this massacre was the fiendish work of a murderous cult that justified its merciless killing as a divine-inspired blood atonement ordained by a maniacal religious crank—Jeffrey Don Lundgren.

Lundgren's group was a splinter of the Reorganized Church of Jesus Christ of Latter-day Saints (RLDS), which is, itself, an offshoot of the Church of Jesus Christ of Latter-day Saints, or mainstream Mormonism headquartered in Salt Lake City, Utah. But Lundgren's bizarre teachings bore little resemblance to the doctrines of these two denominations, both of which renounced any connection with his unholy sect.

As a self-proclaimed prophet and master of the cult, like David Koresh and his Branch Dividians, Jeffrey Lundgren attracted a handful of followers with a mishmash of radical biblical prophecies, blood sacrifices, charismatic preaching, paramilitary exercises to prepare for his apocalyptic, end-times vision, "divine" revelations, mysterious quasi-religious rites, and grotesque sexual rituals to seduce a handful of converts into following him down the bloody path leading to the slaying of the Dennis Avery family . . . and the promise of ten thousand more deaths to follow.

For those five pitiless murders, Jeffrey Lundgren was sentenced to die—five times over—in Ohio's electric chair. But Lundgren's own date with death was yet to come. First, there was an awful business to be done—exhuming the lime-covered, decomposing remains of the five murdered cultists from their mass grave beneath the barn floor. As they dug and gagged and dug some more, authorities searched for answers to the unanswerable: How did such an obscene abomination ever happen? What kind of monster was capable of such atrocities?

The key lay in the twisted psyche of Jeffrey Lundgren, who began his trek to Death Row from his birthplace in Independence, Missouri, on May 3, 1950. The Lundgren family was active in the "stake" or congregation of their local RLDS, so Jeffrey grew up immersed in his church's teachings. He also developed a love for guns and a taste for torturing helpless animals, qualities guaranteed to win him few friends. In fact, his schoolmates generally considered Jeffrey Lundgren remote, arrogant, and an all-around jerk.

When he went off to college at Central Missouri State University in Warrensburg, Jeffrey did nothing to improve his popularity deficiency and spent most of his time hanging around the student house sponsored by the RLDS. Even then, among a pre-divinity school crowd of button-down, blinders-on, short-hairs, Jeffrey Lundgren stood out as a rigid, ultra-conservative ideologue, for whom the only way was Jeffrey's way. Skillful at twisting arcane symbols and ambiguous scriptures to fit his own version of truth, Lundgren became even more adroit at rooting out some obscure Bible passage to prove he was always right and everyone else was always wrong . . . or so said the Bible according to Jeffrey.

Jeffrey Lundgren made few friends at the RLDS house, but he did meet Alice Keehler. In the spring of 1970, both dropped out of school and got married.

Alice was already several months pregnant, and Jeffrey handled his new responsibilities by joining the Navy and shipping out. A few weeks after reporting to San Diego for basic training, his first son, Damon, was born. Eventually, the Lundgrens had three more children: Jason, Kristen, and Caleb.

(Years later, during an appearance on the Phil Donahue show via satellite link from her cell at the Ohio Reformatory for Women, Alice Lundgren told a national television audience that "Marrying Jeffrey was the will of God. I believe I was spoken to and was told that I would marry this man who would be great within the church.")

After four years in the Navy, Lundgren came home to Independence and spent the next several years bouncing from one menial job to another, cheating on Alice, collecting guns, and generally making a nuisance of himself with his increasingly acrimonious quarrels that bordered on violence with elders in the RLDS.

By the early 1980s, angry and resentful that at thirty-something he still hadn't been asked to join the priesthood when most young men were invited in before they were twenty, Lundgren set about creating his own priesthood. Jeffrey formed study groups in which he pushed his radical interpretations of the Scriptures, supporting his version of biblical truth—mainly that Jeffrey Lundgren was a divinely inspired prophet sent by God to cleanse the church of infidels and prepare the world for the Second Coming of Christ.

In those study groups, Lundgren planted the seeds of a murderous cult that would sprout into a deadly Venus flytrap which consumed human beings.

In 1984, Jeffrey Lundgren announced that Scripture passages had revealed he should relocate to tiny

Kirtland, Ohio, once a village unto itself, now mainly a bedroom community of Cleveland, thirty miles to the west. Here, according to his vision, God would reveal himself to his "prophet," as Jeffrey now called himself. Also at Kirtland, there were many more RLDS pigeons for Jeffrey Lundgren to pluck.

Soon after he founded the Church of Jesus Christ of Latter-day Saints (LDS), Joseph Smith, Jr., moved from New York state to this small Ohio village on a command from God, and here the gothic-style Mormon Temple was built. In 1860 the Church split over doctrine, with the new branch becoming the Reorganized Church of Latter-day Saints. Although the two branches disputed its ownership, the Temple at Kirtland remained under control of the reorganized branch of the Church or the RLDS, whose authority Jeffrey Lundgren would soon challenge.

About twenty thousand visitors annually tour the Kirtland Temple and its other historical buildings important to both churches. Temporary guides are employed, given free housing and a small weekly salary to show visitors around and explain the Church's history and traditions.

Jeffrey and Alice Lundgren became guides when they arrived in Kirtland on August 19, 1984.

Almost from day one, Lundgren irritated others with his dogmatic pronouncements and his personal interpretation of holy writ. The same abrasive character defects that had provoked folks in Missouri became even more annoying in Ohio.

"Jeffrey Lundgren was a spiritual bully," declared the Reverend Dale Luffman, the president of the Northeast Ohio chapter of the RLDS. "He wasn't particularly charismatic, but he was very persuasive, and tried to draw into his realm of influence anyone who seemed vulnerable."

Lundgren was scolded several times for expounding on his warped theology to tour groups, mini-sermons that simply didn't square with accepted church teachings.

"He finally started telling people that he had the power to divine what was true in the Bible and what wasn't. When he claimed he had this unique pipeline to God, that, for us, was the final straw," added Luffman.

By late 1987, Jeffrey's heretical views (not to mention some several thousand dollars in missing Temple money) prompted church officials to fire him as a tour guide and revoke his ministerial credential.

The Lundgrens rented a run-down one hundred-year-old farmhouse and fifteen-acre farm on Chardon Road in October 1987, and converted it into a cult compound. At Jeffrey's urging, several former members of his study groups in Independence moved to the farm. Among those uprooting their lives were the Averys, Dennis and Cheryl, both forty-two, and their three daughters, Trina Denise, Rebecca Lynn, and Karen Diane.

In April 1987, Dennis Avery quit his job as a computer operator for the Centerre Bank in Kansas City, sold his home, and moved his family to Kirtland to join Jeffrey Lundgren's growing band of religious fanatics. Avery turned over $10,000 he made from the sale of his home to Lundgren, who went on a spending spree with the windfall. His first purchase was a top-of-the-line, stainless-steel .45-caliber Colt Combat Elite semiautomatic firearm. The pistol became Jeffrey's favorite sidearm that he enjoyed caressing while haranguing his flock with increasingly violent rhetoric and images of blood spilling.

The .45 was the weapon Lundgren used when he slaughtered the entire Avery family, so, in effect, Dennis Avery had paid for his own execution.

Gradually, through threats of hellfire damnation and the kind of insidious mind-fuck games typical of cult leaders, Jeffrey Lundgren gained control over the lives of his followers and ruled his commune with dictatorial powers. He insisted that members call him "Father" or "Prophet." Misbehaving children were severely punished, often beaten with poles, to enforce obedience. Paychecks earned outside the commune were turned over to Jeffrey. All telephone calls were monitored. Individual freedoms were crushed; even mild questioning of Jeffrey's teachings was forbidden.

Lundgren preached that only through the teachings of Father Jeffrey could followers be acceptable to God in the end times soon to be upon them. He drilled into them the dogma that "blood sacrifices" must be made before they could be saved. The theme of violent, Old Testament-style death and bloody retribution were the meat of Lundgren's nightly harangues.

And then there was the sex. Again, Jeffrey was merely following in the tradition of cultists immemorial who used sex—or the need for it or the lack of it—to manipulate their followers, claiming that salvation—mainly for the women in the group—lay in submitting to the sexual demands of Jeffrey the Prophet. The only difference between Jeffrey and his predecessors was in the form those sexual practices took. For Jeffrey Lundgren, that meant some particularly degrading and disgusting rituals.

For example, there was this exchange between Phil Donahue and Alice Lundgren on the program televised in November 1991:

DONAHUE: . . . bizarre sexual demands were made on you including oral sex after he had, you had been obliged to cover him with his own feces. Do I understand this?

MRS. LUNDGREN: That's exactly correct. That is exactly what happened.

DONAHUE: And that you submitted to this bizarre, vulgar activity, why? And you didn't run away, why?

MRS. LUNDGREN: Because, because I thought . . . I thought that was the will of God. I thought . . . I thought that's what I was supposed to do . . . I thought that that was my destiny, that I was supposed to marry this man and that I was supposed to remain loyal to him for the rest of my life regardless of what he did.

DONAHUE: On one occasion, he insisted that you dress in male paraphernalia and take the part of the man so that he could feel what sex felt like as a woman. Is that so?

MRS. LUNDGREN: Yes, I did. It was a situation where I was told, "You put on this apparatus and you perform this sexual act on me, Alice, or I'll get somebody to replace you."

During those episodes, Lundgren loved to dress in a frilly, feminine nightgown, wear makeup and fingernail polish, and have himself tied up with a satin ribbon while his sex partner, a woman, strapped on a dildo and took the male role in the sex act.

According to testimony during Lundgren's murder trial, another of his favorite sexual rituals was to force his women followers to dance naked while he masturbated.

As with nearly everything else he did—including mass murder—Jeffrey Lundgren claimed the kinky sex was okay because the Bible told him so. He called the ritual "Intercession."

In Old Testament days, Lundgren preached, wives were allowed to intercede with the rulers if their husbands were deemed sinful or rebellious. And, of course, the men in Jeffrey's cult were always and abundantly sinful, so there was a constant need for the wives to intercede.

Jeffrey explained that the intercession wouldn't be acceptable to him (or God) unless the women were stripped of all their pride, which, naturally, meant stripping off their clothes while dancing before their Father Jeffrey. If their dancing pleased him, their husbands' sins would be forgiven and their lives spared.

According to the rules of the ritual, the women were told to doll themselves up as attractively as possible for their appearance. When they entered Jeffrey's room, he was seated naked on a bed or couch, with Alice nearby wearing nothing but a loose-fitting housecoat. The women were ordered to strip and give their panties to Jeffrey. Then, while they danced nude (sometimes for up to thirty minutes or more), Jeffrey watched and masturbated into the panties. Sometimes, Alice bent over Jeffrey's lap to help out.

The dancing ended only after Jeffrey climaxed. The women were allowed to dress, but made to wear the panties soaked with Jeffrey's semen. Spilling his semen, Jeffrey asserted, was the same as Christ shedding his blood for the forgiveness of sins. It meant that the women's intercessions were acceptable and their husbands were spared.

Soon after Lundgren was kicked out of the church, RLDS officials and local cops began hearing rumors that Jeffrey was plotting his revenge by taking over the Temple by force. A tipster told Kirtland Police Chief Dennis Yarborough that Lundgren planned to invade the Temple with a paramilitary force he'd been training at the cult's compound and "eradicate the unrighteousness." The invasion was scheduled for May 3, 1988, a date Jeffrey said he arrived at by decoding symbols carved on the front doors of the Temple.

By some strange coincidence, May 3 also happened to be Jeffrey Lundgren's birthday.

Yarborough was skeptical of the rumors, but dropped by the farm just in case. He was shocked to see an arsenal of high-powered weaponry prominently displayed. Convinced now that Lundgren did indeed pose a real threat, the chief warned the prophet that while he might answer only to the law of God, the law of Ohio would be keeping a sharp eye on Father Jeffrey and his collection of oddballs.

About this time, Lundgren also became obsessed with the enigmatic, allegorical—and for many—disturbing account of the Apocalypse found in the Book of Revelations. The more Lundgren studied the passages, the more convinced he became that his destiny was as one of the Four Horsemen who opens the Seven Seals, ushering in Christ's return to earth for a thousand-year reign. (Another interpretation holds that opening the Seals heralds the end of the world, the end of time, a reading that also dovetailed neatly with Lundgren's apocalyptic theology.)

Jeffrey managed to twist the disgrace of his excommunication into one more heaven-sent sign that Apocalypse was just around the corner and that he had been ordained to jump start it. And where better to get the end of the world off and running than at the site of Jeffrey the Prophet's greatest shame, the Kirtland Temple itself now occupied by enemies of the Lord.

Jeffrey convinced his brainwashed flock that they must hold the Temple for three days after which a massive earthquake would destroy unbelievers, and Christ would appear to establish a new Zion with—what else?—Father Jeffrey and the faithful Lundgrenites in charge of the whole shebang.

And while they waited out the three days, there was bloody work to be done. Dale Luffman, his family, staff, guides, and any visitors who might be touring the Temple would be taken prisoner, bound and gagged. The women and children would be gutted. Luffman would be forced to watch the slow execution of his family before he was beheaded, a manner of death that Old Testament warriors deemed to be pleasing in the sight of God, or so said Jeffrey. Chopping off Dale Luffman's head, Lundgren insisted, was divinely ordered retribution. To anyone else, it was revenge, pure and simple. Dale Luffman had pissed off the Prophet Lundgren, therefore he had to die.

In preparation for the Temple takeover, Lundgren beefed up the flock's military training. The men trained constantly with high-powered weapons and on field maneuvers. Alice was the only woman in the group given a gun to carry for any mop-up killing necessary once the takeover began. However, all the women learned how to clean and reload assault rifles in the dark to serve as backups for the men.

Operational code names that sounded like little boys playing war in the backyard were assigned: Talon I, Falcon II, Vineyard IX, Team I, and Team II. The farm was Eagle's Nest. Jeffrey, of course, was Eagle I.

While the women remained at the Eagle's Nest with the kids, the men, armed with guns, knives, and a crossbow, would leave for the Temple at 1:00 A.M. The crossbow was for silently killing anyone who happened to be out on the streets at that hour, especially Chief Yarborough, who often patrolled the village at odd hours.

First, they planned to start a diversionary fire at a service station, and while the attention of villagers was elsewhere, storm and capture the Temple. Anyone found inside was to be beheaded. The cult women would be notified by radio when the Temple was secured and come with the children.

Part of Jeffrey's plan also involved killing members of the cult who had displeased him. Their bodies would be tossed out the front door of the Temple to convince authorities that Lundgren was holding hostages and was willing to kill them.

However, if other members of the group were killed in the takeover, not to worry. The bodies would just be stacked in a corner of the Temple until Jeffrey had a moment or two to go over and raise them from the dead.

As was true with his other crackpot schemes and preposterous prophecies, Lundgren made sure he built in an escape clause to his maniac takeover plan just in case. The takeover of the Temple could only succeed if all his followers were free of sin, just as he was. So when Kirtland police stepped up their surveillance of the group, and after Chief Yarborough hinted to Lundgren that the little village frowned on "armed invasions," Jeffrey abruptly cancelled the operation. He told his followers they were all too sinful to seize and hold the Temple successfully.

The plot to capture the Temple collapsed, but no

problem. Any good prophet worth his salt always has a spare vision or two to pull out in times of need, and Jeffrey Lundgren came up with a doozy. Rather than bringing Christ to Kirtland, Jeffrey Lundgren promised his followers he would take them "to the wilderness" to meet God face-to-face and in the flesh.

Over the next several months, Jeffrey prepared his adherents to go meet God by laying a complex foundation based on his off-the-wall interpretations of Bible passages and his cockeyed translations of arcane symbols and instructions he claimed to find hidden in the Scriptures, particularly the blood-tinged passages from the Apocalypse.

To lead his people, Jeffrey preached that he first had to become "endowed with the power," power bestowed on those who slew the wicked and spilled their blood as a sacrifice to God, a blood atonement for sins of the entire group. According to Jeffrey, all of them must appear before God totally sinless or else God wouldn't see any of them.

Deciding who should be sacrificed wasn't difficult. Nobody liked the Averys, especially Lundgren who had come to detest Dennis Avery's tendency to question Father Jeffrey's dictatorial methods and unorthodox teachings. Also, the Averys weren't attending enough of Jeffrey's classes in which his threats of violence were escalating at an alarming rate. That lack of attention made the Avery family, in Lundgren's eyes, wicked and sinful. Lundgren had long since convinced his followers that God personally told him who was sinful and, therefore, who should live or die. So when Jeffrey said the Averys must die, no one challenged him.

Later, one of the cult members testified: "I remember him (Jeffrey) saying that the Averys were in a state of sin and would die, and it was too bad that because of the parents the children also would have to be killed, because the parents were bringing them up wrong. . . ."

And Lundgren himself explained: "I told my people that they should thank God for the Averys. You see, God had provided the Averys to us to be used as sacrifices."

When the question of the method of execution came up, Father Jeffrey again sought guidance in the Old Testament and concluded that wicked men were beheaded; women were stripped naked, split open, and their guts and internal organs spilled out on the ground; children were swung by their feet and their brains bashed out against a wall.

However, the idea of a mass beheading-gutting-bashing sacrifice was a little too messy even for Jeffrey's bloody tastes. He studied the Mormon Scriptures some more and, sure enough, found a passage that got him off the hook, one that mentioned horns of iron and hoofs of brass. A .45-caliber cartridge was a brass casing holding an iron slug, which must mean that it was okay with God if he used a fancy, semiautomatic pistol to slay the wicked.

Meanwhile, preparations for the trek to the wilderness went forward simultaneously with plans for the murders. The men intensified their paramilitary exercises, and Jeffrey continued to amass huge stores of firepower. He paid $2,700 for a forty-eight-pound, handmade .50-caliber machine gun capable of shooting down a helicopter, and added another four thousand rounds of ammunition to his arsenal.

Jeffrey now envisioned himself as another Moses leading the Jews across the Red Sea and into the wilderness. Jeffrey didn't have a Red Sea, but he did have an old red barn and that's where he ordered a burial pit to be dug. He selected one corner of the barn which often flooded during the spring rains. Here the Averys (Egyptians) would be covered over by a make-do Red Sea while Jeffrey the Prophet (Moses) led his little cult (the Jews) into the wilderness of West Virginia (the Promised Land).

Appropriately, the location Jeffrey chose was the Canaan Valley of the Appalachians, about sixty miles southeast of Wheeling.

The week before the sacrifices were scheduled, Lundgren's followers quit their jobs, took their children out of school, packed up their wilderness gear, and gathered at the farm for the Exodus.

On April 17, 1989, a cold and moonless foggy night, all was ready. Cultists gathered at the farm for what would be the unsuspecting Averys' last supper.

For dinner, Jeffrey had ordered roast beef, mashed potatoes with gravy, corn, and a salad. Dinner was served at exactly 6:30 P.M. During dinner, Dennis Avery mildly reprimanded seven-year old Karen for not eating her corn.

"I don't want to, Daddy," the little girl replied meekly.

Jeffrey, who was having trouble himself justifying the slaughter of little Karen, a sweet, angelic child who had captured everybody's heart, now had his sign from God that the child had to be sacrificed. Because she didn't want to eat her corn, Jeffrey, according to Jeffrey, heard God whisper in his ear, "She is a rebellious and wicked child."

The last supper ended, and the time had come to murder. The blood spilling began with Dennis Avery.

Initially, Jeffrey's plan was to force Dennis Avery to

watch his wife and children being executed, but then he decided to bring them out one at a time, oldest to the youngest, execute them separately and dump them in the pit. Even the hideous murder pit reflected Father Jeffrey's obsession with the Scriptures. Somewhere he'd read that the hole should be six-feet-six-inches-wide by seven-feet-seven-inches-long by four-feet-deep, and those were the precise dimensions of the hole in the barn floor. Groundwater seeping into the hole left a two-inch layer of mud on the bottom.

Assisting the lord high executioner were Jeffrey's eighteen-year-old son, Damon; Ron Luff, twenty-nine; Richard Brand, twenty-six; Danny Kraft, twenty-seven; and Greg Winship, twenty-nine.

As the victims were brought into the barn, they would be held down, bound with silver duct tape, and then carried to the pit for execution. Each man on the murder team had a more or less assigned duty: Damon acted as lookout; Greg ran a chain saw to muffle the shots and any screams; Ron squired the victims to the barn and handled the stun gun meant to immobilize the Averys; Danny, Richard, and Ron did the taping. And Father Jeffrey stood over the pit and performed the human sacrifices.

Murder by assembly line.

After running through the instructions one more time, Jeffrey nodded his head at Ron Luff and pointed at the house. "Let's do it," he said.

It was 7:30 P.M. when the men waiting in the barn heard Ron return with Dennis Avery in tow.

As soon as they stepped through the door, Ron hit Dennis with a charge from the fifty-thousand-volt stun gun which should have been more than enough to flatten the strongest man and possibly knock him out. But Ron Luff's stun gun didn't work properly. All it did was make Dennis Avery lurch and cry out in pain.

"Goddamn it!" he shouted. "That's not necessary! No! No! Goddamn it! Goddamn it! That hurts! No!"

Avery's struggles and cries nearly panicked the killing crew, whose nerves were already jangling over the bloodletting that faced them.

The five cultists leapt on Avery and easily wrestled the slight forty-nine-year-old man to the ground and began taping him. Of all the sacrificial victims, Dennis Avery was the only one who resisted, but not very strenuously and not for long. Cheryl Avery and the three girls went docilely to their deaths.

Avery continued to cry out, "No, goddamn it, no! Please! This isn't necessary!" The cries were finally muffled when the two-inch-wide duct tape was wrapped tightly around his mouth and head.

"Don't blindfold him," Jeffrey had instructed. "I want him to see. I want to look him in the eyes when I break his heart."

Bound hand and foot, Dennis Avery was carried into the execution room where Father Jeffrey waited, twirling his .45, his eyes burning with excitement. In the dim flickering light of a single bulb, with his long flowing hair and wild, bugging eyes, Jeffrey really did look like an old-time biblical prophet, thought one of the awestruck cult members.

Avery was lowered into the pit. He struggled to his knees, but slipped in the mud and tumbled over on his face. As he tried to rise again, Lundgren stepped to the edge of the pit and began firing at nearly point-blank range. A devastating hollow-point slug smashed into Avery's body. The second bullet spun him around in a half-twist, and Dennis Avery splattered facedown in the muck.

Months later, during a diatribe delivered at his murder trial, Jeffrey Lundgren defended the cold-blooded murder of the quiet, God-fearing man, whose only mistake was following a false prophet:

"I had told Dennis Avery what would happen if he continued to sin, continued to deny the truth, continued to reject my teachings, but he continued to choose darkness rather than light, and he had no one to blame but himself for leading himself and his family into this pit of damnation."

Lundgren also later boasted that he looked Dennis Avery in the eye when he shot him dead because, ". . . I wanted him to know who was sending him before God for his wickedness. The Scriptures required me to 'pierce his heart,' so I fired two shots directly into his heart."

A goddamn lie, countered one who was there. Jeffrey shot him in the back. He was too cowardly to look Dennis Avery in the eye.

Although they had been preparing for months for the blood sacrifice, the thunderous roar of the gunshots, even over the keening of the chain saw, stunned the other cult members. Dazedly, like catatonic robots, they stumbled obediently toward the pit on Jeffrey's command, "Come here and see what this looks like!"

For several awful moments, the men stared with morbid fascination at the fresh-dead body in the pit, blood pooling in the mud and spreading across Avery's plaid lumberjack's shirt.

"Okay," Lundgren ordered. "Go get the next one."

While he waited for Ron Luff to return with Cheryl Avery, Jeffrey reloaded the .45. He was experimenting. Because Lundgren believed he was called to slay ten thousand, he wanted to learn which ammunition was the most effective for mass murder. During the Avery executions, he used hollow-points, full-metal-jackets, and silver-tipped slugs. He tried 184-grain and 225-grain self-loads. He carefully placed his shots in the victims' backs, breasts, heads, and legs, then observed how long it took each person to die.

From his lookout post at the barn window, Damon Lundgren turned and called out to the waiting execution party, "Here they come," a procedure he would repeat as each new victim was shepherded to her death.

After Cheryl left with Ron Luff, the other wives and mothers remained lounging in the living room; sewing, chatting, watching Becky and Karen Avery play with the Luff children. Trina sat to one side engrossed in a magazine.

The stun gun still wasn't working, so as soon as Cheryl stepped through the barn door, Ron, Danny, Richard, and Greg surrounded her and began quickly taping her wrists and ankles.

Ron pushed her gently to the floor. "Be calm," he soothed. "Just give it up and it'll be easier. Just let go."

A look of terror leapt to the woman's eyes. It reminded one of the men of a helpless doe suddenly caught in the glaring headlights of a speeding car, too numb to flee. Cheryl couldn't have run even if she'd been able. Conditioned all her life to be submissive to men, Cheryl passively allowed herself to be taped and prepared for execution. During the taping, her eyes were covered. According to Lundgren's reading of the Scriptures, only the male should be forced to watch his own execution.

Cheryl was carried to the pit and lowered into a sitting position against one corner.

Outside, Greg Winship cranked open the chain saw.

Jeffrey Lundgren jacked a shell into the chamber of the .45 and immediately opened fire . . . once, twice, three times. Each slug jolted into Cheryl's frail body, slamming her against the side of the pit. The slugs were full-metal-jackets used for their penetrating power. The bullets that killed Dennis Avery were soft hollow-points that spread when they hit, splattering body parts to mush.

Jeffrey conferred with Ron Luff and suggested they jump into the grave and stab the bodies just to see what it felt like, but then changed his mind. If they had, they would have found Cheryl Avery still alive despite her grievous wounds. The autopsy later revealed that she'd probably lived five minutes or longer after she was shot, long enough to know her children were being butchered and their bodies thrown into the pit beside her, but helpless to prevent the carnage.

Now it was time for the little ones.

Before the next sacrifice was brought before him, Jeffrey told his men to forget the stun gun since it wasn't working anyway. Instead, he instructed, pretend to play games with the Avery girls to gain their cooperation, games like hide-and-seek or hear-no-evil that required blindfolds and that the whole commune had played in the barn last Halloween.

"Now," said Jeffrey, "bring out the next one."

When Ron Luff told Trina Avery her mother wanted her in the barn, the fifteen year-old put aside her magazine and obediently walked out to meet her executioner.

The girl smiled and nodded when the men in the barn said she was part of a new game and started taping her hands and feet. She didn't even protest when they wrapped the sticky tape all around her head, blinding and gagging her.

When that was finished, Richard and Ron picked up the girl and carried her to the pit. She was lowered in next to her parents. Jeffrey had tried body shots on

Dennis and Cheryl, so, with Trina, he aimed for her head.

But the girl jerked just as he pulled the trigger and the bullet grazed her head. Even with her mouth covered by the heavy tape, the men standing around the pit heard her alarmed, but muffled, "Ouch!" Quickly, Jeffrey fired again. The second shot was deadly. The powerful slug struck Trina on the left side of the head and exited under her right ear. She died instantly. For good measure, Jeffrey shot Trina again in the chest as she slumped over.

Only two more to go and the game ruse had worked so well they tried it again. Once more, Ron Luff, playing the part of a human Judas goat, went to the house where thirteen-year-old Becky and seven-year-old Karen were happily playing with a video game.

"Who wants to see the horses?" Ron asked, clapping his hand.

Both girls leapt to their feet, crying, "I do! I do!"

"I can only take one at a time," Luff replied. He pointed at Becky. "You first." Karen, always the quiet, dutiful child, sat down to wait her turn.

Back in the barn again, Becky, known as the feistiest of the Avery kids, jumped up and down when the men surrounded her with the rolls of tape.

"Hey," she laughed. "What's going on?"

In seconds, Becky was securely taped and placed in the pit. She rested across her mother's legs and before she even started squirming, Jeffrey began shooting.

The first shot hit Becky square in the chest, the impact knocking her over against Cheryl's body.

Much later, Father Jeffrey coldly explained to horrified listeners that "I fired again and her hands, which were in her lap, went out like she was reaching for her mother, like she knew her mother was there with her."

Greg Winship also testified that he stood by the pit listening to the rasping, gurgling sounds the child made until she finally sighed heavily and died.

When Ron Luff returned to the house he knew exactly how to appeal to a child like Karen. His own seven-year-old son, Matthew, and daughter Amy, four, adored Ron's piggyback rides.

"Come on," he called to Karen. "Your turn to see the horsey." Ron bent down and the giggly little girl scrambled aboard for her last piggyback ride out to the barn.

And for the fifth and last time that blood-drenched night, Damon Lundgren turned from his lookout window and yelled: "Here they come."

Like her older sisters, Karen was taped quickly and without protest. She weighed only thirty-six pounds, so Ron tossed her across his shoulder and carried her to the pit by himself.

Karen was placed gently in the grave, sitting upright in the mud and the blood, unaware that her dead or dying family lay all around her.

Jeffrey Lundgren wanted to try another head shot. He loomed over Karen, took careful aim almost straight down and popped off two rapid-fire shots.

"I fired straight down into her skull," Jeffrey later explained to an audience, numbed beyond belief by his cold-blooded, emotionless account. "I was less than two feet away and I pulled the trigger, bang, bang. I wanted to put both shots into the same hole."

With the slaying of the tiniest Avery, the terrible blood-atonement ritual ended. Jeffrey pocketed the .45 and told the others to start spreading the bags of lime stacked in a corner over the bodies. On top of the lime came a layer of large stones hauled in earlier from a creek bed for that purpose. The pit was then refilled with dirt and trash heaped over the surface to conceal any evidence of a grave.

While the others worked, Jeffrey returned to the house and told Alice, "It had to be done. It was God's will."

The next day, before leaving for West Virginia, the group carefully erased any trace of the Averys' existence in the commune. The family's effects were sorted out for anything that could be used in the wilderness. What wasn't useful was packed in trash bags that were distributed in Dumpsters as far away as Cleveland.

Before they drove away from the farm, the mass murderers, capable of butchering an entire family of five without batting an eye, left behind a large bag of cat food open in the barn so the commune's three pet kitties wouldn't go hungry.

As a caravan of cars pulled out of the farm's driveway, Jeffrey Lundgren looked back at the barn that was now a tomb.

"Death stinks," Jeffrey murmured. Then he turned to face the road ahead. The killings were behind him. Besides, he shrugged, he had to get used to it because the Scriptures commanded him to slay ten thousand by his own hand.

"Now," Lundgren joked, "I'm down to only 9,995!"

Ironically, almost at the exact moment the Averys were being prepped for their ritual murders, there was a gathering of cops at the Kirtland police department. Chief Yarborough and FBI Special Agent Bob Alvord were troubled by the intelligence reports they were getting from secret tipsters within Lundgren's group and from former cult members. Lundgren's violent ravings were getting worse. The guy was dangerous and the lawmen feared he might explode at any moment unless something happened to chill him down. They believed it was urgent that Lundgren know they were breathing down his neck, and one false move and they'd be on him like tics on a hound.

They planned to confront Father Jeffrey at the farm: all six members of the Kirtland police force backed by sixteen FBI agents. They especially wanted a crack at the weapons cache that informants claimed was big enough to equip a small army. Even if Lundgren didn't allow them to search the property without a warrant, he'd still get the message that they were watching him.

There was some discussion on when to stage the raid. Some officers wanted to go in on Monday; others argued for Tuesday.

The decision was made to go on Tuesday, April 18, one day too late to save the doomed Avery family.

The group didn't remain long in the Canaan Valley when it became obvious that Jeffrey's promise of a sit-down with God was as empty as all his other prophecies. And when Lundgren insisted on more and longer intercessions to satisfy his warped sexual tastes, the realization began to dawn on cult members that maybe this guy wasn't shifting in all gears. Worst of all, maybe the Averys had been sacrificed only to appease Lundgren's raging egomania.

(In fact, cops and prosecutors felt that the murders, disguised as religious hokum, were committed so Jeffrey could save face. None of his other wild prophesies had come true; his harebrained scheme to take over the Temple was stillborn. After all his talk about blood atonement and purification, investigators surmised, Lundgren felt he had to go through with the killings or risk losing his hold over his converts whose faith in Father Jeffrey was already weakening.)

From West Virginia, the group drifted back to its

Missouri roots, and there the disintegration that had begun in Kirtland accelerated. A paranoia festered among followers fearful of being tagged for the Avery murders, but even more terrified that they might be chosen by Father Jeffrey as his next sacrificial offerings for whatever lunatic vision he dreamed up next.

In the end, however, it was neither remorse nor fear that ultimately turned his followers against him, but the far more mundane matter of money. They learned Lundgren had been playing with the sect's cash, just as he had been playing with the women of the group. There was the growing suspicion among skeptics in the cult that Jeffrey's sexual dalliances were more physical and less spiritual than he would have them believe. Under all that pious Bible-thumping, Father Jeffrey was just another crooked con man at heart, an Elmer Gantry with blood on his hands.

By late December 1989, several former members were talking to the FBI and Alcohol, Tobacco, and Firearms (ATF) agents, as well as Kansas City detectives, Kirtland cops, and just about anybody else wearing a badge. Among the informants was Keith Johnson, who had been one of Jeffrey Lundgren's few chums from college days. Now, Johnson's wife, Kathy, was pregnant and the father-to-be was Jeffrey Lundgren.

While some lawmen went hunting for the Lundgrens and their few remaining followers, others, headed by Kirtland's Chief Yarborough, reluctantly took shovels in hand and on the fourth day of the new year went searching for bodies in the barn.

To their dismay they found them.

The horror they uncovered there was seared into their memories for the rest of their days. Yarborough had heard the rumors, listened to the informants' claims, had personally seen the stockpile of weapons at the farm, and was convinced that Jeffrey Lundgren and his cult were entirely capable of violence to support their extremist views. But no one was prepared for what came out of that pit in the old red barn.

Among the officials summoned to the mass grave were Lake County Prosecutor Steven C. LaTourette, who would file charges and eventually win convictions that put the Lundgren cult on Death Row or in prison; Rick Kent, supervisor for the Lake County Regional Forensic Laboratory; and Lieutenant Daniel Dunlap from the Lake County Sheriff's Department, who had trained at the FBI Academy to handle such gruesome crime scenes.

The men first noted a powdery residue in and around the pit, indicating that someone had spread lime in an obvious attempt to speed up decomposition. As the officers began to dig, they encountered layers of seventy or eighty large field stones weighing up to forty pounds each, along with broken cement blocks and bricks.

Next they ran into water flowing through the pit that threatened to destroy evidence and make a systematic exhumation difficult. Boards driven into the ground along one wall of the barn slowed the flow but didn't halt it entirely. Thick, sludgy, sucking clay-like muck made it almost impossible for the diggers to move around in the pit, much less extract the fragile, decaying bodies without damaging them more than they already were.

Not only did they have to fight the overpowering odor of death and the heavy muck, but the weather turned nasty as a harsh wind off the lake brought knifing sleet and plunged temperatures into the low twenties.

When the water was bailed out of the pit, Dunlap and Kent began the odious task of exhuming the first visible corpse. They used small hand trowels to laboriously remove the gummy mud encasing the remains.

From its size, the first body appeared to be a male curled into a fetal position. Near its feet, the workers uncovered the second body. This was a female and as Kent and Dunlap carefully scraped away the muck, they thought at first they'd uncovered some kind of mummy, so completely did the gray duct tape envelop the corpse's head.

Next, they unearthed a third smaller body, obviously a child, resting across the lap of the second body. This was later identified as Becky, reaching out for her dead mother.

One discovery led to another. Exhuming the third body revealed the fourth, smaller than the others, with its head on the hips of the third corpse.

Dental records later proved this was the body of Karen Avery. Because of the corpse's position, Kent and Dunlap decided to remove it before the others. They struggled to lift the tiny body from the muck that sucked and pulled at the decomposed, nearly skeletonized remains like quicksand. The men were as gentle as possible. Nevertheless, as they pulled the corpse free from the mud, the left foot broke off and plopped back into the bottom of the pit.

Since it was the first taken from the pit, this body was tagged Number One.

To prevent the other remains from disintegrating as they were removed, the men carefully worked sheets under and around the second, third, and fourth bodies before they were lifted out of the pit, numbered, and placed in body bags.

The team had gathered at the barn to begin the exhumation before 9:00 A.M. It was after 6:00 P.M. when the first body discovered (and the fourth removed), that of the male, was lifted from the pit in its shroud of fresh, clean sheets.

The searchers were exhausted. The thick mud made them feel like they were wearing lead boots and running through sand dunes. The numbing shock of digging out each decaying body had drained them emotionally. But there was still more nasty work to be done. When they lifted out the male corpse, another body was exposed, a female, also tucked into a fetal position and lying almost face-to-face with the male.

It was the last body, but not the end of the nightmare. As one of the men lifted the head, the entire scalp and its long, braided ponytail came loose in his hand. It was an image none of those hard-bitten lawmen would ever forget.

All the bodies were taken to the Cuyahoga county coroner's office in Cleveland which was better equipped to handle the extensive autopsies that would be required. A team of expert pathologists gathered there to conduct the mass postmortem. Dr. William Downing, the Lake County coroner, observed, while Dr. Elizabeth Balraj, the Cuyahoga County coroner, supervised each autopsy.

The stark, dispassionate clinical autopsy reports entered into evidence at the cult murder trials provided mere shadows of the indescribable horror investigators had unearthed.

The first autopsy started at 11:00 A.M. Body Number One, identified through X-rays as that of Karen Diane Avery, was dressed in a blue jacket with beige, green, and red patches on the sleeves, a white shirt with a purple collar and a picture on the front of a rainbow with red, purple, and green horses on the rainbow.

There were dancing, colored hearts over the main body of the shirt. The pants were light green jeans. The panties were white with purple flowers. The right foot was detached, but remained lodged in a white tennis shoe. The eyes, ears, nose, and mouth were covered with silver-gray duct tape that ran all the way around the head. Beneath the tape, her face was decomposed and unidentifiable. The wrists and ankles were bound with silver-gray duct tape holding the arms and the legs together. The victim had died of two gunshot wounds, one to the head, a second to the chest.

Body Number Two also was identified through dental records as that of Rebecca Lynn Avery, 61½ inches in height and weighing seventy pounds. Clothing included a blue denim jacket, red sweatshirt, blue denim pants, white tennis shoes, white sweat socks, a brassiere, and panties. Yellow earrings remained attached to what was left of the earlobes. The arms were bound at the wrists with duct tape, the left over the right. The legs were bound together at the ankles with duct tape. The head was wrapped with duct tape, completely covering the eyes, ears, nose, and mouth. Rebecca Lynn Avery had been shot once in the posterior trunk (back) and once in the left thigh.

Body Number Three was that of Cheryl Lynn Avery, again identifiable only through dental X-rays. The body was clothed in a hooded, zippered sweatshirt, a white-and-green blouse, a white brassiere, sweatpants, white panties, and a pair of socks and tennis shoes. The hood of the jacket was pulled over the hair; the duct tape wrapped around the hood, completely covering the body's eyes, ears, nose, and mouth. Both wrists were bound using silver-gray duct tape. Cheryl Avery's body contained three gunshot wounds: two to the right breast and one to the stomach.

The autopsy of Body Number Four, positively identified from dental X-rays as that of Dennis Leroy Avery, began at 2:00 P.M. The remains, 67½ inches tall and weighing 124 pounds, were dressed in a black belt, blue jeans, briefs, a black athletic shoe on the right foot and no shoe on the left foot, a white sock on each foot, a camouflage green T-shirt and a long-sleeved flannel shirt. The ankles were bound with gray duct tape. The hands were wrapped in gray duct tape. The same tape was wrapped around the head, covering the mouth but leaving the eyes exposed. There were two gunshot wounds to the trunk.

Dental records were the only means of positively identifying Body Number Five as that of Trina Denise Avery. The remains weighed 145 pounds and was sixty-three inches in height. When she died Trina Denise Avery was wearing blue jeans, a purple-blue-and-red blouse, denim long-sleeved jacket, white brassiere, blue panties, and white gym shoes with white socks. Gold earrings clung to the earlobes. The hands were taped with gray duct tape but were not bound together. There was gray duct tape on the mouth and around the head. Trina Avery had been struck by three slugs: two to the body and one to the head.

Following the lengthy autopsies, prosecutor Steven LaTourette appeared at a news conference to condemn the brutal slayings. Ashen, and in a voice quivering with emotion, LaTourette angrily announced: "These people are the cruelest, most inhumane people this county has ever seen. They're going to die in the electric chair for these crimes."

Within hours, a grand jury in Lake County named thirteen members of the Lundgren commune in indictments charging them with a host of crimes including first degree murder. Immediately, seven former cultists were grabbed in police raids in Missouri: Ron and Susan Luff, Dennis and Tonya Patrick, Debbie Olivarez, Richard Brand, and Gregory Winship.

With the arrests, LaTourette warned that the cult members "are not crazy" and added, "They are the coolest, most inhuman people this town has ever seen."

Even as he spoke, a massive, coast-to-coast manhunt was underway for the remaining cult members, including Father Jeffrey, Alice, and Damon Lundgren.

Cops quickly learned that the cultists had remained in the West Virginia wilderness from April until October 1989. They then returned to Missouri and camped out at the farm near Chilhowee. In mid-December, Jeffrey said it was time to move again. He packed up the family, convinced a couple of die-hard members to accompany him, and left for California. He knew the San Diego area from his Navy days so that's where the group headed.

In early January, the news of the mind-boggling massacre at the Kirtland farm broke nationwide. Holed up in the Sante Fe Motel in National City, California, Jeffrey made plans to skip across the border to Mexico. First, however, he had to do something about Jason, Kristen, and Caleb since they weren't wanted for murder.

When Alice telephoned her mother in Missouri and asked her to come to California and pick up the kids, federal authorities were waiting for the call. The contact number Alice gave her mother was traced to a telephone booth outside the National City motel. The phone booth and motel were staked out in case the Lundgrens suddenly tried to slip across the border.

Just before noon on Sunday, January 8, 1990, Jeffrey Lundgren left room 29 at the motel and strolled out to the phone booth. Agents on the stakeout decided to pounce. The cult was known to be heavily armed, and the cops feared Lundgren would opt for a bloody shoot-out if he felt trapped.

One team of agents rushed the phone booth, grabbed a startled Father Jeffrey while he was still dialing and threw him to the ground. ATF Supervising Agent Richard Van Haelst shoved his pistol in the Prophet's ear. "Jeffrey Don Lundgren," he said. "You're under arrest for murder."

A second squad dashed to the motel and crashed into room 29. Alice leapt from the bed screaming as a shotgun-toting agent burst through the door shouting, "Freeze, bitch, or I'll blow your fucking head off!"

The three younger children were taken into protective custody while Jeffrey, Alice, and Damon were shackled and hustled off to jail. As Damon was being cuffed, he whined, "I didn't do any of the actual shooting."

An agent asked Alice Lundgren if she knew what was going down in the red barn the night of the murders. She snapped, "You would have had to be stupid not to know what was going on."

A search of the Sante Fe Motel room proved that the feds had good reason to worry about a potential shootout. They found an AR-15 assault rifle, two .44-magnum revolvers, a .45-caliber pistol, hundreds of rounds of ammunition, knives, gas masks, camouflage outfits, survivalist gear, and a manual for operating an M-60 machine gun. Agents then went to a storage locker Lundgren had rented in nearby Chula Vista and recovered another weapons cache that included: smokeless gunpowder, reloaders, a .50-caliber rifle with sniper scope, automatic pistols, revolvers, more gas masks and, in the words of one amazed cop, "enough ammunition to ward off an army."

The next day a maid at a Chula Vista motel reported seeing a stash of guns and ammunition in a guest's room. When agents investigated they found a .50-caliber rifle, handguns, and boxes of ammunition. A pregnant Kathy Johnson and Danny Kraft had rented the room to be close to the Lundgrens. An all points bulletin was issued, and a San Diego County Sheriff's deputy spotted the couple a day later. They were arrested without incident, and the mad odyssey of Father Jeffrey and his cult of death was ended.

Over the next year, several cultists were tried for murder and other crimes in Lake County. The overwhelming evidence presented and the testimony of the former members themselves left not the slightest trace of reasonable doubt in the minds of the juries. For example, during one exchange with the prosecutor, cult member Debbie Olivarez was asked:

Q. And every one of these classes you were in attendance?

A. Yes.

Q. Alice Lundgren was there?

A. Yes.

Q. How were the Averys going to die?

A. When it was first discussed, Jeff said he found out that in the Scriptures it is written that people are to be destroyed a certain way; men, women and children.

Q. How were men to be destroyed?

A. That they were to be cut in two.

Q. How were women to be destroyed?

A. That they were to be stripped and have their insides cut out.

Q. How were children to be destroyed?

A. They were to be picked up by the feet and dashed in the head.

Q. What do you mean?

A. Picking them up by the feet and hitting them against the wall.

Q. Do you recall conversations concerning the death of Dennis, Cheryl, Trina, Rebecca, and Karen Avery?

A. Yes, I do.

Q. Would you tell the ladies and gentlemen of the jury about those conversations?

A. One day Jeff and Alice and I were sitting in the kitchen, and Jeff said that he was still looking to see if that was the way that the Averys were to be destroyed. And he said that he wasn't sure about Becky because he didn't know whether to place her in the woman category or the child category.

Q. She was thirteen?

A. I thought she was approximately eleven.

Q. Okay. What, if anything, did the defendant Alice Lundgren say?

A. Alice said that if she . . . that it would depend on whether she had started her period or not, if she would be classified as a woman or a child.

On August 31, 1990, a jury in the Lake County Common Pleas Court began deliberating the guilt or innocence of Jeffrey Lundgren. It took them only three hours and fifteen minutes to decide: On five counts of kidnapping—Guilty. On five counts of aggravated murder—Guilty.

Three weeks later, at the conclusion of the penalty phase of his trial, Jeffrey Lundgren was allowed to make a "brief" statement to the court before the jury decided his fate.

He began by self-righteously proclaiming that "I am a prophet of God. I am even more than that—much, much more."

And then droned on for the next five insufferable hours.

He was justified in slaughtering the Avery family, Lundgren insisted, because "Prophets have been asked by the Lord to go forth and kill since the beginning of time." His conclusion won him no sympathy from the jury: "I cannot say that I'm sorry I did what God commanded me to do," he said.

The jury was more bored than swayed by the sermonizing, and, once freed from Father Jeffrey's bombastic preaching, took less than two hours to recommend he be put to death.

On September 21, 1990, Jeffrey Lundgren returned to court for sentencing. Judge Martin Parks officially pronounced the death sentence, not once, but five times.

He fixed the date for Jeffrey's execution at April 17, 1991 – the second anniversary of the Avery murders.

Those death sentences are under appeal and no one expects Jeffrey Lundgren to fry any time soon. Meanwhile, he continues to study the Scriptures, searching for a way out of the Lucasville prison Death Row. In his spare time, he writes to his ex-followers warning that Christ is coming to set him free and those who have betrayed Prophet Lundgren will be punished.

Alice Lundgren was convicted on multiple charges of conspiracy and complicity. On August 29, 1990, the same day Jeffrey was found guilty in his trial, she was sentenced to twenty years on each of five counts of complicity to commit aggravated murder, and ten to twenty-five years on each of five counts of kidnapping, for a total minimum time of 150 years. The sentences are to be served consecutively. Alice will be eligible for parole after serving the first century.

Damon Lundgren rejected a plea bargain that would send him to prison for thirty years. He opted for going to trial.

Bad move.

A jury found him guilty and the court promptly slapped him with a 120-year sentence, making him eligible for parole after serving 108 years.

Among others charged in the blood-atonement killings, Richard Brand, as part of a plea bargain, was sentenced to fifteen years to life. He's eligible for parole after serving ten years.

Ron Luff stood trial and was found guilty on several counts. He was sentenced to thirty years to life on three counts; twenty years to life on two other counts; and ten years on each of five additional charges. He must serve 150 years before being eligible for parole.

Greg Winship also plea-bargained, and was sentenced to fifteen years to life on each of five counts for a total of seventy-five years to life in prison. He has to serve a minimum of twenty years before he can apply for parole.

Daniel D. Kraft, Jr., is serving fifty years to life and won't be eligible for parole for thirty-seven years.

Kathy Johnson did a year in jail on an obstruction of justice charge. After her release, she and Lundgren's infant daughter moved close to the Lucasville penitentiary so they can visit Father Jeffrey.

In April 1991, Alice Lundgren filed for divorce from Jeffrey Lundgren.

She cited irreconcilable differences.

And imprisonment.

TEN
THE KALLINGERS: COBBLERS AND KILLERS

January 8, 1975. The short, dark, rubbery-lipped man and the slight, youngster with the knit cap pulled down over his long silky hair, both bundled up against the winter chill, attracted little attention as they marched along the tree-lined Leonia, New Jersey, street. Just typical suburbanites, scurrying off to work and school.

Except for this pair, work meant murder and rape; school was a lesson in sexual terrorism.

Shortly before noon, the two turned up the walk leading to 124 Glenwood Avenue. The two-story, tan stucco house was solid middle-class where DeWitt and Edwina Romaine had raised their three daughters and where the close-knit family still cared for Mrs. Romaine's ninety-year-old bedridden mother.

As the two pulled open the storm door and stepped inside the screened-in porch, the front door opened. Edwina Wiseman, the Romaine's twenty-eight-year old daughter, was called "Dede" to distinguish her from her mother who had the same first name. She had noticed the pair coming up the walk and opened the door to greet them. Her four-year-old son, Robert, clutched her skirt and peeked shyly at the strange visitors.

"Good morning," bubbled the man through his thick, blubbery lips. "We're from the John Hancock Life Insurance Company."

Momentarily thrown off her caution concerning strangers, Dede Wiseman relaxed. Insurance salesmen. More door-to-door pests pouring over the George Washington Bridge from Manhattan to pitch New Jersey's suburbanites.

Before Dede could reply, the man shouldered open the door and pushed her inside the foyer. She grabbed the man's wrist and struggled to push him back outside while little Robert, startled, stumbled to the floor and began screaming.

But the man was too strong for Dede. He grabbed her hair, jerked her head back, and spun her around.

"Upstairs," he hissed. "And close your eyes."

"My grandmother's an invalid," she replied. "Leave her alone. She can't do anything to you. And I'm not leaving my baby here alone."

The man momentarily relaxed his grip so Mrs. Wiseman could scoop up her frightened child. Upstairs, the man shoved the two down the hall and into a back bedroom. "Get undressed," he ordered, pulling out a vicious-looking hunting knife. The woman shook her head, too terrified to speak. "Okay," the man shrugged. "I'll do it for you. Holding the knife in one hand, the intruder began ripping Dede's clothes from her body.

His young accomplice, twirling a nickel-plated revolver Western-style, came in just as the man sliced Dede's brassiere off and tossed it in the corner. "Grandma's in the other room on the bed," the boy reported. "Looks like she'll be easy to kill."

The intruders produced large rolls of adhesive tape, and the man began winding the tape around Dede's head and over her eyes. He shoved a discarded sock in her mouth and added more tape to gag the woman. The man forced her to lie on her back on the floor. With his young accomplice helping, the man taped her wrists together then pulled her knees up tight against her breasts and bound her ankles to her arms.

The last thing Mrs. Wiseman saw before the tape was slapped over her face were the man's eyes: cold and emotionless, like flat black marble that reflected no compassion. Later, she recalled from a courtroom witness stand: "You could never forget that person's voice if you were tied up and bound for two hours. You could never forget that face. You could never forget what he had done to you."

When he was finished with Mrs. Wiseman, the man turned to little Robert, who cowered whimpering on the bed. The man disrobed the child, bound and gagged him with the tape, and pushed him down on the bed. "Now," he commanded, "roll over and pretend you're asleep."

Just as he finished, the doorbell rang. The boy stayed to watch the prisoners while the man went downstairs and opened the front door. Another young woman stood there, her eyes widening in fright when confronted by the stranger with the knife in his hand. She was Randi Romaine, Dede's twenty-two-year-old sister, and one of a set of twins in the family. The man grabbed the woman, pulled her inside, and slammed the door. He pushed her ahead of him up the stairs to the back bedroom.

At the sight of her older sister and little Robert, Randi screamed hysterically. "Shut up and strip," the man growled. Sobbing and trembling violently, the young woman complied. Quickly, the two intruders blindfolded, gagged, and bound their second prisoner, also with her knees drawn up against her breasts.

* * *

The man and boy both got down on their knees and examined the naked, helpless women. On their backs, their legs drawn up, both women were shamefully exposed. Both were menstruating. Grinning, the man roughly jerked the tampons from their bodies and tossed them aside. They'd just be in the way when the intruder got around to the cutting work he'd planned. He'd start with the old woman, he decided, then come back and do the boy. Flicking the knife point back and forth between the two vaginas bared before him, the man savored his selection, finally choosing Dede as the third to die. The younger, more attractive woman he'd save and butcher last.

Knife in hand, the man headed for the old woman's room when suddenly the doorbell sounded again.

He looked at the boy quizzically. "More? Maybe," he grinned, "we stumbled into a family reunion. That's good. The more creatures we have, the more we can kill."

Taking the gun from the boy, the man descended to the front door. The boy followed, holding the hunting knife aloft, ready to use it if necessary.

Within minutes, the living room floor was littered with the prone bodies of three more prisoners.

Two more women lay facedown side by side, coats thrown over their heads as blindfolds. Venetian blind cords had been cut down and used to bind the women together at their wrists and ankles. The older woman was Mrs. Edwina Romaine. The younger was her third daughter, Retta, Randi's twin sister.

The man was Frank Jeffry Welby, Retta's boyfriend. He was a big man, over six feet tall and brawny. But with a gun to his head, Welby was helpless to resist when the boy, at the man's direction, tied his wrists and ankles with more green cord cut from the Venetian blinds. A coat also covered his head. But unlike the women, Welby posed a potential threat to the smaller man and the scrawny boy.

"This is just a robbery," the intruder explained. "Behave yourselves and you won't get hurt." As long as his prisoners believed that, the man reasoned, Welby would be less of a threat. If he sensed they were going to be hurt, he might fight to protect the women and himself.

For the next hour, the five hostages listened fearfully as the man and boy prowled through the house, ransacking drawers and closets. They didn't get much for all the tragedy they brought down on the Romaine household: $60 from the family's "mad money" box; $5 from Randi's purse; a few bracelets and trinkets; Dede Wiseman's engagement and wedding rings.

Also, the arrival of Welby and the two women forced the intruder to alter his murder plans. The order of killing would start with Welby, the one prisoner who was likely to cause the most trouble if he got loose. Better not take any chances.

He'd start by cutting off Welby's prick and balls. Later, at his leisure, the man could happily slash into all the cunts that now, unexpectedly, surrounded him.

But just as he turned Welby on his back and started to remove his belt, incredibly, the doorbell rang again!

The man peeked out the front window. A black VW bug was parked at the curb. An attractive, slim young woman with shoulder-length brown hair, round face, and full sensuous lips, stood on the porch. Her dark brown hair was parted in the middle and fell to her shoulders. The flash of a white nurse's uniform peeked through the front of her imitation fur coat.

Maria Fasching, twenty-one, was working as a practical nurse at Hackensack Hospital and studying for her RN degree. Independent and strong-willed, she had learned from her policeman father to stand up for herself and was quick to go to war when she sensed the weak and downtrodden were being pushed around by bullies. In a couple of weeks, Maria would turn twenty-two and already was making plans for a big June wedding.

A lifelong friend of Randi and Retta Romaine, Maria Fasching had promised to look in on their bedridden grandmother on the way to her four-to-midnight shift at the hospital.

Maria greeted the man who opened the door with a warm smile and a friendly "Hi!" The Romaines had many friends. Maybe this was one she hadn't met yet.

"Hi! Come on in," the man waved and stepped aside. He slammed the door behind her. "Just do what you're told, and you won't get hurt," he warned.

Maria took one look at the bound prisoners on the floor and instantly sized up the situation. Disregarding the danger she suddenly had plunged into, Maria whirled on the man and spit: "You don't belong here. Get out!"

The man pointed to where Jeffry Welby lay. "Shut up and get down on the floor right now," he said. "Lay across his legs."

When the woman still resisted, the boy stepped in front of her and, wordlessly, leveled the pistol at her face. Sweat broke out on Maria's forehead. She began to tremble, suddenly aware she was in real danger and that these creeps meant business. She clasped her hand over her mouth and, like the air going out of a balloon, sank to her knees and stretched out at a right angle across Welby's legs.

The man and boy quickly tied her up using electrical cords cut from lamps and appliances in the house. As they worked, Maria whispered, "Please don't make it too tight."

With the boy remaining on guard, the man went to the basement and shrouded the windows with blankets, plunging the two-room space into a deep gloom. Now the butchering could begin.

He returned to the living room, stuffed a handkerchief in Welby's mouth and secured it with tape, pulled him to his feet, and guided him down the steep steps to the basement. The man tied Welby to a water pipe with his hands behind his back. With the coat still covering Welby's head, the man then pulled the prisoner's trousers and undershorts down to his ankles, leaving penis and testicles exposed.

Leering his sloppy grin, the intruder poked at Welby's testicles with the point of the hunting knife. "If you move, you'll lose your balls," he warned.

Back in the living room, the man helped Maria Fasching to her feet. It was merely the bad luck of the draw that the young nurse was selected to die. The other two women in the living room were tied together and the ones upstairs would be too much trouble to move.

With her arms tied in front of her and her legs lightly bound, the man guided Maria down the basement steps with his hands on her shoulders. He stood her facing the boiler room door where Jeffry Welby waited in terror, expecting to die any second.

At first, the family and investigators believed that Maria was murdered when she resisted the intruders' sexual advances and that she died fighting off the would-be rapists. Only later, did they learn the horrifying truth.

"Jeffry's in the boiler room," the man told Maria.

"I want you to go in there and chew his penis off or I'll kill you."

"No!" Maria screamed. "You'll have to kill [me] first."

Without replying, the man raised the long hunting knife and plunged it into the right side of her neck. Maria screamed. The man's eyes glazed over. He drooled and suddenly a powerful erection strained at his pants.

He stabbed the knife into Maria's neck . . . again and again.

"Oh, God," the woman gurgled. "You said you wouldn't hurt me." A scream and then, "I'm choking. You're drowning me."

The knife ripped into her body, stabbing below the nipple of her right breast, below her armpit, into her back, and a final, vicious slash across her throat. As the blood spurted from the multiple wounds and Maria writhed in agony, the attacker grunted in ecstasy and ejaculated in his pants.

Suddenly, the murder frenzy was interrupted by shouting from upstairs.

Edwina Romaine had managed to work loose from the knots binding her to Retta. While the boy stood at the head of the basement steps watching the bloodletting below, Mrs. Romaine struggled to her feet and hobbled out the front door. Her screams aroused the quiet neighborhood and the phone lines at the Leonia Police Department were even then lighting up with frantic calls for help.

"One of them got loose," the boy yelled from the basement door. "She's outside screaming. Let's get out of here!"

As the man dashed up the stairs, he glanced back at his victim. Maria Fasching, her head and body soaked in the blood still flowing from her wounds, somehow had managed to stay on her feet during the vicious attack. Now she swayed back and forth, moaned softly and crumpled to the floor.

The killing team grabbed their loot and bolted out the back door, cutting through neighboring yards until they emerged on a street bordering Leonia's Sylvan Park. In the distance, they could already hear the approaching sirens.

Sergeant Robert MacDougall was one of the first officers to arrive. After freeing the hysterical women and the youngster in the upstairs bedroom, he cautiously inched his way down the basement steps. As his eyes adjusted to the darkness, he made out the form of a woman lying on the vinyl floor. Blood was still dribbling from her nose and mouth, widening the pool in which she lay.

MacDougall squatted by the body and vainly tried to find a pulse. He was sickened by the sight. In all his years as a cop, MacDougall later recalled, ". . . I never expected to see anyone butchered like that."

A muffled moan from the next room drew his attention. He found Welby hog-tied and cut the quivering man free. As MacDougall peeled the tape from his face, Welby said, "I heard Maria scream in the next room. Is she alive? Did they kill her?"

"I'm afraid she's dead, son," MacDougall answered. "But she's really messed up. Who is it?"

"Maria Fasching," Welby said.

Sergeant MacDougall sat back on his heels, stunned as though someone had punched him in the belly. Al Fasching, Maria's dad, had been his partner and one of his oldest friends on the Leonia police force. MacDougall had known Maria since she was born, longer even, because he remembered clearly the day Al announced with bursting pride that he was going to be a daddy.

A spontaneous grief overwhelmed him and blind rage exploded in his belly. Maria was like one of his own. He felt like one of the killer's knife strokes had jabbed into his own heart. Get the son of a bitch! Kill the cocksucker if it's the last thing I do, he thought.

MacDougall helped Jeffry upstairs and then called headquarters. Reporting directly to Chief Manfred Ayers, MacDougall broke the news. "Better get some more people out here," he advised. "We got a goddam psycho loose. And somebody'd better find Al fast."

Homicide detectives were soon on the scene. Like MacDougall, they had known Maria since she was a toddler swinging on the playground swings. And like MacDougall, they went about their grim work sick to their stomachs and seething with vengeance.

Meanwhile, Retta Romaine, who thought Maria was still alive and tied up in the basement, had called the Fasching family. Minutes later Al Fasching burst into the living room.

"Where's Maria?" he cried.

MacDougall and other cops restrained their friend and pulled him outside. "No, you don't want to see her this way," MacDougall said. "You'd do the same for us. We'll get this guy for you."

When news of the shocking murder spread, a sense of calamity descended on the small town. And when word circulated that the child of a brother officer had been savagely slain, cops from surrounding communities rushed to man roadblocks and aid in the investigation.

The next day, Dr. Thomas J. Lynch of the Bergen County Medical Examiner's Office performed an autopsy on the murdered woman. His report noted that "There was no evidence of rape. There was no evidence of any attempt that we could see of any kind of sexual invasion. . . . No seminal stains were detected on the mouth swabs, the vaginal swabs, the rectal swab, the pantyhose or on the white underpants."

Nevertheless, as far as the cops were concerned, the murder of Maria Fasching was a "sex killing," as indeed it was. But the killer's demand that Maria bite off Jeffry Welby's penis and eat it was so alien, so loathsome, that that sexual aspect of the slaying wasn't talked about until years later.

Because the pairing of a man-boy murder team was so remarkable, it immediately attracted the attention of other police agencies in widely separated jurisdictions that were investigating suspiciously similar crimes by a man and his underage accomplice. Two days after the Fasching murder, the *New York Times* reported that the Leonia murder suspects had been tied to at least eight other robberies and sexual assaults:

"Joseph C. Woodcock, the Bergen County Prosecutor, said . . . a 13-state alarm was out for the two, whom he described as nomads and highly mobile," the *Times* continued.

"He described the older man as about 40, 5 foot 5 inches tall, greasy, slicked-back black hair and blue eyes. The boy was described as 11 or 12 years old, with a 'kind face' and long blond hair that gave him a girlish appearance. . . .

"Mr. Woodcock said that in each of the incidents, except two, the pattern had been the same: the young boy or sometimes both would canvas a neighborhood under the guise of a salesman and both would later force their way into a home deemed a good target.

"And in each case, women hostages were stripped of their garments, tied to the bed and either raped or forced to submit to other sexual abuses while the youth ransacked the house in an orderly manner . . . telephone, venetian blind, lamp and other cords in the houses were cut and scattered about the house."

According to the *Times,* the strange team of marauders may have been responsible for the following:

•On November 22, a youth went from door-to-door in Lindenwold, New Jersey, pretending to sell tie clasps, then returned to one house with a man, and the two forced their way in past a woman. The woman was tied to the bed and raped, and $500 in cash and jewelry were stolen.

•On December 3, after posing as insurance salesmen, a man and boy forced their way into a house in Harrisburg, Pennsylvania, and held four women hostage. One was tied to a bed and sexually abused.

•On December 10, in Baltimore, Maryland, a pair fitting the description forced their way into the home of a woman, stripped her, tied her to the bed, raped her, and escaped with money and jewelry.

•And on January 6, in Dumont, New Jersey, a few miles north of Leonia, a man and a boy entered an unlocked home while the woman occupant was in the bathtub. When she came out, she was tied to the bed, her eyes were taped closed, and she was sexually abused. Later, a bus driver reported picking up a man and a boy matching the description near the scene of the crime in Dumont and dropping them off at the George Washington Bridge bus terminal on Manhattan's Upper West Side.

Only two days later, the same man-boy team invaded the Romaines, apparently intent on killing everyone they found at home.

"The pair remained cool during the entire episode," Woodcock said, "and the eleven-year-old performed his role as if he knew exactly what to do and showing no signs of emotion as one would expect from someone that age."

Because of the youth's long hair, many of the victims were uncertain at first whether he was a boy or a girl. Conceivably, Woodcock added, there may have been other assaults, but the women may have been too embarrassed to report the sex crimes to the police.

There was one more ominous pattern to the pair's home invasion technique: Like the infamous "Boston Strangler," the man seemed to relish tying his victims on a bed and toying with them, often for hours. Once, he ordered his young companion to rape a woman captive.

After they fled from the Romaine house, the man and boy ran until they came to the park. There, next to a baseball diamond, they stopped while the man tore off his wide, blue-gray tie, and his black-and-white plaid shirt now soaked with Maria Fasching's blood.

He knelt at a puddle of water, washed off the blood that covered his hands and urgently tried to scrub the shirt clean, but the shirt was too heavily stained and his efforts were in vain.

The two continued through the park, ducking into bushes wherever a police car, siren screaming, raced through the neighborhood. The cops seemed to be everywhere, but they all rushed by with barely a second glance at the man and boy.

Somewhere along the way, the man tossed the bloody shirt aside and buttoned his doubled-breasted overcoat up to his chin so no one would notice he was bare-chested. They finally came to a busy thoroughfare and, after a short wait, caught a bus for New York City.

At the terminal, the man waited in the rest room

while the boy ran down the street and bought him a new shirt to wear. They grabbed a slice of pizza at a street stand and walked over to Penn Station. From there, they took a train to Philadelphia's Thirtieth Street Station, caught the El to Huntington Street, and walked the few blocks to home.

There, the man's wife noticed he was wearing a new shirt but didn't comment on it. After supper, the boy rushed off to meet some buddies at the Lighthouse, a neighborhood center. The man lay down for a nap.

Meanwhile, New Jersey cops tore into the investigation like enraged hornets whose nest had been kicked over. One of their own had been brutally butchered and everyone, from the chief down to the lowest rookie walking a beat, swore an oath to get the bastards.

Police immediately picked up the scent the evening of the murder when one of Sergeant MacDougall's neighbors called him to report something strange she'd noticed that afternoon while walking her dog in Sylvan Park. A man and boy, running through the park hand in hand, had stopped at a puddle of water to wash out what looked like a shirt. As they ran off, the woman thought she saw the man throw something in the bushes.

MacDougall and the woman retraced her steps through the park. She pointed out the site, and, after a brief search, the sergeant found the bloody shirt just where it had been discarded.

The garment, bearing a wealth of clues, was rushed to the New Jersey Crime Laboratory. Within days, experts had located the manufacturer who pinpointed a store in Philadelphia where it had been purchased. The shirt also carried a distinctive laundry mark that investigators traced to the Bright Sun Cleaners in Philly's Kensington section.

The owner of the shop instantly recognized the marking.

"Yeah, that's mine," he told detectives. "See, my machine has room for only seven letters so I had to leave out one 'l'—Kalinger instead of Kallinger. This is Joe Kallinger's shirt. He owns the shoe shop over on the corner of Front Street and East Sterner, the one with the big sign in the shape of a shoe hanging over the door. Good cobbler. Best in the neighborhood."

On the night of January 17, nine days after Maria Fasching was butchered, a raiding party of more than twenty angry cops kicked in the door of a run-down apartment in the working-class Kensington section of Northeastern Philadelphia, leveled shotguns at the meek-looking cobbler, who lived there above his shoe repair shop, and shouted, "Freeze, motherfucker!"

The manhunt for the Leonia killers and the man-boy team that had terrorized three states was over. Joseph Kallinger and his thirteen-year-old son, Michael, were arrested.

Even the usually unflappable *Time* magazine could barely conceal its surprise and outrage over the Kallinger depravities when it reported the capture:

"A father's slinking off with his scarcely teen-age son to commit various alleged acts of robbery, sexual brutality and finally murder may be a new twist in the already sufficiently demented and bizarre annals of crime. But it is, astonishingly, only the latest episode in a series of events that, at least to Philadelphia newspaper readers, have made the whole Kallinger family well known over the past few years."

Indeed, the arrests were only the beginning, as the secrets hidden in the depths of the Kallinger clan cesspool slowly bobbed to the surface; the facts were even

more foul and appalling than anyone, even the cop
who thought they'd seen it all, could imagine.

While they hate them, cops can at least understan
what motivates most rapists and killers.

But police had trouble comprehending Michael Kal
linger, this sandy-haired, angelic-looking youngste
who eagerly participated in the nightmarish crim
spree. Many victims weren't even sure the youth was
boy or a girl. His long, silky hair confused them . .
until he exposed himself and began pawing at their pri
vates.

But then, nothing in their training or experience ha
prepared the cops for the likes of Joe Kallinger and hi
ghastly "family values."

Joe Kallinger was born in Philadelphia in 1936 an
was surrendered for adoption while still an infant. Hi
new parents were Austrian immigrants Stephen an
Anna Kallinger. The couple lived above the shoe repai
shop they owned, where Joe lived most of his life, eve
after he was grown and with a family of his own. Ex
cept for a brief period in his twenties, Joe Kallinge
never really left home and remained bound to his cob
bler bench until the cops came to haul him away.

Kallinger's lifelong obsession with sex organs, espe
cially penises, and castration fantasies began as
child. He claimed he was a victim of child abuse him
self, which included repeated threats by his adoptiv
parents to cut off his penis when he misbehaved.
childhood hernia operation left him convinced tha
he'd been surgically altered and a smaller penis ha
been attached replacing his own. In 1944, Joe als
claimed, he was sexually assaulted at knife point by
gang of older kids. Sodomized and forced to suc
cock his obsession was fueled. In Kallinger's twiste
mind, the final blow that pushed him over the edg

came when his first wife left him. She was leaving, she told Kallinger, because his penis was too small to satisfy her.

Kallinger and his first wife married when they were both only seventeen years old. After a couple of kids and a few years of a stormy marriage, the woman left him for another man. Kallinger met his second wife, Elizabeth, also called "Betty," in 1957. They were soon married and had five kids: Mary Jo, Joe, Jr., Michael, James, and Bonny, the baby, who was only eighteen months old when Kallinger went out to kill. For a time, Stephen, the son from his first marriage, lived with the Kallingers until he got fed up with his father's beatings and took off.

All the Kallinger kids had the same sickly look: undersized for their ages; undernourished with dark, haunted circles around their eyes like prisoners of war, who have suffered psychological torture by being deprived of sleep.

Little wonder, since Joe Kallinger wrote the book on child abuse. The horrors that he inflicted on his own kids were revealed when three of them filed charges against their father in 1972. Kallinger went to jail for seven months, until an attorney talked the children into recanting and Joe was released.

In the basement of his shoe shop, Kallinger had installed what the kids referred to as "the torture chamber." A metal table held Joe Kallinger's "educational material": sections of heavy rope, rubber hose, a box of straight pins, strips of leather and shoe soles, and a homemade cat-o'-nine-tails.

Beginning in 1969, Stephen, then about thirteen, Mary Jo, ten, and Joey, about nine, were repeatedly summoned to the cellar for "instructions" in family loyalty and discipline. The brutal "reeducation" session continued for three years. Almost every night after midnight, one of the children was dragged from bed and marched down to the dreaded torture chamber to be punished for some infraction. If Joe couldn't find any wrongdoing, he invented some. And all the while her children were being brutalized, Betty Kallinger turned her back or silently rocked in front of the television set.

(Years later, Joe Kallinger recalled, "I took great pleasure in punishment that combined sex and sadism. I threw pins at Mary Jo's exposed body, and flogged Joey with my homemade cat-o'-ninetails. I also brutalized Stevie, though I don't remember how.")

Punishment was meted out when the children, in Kallinger's eyes, disobeyed; when they failed to sell their quota of shoe polish he forced them to peddle door-to-door; when they played hooky, which was frequent; or just for "doing stuff."

Special "instructions" were reserved for Mary Jo when she failed to pick winning horses during racing seasons. Late at night, Joe would awaken Mary Jo and order her to select horses from the Racing Form for the next day's races. For three years, beginning when she was ten, Mary Jo sat at her little table in the living room trying to stay awake while she picked winners.

When the horses didn't win, Kallinger beat her. Sometimes he made her stand in front of him while he threw straight pins like darts at her naked, little body. The more pins Joe could stick in her flesh, the happier he was.

Stuff that merited reeducation punishment also included a variety of sexual activities, both heterosexual and homosexual, that for street urchins like the Kallinger kids was as common as dirt.

There was the time, for example, when Joey, eleven, and Mary Jo, twelve, were caught selling blow jobs to fourteen neighborhood boys on a tenement roof next door to a playground. Mary Jo collected 50¢ from "customers" and sent them up the stairway to where Joey waited to service them.

One Saturday afternoon in 1972, Mary Jo and Joey ran off with friends and stayed away all night. Joe spent most of Sunday cruising Kensington by cab searching for the "traitors." He found them with three other kids, one who Mary Jo called her boyfriend.

Dragging his children home, Kallinger handcuffed Joey to the refrigerator and took Mary Jo to the cellar and tied her up. Joe fired up a small kerosene stove and placed a kitchen spatula on the flame. When the implement was heating up, Kallinger flipped open a switchblade knife he habitually carried, the one that he had to hold in his hand in order to become sexually aroused during intercourse. He scraped the edge of the razor-sharp blade across Mary Jo's throat and warned her not to scream.

Then he stripped off her clothes.

When the spatula was hot, Kallinger kneeled in front of his daughter and pressed the blistering metal against the inside of her thigh, barely a quarter of an inch from her exposed vagina.

Despite his warnings, Mary Jo screamed in agony and writhed against the ropes that held her securely. But Kallinger wasn't satisfied she'd learned her lesson. He reheated the spatula and pressed it against the same seared spot. When he removed the spatula, bits of burnt flesh clung to it.

Years later, Kallinger admitted to a biographer that

he tortured Mary Jo because he was jealous of her boyfriend.

"I did it so she wouldn't fuck," Kallinger said. "It would hurt her and when you're hurt, you can't fuck.

"But she was lucky I didn't do what I started out to—stick the hot spatula up her vagina, shove it right on up into her guts and sizzle the badness out of her."

The punishment for Joey maybe wasn't quite as terrible, but was just as excruciatingly painful. Kallinger beat the boy with the handle of a hammer—every hour on the hour for the rest of the day.

Not long after this episode, the children had their father arrested.

Despite the constant threat of torture, Joey, among all the Kallinger kids, remained resolutely defiant, often mocking and cursing his father openly. Finally, Kallinger decided the insubordination had to be stamped out once and for all.

Joey had to die.

But first, to make his efforts worthwhile, Kallinger took out a $59,000 double indemnity life insurance policy on his son's life. Kallinger also figured he needed help with the killing so he recruited his next oldest son, Michael, who was only thirteen years old at the time.

The schemers tried to bump off Joe, Jr., three times in July 1974. The first attempt was during a weekend sight-seeing excursion to the old coal mines and slate piles near Hazleton, Pennsylvania. At the peak of one of the highest mounds, almost a mountain, Kallinger and Michael urged Joey to stand closer and closer to the edge, hoping he'd back off the cliff and fall to his death. Michael even threw rocks at his brother to force him backward. But Joey thought it was all a big joke, and the ludicrous murder plot flopped.

The following Thursday, July 25, Kallinger hatched another harebrained scheme. Before dawn, Kallinger got Joey out of bed. He and Michael had decided, he said, to burn down some construction trailers parked nearby and they wanted Joey to be in on the fun.

Joey was sent ahead with a can of gasoline, cigarettes, and matches. His job, Kallinger instructed, was to slosh the fuel around the trailer and, on Michael's signal, set it ablaze. What Joe, Sr., and Michael hoped would happen, knowing Joey, was that he'd start smoking before he left the trailer and conveniently blow himself up. It almost happened that way. Joey started the fire, and, although his pants' legs were singed in the sudden blaze, he escaped without harm.

Frustrated that Joey refused to roll over and die as planned, Kallinger's schemes were forced to take more drastic and direct action.

That July, buildings were being razed all along Market Street. The morning of the twenty-eighth, a Sunday when the demolition sites would be deserted, Joe gathered up chains, handcuffs, ropes, flashlights, and a camera, stuffed them in a canvas bag and summoned Joey and Michael. "Let's go get some pictures of the old buildings before they're all gone," he told the boys. "Maybe we can find some good stuff in there."

The picture taking appealed to Joey's ego. Earlier, photos of him in chains and handcuffs had made him a star among the street gangs of Kensington.

At the demolition site, the three found a circular stairway leading down into the dank recesses of a water-filled subbasement. Just where the steps met the water, Joe spotted a ladder. "Go stand on the ladder," he urged Joey. "It'll make a great picture with you all chained up." Joey complied, but as soon as the boy was fastened tightly to the ladder, Kallinger stepped back and toppled it into the dark, smelly sludge.

Joey struggled facedown for several minutes while his father and brother watched the ladder bob on the slimy surface. Once, Joey managed to turn his face up and call in a weakening voice, "Daddy, please help me."

Then he rocked back over with his face in the black water and was still.

When Joe was sure his son was dead, he pulled the ladder to the stair landing, removed the chains, and went home with Michael.

Late that night, he called police to report his son was missing. Police searched but found no trace of the youngster. Not long after, Kallinger filed for payment of the insurance on Joey's life, but the life insurance company raised serious doubts about Joey's death and never paid the claim.

Early on the morning of August 9, the body of a young, white male, weighing only about seventy pounds, dressed in a brown short-sleeved shirt and red-white-and-blue-checkered pants, was found rotting on a slab in the subbasement of a building at Ninth and Market.

The Office of the Medical Examiner assigned case number 4003-74 to the body. Deputy Medical Examiner H.E. Fillinger did the postmortem, but stated that putrefaction was too far advanced to determine the exact cause of death. The cops suspected murder.

On August 12, Homicide Detective James O'Neill checked the reports of teenage runaways and came up with the name of Joseph Kallinger, Jr., fourteen, of 2723 North Front Street. The father, Joe Kallinger, was summoned to the city morgue and identified photographs of the remains as his son.

The "grieving" family buried Joey in the family plot.

According to O'Neill, Kallinger refused to cooperate with the investigation and remained a prime suspect. But the cops didn't have the evidence to back up their suspicions, and Joe Kallinger arrogantly defied them to prove he was a killer. They couldn't, and he was never charged with Joey's death.

But maybe the cops didn't look close enough. If they had, they might have discovered that Joey wasn't Kallinger's first murder victim. As a tune-up to killing Joey, the father-son team had gone out two weeks earlier searching for a victim to practice on. It was also an opportunity for Kallinger to try something that had fascinated him for years—what would it be like to chop off somebody's penis.

Long after he was convicted of Maria Fasching's murder, Kallinger related details of that first slaying.

It happened on a warm Sunday evening in the early summer of 1974. Kallinger said he was in his shop toying with a new type of cobbler's tool used for cutting through heavy materials such as layers of leather. Michael lounged on the cobbler's bench, watching. The shape of the tool reminded Kallinger of a tiny guillotine, and the notion suddenly struck him that this would be a good time to kill someone and use the cutter to fulfill his long-suppressed urge to cut off a penis.

He told Michael what he had in mind, and, according to Kallinger, his son eagerly jumped off the bench. "Good, Dad," he replied. "I'll help you." Kallinger pocketed the handcutters and a roll of black tape, and the pair set out in search of a victim.

They found him standing cutside the Mann Recreation Center at Fifth Street and Allegheny Avenue. Jose

Collazo, a short, skinny Puerto Rican kid, was only ten years old.

The Kallingers told the boy they needed help moving some boxes, and, when they offered to pay him, the youngster willingly tagged along. Not far away was an abandoned rug factory Joe Kallinger knew about and that's where they headed.

Once inside the dusty, old building, Jose apparently sensed he was walking into a trap. He drew back and began to whimper that he wanted to go home. But the Kallingers took him by each arm and marched him up some rickety stairs. On the second-floor landing, they forced the boy to disrobe. Joe found a discarded electric fan and used the electrical cord to tie the boy's hands and feet. They stuffed one of the child's socks in his mouth and secured it by wrapping layer after layer of the black tape all around the child's head.

Then, Kallinger claimed, Michael rolled Jose over on his stomach and used the handle of the cutting tool to violently sodomize the boy. Jose struggled and tried to scream through the choking gag as the handle tore into his rectum.

When the boy stopped struggling, they turned him over and Kallinger used the handcutters to snip off about half an inch of the boy's penis. The youngster didn't flinch. Apparently, Kallinger thought, the kid had suffocated from the tightly taped gag, or maybe shoving the handle up his rear had killed him.

Whatever, Kallinger now had his grisly trophy that he carried home triumphantly. He quickly forgot about the tortured, mutilated body of the murdered child left to rot in the empty factory.

The next day the piece of flesh started to smell bad. Kallinger encased it in plaster of paris and kept it near his workbench. A couple of weeks later, he threw it down a sewer.

About three months after Joey's funeral, and after the pressure from the Philadelphia cops to pin Joey's death on him had eased, Joe Kallinger decided the time had come to kill again. But this time not so close to home. There was too much heat on him already.

So in November 1974, father and son launched their campaign of terror against suburban housewives. This time, Joe wanted to mutilate women. He also had another reason for going after women. Kallinger needed specimens of fresh vaginal fluids, mixed with sperm, for a revolting experiment he hoped to try out on Bonny, his youngest daughter. The toddler suffered from a congenital condition that left her skin covered in ugly purple splotches. Joe believed he could heal her with a salve consisting of vaginal fluid, sperm, and perfume stolen from his female victims.

Joe began by picking out a town on the map that was easily accessible from their Kensington home via public transportation since Joe didn't know how to drive and Michael was too young to get behind the wheel. His first choice was Lindenwold, New Jersey, a village southeast of Philadelphia. The pair arrived there by the High Speed Line Railroad early on Friday, November 22, and began roaming the streets searching for likely victims, or "delegates," as Kallinger called them.

This was meant primarily as a murder raid, but the Kallingers also had an eye out for profit, mainly jewelry, so they carried a large, blue suitcase to haul away loot. Joe also had a brown paper bag holding a large butcher knife, several bootlaces, tissue, and a pair of rubber gloves. The knife was for slicing off breasts and slashing open vaginas (or penis and testicles if the man of the house was at home). The tissues were for soaking up the excess vaginal fluids and sperm after Joe had come in his victim, and the gloves were for carrying the "healing balm" home safely.

Jane Forrest (not her real name) on Carlton Street, stepped out the back door to empty her cat's box. She didn't notice the man and boy who paused across the street to watch. Back inside, Mrs. Forrest put her two toddlers down for their naps and had just turned on her favorite soap opera when a thin, pale youngster wearing a tasseled stocking cap knocked on her door.

Behind him stood a dark man in an overcoat. He looked vaguely like a policeman, Mrs. Forrest thought, so she opened the door.

The man smiled and put his hand on the boy's shoulder. "Has this kid been trying to sell you things?" he inquired. Before she could answer, the two pushed against the door, bowling her over.

In minutes, the woman was stripped and lashed spread-eagled to her bed. She was gagged, and a pillowcase covered her head as a blindfold. While Mrs. Forrest lay helpless, the Kallingers rummaged through the house, filling the suitcase with cash and jewelry and any trinkets that struck their fancy.

Returning to the bedroom, Joe began to undress, his eyes feasting on Jane Forrest's breasts and between her widespread legs. She felt fingers brush over her nipples and heard the boy ask: "Dad, can I fuck her?"

"No," she heard the man answer. "I've got to do this alone."

Joe Kallinger climbed on the bed, butcher knife in hand, and rubbed his erection over the woman's genitals until he ejaculated. He pulled on one of the rubber gloves and worked his fingers around inside Mrs. Forrest's vagina until the rubber was well lubricated. He carefully removed the glove, turned it inside out to preserve the precious fluids, added a few drops of perfume from a bottle on Mrs. Forrest's bureau, and stored it away in his overcoat pocket.

The Kallingers strolled away with the suitcase stuffed with loot, leaving the gagged and blindfolded young mother still lashed obscenely to the bed.

They arrived home on the 5:45 P.M. train.

After dinner, Joe took a box of cotton balls from the bathroom, a pan of water, and the glove holding the sexual fluids. He sat Bonny in a chair next to his workbench and began swabbing the purple splotches with his "miracle" cure.

In a few days, it became clear the cure wasn't working. Joe needed more fluids. Besides, he and Michael both were becoming addicted to the power trip, the thrill of taking over a home and holding helpless women hostage and in terror.

On December 3, they went west, all the way out to Harrisburg. And struck pay dirt.

The Kallingers arrived at Susquehanna Township by bus about 10 A.M. The township, just north of Harrisburg was a fashionable, upper-middle-income enclave of prominent Harrisburg businessmen, professionals, and state officials. The tidy, upscale boulevards, lined by spacious, manicured lawns, were a far cry from the crowded, debris-strewn streets of Kensington. Joe was envious of all this affluence and vowed to make the delegates he found that day pay for their privileges.

Walking along Green Street, Joe and Michael spotted an attractive middle-aged blond woman leave her two-story, white, brick house and drive off. She appeared to be running an errand, so Joe surmised she'd probably be back soon. Acting as though they belonged there, the Kallingers strolled up the driveway and broke into the house by the back door. The house was empty, but the breakfast table was set for four. The green placemats and fine china told Joe company was expected.

At 11:30 A.M., the woman returned. As she unlocked the front door, Joe was there waiting. He grabbed the woman, pulled her into the hallway, and pushed her to the floor. He jabbed the point of his butcher knife against the woman's cheek and snarled, "If you scream, you're dead."

Shaking with fear, the woman struggled to stay calm. "Why are you doing this?" Helen Bogin asked.

"Get up the stairs and be quiet," Kallinger answered. Out of the corner of her eye, Helen Bogin caught sight of Michael pointing a pistol at her. She knew better than to resist. In response to Kallinger's questions, Mrs. Bogin confirmed that she was expecting three members of her bridge club for lunch. They were due any minute.

Upstairs, Kallinger stripped the covers off a bed and flipped the metal frame upside down. With Michael standing guard, he used wads of cotton and two-inch-wide adhesive tape to blindfold the woman. A man's handkerchief and more tape served as a gag. He forced her to lie on her back on the bed frame, spread her arms and legs, and tied her securely.

Before leaving her, Kallinger pulled up the woman's sweater and shirt and pushed aside her bra, exposing her breasts. The prick of the knife point beside one nipple was just enough to break the skin, Mrs. Bogin later testified.

"This is just a sample of what will happen if you don't behave yourself," Kallinger growled.

Then father and son adjourned to the living room to await the luncheon guests.

One by one they arrived, and one by one each was taken prisoner.

* * *

Ethel Fisher Cohen was the first to be taken prisoner; Thelma Suden a few minutes later, and finally Annapearl Frankston. As each guest arrived, she was taken to different rooms on the second floor, blindfolded and gagged. Kallinger stretched coat hangers into long pieces of wire and painfully twisted the wires around the women's wrists and ankles. While he worked, Michael followed along, methodically removing diamond rings and other jewelry from the women. These he tossed in a canvas bag along with a cache of jewels he'd found in a bureau drawer and $700 in cash one of the women carried.

According to later testimony, the Kallingers got away with over $20,000 in cash and jewels.

On this raid, Kallinger also carried a can of lighter fluid with the intention of cremating his victims when he was finished with them. But by the time he and Michael were done ransacking the house, it was too late to play. They hurried off to catch the bus back to Philly and be home before dark.

A week later, on December 10, the pair took a bus to Baltimore and broke into a residence in Homeland, a wealthy suburb north of the city.

There they again found a woman home alone, tied her up, and stole her jewelry. Then, with his pistol jammed against the woman's forehead, Joe Kallinger forced her to suck him until he came in her mouth. The sexual ravishment seemed to dilute Kallinger's murderous mood, and he left without killing the woman as he had planned to do.

On January 6, 1975, the Kallingers raided into the Northeast. About 9:00 A.M., a bus dropped them off in Dumont, New Jersey.

Once more, purely by happenstance, they stumbled over the ideal target: a woman alone. Mary Randal (not her real name) was in the bathroom when the pair entered through an unlocked door. They grabbed her when she stepped from her bath, and, while she was still nude and dripping, tied her to her bed.

After rummaging through the house, Joe again forced the victim to perform fellatio at gunpoint, warning that if she used her teeth on his penis he'd kill her. But this time, one blow job wasn't enough to sate him. Kallinger wanted to sexually humiliate the woman even more, so he called Michael into the room.

"Do whatever he wants you to do or I'll kill you," Kallinger told the woman.

The frail, thirteen-year-old boy pulled his pants down and climbed on top of the helpless victim. For ten minutes he struggled to rape her but couldn't stay hard long enough to penetrate. In frustration, he leapt from the bed and left the room. Soon after, the Kallingers fled with their loot.

Once more, Joe Kallinger had been diverted from his mission to murder by oral sex. Two days later, however, he headed back toward Dumont, vowing this time to kill. Along the way. he detoured to Leonia and because he did some unknown woman in Dumont lived.

But Maria Fasching died.

The night the cops came, Joe had just closed his shop for the day, and the family was settling down in front of the television. Suddenly there was a pounding on the door. Betty jumped up and called, "Who is it?"

"Police! Open the door!"

"You got a search warrant?" Betty yelled back. She knew that Joe and Michael had been out robbing. She even got up early to fix breakfast for them before they set off on their raids. Besides, the house was full of loot, so Betty was expecting the worst. But before she could open the door, the police broke it down.

A small army of cops poured into the living room: FBI agents and state police from Pennsylvania, New Jersey, and Maryland, six Philadelphia homicide detectives, officers from Dumont and Baltimore, plus investigators from the Bergen County Prosecutor's Office.

And they did have search warrants.

At first, Kallinger denied he was the man they were looking for. But the charade quickly crumbled.

One member of the raiding party was Lieutenant James O'Neill, the tough homicide cop who was convinced Joe had killed Joe, Jr., and had sworn to get him.

O'Neill got up in Kallinger's face and growled, "I know you, Kallinger, don't try to bullshit me. You killed your own kid and you killed that woman in Leonia."

Joe and Michael were taken to the main police lockup where more officials from the tri-state area waited to question them. They were arraigned before Judge Thomas P. McCabe who ordered Joe held on $100,000 bail and turned Michael over to juvenile authorities.

Kallinger's fingerprints had been found at the Susquehanna Township crime scene, so the pair was charged first with that robbery to make sure Pennsylvania got first crack at them. They were immediately transferred to the Dauphin County Jail in Harrisburg.

Meanwhile, the other jurisdictions lined up with their complaints: New Jersey rushed in to charge Joe with the murder of Maria Fasching and two armed robberies at Dumont and Leonia.

* * *

On January 28, 1975, Joe was indicted by a Camden County, New Jersey, grand jury on charges stemming from the assault on the Lindenwold woman. The seventeen counts included conspiracy, burglary, armed robbery, rape, assault, possession of a gun and knife, contributing to the delinquency of a minor, debauching the morals of a minor, and threatening to kill.

On January 28, 1975, Baltimore authorities hit Joe with their robbery charges.

Michael remained in Pennsylvania state custody until September 1976, when he was sent to live with foster parents.

New Jersey wanted him in connection with the murder and the two armed robberies there. However, during a closed hearing in January 1979, Michael pleaded guilty to armed robbery in Leonia and Dumont. In exchange, the murder charge was dismissed. No action was taken in the Dumont or the Baltimore sexual attacks.

Pennsylvania courts placed Michael on probation and retained jurisdiction over him until he turned twenty-one on December 25, 1982. One condition of his probation was that he could never write anything about the case.

But Joe Kallinger wasn't getting off with such a slap on the wrist.

He went to trial three times and tried to feign insanity each time. And each time the juries flatly rejected his innocent by reason of insanity claims. Kallinger may have been a full-blown cuckoo, but in the eyes of the juries he wasn't legally insane.

During the trial on the Susquehanna Township charges, Kallinger insisted that he talked to God and God talked back, that he was one thousand years old and that he was previously a butterfly.

The jury didn't buy it. It took them only an hour to find Kallinger guilty on all nine counts of burglary, robbery, and false imprisonment.

At sentencing, Judge John C. Dowling admonished, "You are an evil man, Mr. Kallinger . . . I say evil not just because of your crimes but because you actively involved a twelve-year-old boy in these infamous deeds. To so corrupt your own son is utterly vile and depraved. . . . The cutting of Mrs. Helen Bogin, the threats to kill, the assaults, the binding and gagging, and other indignities heaped on four defenseless women stamps you as a violent and dangerous criminal from whom society needs protection."

He sentenced Joe to a minimum of thirty and a maximum of eighty years in prison.

Judge Dowling later confided, "I wanted to make sure he would never be on the street again."

At his murder trial in New Jersey, Kallinger switched tactics. Instead of talking to God, he foamed at the mouth and fell off his chair. Rather than a butterfly, he now chirped like a bird until the exasperated judge ordered him caged in an adjoining room.

The jury deliberated on five charges: murder, robbery, armed robbery, possession of a dangerous weapon, and contributing to the delinquency of a minor. It took them only an hour and forty minutes to reach unanimous, first-ballot decisions on each charge: guilty on all counts.

On October 15, 1976, Judge Thomas F. Dalton sentenced Joe to a mandatory life sentence at New Jersey State Prison. The sentence was to run consecutively to the thirty to eighty years Judge Dowling had imposed in Pennsylvania.

On July 22, 1977, a jury trying the Carty case again

found Joe guilty, this time of breaking and entering with intent to steal; breaking and entering with intent to steal while armed; robbery while armed; assault with intent to commit rape; assault with intent to commit rape while armed; and the threat to kill.

Judge I. V. DiMartino sentenced Joe to not less than forty-two nor more than fifty-one years in New Jersey State Prison. He said, "I do not believe Mr. Kallinger will ever be rehabilitated. I do not believe any sentence will ever deter him."

DiMartino also ordered the sentence to run consecutively to all others imposed by courts in Pennsylvania and New Jersey.

But even safely locked away, the world hadn't heard the last of Joseph Kallinger. In 1988, he announced in a television interview that when he is set free, he still planned to butcher everyone on earth.

BIBLIOGRAPHY

Clarke, James W. *Last Rampage: The Escape of Gary Tison.* Boston: Houghton Mifflin Co., 1988.

de Ford, Miriam Allen. *The Real Ma Barker.* New York: Ace, 1970.

Earley, Pete. *Prophet of Death: The Mormon Blood-Atonement Killings.* New York: William Morrow and Company, Inc., 1991.

Fox, James Allen and Levin, Jack. *Mass Murder: America's Growing Menace.* New York: Plenum Press, 1985.

Gentry, Curt. *J. Edgar Hoover: The Man and the Secrets.* New York: W.W. Norton & Company, 1991.

Godwin, John. *Murder USA: The Ways We Kill Each Other.* New York: Ballantine Books, 1978.

Kobler, John. *Capone: The Life and World of Al Capone.* New York: G.P. Putnam's Sons, 1971.

Kohn, George C. *Dictionary of Culprits and Criminals.* Metuchen, New Jersey: The Scarecrow Press, Inc., 1986.

Lane, Brian. *Murder Update: The Full Stories of Today's Most Famous Cases.* New York: Carroll and Graf, 1991.

Nash, Jay Robert. *Almanac of World Crime*. Garden City, New York: Anchor Press/Doubleday, 1981.

———. *Bloodletters and Badmen*. New York: M. Evans and Company, 1973.

———. *The Encyclopedia of World Crime (Vol. I-VI)*. Wilmette, Illinois: CrimeBooks, Inc., 1990.

———. *Murder, America: Homicide in the United States from the Revolution to the Present*. New York: Simon & Schuster, 1980.

Newton, Michael. *Hunting Humans: An Encyclopedia of Modern Serial Killers*. Port Townsend, WA: Loompanics Unlimited, 1990.

Newton, Michael and Newton, Judy Ann. *The FBI Most Wanted: An Encyclopedia*. New York: Garland Publishing, 1989.

Norris, Joel. *Serial Killers: The Growing Menace*. New York: Doubleday, 1988.

Powers, Richard Gid. *G-Men: Hoover's FBI in American Popular Culture*. Carbondale and Edwardsville: Southern Illinois University Press, 1983.

Sasse, Cynthia Stalter and Widder, Peggy Murphy. *The Kirtland Massacre: The True and Terrible Story of the Mormon Cult Murders*. New York: Donald I. Fine, Inc., 1991.

Schoenberg, Robert J. *Mr. Capone: The Real—and Complete—Story of Al Capone*. New York: William Morrow and Co., 1992.

Schreiber, Flora Rheta. *The Shoemaker: Anatomy of a Psychotic*. New York: Simon and Schuster, 1983.

Sifakis, Carl. *The Encyclopedia of American Crime*. New York: Facts on File, Inc., 1982.

———. *The Mafia Encyclopedia*. New York: Facts on File, Inc., 1987.

Trainer, Orville. *Death Roads: The Story of the Donut Shop Murders*. Boulder: Pruett Publishing

Company, 1979.
van Hoffman, Eric. *A Venom in the Blood.* New York: Donald I. Fine, Inc., 1990. (The Gallegos)
Wallis, Michael. *Pretty Boy: The Life and Times of Charles Arthur Floyd.* New York: St. Martin's Press, 1992.
Wilson, Colin and Seaman, Donald. *The Encyclopedia of Modern Murder.* New York: Arlington House, 1988.